THE PRICE OF DESIRE

"We are of a kind, you and I," Griffin said quietly. "I think you know it's true."

Then he bent his head and laid his mouth over hers. There was very little pressure in the kiss, just a touch, a tender brush. Sweetness and solace. He offered only as much as he thought she could accept and was uncertain from the beginning if she could accept any of it.

His hands slid from her elbows to the small of her back. He resisted the urge to pull her closer and instead let her find her own way into the shelter of his embrace. She edged closer, her mouth parting. He changed the slant of his mouth, licked her lower lip with the damp edge of his tongue.

He caught the scent of lavender on her skin and the taste of mint on her mouth. The fragrance made him think peculiarly of innocence—the taste of things fresh and unsullied.

Olivia raised her hands, then let them fall back to her side. She hadn't quite known what she wanted to do with them. Touching him, her fingers on his shoulders, at the back of his neck, drifting into the curling ends of his dark hair, all of it seemed too much, or possibly it was that it wouldn't have been enough.

His kiss made her remember emptiness and longing. It made her think of what she could have in the moment, but would always be denied in the forever. In spite of that, or perhaps because of it, the kiss stirred her. . . .

Books by Jo Goodman

The Captain's Lady
Crystal Passion
Seaswept Abandon
Velvet Night
Violet Fire
Scarlet Lies
Tempting Torment
Midnight Princess
Passion's Sweet Revenge
Sweet Fire
Wild Sweet Ecstasy
Rogue's Mistress
Forever in My Heart
Always in My Dreams
Only in My Arms
My Steadfast Heart
My Reckless Heart
With All My Heart
More Than You Know
More Than You Wished
Let Me Be the One
Everything I Ever Wanted
All I Ever Needed
Beyond a Wicked Kiss
A Season to Be Sinful
One Forbidden Evening
If His Kiss Is Wicked
The Price of Desire

Published by Zebra Books

THE PRICE OF DESIRE

Jo Goodman

ZEBRA BOOKS
Kensington Publishing Corp.

ZEBRA BOOKS are published by

Kensington Publishing Corp.
850 Third Avenue
New York, NY 10022

Copyright © 2008 by Joanne Dobrzanski

ISBN-13: 978-0-7394-9948-1

Printed in the United States of America

For some of the people who've dropped seeds in my life.
You may never see this,
never know,
that your seed was nourished and thrived.
Recognition is long overdue.

Mary Alice Dambaugh
Barbara Keller
Dr. Dietrich
Amy Yohn

Prologue

London
January 1823

"The debt is £1,000."

Griffin Wright-Jones, Viscount Breckenridge, closed the book of accounts slowly, running his forefinger along the spine before he neatly squared it off so it was parallel to the edge of his desk. He set himself back just a fraction in his chair, inclining his back and resting his elbows on the wide, burnished leather arms. It was only then that he deigned to look up, one dark brow lifted in an expression of such mild curiosity that it could have been mistaken for indifference. He did not expect that the man standing at attention on the other side of the desk would make that error. Alastair Cole had too much at stake—£1,000, to be strictly accurate—to misjudge the situation.

"I admit that at long last you have impressed me," Breckenridge said.

Alastair Cole said nothing. Did nothing.

"If you schooled your features so well at the table, you would have discharged this debt handily. Mayhap you would not have amassed it."

"I will honor it, of course."

"Of course." Breckenridge paused deliberately, though not overlong. Still, it was enough time to observe Mr. Cole shift his weight ever so slightly from his right foot to his left. This infinitesimal movement was accompanied by a shift in Cole's gaze. "You are a gentleman, after all," Breckenridge said. "I would expect nothing less."

"I am gratified you know it."

Breckenridge nodded slowly. "Your reputation is important to you, I imagine." He noticed that Alastair Cole did not flinch, but he did blink. Twice. Breckenridge's hands closed soundlessly in an attitude of prayer. He pressed the tips of his fingers together, making a steeple of them as he continued to regard Cole, considering. "You will likewise be aware that my reputation is important to me."

"My lord?"

Breckenridge was now quite certain that Cole's voice box was as tautly stretched as his nerves. There had been an alarming squeak as the man had uttered these last words. Judging by the scarlet color that rose above the stiff points of Cole's collar, he had heard it as well.

"I collect what is owed," Breckenridge said. "That is *my* reputation. Do you understand?"

"Yes."

"Good. Then you will not take offense when I ask how you plan to cover your losses." Breckenridge permitted himself a small smile at Cole's discomfort. Clearly the young man was offended at having the question put to him—a gentleman was taken at his word, after all—but he also seemed to sense that a toplofty tantrum was an indulgence he could ill afford. Breckenridge held up one hand, palm out, forestalling Cole's answer just as the man's lips parted around the lie he was about to tell. "And, pray, do not say you mean to ask for an advance on your quarterly allowance. We both know that such a request is unlikely to be granted."

Alastair Cole brought his fist to his mouth as he cleared his throat. "Pardon me, my lord. A tickle in my throat."

Breckenridge watched Cole's eyes drop briefly to the tumbler of whiskey on the desk and the decanter beside it, but he did not offer libation and Cole did not ask for it.

"Unless you are in possession of facts unknown to me," Cole said, "I have every reason to anticipate my request will be met favorably."

Breckenridge made no response save for raising his arched eyebrow a fraction higher.

"*Are* you in possession of such facts?" Alastair Cole asked.

"I don't believe so. I know what you know. Our opposing views suggest we interpret the facts differently."

"I'm certain that is the case."

Breckenridge thought Cole looked relieved. "I hope for your sake that you are in the right of it." His expression remained unchanged as he added quietly, "You would not want to be wrong."

Cole teetered slightly. The flush that had suffused his skin vanished, leaving him pale except for the sprinkling of freckles across his nose. "No, my lord. That is, I'm *not* wrong."

The viscount nodded. He dropped his hands to the arms of his chair. "Then I can expect payment tomorrow?"

"Tomorrow?"

The soprano note of panic had returned to Alastair Cole's voice. It required effort of will for Breckenridge not to wince. He consulted his gold fob watch instead. "It is long after midnight already," he said. "I did not realize. In that case I will expect payment in the morning. I am given to late risings. It is the hours I keep, I suspect. Let us say eleven, shall we? Something less than twelve hours from now. That should be sufficient."

"Eleven? I couldn't possibly."

"I don't believe I could have heard you correctly."

Cole swallowed hard. The flush was back in his cheeks. "I require more time, my lord."

"Do not keep it a secret, Mr. Cole. Out with it."

"A day," Cole said quickly. "A few days at the most."

"A day? A few days? Which is it?"

"A few days."

"Three? Four? Be specific, man."

"Four."

"Four days to secure an advance on your allowance seems excessive."

"There are arrangements that must be made."

Breckenridge considered this. "Travel arrangements, no doubt. In four days you could be in Liverpool. You could be in France."

"No." Alastair Cole shook his head vehemently. A lock of red-blond hair fell across his brow, making him look even younger than his twenty-one years. "That is not my intention. I swear to you, you shall have your money."

"You would have me believe you are in earnest."

"I *am* in earnest."

Breckenridge did not respond immediately. He allowed silence to fill the space until it became as thick and cold as day-old porridge. It was an underrated tool, silence. At least Breckenridge had always found it so. People were often discomfited by it. Society sought to fill the void with chatter and tattle, tongues wagging as they were wont to do. Alastair Cole struggled to remain upright under the weight of it. Breckenridge could see that he was worrying his lower lip, probably drawing blood. God's truth, there should be blood, Breckenridge thought, when gentlemen made wagers beyond their means to pay. No exception could be made for youth or inexperience, both of which afflicted Alastair Cole.

"Very well," said Breckenridge. "You shall have your four days. Mark it well in your mind that I mean to have my money by this hour on Thursday."

"Thank you, my lord." Alastair bobbed his head. "Thank you."

"And what do you propose to exchange for the four days?"

"What?"

"Quid pro quo. You know the phrase, do you not? Recently come down from Cambridge as you have."

"Something for something. Yes, I know it." Alastair Cole pushed the wayward lock of hair back into place. "But I thought I explained myself. I don't have the money now."

"That has been made clear to me, but I don't have four days to surrender to you without something in return."

"You want interest? Is that it?"

"I'm not a bloody moneylender, Cole. This is business." Breckenridge knew the impact his dark, remote gaze had on gentlemen of Alastair Cole's ilk. He used it now, not at all disappointed with the result. Small beads of perspiration formed on Cole's upper lip, glistening in the firelight when the young man turned his head. Breckenridge allowed his glance to drop to the ring Cole was wearing on his right hand. "Tell me about that bauble."

Cole jerked as if pulled from a trance. "Bauble?" He followed Breckenridge's line of sight to stare at his own hand. "The ring?" he asked weakly.

"Yes, of course, the ring."

"It was my father's."

Breckenridge waved that response aside and bid Cole come closer. "An emerald. Very nice. Solidly square cut. Unimaginative but suggesting strength. I make it to be set in a bed of—what?—twenty diamond chips?"

"Twenty-one," Alastair said on a thread of sound.

"I see. Not at all the usual thing. Meant to mark an anniversary?"

"A birthday."

"Even better. I believe it will do." He put his palm out to accept the ring and waited.

Alastair Cole did nothing at first. "I don't think—"

"No, you don't," Breckenridge said, interrupting. "Perhaps in the future you will."

Jo Goodman

Flushing deeply, Cole nevertheless managed to mount an argument. "The ring is worth a good deal more than my debt."

"I hope so, else where is the incentive for you to return with my money?"

"I couldn't possibly give it to you."

Breckenridge sighed. He did not fail to notice that Cole made no move to withdraw his hand. "So that it is the way it is to be. I had hoped for more, some evidence of backbone, mayhap." He removed the ring from Cole's finger and slipped it onto his own. "We are of a size. That is good."

Except for a hand that trembled slightly now, Cole did not move.

Breckenridge glanced once in the younger man's direction, evincing mild surprise that Cole was still there. He said nothing, merely inclined his head toward the door.

Alastair Cole's hesitation only lasted a moment, and he exited the room a moment after that.

Griffin Wright-Jones waited to hear the door click into place and Cole's heavy footfalls recede before he removed the ring and placed it in a cleverly hidden drawer in his desk. It was then that he permitted himself the luxury of slumping back in his chair. Closing his eyes, he rubbed them gently with his thumb and middle finger in an attempt to ease the ache that had grown steadily behind them.

His lips moved the smallest fraction around words that were merely an expulsion of air. "God's truth, do they never learn?"

Chapter One

Olivia Cole caught her reflection in the cheval glass and paused to take account of herself. She was not by nature a vain woman, but circumstances were such in her life that she could ill afford to present herself in a poor light. It was not possible to hide every aspect of her worry from the servants. She had no illusions that she would ever trod the boards at Drury Lane, but she had hoped she was offering a more untroubled countenance than the one she observed now.

There was no disguising the fact that she had been weeping earlier. Her eyelids were still faintly swollen and the lashes clumped in small, dewy spikes. Swiping at her eyes did not diminish the effect. Her knuckles left pronounced color in an otherwise pale complexion, emphasizing violet shadows beneath her eyes and lending them a bruised, injured look.

Her ginger-colored hair, a fiery problem to be contended with on any given day, had escaped the moorings of all three tortoiseshell combs so that far too many strands were licking at her temples, forehead, and nape like flaming tongues. She raised one hand to make an adjustment, intending to smooth and secure the firestorm, but let her hand fall back to her side when it occurred to her it was too small a gesture and far too late in coming.

The scratching at the door was insistent. Olivia moved slowly in that direction. It was disconcerting to realize that her palms were damp, a condition she noticed when she attempted to press out a wrinkle in the bodice of her day dress. The fold only existed because the incongruously bright, apple-green gown hung on her frame in a way it had not done since she stood for its fitting. She unfastened the grosgrain ribbon beneath her breasts and tied it again, this time more ruthlessly than her maid had done earlier. With the bodice snugly secured, she squared her shoulders and made to reach for the door handle. At the last moment she stopped and reached for the shawl that had been thrown carelessly across a nearby chair. She could pretend at least that she was chilled, when in truth she had a need to hide the collarbones that four days of almost no nourishment had made prominent.

Olivia steeled herself as she opened the door. It was in every way a condition of the mind. Her limbs were in fact trembling.

"Yes, Mrs. Beck?"

The housekeeper bobbed her head once. "Begging your pardon, but there's gentlemen come to inquire after you. I thought I should tell you myself."

"Thank you. That was good of you." Olivia's own maid, to demonstrate her self-importance, had a regrettable tendency to say things she ought not in the servants' hall. Chastisement had had little effect on Molly Dillon, placing Olivia in a position of releasing the girl from service or guarding her own tongue in Molly's presence. Against the advice of Mrs. Beck, Olivia had become more circumspect and Molly remained employed.

"Gentlemen, you say?" asked Olivia. Her mouth was dry, but she resisted the urge to lick her lips. "How many exactly?" Had her father sent them? It was the question uppermost in her mind, and she couldn't pose it to Mrs. Beck without giving more of herself away than she ever had to Molly Dillon.

"Two." There was a small hesitation. "I can't be certain, but I think they might be from Bow Street."

"Runners?" Olivia was glad she'd had the foresight to keep one hand on the door frame and the other resting on the handle. The tenacity of her grip made her knuckles briefly turn white. "Alastair, then. They've come about Alastair." She felt no relief at the thought. As much as she feared they'd come for her, that outcome was preferable to the one that seemed more likely.

"I'm thinking that's so."

Olivia nodded absently while she considered what she must do. "Show them to the drawing room. I will receive them there."

"As you wish." Mrs. Beck bobbed her head again and turned to go, only to be brought up short by Olivia's entreaty.

"Have you a sense of what their purpose might be?"

The housekeeper had drawn up her apron and was twisting the hem in her hands. Anxiety deepened the careworn lines around her eyes and mouth. "I can't say. I tried to get a word from them, but they are like the sphinx, all stone and silence. They don't seem entirely comfortable, I know that. I can't make out what it means, though."

Olivia's breath caught, imagining the very worst.

Mrs. Beck shook her head vehemently. "And you shouldn't make it out to be something that it is not. Oh, I wish I'd left well enough alone." She turned on her heel and this time fled.

Olivia closed the door and leaned against it. There was nothing for it but that she would have to meet her visitors. She might fear what they would say to her, but she had to hear it nevertheless.

Returning to the cheval glass, Olivia made the adjustments to her hair that she had been too weary—no, too *discouraged*— to make earlier. Fixing the combs in their proper position did not greatly improve her appearance, but at least she no longer looked as if she'd just tumbled out of bed. In truth, she'd never been to it, having spent the night sitting in a chair by the fireplace with her feet resting on a hassock.

Olivia applied a bit of powder to her nose and made a swipe under her eyes. The bruised look was marginally erased. She pinched her cheeks to good effect and pressed her lips together to raise a modicum of color.

Her nostrils flared slightly as she took a deep breath. Releasing it slowly, she pronounced herself fit enough to greet strangers, though in no wise of a mood to converse at length. She hoped these runners—if that's what they were—had come without expectations.

Although she approached the drawing room as she imagined the wrongfully condemned approached the gallows, upon opening the door Olivia managed a gracious though somewhat grave smile.

"Gentlemen," she said easily, "I am consumed with curiosity as to your presence in my home. I hope you mean to enlighten me quickly as I am obliged to visit Lady Fontanelle for elevenses."

Neither man spoke for a moment, although they did exchange unreadable glances. Olivia was not at all certain Mrs. Beck was correct in her estimation that they were from Bow Street. For one thing, they dressed rather better than the runners she'd seen mingling with crowds at Vauxhall Gardens or strolling in and around Drury Lane after the theatres released their patrons. These gentlemen wore clothing cut from a different cloth; frock coats that looked as if they'd been tailored to fit comfortably on broader shoulders, waistcoats that did not hang too loosely nor strain the fabric around Corinthian physiques.

The gentlemen were of an age and attitude that reminded her of Alastair. It occurred to her that they might be his intimates, though caution kept her from advancing this assumption.

"Mrs. Cole." The gentleman with russet-colored hair and a nose that looked to have been broken, perhaps several times, made a slight bow as he stepped forward to separate himself from his companion. "I am Stephen Fairley. I was instructed most particularly to speak to you."

Olivia wondered how that could be. He was under the misapprehension that she was *Mrs.* Cole. She did not correct him. "And so you are, Mr. Fairley." She glanced in the direction of his partner. "You, sir? Were you similarly instructed?"

"I was. Patrick Varah, Mrs. Cole." Mr. Varah's clipped blond hair fell across his sloping brow as he bent his head to make his introduction.

Olivia had no intention of making them easy in her presence. She certainly was not easy in theirs. Crossing the room to the small tea table near the fireplace, she deliberately chose a path that forced her visitors to make way for her. Divide and conquer, she reasoned, was always a wise course, even if the effect was short-lived.

"Please state your purpose," she said, turning on them.

"It's thought that you'll already have some notion of that," Mr. Fairley said carefully. "But I was told that if it must be refined upon, I should say that we've come on the matter of a certain emerald ring and a debt of considerable consequence."

Olivia was glad of her foresight to put the table at her side. By placing her right hand on the polished cherrywood top, she was able to keep herself upright. "I see," she murmured. No other response occurred to her. Her mind had become a perfect blank slate.

"You'll want to fetch your pelisse and bonnet," Mr. Varah told her. "Gloves, also. The air is bracing. I shouldn't be surprised if it snows this afternoon." When she didn't move, he prompted rather gently, "You understand we've come for you, don't you? It's expected that you'll return with us."

She nodded once, slowly, though there was no real comprehension behind the movement. Her head ached abominably.

Mr. Fairley took a small step toward her, one hand raised as though to offer support. "Perhaps you should sit." He glanced at his companion. "It cannot hurt to wait for her to recover her wits."

In other circumstances, Olivia would have taken umbrage with Mr. Fairley's characterization of her as witless. The sad truth of the matter, she reflected, was that he had named the thing correctly. When Mr. Varah slipped a claw-and-ball-footed chair behind her knees, she dropped like a stone. The gentlemen hovered momentarily, uncertain, then backed away. She drew a deep, settling breath.

"Rest easy, sirs. I have no intention of fainting." She glanced up in time to witness their relief. Clearly they were not prepared for any reaction from her save for acceptance and co-operation. It made her wish she were given to brief moments of blissful unconsciousness just to test their mettle. High drama did not suit her either, so there would be no wailing or wringing her hands. She resisted even the small urge to press one hand to her forehead, thinking it was precisely the sort of gesture that was overdone on the stage to convey moments of great anxiety.

"I must know about Alastair," she said quietly. "The ring means nothing, the debt less than nothing, if you cannot tell me how he fares."

Mr. Fairley cleared his throat, betraying his discomfort. "I can say, quite truthfully I promise you, that when last I saw your husband he was having a run of good luck at cards and in fine spirits."

Olivia could not divine the exact meaning of that. It seemed to her there was a greater truth that Stephen Fairley was neatly sidestepping. The phrase "in fine spirits" resonated with her, prompting her to wonder if Alastair had been deep in his cups. "You are not from Bow Street, are you?"

"Certainly not," Fairley said, bristling slightly at the suggestion.

As if to ward off a similar insult aimed at him, Mr. Varah interjected, "We are friends of your husband, come to do him a favor."

"I doubt that," Olivia said.

Fairley offered an alternative description. "Amiable acquaintances. I could not say whether your husband counts any man as his friend."

Olivia pressed her lips together and nodded briefly, satisfied Mr. Fairley was in every way more accurate than his companion. "I imagine you play cards at the same table now and again. Mayhap place wagers on the horses."

"Yes."

Taking this in, Olivia tightened the hands folded in her lap. "Did you know him at Cambridge?"

"I did," said Varah. "Fairley here was an Oxford man."

"He told you he was married?" asked Olivia.

"Never breathed a word of it, Mrs. Cole. Fairley and I only learned of it this morning when we were called upon to perform this small service."

"A service, is it? No longer a favor?"

"It can be both," Fairley said. "And it is. I hope you will believe me when I say that your cooperation will be of considerable benefit to your husband. I imagine it is the very thing he is counting on."

Olivia made no reply and allowed silence to settle heavily around her. She drew a modicum of comfort from it as though it were as tangible as the shawl about her shoulders.

After several long moments, Mr. Varah tread lightly into the quiet, tipping his head toward the door. "We should be off, Mrs. Cole. Shall I ring for the housekeeper? You really must dress for the weather. The hack can provide but a thin shield from the wind."

Stoic and graceful, Olivia stood. She forbade to answer Mr. Varah but crossed the room and rang for Mrs. Beck herself. She made no attempt to leave their company in order to prepare for her departure. It occurred to her that she would not tolerate well the humiliation of not being allowed out of their sight. Mr. Fairley and Mr. Varah had been unfailingly well mannered, but she did not mistake that it meant they trusted her. Indeed, she suspected they had been cautioned against it.

For Olivia it was further proof they did not comprehend the nature of her relationship with Alastair. Far from desiring to bolt, she was prepared to surrender herself in whatever manner was required. Alastair would have known that; whoever sent Fairley and Varah did not.

The ride in the hack was rather more brief than Olivia anticipated, lasting not above thirty minutes. She thought it probably seemed much longer to her companions, or at least she hoped that it did. Since leaving the comparative safety of her home, Olivia fancied Varah and Fairley were proving to be more like gargoyles than guards. They sat stonily on either side of her, crowding her with their shoulders and elbows and making no allowance for the fact that she was already occupying very little in the way of space. She ignored the hammering of her heart and tightness in her throat and told herself she was glad of the warmth their proximity provided.

Something good could come of something bad.

She held this thought, as she often did, until she believed it was so.

"What is this place?" Olivia asked, confronting a row of houses as she alighted from the hack. She stiffened a bit as she came to the answer herself. In the light of day there was nothing to obscure the genteel shabbiness of the street or the residences that lined it. The gray stone houses might have been home to gentry half a century earlier, but they were let out as business establishments now. Twin lanterns fitted with red glass were affixed to more than one dark entrance. Curtains were drawn while the occupants of those houses slept on, oblivious to the late hour of the morning.

Glancing on either side of her, Olivia saw that she and her escorts were alone. The hired hack was the only one of its sort on the street. Its noisy approach was probably most unwelcome even as the time was nearing eleven.

She imagined—and she had experience enough to imagine it well—that with a bank of fog rolling up from the river and the forgiving cloak of night, this particular street might present itself as infinitely more appealing, certainly more exciting. Gentlemen about town, especially young gentlemen, would gravitate to this place, called here by the intrigue of something illicit, the hope of something winning, and the promise of something adventurous. If they were fortunate, Olivia supposed, they would leave wiser for the experience without having to explain away the pox to their wives, empty pockets to their creditors, or the lump on their head to their physicians. All of that and more was to be had on a street like this when day gave itself over to night.

Olivia actually sighed, holding up one hand to stave off Mr. Fairley's answer to her question. "It is of no import," she said. "I can't think that it matters where we are. One enterprise is very like another."

Fairley looked pained. "That's not quite so, Mrs. Cole, but it's not for me to explain. We're not much more than a well-pitched stone from Covent Garden. We're standing in Putnam Lane off Moorhead Street." He pointed to the unremarkable gray stone townhouse directly in front of them. "This is Breckenridge's establishment. If it has another name, I've never learned it."

"Pray, Mr. Fairley, how much information would you have felt compelled to impart if I had shown the least interest?" Olivia was gratified to see Stephen Fairley flush at her rebuke. It was a modest sign that she was regaining the use of her faculties.

Varah paid the driver and waved him on. "This way, Mrs. Cole. Mind the steps. I see a glaze."

Olivia ignored the elbow he offered but took his advice to be careful. Mr. Fairley, she noticed, hung back a little. She hoped he was still stinging from her reproach. She swept past Mr. Varah when he threw open the door for her.

The entrance hall was lighted by a single stub of a candle in a wall sconce. It provided enough light for Olivia to avoid bumping into a table set just inside the door but was insufficient to prevent her from catching the toe of her boot on the fringed carpet and stumbling into the newell post. Straightening, she discreetly massaged her hip and fended off Mr. Varah's concern.

The air was stale with the lingering scents of tobacco, alcohol, perfume, sweat, and something oddly sweet that she could not identify. A second sniff assured her that she did not want to apply herself to making that discovery.

When Fairley and Varah had finished stamping their feet and brushing off their hats, Olivia became aware of the inordinate quiet in the house. No one, it seemed, was stirring above or below stairs. No one had come forward from the back of the house to greet them. She regarded her escorts with a new wariness in her eyes, wondering far too late if she was safe to be alone with them.

"We're expected upstairs," Varah said.

Olivia shook her head. "I think I'd like to remain here."

Both Varah and Fairley were prepared to present their argument against it, but they stopped even as their mouths began to shape the protest. Their gazes were drawn upward over the velvet crown of Olivia Cole's bonnet to the top of the stairs.

Viscount Breckenridge nodded once in the way of dismissal. "You've discharged your debt, gentlemen. I can think of no reason we shall have to speak of it again. Ever. That's clear enough, isn't it?"

Olivia had turned her head to follow the line of sight of

Varah and Fairley; now she twisted back to look at them. They were nodding in unison and already replacing their hats. They managed to look at once apologetic and deferential. It was unseemly how quickly they made their departure.

"Olivia Cole?"

Olivia lifted her face in the direction of the voice again. "That's right."

"Good. I'd hate to think they'd gotten it wrong, what with me having just let them go. It's gratifying that my trust in them wasn't entirely misplaced." His dark eyes bore into hers. "It remains to be seen about you."

Olivia wondered what reply she might make to that, but before one occurred to her he was gone and she was left staring at the space he'd occupied. She stood at the foot of the steps for several minutes, determining her course of action. She had the oddest sense that it was a test of sorts, but no sense of how he meant to take her measure. Leaving the townhouse seemed the only sure way she could fail.

Olivia unfastened the ribbons under her chin and removed her bonnet before she began to climb the stairs. She found him in a room that bore a passing resemblance to a place where one might conduct affairs of business and commerce. A large desk was central to the room. Much of its surface area was covered by ledgers, writing paper, and pots of ink. Bookshelves occupied two full walls, and many of the volumes lay on their side to make as much use of the available space as possible. Still, a stack of books rested beside one of the room's two wing chairs, carelessly doubling as a side table complete with an empty cup and saucer on top. The teapot, cream pitcher, and sugar bowl remained on the silver serving tray that rested on a more traditional oval table near the fireplace.

A mirror almost as long as the mantelpiece hung above the hearth. It was mounted in an elaborately carved gold leaf frame and served no purpose that Olivia could divine except to reflect the light of the three silver candelabra situated at

evenly spaced intervals on top of the mantel. Their position-
ing seemed to be exact: three points of order in a room that
might kindly be spoken of as comfortable or cozy, but could
more accurately be described as cluttered. Olivia followed the
cast of light reflected in the mirror and discovered it brightened an area around one of the reading chairs where a footstool had been overturned and a book lay open on the floor.
A wool rug also lay discarded in a heap beside the stool.

The tableau suggested to Olivia that her host was more
eager for her arrival than his disinterest at the top of the stairs
indicated. Of course it was entirely possible that the stool,
rug, and book had been lying there for days and had nothing
at all to do with her presence in the townhouse.

She was aware of her host's interest now. He was comfortably ensconced in the leather armchair behind his desk.
Except to raise one dark eyebrow when she entered the room,
he gave no other indication that he'd noticed her presence.
Nevertheless, she felt his gaze following her as she took a
turn about the room. If he expected her to speak before he
did, he was sadly out of it there. Olivia knew her place, knew
that she could remain silent until she understood the purpose he had in mind for her.

Alastair would be depending upon nothing so much as her
circumspection.

"Is it your nature to be so tolerably composed?" he asked.
"Or must I anticipate that you will fly into the boughs at any
moment?"

"Fly into the boughs?" she said, turning to face him. "No.
That is not done. Not by me."

He stood suddenly, taking note that she held her ground. If
she flinched, it was quite literally only in the blink of an eye.
"Griffin Wright-Jones." Coming around the desk, he made a
small bow. "You look puzzled, Olivia Cole."

"I understood this place to be Breckenridge's establishment."

"It is."

"But you're not Mr. Breckenridge."

"That might be a comfortable fit, but alas, I am not. You must try not to judge me too harshly when you hear the truth of it. It is my dubious honor to be the Viscount Breckenridge. Ahh, yes, well, there you have flinched. It is not an exalted title as these things go, so I don't allow myself to believe you are intimidated by it. You've had some experience with members of rank, I expect, and it did not go well for you."

His glance dropped to her hands. She had long, beautifully tapered fingers that had whitened where she was gripping her bonnet. "You are clutching."

"I beg your pardon?"

"Clutching." He indicated the black velvet brim of her bonnet. "Is that why you removed it? So that you might have something to do with your hands? Or did you think that by making a display of your hair I would be persuaded not to look elsewhere?" He watched her stir a bit uncomfortably as his deliberately narrowed gaze made a slow assessment of her person. "I am credited to have an eye for a woman's true beauty, and I judge that on a day less fraught with tension than this one, your hair is the very least of it."

It was a pretty compliment in a peculiarly left-handed fashion, Olivia thought. She gave it the credence it deserved, which was to say she gave it none at all. He might just as well have picked up a stick and poked her with it. The only recourse she had to spite her tormentor was to relax the grip on her bonnet. To remain unaffected in the aftermath of such a casual and demeaning study was the best revenge.

"Please, won't you be seated?" he asked. "While I applaud your effort, you are not so steady on your feet as you would have me believe."

Olivia would like to have denied it, but being caught in an obvious lie always had unpleasant consequences. Although her pride was wounded, it was relatively unimportant that he correctly surmised that she had yet to get her feet firmly under her.

"Allow me to take your coat," he said. "And the bonnet. You are yet wont to crush it."

Olivia was afraid that even the thought of flinging it at his head would be revealed in her face. She made herself think of jonquils instead, picturing the slim green stems and yellow buds just as they might be moments before flowering. At peace with this vision in her mind's eye, she released the bonnet and permitted him to help her remove her pelisse. Her kid gloves fell out of the pocket where she'd stuffed them earlier, and she almost collided with him in her haste to pick them up.

It was too much to hope that he would not notice the loose stitching on the seams of the second finger and thumb, or that he would not see the palms were shiny with wear. "I was asked to make a rather hurried departure," she said by way of explanation for the poor condition of her gloves. "I took what I was given, I'm afraid. A pair of old favorites."

Olivia watched, vaguely disturbed as he turned them over and touched the back of one with his fingertips. The sensation was such that he might well have been brushing her own hand.

For the second time in the matter of an hour, Olivia dropped heavily into a chair behind her. She followed her host's progress to the door where he pulled the bell cord. In just under a minute a footman appeared in the doorway. Breckenridge gave him the pelisse, bonnet, and gloves and some instructions that Olivia could not properly hear before sending the servant away again.

She had not given a thought to servants before Breckenridge's man made his appearance. Although she had no intention of calling upon one to lend assistance in any circumstance, she was moderately calmed by the knowledge that she and the viscount were not alone in the house.

She'd made her own study of the viscount as he'd stood waiting for the bell to be answered. If he'd noticed her stealing glances in his direction, he'd given no indication that he was the least bothered by it.

Olivia was certain that she'd never seen him before, not that there would have been many opportunities to cross paths. Alastair did not introduce her to his friends, or even his amiable acquaintances, of whom she was now sure Breckenridge was not one.

He did not cast his profile in a way that made him an imposing figure, merely an intimidating one. His dark, chestnut-colored hair was longer than was the current fashion and carelessly furrowed by the fingers he'd plowed through it. His eyes were darker yet and given to narrowing so they did not simply gaze upon the object of his study, but secured it. His features were strong, angular, and except for a pale, thin scar bisecting his left cheek from the temple to the corner of his mouth, perfectly symmetrical. The scar saved him from the beauty that was the marble work of master sculptors and lent him something that was at once more striking and more human, the work of God twisted by man.

Olivia judged him to be not yet thirty, though it was a narrow thing. There was a weariness in his expression as he waited that he had taken pains to hide from her earlier. Even as she wondered at its source, it vanished. If it were not for the fact that she'd glimpsed a similar look in her own mirror, she could have been convinced that she'd imagined it. This commonality did not cheer her in the least. There was no conceiving of what harm might be done by two people with these unfortunate dispositions.

She thought he held himself in a posture of such correctness that it was most likely the product of the combined efforts of nannies, tutors, and a martinet of a mother. His stance lent him height and a certain polish. He made to carry himself in a manner that looked supremely natural, without a hint of the tension, superiority, or self-consciousness that she'd had occasion to observe in others of privilege and formidable education. Then, just as if to dismiss Olivia's notion that he was uncommonly unconstrained, he rolled one of his shoulders and rubbed the nape of his neck with his palm.

The scar was proof that he'd been vulnerable once. His brief massage of corded muscle reminded her that he was vulnerable now. It struck her that it was little enough advantage knowing this fact, but she would accept every scrap he gave her.

When Griffin returned to his desk, he took up a position in front rather than behind it. He pushed aside a stack of ledgers and made room enough for him to rest one hip on the edge. Bracing himself by extending his other leg, he folded his arms across his chest and regarded Olivia Cole with a frankness that had been absent in his earlier scrutiny.

"Have you arrived yet at the reason you are here?" he asked.

"If I am to judge by the interview thus far, I would say it is because you are singularly self-indulgent."

He actually smiled. The impact of the scar was visible now as the left corner of his mouth lifted a bit higher than the right, tugging his grin at a decidedly rakish angle. "Given your experience, it's a fair observation," he allowed. "It is also incorrect, but it is of no consequence to me if you choose to believe differently. Mr. Varah and Mr. Fairley were permitted to give you enough information to secure your cooperation. What did they tell you?"

"Mr. Fairley, I believe it was, informed me it was regarding the matter of a ring and a debt."

"And so it is, and here you are." His eyebrows knit slightly as he continued to regard her. "You're not Alastair Cole's wife, though, are you?"

"No."

His expression cleared as he nodded. "I wasn't certain. The note in my possession only references Olivia. When my sources learned that you shared a residence with Mr. Cole, it seemed the most respectful course to assume you were his wife."

Olivia volunteered no information.

"It occurs to me now that you are also not his mistress."

"No, I am not."

"A relative, then. There are similarities of appearance. His hair is a pale imitation of yours, but the proper coloring is there. The shape of the eyes, I think, is also somewhat alike. Yours are green, are they not?"

"Yes."

"I can't say that I recall his. Perhaps green also, like the emerald he was wearing."

Olivia realized she was gently worrying the inside of her bottom lip with her teeth. She released it and affected a calm she did not feel.

"You are rather tall, also like him, though I believe it attracts more attention when a woman is of a certain height, especially when she is of such a narrow frame that a willow branch could hide her figure. When did you last eat, Miss Cole?"

She blinked, startled by the question. Had she taken more than tea at breakfast? And what of supper yesterday?

"Never mind. Your hesitation speaks for itself." He pushed away from the desk and pulled on the bell cord again. This time his summons was answered by a different servant. He gave instructions for a repast of baked eggs and toast, but before he let the young man go, he asked Olivia, "Do you care for hot cocoa?"

It was an extravagance she rarely indulged. The thought of it made warmth and sweetness settle lightly on her tongue. She had to press her arm against her stomach to quell the rumbling sound.

"Bring the cocoa. Tea as well. Here, take the tray." He stepped aside to permit the servant to enter and remained there until the lad had carried out the task of collecting the service. After closing the door, he returned to his perch on the desk and assumed the exact position he'd had before. "You look as if a draft could move you from that chair."

"You needn't have troubled yourself or your staff," Olivia said. "I'm not hungry."

"A matter of no account. It remains that you'll eat."

"High-handed," she said.

"There you have me." Shrugging, he picked up the conversational thread as if he'd never abandoned it. "Would I be correct that you are Alastair Cole's cousin?"

"No."

"His sister, then. I should have trusted my first notion. I gave too much weight to the physical differences."

Olivia thought he seemed disappointed in himself. A game played and lost. She wondered at it, wondered how much he'd played to amuse himself and how much was done to unsettle her. Perhaps doing both was the point of it all.

"Though why I should have done so," he went on, "does not make practical sense. I have sisters of my own. Three, in fact, and we could not be more dissimilar in appearance or inclination. I take by your expression that you consider it a fortunate turn for my sisters. You would be right, of course. They are wholly respectable, while I . . ." He lifted his hands, palms up, to indicate the entirety of his establishment. "While I, for reasons that are obvious to the meanest intelligence, am not."

As Breckenridge had correctly divined the bent of her thoughts, Olivia decided that saying nothing was the wiser course.

"I should like to hear your opinion on a particular matter, Miss Cole. It *is* Miss Cole, is it not?" When she nodded, he continued. "I'd like you to tell me in which of these three respects the gentleman is the most complete bounder. He surrenders his wife to a man he owes payment. He gives over his mistress to discharge his debt. Or he sacrifices his sister to spare himself a very bad end. I confess, I cannot work it out myself, but it occurs that you might have a cogent position."

Olivia realized she was worrying her bottom lip again. This time she didn't attempt to stop. She drew blood instead.

Her silence did not deter him. "It's a puzzler, isn't it? I have been thinking that if I could arrive at some clever answer, it might make an acceptable teaser in society. Riddles are popular with a certain crowd and their parlor games. It would be a thing oft repeated. The wife. The mistress. The sister." He feigned disappointment when Olivia offered no reply. "It seems nothing occurs to you either. That is too bad. It will have to remain between us, I'm afraid. At least for the nonce. Is your standing in society a concern to you, Miss Cole?"

"I have no standing in society."

"Then perhaps you are fortunate."

"I have never thought about it."

"Truly? Then you are singular. Standing and reputation account for the greatest part of what passes for thinking among the ton."

"I wouldn't know."

"I believe your brother would, though. He has cut a wide swath in society since he's finished university."

"Your sources again, I collect."

"Yes. I have many at my disposal. Knowing one's patrons is part and parcel of operating this establishment."

"If you say so," she said, her tone carefully neutral.

"I do. There are patrons with deep pockets that will never go owing the house. Others whose pockets are considerably lighter and want credit to compensate. Some enjoy long runs of good fortune, and there are those who seem to take perverse pleasure in losing time and again. Both present problems in their own right. Then there are the cheats. Attention must be paid, of course. The surest way of keeping out the deep-pocketed players is to entertain the cheats. So, yes, I find it important to learn something about the gentlemen who frequent my establishment. Prudence dictates it."

"You speak only of gaming."

"And why would I speak of anything else? You do know you're in a gaming hell, don't you?"

"I feel certain that is the least of it."

"Do you? Are your first impressions never wrong?"

"I saw the red lanterns. I know their purpose."

"You did not see them on my door, did you?"

"No."

"But you concluded you were being escorted to a brothel anyway."

She had. "It was not an unreasonable assumption."

"Perhaps not, but it is *not* my business. Did someone tell you otherwise?"

"No."

He nodded once, satisfied that he had impressed the truth of the matter upon her. "Do you want to know the size of your brother's debt?"

"If you'd like to tell me. In truth it doesn't matter if it's one pound or one thousand. I have no money of my own to compensate you."

"As it happens, it is £1,000."

Olivia felt herself in the grip of a chill as color drained from her face. She wished she had chosen a chair closer to the fire.

"If you think you might faint," Breckenridge said, "lower your head to the level of your knees."

She thought people were inordinately worried about her fainting today. "I am not going to faint." She noticed he was as skeptical of her assertion as Varah and Fairley had been.

"My sister Jenny requires almost no provocation to swoon. It's fascinating, really, how she has mastered the art of it. The physicians say they can find nothing to account for it, but then they are forever examining her without her corset. Her husband shares my opinion that she instructs her maid to pull the strings too tight."

"She would not thank you for imparting that information."

"It is by way of educating you. Jenny approves of education. She has a prodigious intellect." One side of his mouth twitched. "Which we all support since she has little in the way of common sense."

"It must gratify her," Olivia said dryly. "Your support, I mean."

The grin deepened momentarily, then was gone. "As it is now a certainty that you will not faint, let us return to the problem of the £1,000. Your brother volunteered that he could pay the debt with an advance on his allowance. I knew that such a large advance would not be forthcoming. Your father is by reputation a clutch-fisted individual, and there appears to be support for the rumor that Alastair has fallen out of favor with him."

"You think you know rather quite a lot."

"I do not require that you confirm or deny anything I am telling you, so ease your mind on that score. I merely present the whole of it as a caution. You will be pleased, I think, to know that as much as I learned about Alastair, I never once received any particulars about you. The most surprising thing to learn about you being Alastair Cole's sister is that it makes you Sir Hadrien Cole's daughter. I wonder that it is not common knowledge."

"I fell out of favor with my father some years ago." Olivia offered Breckenridge this small bone to keep him from digging for a bigger one. She was careful not to hold her breath as she waited to see if it would be enough for him.

"Perhaps that is why your brother came to the conclusion that he could offer you in his stead."

Olivia was on the point of seizing this opportunity to inquire after Alastair when the door opened and the lad who'd removed the tea service appeared on the threshold with a large tray laden with the repast the viscount had ordered.

Griffin Wright-Jones pushed aside more items on his desk and dropped a short stack of account books onto the floor. He pointed to the clearing and removed himself, then he indicated to Olivia that she should take up the chair behind the desk. When she didn't move quickly enough to suit him, he said, "I will not hesitate to put you in it."

Olivia saw the young man bobble the tray on his way to setting it down as he regarded his employer with surprise mixed with wariness. She took that as an indication that the viscount was not in the habit of making threats. She wished she might know better if it was Breckenridge's habit to carry them out. Olivia came to her feet in what she hoped was a dignified manner. It was important to her that her host did not mistake cooperation for intimidation. She had a kind smile for the bearer of the tray as she skirted the desk, but she waited until he was gone before she took her seat.

Aware of Breckenridge's narrowed gaze, Olivia picked up a fork before she was ordered to do so and stabbed at the yellow curds of baked egg. "To spare you from feeding me as well," she said before placing the egg in her mouth.

Griffin slipped into the chair she had occupied and watched her eat. She had no enjoyment of the food, of course, but that was not the point. The point was that she truly looked as if a sudden draft would lift her off her feet.

She wore a shawl about her shoulders, but it had slipped when he'd helped her out of her pelisse and he'd seen the unnaturally prominent line of her collarbones. It was true that her figure did not lend itself to the fullness of sensual beauty, but judging by the bruised shadows beneath her eyes, she had recently acquired an appearance that suggested starvation.

"You're staring," she said.

"Am I?"

Of course he was, and he knew it. "Yes. Has anyone commented that it's impolite to do so?"

"I find that women are glad for the attention."

Olivia thought she might choke on the bite of toast she'd just taken. She managed to push it down with a sip of the cocoa. "You find that . . ." She stopped, unable to repeat the whole of it even to be certain she had not mistaken the words. She simply shook her head and took another sip of her hot drink, nearly closing her eyes with the pleasure of it.

"I may have overstated it," he allowed. He observed that she was not proof against the sweet cocoa. A thin mustache of liquid chocolate appeared just above her upper lip, and even as he wondered if she would raise her serviette or lick it away the tip of her tongue appeared to do the deed. He knew himself to be most grateful. "There are naturally exceptions."

"I wish to be in the category of exceptions."

Griffin gave in easily, but only because the fire was in want of tending and he'd already witnessed the flicker of her tongue along her lip. He rose and crossed to the fireplace where he poked at the coals, then added more from the scuttle. He stood there wondering what he might reasonably expect from Olivia Cole while she cleaned her plate and tipped her cup to swallow the last mouthful of cocoa.

"Will you take tea with me?" he asked when he returned to remove the tray.

"I couldn't possibly."

He did not insist. "Very well. You may remain there. It is a comfortable chair, is it not?"

It was, but the soft leather also held the faint scent of him. There was nothing comfortable about that. "I think I would prefer a turn about the room."

"As you wish." He set the tray on a side table and poured himself a cup while Olivia picked her way among the detritus that was the evidence of his work. "The servants dust and polish only. I don't allow them to move anything."

It was unnerving the way he seemed to respond to her thoughts as if she'd spoken them aloud. "It seemed that might be the case. There is some method, I expect, to your placement of papers and journals and accounts."

"I begin a new pile and never move it."

"I suppose that system has merit."

"Do not tempt fate by shifting even so much as the quills on my desk. The one servant who disobeyed me was summarily discharged."

"Then I beg of you, make me your servant."

Her quick response reminded Griffin that Alastair had written that she was both clever and resourceful. She had given him ample proof of the former. He decided to accept her brother's word on the latter.

He added a dram of whiskey to his tea before settling in the leather chair she'd given up. Observing her interest in the wall of books, he said idly, "In truth, I haven't determined what use I might make of you, but you can be confident it will not be as my servant. I am a generous employer, still, you would have to give over the rest of your life to service if there were to be a prayer of repaying your brother's debt."

Olivia was not unaffected by his words. She adjusted the shawl about her shoulders to retain some semblance of warmth. "You have not told me where Alastair is."

"You have not asked."

She thought she could wait him out, but he was sipping contentedly from his toddy and appeared in no wise ready to offer information. "Where is my brother?"

"I haven't a notion."

"He's not here?"

"I know everyone who is under my roof; if he was one, I would have a notion, wouldn't I?"

Olivia frowned. "Then you don't mean to exchange me for my brother?"

"Is that what you thought? I hadn't realized. You're here because your brother expressly said you should be. You don't believe me? Come. Read this for yourself."

Griffin set his cup down and opened the hidden cubby in his desk where he'd secreted Alastair Cole's ring. What he drew out was not that piece of exquisite jewelry, but a slip of neatly creased tri-folded paper. He held it out to Olivia. Hesitation was evident in every one of her steps. "You don't look particularly eager to read it. I can find no fault with that. Would you rather I summarize?"

Shaking her head, Olivia took the last few steps to the desk and removed the paper from his hand. To afford herself some small privacy, in spite of the fact that he knew the contents very well, she gave him her back as she read.

Dear Breckenridge,

I pray that you will understand that I could not abandon the ring. It is an heirloom entrusted to my care. When I learned that you were not wearing it, I knew what I must do. If there is to be the slightest hope that my allowance will be advanced, I must make the request in person, and I cannot do that without the ring in my possession.

In place of the ring, I suggest you seek out Olivia at my Jericho Mews residence. While the ring's value can be measured, Olivia's cannot. She is vastly clever and resourceful, a gem rarer than the one I bear once again on my finger. Take her to your hell, but show her more care than the disdain you showed for my bauble. She will reward you in ways you cannot imagine. You have my word that I will come for her with every shilling owed.

Your servant,
Alastair Clark Cole, Esq.

It was on Olivia's second reading of her brother's missive that her hands began to tremble. She dropped the paper, and when she stood up from retrieving it, she felt peculiarly light-headed. The floor listed, then the wall of books shifted in a like manner. The volumes lying on their sides suddenly stood upright. The mirror tilted at an angle that should have sent it crashing to the floor. The logs in the fireplace were vertical while the flames flickered on the horizontal.

The perspective that guided her steps, controlled her balance, and made it possible for her to know up from down failed her in every conceivable way.

Griffin acted quickly, reaching her side in time to prevent her from hitting the floor in the event she fainted. True to her word, though, Olivia Cole did not faint.

She surrendered the most recent contents of her stomach instead.

Chapter Two

Embarrassment flushed Olivia's cheeks. She stared at the mess she'd made, some of it on the black wool waistcoat of his lordship, and thought she might be sick again. Apparently Breckenridge thought so too, because he quickly pushed her back into a chair, grabbed the silver dome used earlier to cover her plate of baked eggs and toast, and, turning it over, pressed it into her lap like a bowl.

She clutched it against her midriff, lowered her head, and was sick a second time. Breckenridge did not leave her side, though she wondered how he was able to stand there. Perhaps he'd closed his eyes. She risked a glance upward and saw that, no, he hadn't. His concern seemed genuine, then she remembered she was worth £1,000 pounds to him, more in fact if he expected to collect interest. Olivia had a suspicion that he did.

She accepted the handkerchief he held out to her but retained her possession of Alastair's marker. Although she'd memorized the contents, she was not eager to part with it.

Olivia pressed the handkerchief against her mouth, blotted her lips, then offered it back. The gesture was refused.

"You may keep it," Griffin said.

When Olivia glanced up a second time, she saw he had already removed his frock coat and was carefully unbuttoning his ruined waistcoat. Once he'd shrugged out of it, he held it by the collar between his thumb and forefinger and carried it to the door. He released the waistcoat, allowing it to fall in a heap on the floor, then rang for assistance.

Olivia's embarrassment grew as she watched Breckenridge remove his stained chitterling and discard it on top of the waistcoat. She found a soupçon of comfort in the fact that she had missed his boots and trousers. He might very well have stripped to his linen and stockings if she had not.

"You should not have insisted that I eat," she said, her tone more defensive than accusatory.

"You neglected to mention that you are unwell."

"I am *not* unwell."

Griffin cast a dubious glance in her direction. "Then it was your intention to serve me breakfast, I take it."

She flushed. "Do not be ridiculous." Leaning forward, Olivia placed the overturned cover carefully on the floor. It tipped a bit to one side but its contents were not lost. She looked away and sat up slowly so that she would not be sick again. "It gives me no pleasure to admit it, but the room simply tilted on its axis and I had no bearings. That is what made me ill."

"Perhaps."

"You don't believe me?"

"On the contrary. As an explanation, though, it begs the question of what caused the room to tilt. I could advance my theory, but I will wait to hear what my physician thinks."

"Physician?" It required considerable effort for Olivia to remain seated. "I do not think a physician is at all necessary."

"Then it is a good thing you have no say in the matter." Griffin gave her his back as he opened the door for the approach of his valet. "Mason. Good man." He stepped aside to permit his manservant's entry. "I'm afraid there's been a bit of a—" Griffin was not certain how he wanted to describe it, so he merely pointed to the discarded items of clothing and allowed Mason a moment to make his own assessment.

"I see, sir. I'll take care of it." He made a sweep of the room with a glance that missed nothing, barely resting on either his lordship's guest or the bits of vomitus on the Aubusson rug near her feet. The overturned dish cover gave him brief pause, then he quickly moved to see that all else was in order. "I'll send one or two of the lads to make short work of the rest." Stepping closer to Breckenridge, he made a discreet inquiry. "Is the lady still unwell?"

"All evidence to the contrary, she says she was never unwell in the first place." Unlike his valet, Griffin did not set his voice at a pitch that could not be overheard. "She says the room tilted."

"Foxed, then," Mason said without inflection.

"I had not considered that." Behind him, Griffin heard Olivia's sharp intake of breath. He smiled, but it was for Mason alone. "Send for Pettibone anyway and have someone prepare a room for our guest. It is a certainty that she will be with us for at least a few days, possibly as long as a fortnight."

Mason's rounded features showed the first hint of discomfort. "I feel I must remind you that there are no females among the staff here. You said you didn't want—"

"Yes, yes. I recall what I said. God's truth, but this is an inconvenience I have no liking for." He glanced back at Olivia and asked somewhat impatiently, "Do you require your maid?"

Surprised in equal parts by his question and his tone, Olivia's lips parted around an indrawn breath even as her chin came up. Neither action served to provide an answer.

Griffin plowed a hand through his hair, deepening the furrows. "It's a certainty that she will require clothes and sundries. You may as well arrange for her maid to be brought here along with whatever —"

Now Olivia did come to her feet. "No!"

Although it was Griffin's tendency to arch one dark eyebrow, the effect of Olivia's outburst was to cause him to raise both. If she continued in such a manner the effort required to restrain himself would likely exhaust him. His look pinned her back, and while she did not sink into the chair she'd vacated, neither did she step away from it or voice a second protest. Watching her still, he spoke to his valet. "The physician only for now. I will let you know about the other later."

"Very good, my lord." Mason stooped to pick up the clothing and backed out of the room, leaving a lingering impression that he was glad to do so.

Griffin waited until Mason's steps receded before he advanced on Olivia. He pointed to the chair at her back. "Sit." While his voice made it clear he would brook no argument, he noticed that she was slow in complying. He chose to believe it was the last vestige of her illness that made her so. The thought that she would prove to be difficult at every turn was not one he wanted to entertain.

"I do not want you to bring my maid here," Olivia said, staring at her hands.

"No one has ever accused me of being a slow top. I gathered that was what you meant when you said *no*."

Olivia did not have to look up to know that he was still out of patience with her. "She would not manage herself well in your establishment."

"She only has to manage you," said Griffin. "I don't care—" He stopped because in point of fact he *did* care. "Not manage herself well *how*? Speak plainly, Miss Cole, else I will put my own construction upon it."

"It pains me to speak ill of her, but she is a gossip and engages in flirtations." She could have added that Molly Dillon was barely adequate as a lady's maid, but it seemed a harsh judgment and Breckenridge was sure to inquire why she hadn't been dismissed already. Olivia did not want to tell him that she simply hadn't the heart for it. It did not bear thinking what he would make of that aspect of her character. "Dillon might prove to be an unsettling presence."

That would make two of them, Griffin thought. *Bloody hell.* "Very well. I will ask Truss to inquire after a more circumspect female, though where he will find one in this part of London is a mystery to me. It is my good fortune that it will be his problem. As butler, it falls on him to make those choices."

"How convenient for you."

Nothing in her tone suggested sarcasm, and Griffin allowed that she was able to make her point without it. It was his unhappy observation that too often people were compelled to underscore their meaning with a certain heaviness of inflection, especially those of his acquaintance who mistook sarcasm for witticism. He made a point to avoid their company as the comments from those impoverished minds failed to amuse him.

The door rattled, drawing his attention to it. "Enter!" A pair of lads from the kitchen hurried into the room. "So it fell to the two of you to manage this bit of business. You have must have sorely displeased Cook."

They ducked their heads in unison and mumbled something about a meat pie as they set about wiping the floor and carrying off the dish cover. The younger one, a boy of ten with a gap-toothed smile and a smudge of freckles and something else across his cheeks, politely asked Olivia to set her right foot forward. "It's just that I'm noticing a bit of muck here, miss. Don't want you bothered by it later."

Olivia raised her hem just enough that she could see what he did. Cheeks flaming, she pushed the foot forward as he'd asked. It was quickly wiped clean.

"Thank you, miss." The gap-toothed grin was gone as he made a last swipe at the floor and folded his large rag around the offending bits of egg and toast. He took a brush from the water pail he'd carried in and just as efficiently dealt with the stain on the carpet. "Like it never happened," he said. "Once the water dries, that is." He turned his shoulder so Breckenridge could cast a glance at the spot. "Is it all right by you, m'lord?"

"It is." Griffin tipped his head toward the door. "Go on. Both of you. Leave the teapot, though. And both cups. Take the rest."

The second lad pushed his tongue to the corner of his mouth as he carefully balanced the tray while removing the delicate teapot and china. That little pink tongue disappeared once he'd accomplished the task. He bobbed his flaxen head in acknowledgment of his dismissal and hurried to follow his compatriot into the hallway.

Olivia thought she spied a hint of amusement in the shape of Breckenridge's mouth. She couldn't be certain as she only caught it in profile as the boys were taking hasty leave of him. The speed of their retreat probably had something to do with the stolen meat pie, but whether they were hurrying away from his lordship's discipline or racing for the pie while it was still warm was something Olivia did not expect that she would ever know.

Griffin returned to the chair behind his desk and lifted his teacup. "I would consider it a rare piece of luck in this morning's work if we were not visited by another interruption until the physician arrives."

It put Olivia in something of a bind to make any response at all. She would welcome a series of interruptions as long as none of them was the physician. She suspected he knew it well enough, so she forbade to comment.

"Will you take tea now?"

"I believe I will."

"Whiskey?" Griffin rescinded the offer when he saw her blanch. "Perhaps not." He poured her a cup without benefit of cream or sugar and slid it across the desk toward her.

Olivia reached for it, tempted to push her tongue to the

corner of her mouth to aid in balancing the saucer and cup in the same way the kitchen lad had sought to balance the tray. "Thank you." She was gratified to see the cup didn't tremble as she lifted it to her lips. The taste of it was welcome, washing away the unpleasantness that lingered in her mouth and throat.

"I should like to discuss your brother's marker," Griffin said. "You realize that's what it is, don't you?"

She nodded. "I'm familiar with the term. I'm afraid I don't understand the whole of what happened. He lost money at your games, that much is clear, though why you permitted him to amass such a debt is not. Did you not make a point earlier that you knew your patrons?"

"I wasn't present, else it would not have occurred. I had to be away from town that evening. It was upon my return that Mrs. Christie informed me of what had transpired."

"Mrs. Christie?"

"A friend," he said shortly. "She is sometimes called upon to observe the play in my absence."

Olivia thought she should refrain from advancing any observations regarding Mrs. Christie. Though she dearly wondered if the woman was a partner in Breckenridge's business, she did not put the question to him either.

"She did not know the extent of Mr. Cole's existing debt until she laid the whole of the evening's play before me. I take responsibility for the oversight, but not responsibility for the debt. That is your brother's."

Olivia did not argue the point. He was right. "It is difficult to imagine that Alastair willingly parted with the ring. As he mentioned, it is an heirloom."

"He told me it belonged to his father."

"Yes. And his father before, and so on. That is what qualifies it as an heirloom."

Griffin thought she delivered her darts with a gentle touch.

He would check himself for wounds later. "Yes, well, he didn't precisely offer," he admitted. "He didn't resist either."

"Were you threatening to cut off his finger?"

"It didn't come to that."

But it might have. The thought came so strongly to her that Olivia wondered if she'd spoken it aloud. Breckenridge's unapologetic, matter-of-fact expression told her that she may as well have. He'd plucked the thought just that easily from her head.

"As I recall," Griffin said, "I admired the ring, he protested for form's sake, I asked for it, and he held out his hand for me to take it. It was accomplished with a minimum of fuss. I wore it until he left the room, then I put it away." He held up his hands to show they were bare. "I gave your brother four days to come up to snuff. He benefited by the fact that I was called away again so that I did not discover the ring had been exchanged for his marker until very late last night. You benefited because I waited until this morning to make you account for it."

Olivia trusted that was so. His anger was well checked today, but she did not think she would have cared to witness it last night when every one of her own nerves was so tautly stretched. She acknowledged his restraint. "It was a kindness that you waited. Thank you."

"I didn't do it for you."

She nodded. "I know, but it's true I benefited."

A small crease appeared between Griffin's eyebrows as he continued to regard her closely. "Are you being clever, I wonder. If so, you should know that I am not easily taken in."

"I thought I was being honest. If you think there is something clever in that, I will not attempt to dissuade you."

He raised his cup once more to his lips, wishing—not for the first time—that he had more whiskey in the thing than tea. He drank, set the cup down, and allowed himself a small admission. "I cannot say that you have met or exceeded my expectations, Miss Cole, since I conceived of none, but I think there is no harm in telling you that I find you to be a most singular individual. I offer no judgment as to the good or bad of it. It is simply that I want to acknowledge a certain peculiarity of character about you that I find more intriguing than annoying."

Olivia tilted her head a fraction as she took in the import of his words. "Then I have missed the mark, my lord, for I did so wish to be annoying."

A glimmer of a smile played along his mouth. "It is my perversity, I'm afraid, not yours, that makes it thus. We shall have to, both of us, endeavor to go forward. Now, I should like to have your brother's marker returned to me. It is crushed in one of your fists, I believe."

Olivia saw no merit in pretending to be surprised by his observation. She would have liked to destroy Alastair's marker, true, but she also would have liked to have accomplished the thing without being caught out. It was borne home to her once more that very little escaped his lordship's notice. She stood and handed over the note.

"You show considerable restraint yourself, Miss Cole. For a moment I thought you might dunk it in your tea."

She might have, had it occurred to her. "It's yours," she said simply.

"So was the ring . . . briefly." He ran the side of his hand over the note, smoothing it out so he could then fold it neatly. When he was done he returned it to the cubby he'd taken it from, then sat back in his chair and made a steeple of his fingers as he considered what must be done.

"I presume you know your brother better than I. What do you predict he will do?"

"He will speak to our father."

"Will he? You don't think he'll run off? I had the sense that he was almost pleading with me to take you. I considered that he wanted to relieve himself of the responsibility, though how he can be your caretaker or guardian surpasses my understanding. He is an unlikely candidate for the role since he is in no fashion responsible for himself."

"He won't run off."

"Even if Sir Hadrien refuses his request?" Griffin saw her hesitate and knew he had hit the mark directly. "You are not so certain now, are you? Has Mr. Cole any other means of raising so much of the ready?"

"I cannot say."

"Which means he doesn't."

"It means I cannot say. My brother does not confide everything to me."

"Why not? He writes that you are clever and resourceful. Vastly clever. Why does he not avail himself of such intelligence as you are alleged to possess?"

"Although I am older by three years, Alastair has recently come to fancy himself my protector."

So she was four and twenty. He'd wondered. "God help you, then."

Olivia set her mouth in a disapproving line. "You tell your sisters all, I collect."

Hoist by his own petard, Griffin admitted that he did not. His exact words were, "Perish the thought."

"Just so. My brother determines what I must know. It is frustrating and worrisome, but telling him that changes nothing. He promises he will do better, but he is a man, and thinks he must have his secrets from me."

Griffin considered this, uncertain what he could believe. "Would regularly visiting this establishment and others like it be one of his secrets?"

"In a manner of speaking. I knew he enjoyed making wagers and participated frequently in the sort of silly speculations that young men take into their heads. You must be familiar with such things. Will the hack driver turn right or left at the next crossroads? How many pitchers of ale can the serving girl balance on her tray without mishap? Will it rain before noon, do you think? Snow? Hail? Can a certain gentleman deep in his cups still have his way with the—"

Raising one hand, Griffin stopped her. "I am familiar," he said dryly. "The hack driver, by the way, usually turns left, and four pitchers is generally as many as a serving girl can manage."

"It is good information to have." Given a tray large enough, she could carry six pitchers. That peculiar talent was not something she intended to share with the viscount. "My point is that I was aware of Alastair's wagering. That he was frequenting your establishment or any other hell was unknown to me."

"You lived in the same house."

"Yes."

"Where did you think he was going of an evening?"

Olivia's eyes dropped to her hands. The teacup she was holding between them was growing cold. There was little enough of the tea left, and she determined that she must drink the last of it.

"Your avoidance of an answer can only be temporary at best," Griffin pointed out. "I will have the truth—or some version that passes for it—from you."

Olivia smiled politely, if somewhat coolly, and finished her drink. She replaced the cup in the saucer and moved both to the desk, resting them on top of a short stack of papers so there would be no risk to the finely polished wood grain. "Is it your practice to use thumbscrews?" she asked, sitting back once more. "Or must I steel myself for the rack?"

Griffin said nothing for a moment. His sigh conveyed more in the way of disappointment than frustration. "You are least amusing when you are trying be."

Olivia felt her cheeks warming. Effort was required not to flinch in response to his dark, unwavering gaze. With a stare such as he possessed, thumbscrews and the rack were superfluous.

"If you must know, and apparently you must," she said, "I believed my brother was visiting a lady friend."

This was a bit of intelligence that Griffin had not anticipated. The larger question for him was if it had any basis in fact. "What made you think so?"

"Small things. His attention to his appearance. His restlessness of an evening as the hour grew late. The time he spent at his desk dealing with correspondence. I don't believe he was ever so diligent as he appeared to be recently. It may be that he was only preparing markers similar to the one he left for you. I couldn't know that, naturally. I imagined he was writing sonnets."

"Sonnets."

"Do young men not compose them any longer?"

"Not since Byron set the standard beyond what mere mortals can put to paper."

"Well," Olivia said flatly, "I thought he was writing sonnets."

"Let us pursue what you thought a bit longer. Was there a particular female you considered a candidate for your brother's affections?"

She shook her head. "No one, I'm afraid. There were no introductions. I am . . . I am not often about in society."

Griffin wondered at her hesitation. There was a moment there when he was certain she was choosing her words carefully. He decided not to press further into the reasons for her isolation. It was true enough, he knew, else how had she not come to his attention when he'd first made inquiries about her brother? Neither had those inquiries revealed evidence of a paramour or mistress. The absence of such information was troubling, although he allowed that Olivia Cole's assumptions could be without foundation. It did seem possible, however, that Alastair Cole's evenings out were occupied with more than visiting the gaming hells, and Griffin realized that in addition to everything else he was confronting of late, he now had to concern himself with the reliability of his sources. If he could not trust that he was being given all the information, then he could trust none of it.

"It may be that your brother did not consider his lady friend suitable for introduction," Griffin said. "That must have occurred to you."

It was just as likely that the reverse was true, but Olivia did not offer that. "It did enter my mind that Alastair had set up a mistress. I suppose that when I noticed there were less funds to deal with the household accounts, I considered it more acceptable that he would squander his allowance on love of a woman than love of gaming or drink."

Griffin's narrow, crooked smile held a hint of derision. "You are a romantic, then."

"No. Not at all. But I hold out hope that others might be."

She had surprised him again. Intrigued him, really. "I confess this day is turning out as nothing I could have foreseen."

Did he imagine it was any different for her? In spite of Alastair's note stating his intentions and her own words to the contrary, she was not convinced that her brother was on his way to Sir Hadrien's. If he'd thought of some other scheme to raise the money, he would be engaging in it now rather than journeying to their father's.

"Can you tell me what your brother meant by the turn of phrase: *she will reward you in ways you cannot imagine?*"

Olivia saw that Breckenridge did not consult her brother's marker. Evidently he had memorized the contents as well. She sought out a place of tranquility in her mind—this time a wheat field made golden by sunshine—and lay herself down at its very center. With panic momentarily quelled, she answered with preternatural calm. "You must not make too much of it. It is the sort of hyperbole that Alastair is wont to make when the truth does not serve."

"And the truth in this case would be . . . ?"

"That I am of no particular value to anyone, my lord. I have no funds, nor any hope of securing them. I have no happy talents. My interests are pedestrian and unlikely to change. I cannot say that I have any particular accomplishments. I do not play the pianoforte. Neither do I sing, paint, embroider, or ride. It would take considerable time to name all the things I cannot do, do not want to do, and will not do, so I hope you will spare us both that exercise."

Griffin was silent a moment, taking it in. "I see. Then tell me why I should keep you here."

"I can think of no reason." She all but leapt to her feet.

"You are not an exclamation point, Miss Cole. Sit down."

She sat. Slowly. "It seemed you were on the point of dismissing me."

"You would do well not to assume you know the bent of my mind." He leaned forward in his chair and set his forearms and folded hands on the desk. Tapping his thumbs lightly, he regarded Olivia Cole without expression. He owned that she suffered his direct study without demonstrating the least discomfort. Judging by the angle of her chin and the brightness in her eyes, she was preparing to challenge him if he gave her cause.

"Let us be clear, Miss Cole, that even if you are the single most unaccomplished female of my acquaintance, you are still worth a sum of £1,000. That your brother would have me believe you are worth something more than that, I am willing to credit to his affection for you and a healthy regard for his own skin. He could hardly say you were worth less, then offer you—however temporarily—in place of his debt. You can agree with that, can't you?"

Although it was reluctantly offered, Olivia nodded shortly.

"It is also true, though perhaps not so obvious, that the longer you remain under my roof, the larger your brother's debt grows and your worth increases. I cannot conceive that you are less expensive to accommodate than any other of the females that I know."

"Perhaps you will be pleasantly surprised, my lord. I do not require that you accommodate me. In deference to my brother's predicament, you can rest assured that I will ask for as little as necessary to assure my survival."

"Then I will be surprised. It is my experience that women who begin by having the fewest needs soon come to a place where they must needs have it all. If you prove to be the exception, your brother and I will both have cause to thank you."

"Might I know what your intentions are?" asked Olivia.

"My intentions? Yes, I suppose they are uppermost in your mind. I believe I mentioned that you will have a room prepared for you, be attended by a physician, eat a meal that you can keep down, and have the comfort of your own possessions as they will be brought here. Other than the visit by the physician, I imagine every day will be like every other. You will eat, rest, entertain yourself, and stay well away from the activities in this house."

Olivia listened to this and knew a profound sense of relief. It struck her that perhaps she should have had more faith in Alastair's judgment. He had been in desperate straits, true enough, to suggest that Breckenridge accept her in place of the ring, but he hadn't precisely sent her into a lion's den. The viscount was not without scruples, it seemed, and he appeared to have no designs upon her person. She was under no illusions that Alastair's admonition to Breckenridge that he show more care for her than he'd shown for the ring carried the weight of threat with his lordship. He would do as he pleased.

"I should like to return to my residence to pack my things," Olivia said. She held out no real hope that he would allow it, but it was not an unreasonable suggestion.

"No. Your maid, or someone you deem better able to make decisions regarding your wardrobe, will have to do it. Otherwise, the task will fall upon someone of my choosing."

"As you wish. I think I should offer some explanation for my absence, don't you?"

"And so it begins," he said under his breath. "She who has no needs is already asking for paper, pen, and ink." He pushed all of it in her direction. "You may compose your missive here. Be certain that I intend to read it."

Pulling her chair closer to the edge of his desk, Olivia murmured her agreement. With Breckenridge poised to take the paper immediately from her possession, she had little choice but to be brief and believable. She considered several different introductions, then decided that bold was best.

Olivia barely lifted the quill as she wrote, waiting until her words disappeared to nothingness before she deigned to dip her pen in the ink. She scratched out five sentences, read them over for legibility and accuracy, then signed her name. The ink had not yet dried when Breckenridge took it from her.

"Who is Mrs. Beck?" he asked, glancing up at her.

"Our housekeeper."

"She will not question this?"

"I don't believe so. She suspected Mr. Fairley and Mr. Varah were from Bow Street, and she is aware we spent very little time together before I left with them. I think she will be relieved to learn that they were friends of Alastair come to take me to him. As he has been gone from the house most of this last sennight, it seems reasonable to suggest that he has fallen ill and that I am to attend him."

"You make no mention of where that is precisely."

"I thought you might suggest something. It is not appropriate that I should put this residence."

Griffin conceded the point. "Very well. To allay the concerns of your staff and avoid any true confrontation with Bow Street, let us agree your brother is recuperating at Wright Hall in Surrey."

"Really?" she asked. "Surrey? Why there?"

"Because that is bloody hell where I say he is."

She blinked.

Ignoring her startled look, Griffin bent to the task of adding the address as a postscript. He glanced over the missive and decided it would do. Tempering his impatience to be done with this thing, he said, "You have requested only one trunk. Will that be sufficient?"

"I will not be here long."

He made a sound at the back of his throat that she was meant to take for skepticism and put the letter aside. "Someone will show you to your room directly. It should be ready by now, and you will wait there for my physician."

It was the butler Truss who escorted Olivia to her room. He hadn't much to say as he was clearly discomfited by her presence. Her bedchamber, he told her, was on the same floor as the viscount's, but at the rear of the townhouse. He mentioned it only because he wanted her to know that he hadn't put her in the servants' quarters as it didn't seem fitting. He made a point to explain that every other room in the establishment had a most particular purpose and that she wasn't to be in any one of them without the express consent of Breckenridge himself.

Olivia had no reservations about agreeing to that.

The bedchamber was more than adequate for her needs. She was surprised to find that a small bathing room adjoined it. The copper tub was of such ridiculously large dimensions that she was sure the water would be cooled before it could be sufficiently filled. She had to squeeze around the tub to reach the washstand. Bracing her arms on the marble top, she confronted her reflection once again. In spite of her embarrassing bout of sickness, she could see that her color had improved since earlier this morning. Such was the influence of the viscount. Olivia counted it as a good thing she would not have to endure another interview with him during her stay. He was as desirous of ignoring her presence as she was desirous of being ignored.

All things considered, it could be much, *much* worse.

Olivia removed the tortoiseshell combs from her hair. She glanced around and saw that no brush had been provided. Using one of the combs and her fingers, she managed to weed the small knots from her hair and finally tamed it in a thick braid. To secure the plait, she removed the ribbon that defined her bodice and wrapped it around the tail. Satisfied, she poured water into the washstand bowl and applied a damp flannel to her face and throat.

Moderately improved in spirit, if only temporarily, Olivia returned to the bedchamber. It was comfortably appointed with a neatly made bed and night tables on either side of the plump pillows. A blue-and-brown plaid wool rug lay folded at the foot of the bed. A fire had been laid and there was a stack of logs on the marble apron. The armoire was sufficiently large to store what belongings would be brought for her and a narrow chest of drawers would hold incidentals and sundries.

There was only one painting and it hung on the same wall as the door. She would be able to see it when she woke and the thought cheered her. The artist had used the brightest colors in his palette to create a scene of kites flying in the park. It was easy to imagine the dizzying motion of the kites and the children who ran after them, arms stretched, clutching their strings in small fists. She thought it was an odd choice for a room that probably rarely saw visitors, but then it was also safe here, and it was unlikely to have drawn the notice or approval of Breckenridge's gamers.

The bedroom's sole window overlooked the small garden and alley beyond. Olivia tied back the heavy velvet drapes to allow the modest light of an overcast sky to enter. There was but a single chair and it was situated too close to the bed and not close enough to the fire. Olivia changed that, turning it so she could have all the benefit of the flames, then tested it for comfort.

When she sat down she did not imagine she could fall asleep, or even that she would want to, yet once she had fit herself between the wings of the chair and curled her feet under her it was as if the choice had been taken from her. She did not recall her head tipping to one side or her eyes drifting closed. Sleep came upon her surely and deeply and led her to a place without dreams, without cares, but also without hope.

"She didn't rouse easily," Dr. Pettibone said. "I didn't know what to make of it at first."

"Exhaustion," Griffin told him.

The doctor nodded. "I did not assume that she was drugged." He was slight of stature but had an air of great consequence about him. It was not without reason. His reputation was one of caring and competence, and he confounded his colleagues by his willingness to enter the brothels and gaming hells on Putnam Lane. "That is what she said as well, though she gave me cause enough to wonder if she was lying."

Griffin turned away from pouring the doctor a small whiskey. "How so?"

"She was adamant that she did not want to be examined."

"I warned you." He finished pouring the drink and carried it to Pettibone. "I hope you did not let her protestations sway you."

"No, but I was ever mindful of her modesty. I found her to be peculiar in that regard. The ladies here in the lane are rather more indifferent to stripping to their chemises. I'm afraid I expected the same from her. You did not tell me she was no whore."

"Bloody hell, Pettibone. I didn't tell you she was."

The doctor knocked back half of his drink. "Yes, well, as I mentioned, I was able to make my examination, though not as thoroughly as I might have otherwise done. You understand, don't you? I cannot say with complete confidence that she is or is not pregnant. I believe that was your first concern."

Griffin actually closed his eyes and put a hand to his temple. "I don't believe I voiced my concern. I said she became violently ill after breaking her fast. I sent for you so that I would know the cause."   ,

The thin line of Pettibone's lips disappeared as he flattened his mouth. The expression was equal parts defensive and disapproving. "Pregnancy *is* a cause of such sickness. I had to consider it."

"Then give me your considered opinion," Griffin said wearily. "Not what you know or can prove, but what you think."

"That is rather backward from the way one normally arrives at these things, but for you, Breckenridge, I will make an exception. Your guest—and I do take umbrage that neither you nor she saw fit to share her name—is likely suffering from nerves. I concluded this after eliminating drink and opium use as other possibilities. She owned that she has not slept well these last few evenings and that she has very little appetite. She has also had headaches. A small one today; a violent one only yesterday. These are often the physical manifestations of a nervous condition."

Pettibone finished his drink and set his glass aside. "She masks it well in some regards, though it is probably not in her best interest to do so. Such anxieties as she has will express themselves whether she wishes it or not. Straightforward or sideways. She cannot hope to contain all her apprehensions without suffering for it."

Frowning, Griffin set himself on the edge of his desk. "You entertain the most singular notions, Pettibone."

Not at all offended, the physician nodded. "I do not bleed my patients either. You will want to know what is to be done, of course."

"Of course."

"I gave her a small bottle of laudanum. Used sparingly it will help her sleep—which sets the stage for her recovery—and relieve such megrims as she has from time to time. Naturally, you must insist that she eats. Toast and broth at first, I think, then as her appetite improves she may have whatever she likes that her stomach will tolerate."

Griffin watched Pettibone shift slightly in his chair, unwittingly signaling his discomfort with what must be said next. "Out with it," Griffin said. "I am paying you to hear it all."

Pettibone cleared his throat. "If I understood correctly, then she is to be your guest for several days. Truss informed me it could possibly stretch a fortnight." When Breckenridge did not interject information to the contrary, Pettibone continued. "She will not be improved by being confined to a single room. I believe—"

"Did she complain?" Griffin asked sharply.

"No. No, not at all. Quite the opposite. She remarked that she found her accommodations perfectly agreeable and was untroubled by your insistence that she should not leave her room."

"Then what is the problem?"

"The problem is that she *must* leave from time to time. It is critical for her condition that she take regular exercise. That cannot be accomplished by taking a turn about a room so small as the one she is in. Fresh air will do remarkably well for her. Once a day will be sufficient. Twice would be ideal."

Griffin had thought the headache he was nursing could not become worse. Here was proof that he was wrong. "She said it was out of the question, didn't she?"

"What she said was that she would do whatever I recommended, but that permission for such daily outings was only yours to give."

"Good lord," Griffin said, more to himself than the doctor. "But she can make a thing turn back on itself."

"How is that again?"

Griffin shook his head. "It is unimportant. What else came of your examination?"

"It is just as critical that she have some means of occupying herself, else she will have no thoughts but the ones that are troubling her. The nervous condition will worsen. She won't sleep, eat, or—"

"Yes, doctor, I see the picture you are painting; however, she has already informed me in words plain and firm that she has no interests or accomplishments one might associate with her sex."

"She indicated as much to me, though she did mention rather reluctantly that she likes to read."

Griffin very nearly rolled his eyes. He remembered her studying his library, tilting her head first one way, then the other, to read the titles of the books he'd stuffed on the shelves on their sides. "She mentioned this reluctantly, did she?"

"When I pressed, yes. She seemed a bit embarrassed by it."

"Indeed."

"You might consider allowing her to choose some books."

"I'll choose the books." With that statement he realized he had given in. Truly, Olivia Cole was proving herself resourceful.

"I am certain that will be agreeable."

"It will have to be," Griffin said shortly. "I am not feeling in any way charitable toward her."

"That did not go unnoticed by me, although I confess I see no reason for it. In spite of her distrust for physicians, I found we were able to establish a mutual regard. Under the circumstances, her affability is remarkable."

"Circumstances?"

"The state of her nerves."

Griffin found himself on the receiving end of Pettibone's rather sharp stare. It was so pointed in fact that the doctor may as well have been wagging a finger at him. Griffin was forced to acknowledge to himself that the state of his own nerves could most politely be described as frayed. It was also no reason to be out of sorts with Pettibone.

"Is there anything else?" Griffin asked.

"Not about my patient."

Griffin waited.

"You had news from Paris. You were gone from town, I heard. Did it raise your hopes?"

Trust Pettibone to examine the open wound. Griffin harbored some regret that he'd ever confided in the doctor. It was not that the scandal that touched his life was unknown in society, only that Pettibone was one of the few privy to Griffin's own telling of events. "Briefly. And dashed them again. Nothing came of it. Nothing ever comes of it."

"It doesn't stop you, I've noticed."

"No," Griffin said quietly. "It doesn't." He visibly shook off the feeling of hopelessness, rolling his shoulders and rubbing the back of his neck. His mouth curled to one side, an expression rife with self mockery. "Is it madness, do you think?"

"A fine one, if it is."

He nodded. "As it should be then." He stood and thanked the doctor. "Truss is prepared to pay your account in full."

"Very good." Pettibone gathered his small black case and was on the point of showing himself out when the viscount called his name. He turned. "Yes?"

"I was wondering how you learned about Paris."

"Mrs. Christie."

Griffin showed no surprise because he felt none.

"Was she wrong to mention it to me, my lord?"

"No. In some manner it concerns her as well." Or at least she believed it did. Griffin had not been able to convince her otherwise, and perhaps she wasn't wrong to disbelieve him, because with this last bit of information from the well-meaning Dr. Pettibone, Griffin resolved he must end his arrangement with his mistress.

Olivia had not considered how loud and raucous the hell might be with the onset of evening and the tide of patrons spilling in from the street. To be fair, not all of the noise came from below stairs. Even situated at the rear of the house as she was, she could hear boisterous laughter and drunken rough play and challenges coming from Putnam Lane.

She added more logs to the fire and stood warming her hands. The house vibrated with the steady movement of those below. She felt the tiny trembling of the floorboards under her. Occasionally there was a thump that she liked to imagine was a young man falling on his face from too much drink.

It was not only the drone of male voices that she heard. Olivia was easily able to pick out the feminine vocals as well. Breckenridge insisted that he did not operate a brothel, but she believed there were gradations of the truth in that assertion. If no money exchanged hands within the establishment it seemed a certainty that money was exchanged elsewhere. Mistresses. Courtesans. Adventurous widows. Eccentric and free-thinking women of a certain age. Olivia supposed these were the sorts of females who accompanied their gentlemen of an evening.

She was relieved to be well out of it.

Even as she thought it she heard the tread of footsteps in the hall. One pair light, the other with a distinctive cadence that signified a limp. A man and woman, for that is what she presumed the steps to represent, passed her door after the briefest of pauses, and continued a short distance to the stairwell at the end of the hall. Olivia could hear them climbing the steps, then followed their progress across her ceiling. Silence fell for a few blessed moments, but it was broken with a shudder that rippled her drapes.

Olivia supposed it meant the couple had found the bed.

She closed her mind to it, glad for the books one of the servants had delivered earlier in the day. She'd permitted herself a small smile when they arrived, though with her back turned to the man who'd carried them in. It seemed the cautious thing to expect that Breckenridge might quiz him. Certainly,

given the titles the viscount had provided, Olivia had reason
to question his generosity and his motives.

Thomas Brown's "Lectures on the Philosophy of the Human
Mind," the selected essays of T. R. Malthus, and a slim volume
of three plays by Shakespeare—all of them tragedies—seemed
to suggest that Breckenridge was getting a little of his own
back or providing her with the means to sleep without benefit
of Pettibone's laudanum.

Olivia plucked the wool rug from the foot of the bed and
carried it and the Malthus essays to the chair. In very little
time reading acted as a barrier against all the distractions of
her surroundings. She ceased to hear the rhythmic thumping of the bed above her, or the cries of the coupling partic-
ipants as they urged each other on. She did find it darkly
humorous that by the time they would come to crisis, she
would be deep into reading the edifying "Essay on the Principle of Population."

"You permitted them to go up to the rooms?" Griffin demanded. "I thought I was clear on that point, Mrs. Christie. I
do not want my patrons coming upon her on their way to the
private rooms."

"You told her not to leave her room, didn't you? I fail to see
that it's a cause for so much displeasure. The gentlemen
expect to have a private place for an interlude if they're so inclined."

"And I am not inclined to provide it at the moment. That is
cause for displeasure."

Alys Christie's nostrils flared. She was never served well
by an angry countenance as it flushed her complexion unevenly and creased her brow. Because she had good reason to
know it, she strove mightily to tighten the reins on her temper.
It was never an encouraging sign when Breckenridge called
her Mrs. Christie. It not only meant that he was put out with

her, but that he was once again contemplating ending their arrangement. Hanging on seemed to be what she'd done these last two months, and after nearly a year under his protection, and the experience of having three previous gentlemen protectors and a husband besides, she knew the signs that she was about to be cast aside.

Arguments over trivial matters were the death knell, she had learned, and there could be no subject as inconsequential to her as the offended sensibilities of one Miss Olivia Cole.

Chapter Three

It was still dark when Olivia awakened. Snugly coccooned in the bed as she was, she allowed herself the luxury of remaining there a few minutes longer. The fireplace was cold and the stub of a candle she had placed on the bedside table had extinguished itself while she slept. She had wondered if she would wake disoriented to her new surroundings, but this was not the case. She knew immediately where she was and found some comfort in that, though it was short-lived. It was tempting to mistake this sense of familiarity for a sense of well-being. She could not do it, of course. The circumstances of her life were such that the moment she believed she was safe she was at her most vulnerable.

Olivia turned on her side and faced the window. She'd pulled the drapes closed before she retired but was careful to leave a sliver of an opening between them. As she lay watching, a crease of morning light slowly filled the space. The diffusion of the light, as though it were being filtered through frost flowers that had formed on the window, made her think it might have snowed overnight. She hoped it had. There was no part of London, from the tenements in Holborn to the palace at St. James, that was not improved by a blanket of snow. While fog had the ability to shroud the city's landscape and make every distinction of architecture disappear, it seemed to Olivia that snow both illuminated and softened it. The townhomes along Putnam Lane would look just as respectable as those bordering the park once they were iced like party tea cakes.

The impulse was upon her to take in that vision, but she resolutely quelled it. If she had awakened in her own bed, she would have already thrown off the covers and completed her morning ablutions. Molly Dillon would have arrived in her room—a bit sullenly perhaps because she so disliked early risings—and helped her dress and arrange her hair, then Olivia would have asked for her pelisse, bonnet, and gloves and left the house for a morning stroll before the snow was trampled and made black by the smoke and soot rising from thousands of chimneys.

Olivia snuggled deeper under the covers. She was struck anew by the silence of the residence. Now that she had experienced the din of activity that filled the hell at night, she imagined this quiet was greatly prized by Breckenridge and his staff. She had an appreciation for it as well, finding these moments were to be savored if one could concentrate on one's breathing and not on the thoughts spinning like dervishes in one's mind.

It was inevitable, though, that one thought would demand attention above all others.

Alastair.

Now that it seemed he had not come to physical harm, she could permit herself to be furious with him. And disappointed. He should have told her what was toward rather than attempt to settle his debt in this havey-cavey fashion. More to the point, he should not have been making wagers, especially when he knew he was extending himself beyond his means.

Olivia realized that Alastair had not considered he would lose, certainly not to the degree that he had. A loss now and again was inevitable, and he would have anticipated that, but his general optimism, and yes, his naïveté, would have blinded him to the reality of the deep losses he was sustaining. His good fortune would return because he believed it would, because it always had. He did not see what she saw, or rather he did not draw the same conclusions that she had.

It was Olivia's view that her entry into Alastair's life had turned the tide of his fortune, beginning with his falling out with their father. It was inevitable, she supposed, that Alastair would eventually come to it, and she did not want to think what his response would be.

The thought of Sir Hadrien darkened her mood. She flattened her lips, suppressing the small moan that would have otherwise escaped. She hoped that one day she would be able to think of him without this bitterness in her heart, for it afforded him too much influence over her, but apparently this morning was not the start of that day.

Drawing in a bracing breath, Olivia lifted the covers and made herself leave the warmth of her bed. She thrust her feet into her slippers and put on her robe, then dealt with the tinder and logs to build a modest fire in the fireplace. It was impossible to stay still for long—the cold was simply too penetrating. She hurried on tiptoes into the bathing room and prepared herself for the day.

Olivia did not miss her maid's services until it came to dressing her hair. No elaborate knots were possible, so she simply wove a dark green ribbon into her hair as she refashioned her braid. She liked the weight of the plait at her back and decided then that it would be acceptable to wear her hair in such a manner until she was returned home. The likelihood that Truss would be able to secure the services of a maid for her seemed small. Olivia also deemed it unnecessary. She had many more years of experience doing for herself than she did having anyone do for her.

She had returned to warming herself at the fire when her door rattled gently at a knock from the hallway. She opened it cautiously, needing to assure herself it was not some late-night reveler still stumbling about Breckenridge's hell looking for an exit. It wasn't. Olivia recognized the footman as the one who'd carried the tea service into the viscount's study yesterday morning. She nodded a greeting and bid him enter.

"It's tea and a few points of toast, miss, just as the doctor bid us prepare for you. Cook allowed that you might be feeling more the thing this morning and added a bowl of porridge. You can eat it or not as you wish."

"Thank you."

He set the tray down on the bedside table nearest him. "It seems you should have a proper table in here, miss, and another chair to sit at it. I'll see what I can find." His face reddened as he was unable to stifle a yawn. He ducked his head. "Pardon me."

"Of course. I feel quite certain this service falls outside the hours you typically keep."

"It does that."

"Then I'm the one who should beg your pardon. I have no liking for being a bother to others."

"I didn't mean it was a bother, miss."

"I know." And she did. "What is your name?"

"Foster."

"And what are the names of those young lads I saw yesterday?"

"They'd be Wick and Beetle. Wick, because he cleans the lamps and sees after the candles, and Beetle . . . Well, that is because he scurries about like one."

Wick and Beetle. Hardly the names their mothers would have given them. "Thank you, Foster. Will you come to take the tray or should I ring?"

"I'll come back directly but ring if you require something. Mr. Truss informed us that we'd hardly know you were here, and he had that from his lordship. I don't mind, though, if you come to realize there is a service I can do for you. Pulling on the cord will bring me here."

"That is very generous, Foster, but I shouldn't like to make trouble for you. I will manage, I'm sure."

"Just the same," he said, backing out of the room. "Truss says I'm to look after you and one pull will do it."

"One," she repeated, smiling gently. "That is good to know."

Once she was alone, Olivia sat on the bed and ate. She was actually quite hungry and had to restrain herself from eating too quickly. The tea, toast, and milky porridge all settled reasonably well in her stomach. Had the cook provided a more generous serving of the last, she still could have eaten all of it.

She had removed herself to the chair and was reading from the Malthus when the door rattled again. Thinking it was Foster come to take away the tray, she bid him enter. Her eyebrows lifted when she saw it was Breckenridge's valet.

"Mr. Mason," she said, setting her book on the floor. "I did not expect that it would be you."

"I had not meant it to be a test, Miss Cole, but it is just as well that it happened in this fashion. I feel strongly that his lordship would want me to caution you to see who it is at the door before allowing anyone to enter."

"That is good advice, Mr. Mason. I was careful earlier, but you have seen for yourself that I lowered my guard." She offered a small, slightly perplexed smile. "Do you suppose his lordship has considered the benefits of a key?"

"If he has, it would be to lock you in, I'm afraid."

"Oh." That wasn't what Olivia had in mind. "Then I hope you will not mention it."

"No, Miss Cole, I won't."

Had his eyes danced? Olivia thought they might have. His mouth, though, remained flat. "Why are you here, Mr. Mason, if not simply to caution me?"

"Dr. Pettibone's instructions are that you should take a

daily constitutional. It's his lordship's wish that I accompany you on your walk."

"Really?" It was difficult not to be skeptical. "Lord Breckenridge wishes that?"

"He does. Are you agreeable?"

"Yes! Oh, yes! Allow me to get my pelisse." She stopped suddenly, remembering that her outdoor garments were not in the armoire. They had been taken away yesterday after her arrival and not been returned to her.

"I have your things, Miss Cole. This way."

The things Mason had for her were not precisely *her* things. Instead of her pelisse, a hunter green cloak was held out to her. The attached hood was trimmed in red fox fur, a color that very nearly matched her own hair. Mason also showed her a red fox muff to replace her worn kid gloves.

"I can't accept these," she said, trying to push them back. "Where are my garments?"

Mason gave no quarter. "They're not fit for walking in this weather. You must have noticed that it snowed overnight." He glanced toward the nearest window. "It's snowing yet. Lightly, to be sure, but enough that heed must be paid."

"I've walked in my things many times."

"Yes, miss. It looked as if you had."

Olivia flushed. She was aware that her garments were gently worn and no longer of the latest fashion, but that Mr. Mason should be moved to comment, however carefully, stung.

"I meant no offense, Miss Cole. His lordship thought that you—"

"Pray, do not trouble yourself to explain, Mr. Mason. I will accept them, now that I know their full cost."

"I don't think you under—"

Olivia turned her back on him, effectively cutting him off.

She allowed him to place the cloak on her shoulders, but she fastened the silk frogs herself. The wait by the door seemed interminable as Mason put on his own coat, scarf, and hat.

The bracing air did not do as much to improve Olivia's mood as the walk itself. By the time she and Mr. Mason reached the end of Putnam Lane she was regretting her churlish behavior and prepared to apologize for it. While the valet most kindly assured her that no apology was necessary, Olivia made him listen to the whole of it anyway.

"It must be entirely confessed," she told him, "else it will always weigh on my mind."

When she finished, his grave acceptance brought a smile to her lips. "How is it that you became my escort this morning?" she asked as they crossed Moorhead Street. "The truth, Mr. Mason. I am glad of this opportunity so I will not be put out if you came to it with all the enthusiasm of a young man confronting a press gang."

Mason's prominently rounded chin puckered a bit as he chuckled. "It was with rather more willingness than that. His lordship could not escort you, of course. He has that much concern for your reputation, and he is known by sight in this part of London."

Olivia was unsure what that meant precisely, but she was loath to ask for an explanation. Was Mason saying that *she* would be seen in a poor light if the viscount accompanied her? It was difficult to fathom. He had rank, after all, and much was forgiven because of it. As she tried to work it out she was aware that Mason was continuing his explanation.

"There was naturally a concern for your safety. Even if there was no question that you would return, he would not have allowed you to walk the streets alone."

Olivia freed one hand and lifted it to indicate the street ahead of them and the small park beyond. "It cannot have escaped your notice that there is almost no one about."

"It is not a risk worth taking, Miss Cole. There are footpads alert to opportunity at any hour of the day."

"And I *am* worth £1,000." She looked at him sideways, wondering if she had misspoken. "You were aware of that, weren't you?"

"I was. His lordship told me. You needn't be concerned that it is common knowledge among the staff. It is yet another reason why I was chosen to act as your escort. You will find that Lord Breckenridge values discretion."

"I see." Olivia stepped over a mound of snow that had been pushed street side. Ahead of her an eddy of snow was lifted into the air. "How long have you been in his employ?"

"He was still in short pants."

"Long ago as that?"

"I was his father's man then."

"His father's dead?"

"Almost ten years now."

She felt oddly dismayed to hear of it, though why that should be so she couldn't say. "So young."

"For both of them," Mason said. "One too young to die; the other too young to take the mantle."

When Olivia looked askance at Mr. Mason, she saw that he seemed surprised that he'd spoken so openly. She watched him press his lips together and knew there would be little else forthcoming. She ducked her head against the wind while he clamped one hand on his hat and used the other to raise his scarf to the level of his nose. With his mouth so effectively covered, they continued on just as if no words had ever passed between them.

Griffin waited until afternoon before he called upon Mrs. Christie. Nothing had been settled between them last evening. She had thwarted his every effort to end the affair. Because their confrontation had taken place at such a late hour, Griffin had not pressed his argument forcefully. Rather than utter sentiments that he still hoped might be left unsaid, he'd allowed her to believe she had won the day and his affections for that much longer.

He entertained no doubts that Mrs. Christie thought she had secured as much as another month under his protection. She set that much stock in her persuasive powers. To be fair, she had not tried to seduce him, though whether she thought she was punishing him or had correctly divined that his ardor for her had cooled he had no way of knowing. What she had done was to put forth the notion that she was his partner in business, that their association transcended the mere physical, and that her presence each night in his establishment was critical to his continued success.

He'd been struck by the complete conviction with which she set forth her argument and could think of no response save for those he would regret. Now, mounting the steps to her home, he wondered if he had done right by her, for it was in his silence that she perceived herself the victor.

Griffin had purposely chosen the afternoon hour to call upon her because he knew she would no longer be abed. The mantel of snow aided his cause, making it unlikely that she would have yet stepped out. Still, after she'd been informed of his arrival, she sent down the message that she was late in rising and would not be quick to join him. He supposed that he was meant to infer that he was free to go. Although he had every right to join her in her bedchamber—and had done so on many occasions when she thought to tease him in such a fashion—he allowed the housekeeper to show him to the drawing room where he knew he could expect to wait above an hour for her.

"So you are still here," Alys Christie said when she finally saw fit to seek him out. She managed to infuse a note of surprise in her greeting. "I was not at all certain you would be. You have a tendency toward impatience of late." She walked directly to him and gave him a kiss full on the mouth.

Griffin did not pull away but neither did he respond. If she noticed, she was not allowing him to see it.

"Will you take tea?"

He shook his head.

"A whiskey, then."

"No, nothing for me."

Her pale eyebrows lifted slightly. "Very well, but you would not deny me, would you?" Not waiting for an answer, Alys went to the drinks cabinet and poured herself two fingers of whiskey.

Griffin smiled slightly. He'd always been amused that she preferred hard liquor to sherry. In the beginning she'd tried to hide it from him, concerned that he would judge her as not being as refined in her tastes as she ought to have been. To Griffin's way of thinking it made her more interesting rather than the opposite, and he'd told her so. That he was prepared to end their association did not change his thinking about her tastes. It was just that there was so little else that he found in any way attractive.

There would be those among his acquaintances who would wonder at this perception. By every standard of fashion, manners, and beauty, Mrs. Christie was acknowledged to be a diamond. At thirty years of age, she had the experience of being so well admired as to give her a surfeit of confidence. She exhibited the heritage of her Viking forbears in her pale coloring and smooth complexion, and while her hair was very fine, she had it in abundance. Even plainly arranged it called attention to itself. When she wore it adorned with flowers and beads it resembled nothing so much as a crown. Her figure was womanly in every regard: rounded arms, hips, and bosom. She knew what fashions and fabrics accentuated the features that made men shift their glances in her direction. The turn of her ankle was delicate; the curve of her waist pronounced. With shoulders held back and her chin lifted at an angle that suggested condescension, her manner of carrying herself was often referred to as regal.

Her standing in polite society, though, would never put her in the same circle as the royals. Griffin could not imagine that she would ever admit it, but she stood poised on the edge of the ton like a beggar at a baker's window. And like that poor soul, she longed for entry, not mere crumbs.

Griffin had no illusions as to why she agreed to leave her former protector and accept his offer. She had observed that his own standing in society possessed a certain fluidity. He had rank, which gave him entry and a reputation that kept him closer to the periphery than the center. He enjoyed the freedom to step outside the ton altogether as he did when he took up the gaming hell, but he also was greeted by his peers as a prodigal son on any occasion that he returned to their fold.

Some of rank and privilege envied him for shrugging off the strictures that set their life on such a narrow path. Others, like Alys Christie, envied him his access to that path.

"We are done, Mrs. Christie," Griffin said. He had not anticipated putting it before her quite so baldly, but once said he did not try to soften it. He watched twin sovereigns of pink appear in her cheeks. Her fine china-blue eyes, arguably her best feature, brightened with a sheen of tears. At one time he would have mistaken them as an expression of disappointment or sadness. What he had learned was that they appeared out of deep frustration and were the precursor to a fit of temper that few young children could match for ferocity and duration.

Griffin decided a warning was in order. "I will not suffer one of your rages, Alys, so think before you fly into the boughs."

Taking a deep breath, she held herself in check for the moment. The note of caution in his voice meant little to her, and the threat less than nothing, but the fact that he had called her Alys was enough to give her hope. "We can discuss it, can we not, Breckenridge? I thought we had reached an under-standing last evening."

"There was no understanding. You made your argument, and I did not gainsay you. It is not the same as reaching an accord. We are done."

Alys pursed her lips. Her fingertips tightened on the tumbler in her hand. "I don't see how that can be. You need me."

"Oh, Mrs. Christie, do not make me say otherwise. Let us at least agree that we might remain on friendly terms."

"Is it because there was no good word from Paris? Have you now given up hope on everyone?"

Griffin was aware he was being drawn in and still could not hold his tongue. "You told Pettibone. That was not your place."

"It *is* my place. Your wife—"

"My wife is nothing to you."

"But if she's dead— If you can prove that she's—"

"It changes nothing." In contrast to his eyes, which were hard, his voice was dangerously soft. "She is already dead to me, and it makes no difference. I will not marry you, Mrs. Christie."

"Have I spoken of marriage?"

"Even you have moments of restraint."

Alys's nostrils flared. He'd raised the point of restraint at the very moment she was rearing back her hand to throw her glass at him. She caught herself and drank half of what she'd poured instead. Above the rim of the tumbler her pale blue eyes glittered. It was rare that there was heat in her anger. What she invariably felt was ice cold, and this was no excep-tion. The whiskey did not warm her.

"What of your business?" she asked. "Have you considered at all what I said last night? We are partners, Breckenridge. You cannot deny that I have been an asset to you in the oper-ation of the hell."

"I do not deny it. It does not make us partners. Your contri-bution was not financial, and it was not asked for."

"God's truth, but it was not refused," she snapped. "You appreciated my presence in your place. You even were moved to remark that your patrons wagered in a most excellent fashion when I was in the room. That was more of the ready in your pockets, Breckenridge."

"And you were recompensed handsomely for it. Never say to me that you did not benefit from our arrangement. You have a house for which you owe nothing. Fine clothes. Jewelry that you may keep or sell at your pleasure. Your staff receives their wages from me and your allowance defines the very word generous."

Hearing his voice begin to rise, Griffin took a leveling breath. "The house. The clothing. The jewelry. All of it is yours, Mrs. Christie. I will see that your allowance continues throughout this quarter, but you will have to pay your household accounts and staff out of it. It is still a most liberal settlement, I believe."

It was not enough, not nearly enough. What she said was, "It is nothing! What you offer is an insult!"

"Do not pretend that you haven't been preparing for this day, Mrs. Christie. You may have allowed yourself to hope for a different end, but you are an intelligent woman who is well able to assess the risk of doing naught but hoping. I cannot help but think you have made some profitable investments. Certainly you asked for such advice as I was able to give on a number of occasions. If you but heeded half of it, you will have amassed a tidy sum. It also occurs that you will have already set your sights on another gentleman to take my place, and I do not fault you for it. If you can bring him up to snuff and put yourself in the society you crave, then I will be happy to dance at your wedding."

Griffin picked up his coat and folded it over his arm, then retrieved his hat and gave it a tap against the side of his knee. "Our arrangement has never been more than what it is, Mrs. Christie. It was predicated on a mutual appreciation for what we can *do* for each other, not for what we can *be* to each other."

There was no mockery in the slight bow he made her. He gave her this final respect as her due, then began walking toward the door.

"Bastard!" She flung the tumbler at his back and was angry when it missed him, angrier still that he must have anticipated she would do it and didn't trouble himself to flinch. "You will regret putting me aside, Breckenridge."

He paused on the point of leaving to glance back at her. "I know you believe that, but I am certain now of exactly the opposite." His dark eyes narrowed briefly on her frozen attitude of outrage. "It was the ring, Mrs. Christie. Or did you think I didn't know?"

He stepped over the fallen tumbler and puddle of whiskey and let himself out.

Olivia appreciated that her second and third day in the gaming hell proceeded uneventfully. Mason escorted her on a walk twice each day, making certain that she went unmolested. He was not given to many words and after she had exhausted the topics of weather, Malthus, and the butler's frustrating, ultimately fruitless search for a suitable maid for her, there was nothing he cared to talk about.

The snow ceased to fall on the second afternoon. As much as she had appreciated it, she was concerned that it would delay Alastair's return. *If* he meant to return at all. That niggling thought would not be permanently quelled. She hated that the viscount must be thinking it also. He had to have already calculated the length of the journey Alastair would make to reach Sir Hadrien as well as the time it would require. Sir Hadrien detested town and spent almost the whole of the year at his estate in Sussex. With no mishaps, she could expect Alastair to be gone at least five days. If their father proved difficult—and it was almost a given that he would—it seemed unlikely that her brother could return before a full sennight had passed.

She finished the essays by Malthus and began Brown's. Soon after she mentioned to Mason that it might be pleasant to write down her own thoughts on the philosophy of the human mind, Foster appeared at her door bearing paper, quills, and a full bottle of ink. The small table he'd procured for her earlier so that she might take her meals in comfort also served well as a desk. She wasn't sure what she might put to paper concerning philosophy, but she heard enough coming from the floor below each evening to venture some thoughts about the human mind.

On the evening of her fourth day, Olivia had a surprise waiting for her when she returned from her late outing with Mr. Mason. It had not occurred to her during the walk that the valet's rather jovial mood—which regarding Mason meant that he tipped his hat and ventured a smile when he greeted her—had anything to do with his knowledge of what would be taking place during their brief absence.

Immediately upon her arrival at the threshold to her room, she knew something was different. She could quite literally smell it in the air. The breath she drew was changed by the scent of lavender and moist with steam from—could it truly be?—the water-filled hip bath.

Olivia had been so moved by this gift, knowing what pains had been taken to haul so much heated water to the tub, that she was possessed by the urge to throw her arms about Mr. Mason's shoulders and plant a kiss on his cheek. Had she given into the impulse it would have been a novel experience for both of them, but her own natural restraint was reinforced when Mason, having some sense of how she might be moved to express her gratitude, cautiously stepped back out of arm's reach.

As she thought about it later, a smile tugged at Olivia's lips.

She slipped lower in the tub. She doubted Breckenridge had ever known an urge to hug his valet.

In the end she had never properly thanked Mr. Mason. Although she felt as if she were dancing in place with excitement, she had in fact simply stood in the doorway unmoving. What she offered him was a watery smile, hardly an adequate demonstration of the gratitude that was in her heart.

The scent of lavender rose deliciously from the bath as Olivia stirred the water with her fingertips. She tried to imagine whose idea it had been to add bath salts. Similarly, someone had thought to line the copper tub with linens. Sitting almost shoulder deep in warm and fragrant water was as decadent a luxury as she had known.

Olivia picked up a sponge and sliver of soap and made a lather that she applied to her arms. She set her mind once again to wondering at the origin of the salts and linens. Owing to the fact that she was a curiosity, she'd had brief contact with most of the staff. It wasn't that a woman had never stayed in the gaming hell that made her an unusual guest and the subject of speculation. It was the mystery surrounding her presence that created the stir.

Mrs. Christie, the woman whom Breckenridge had named as a friend, Olivia had learned was a frequent visitor to the hell but only occasionally remained there until morning. That she was his lordship's mistress was understood, and the servants, Beetle most particularly, let such words drop that Olivia came to understand it as well.

Her own connection to the viscount was not a matter of easy comprehension for the household staff, especially as Breckenridge had nothing at all to do with her. Except for Mr. Mason, who knew the truth of it and wasn't sharing, everyone else was left to wonder.

It amused her to think that the bath, the salts, and linens may all have been in aid of softening her own defenses so that she might answer their questions rather than have so many of her own. She had it from Wick that there was a small, friendly wager among the servants as to the nature of her presence in the gaming hell. The hypothesis that currently curried the most favor was that she was in fact a relation to his lordship, a distant cousin whose lack of marriage prospects and financial straits were an embarrassment to the family. Apparently she had been thrust upon Breckenridge as a punishment of sorts to both of them.

Olivia thought that if she'd had only one shilling to her name, she still would have been moved to place it in support of that particular theory. It seemed a more likely turn than what she knew the truth to be.

Olivia kept at the puzzle of the salts and linens while she washed and rinsed her hair, regretting for the first time that she did not have Dillon's help with the task. The most likely candidate to have contributed the additional amenities was Beetle, she decided. The boy had informed her by way of making conversation that his mother was a whore at Mrs. Tittle's fine house here in Putnam Lane. From the way he'd told her, she gathered it was an establishment of some renown, popular with a certain set of privileged gentlemen. Beetle had been wont to impress upon her the elegant fashion of the place. It was turned out as well, on the inside at least, as Breckenridge's own establishment.

Although the salts and linens probably had been lifted by Beetle rather than willingly donated by Beetle's mother, they were the bath's defining touch. She supposed that thanks were in order also to the proprietor of the house. Mrs. Tittle obviously saw advantages to creating the illusion of a fine lady's boudoir for her patrons rather than reminding them in every way that they were naught but among whores.

Olivia allowed that it was probably a good strategy.

She closed her eyes and rested the damp twist of hair that she'd made at the back of her head against the tub's lip. The water cooled, but even then she was reluctant to leave her bath. It was not until gooseflesh appeared on her arms that she made to stand.

Towels had been placed for her on a footstool at the side of the tub. She chose one to wrap around her hair and the other to dry herself with. She shivered, feeling the cold in earnest now and quickly pulled her nightshift over her head. Her robe added another layer of welcomed warmth. She padded barefoot into her bedchamber and found her slippers, stood in front of the fire for a few moments, then began to gently rub her hair dry.

"I have your dinner, Miss Cole."

The voice from the other side of the door startled her. She hadn't heard a knock, and Breckenridge's staff was scrupulous about knocking. An ember popped loudly in the fireplace, forcing her to step back. "A moment," she called, quickly plaiting her hair. "I just need a moment to—"

Olivia froze, her fingers still wound in the tail of her braid, as the door was pushed open. The entry of anyone into the room should have been preceded by a tray. The absence of one was the first thing she noticed.

The unfamiliarity of the face was the next detail to have impact.

In moments the whole of it registered. The intruder was elegantly attired in evening clothes, not the livery the footmen wore when they were at post in the gaming rooms. The gentleman's expression was not one of surprise at making the discovery of her presence, but rather satisfaction that he had arrived at this end expecting it. And finally there was the step he took into the room, a step both assured and deliberate. Here was a man whose arrogance did not allow him to conceive that his entry would be unwelcome.

Olivia understood that he presented every sort of danger to her because of it.

Unable to move, she watched him close the door. He stood

with his back to it, his hands disappearing behind him as he fiddled with the knob. She frowned. "What are you—"

The voice she'd found was silenced when he brought his fists to the forefront and turned them over, unfolding them slowly. The right one held a key.

Olivia's hands dropped to her side. The towel that had been folded around her neck fell to the floor. She didn't know why she did it, but she found herself stooping to pick it up. Perhaps it was because she needed something to clutch, she thought, just as Lord Breckenridge had pointed out. She straightened and twisted the towel in her hands.

"You should leave," she said. And as if it would make any difference to him, she added, "If you leave now no one has to know you were here." Her eyes darted to the bell cord that would bring Foster or someone else from the servants' hall to her room if she could reach it.

The gentleman followed her glance, understood its import, and merely shook his head. He unbuttoned his frock coat and slipped the key into a crescent pocket in his waistcoat. "I suspect that who knows I am here is more your concern than mine."

He had a sweet, almost shy smile that Olivia found perfectly incongruous to the import of his words and the intention she could see in his eyes. He was of an age with her and handsome enough that young ladies of little experience were probably desirous of his attention. Whether his pockets were deep enough to attract the notice of their mothers and make him a truly desirable connection was not immediately apparent to Olivia. The cut and detail of his clothing suggested a living that was more than sufficient to set a standard in fashion, but she recalled that Alastair often went about similarly turned out, even as she was struggling to settle their account with the greengrocer.

"Please leave," she said.

"You say it prettily." He smiled. "Say it again."

Olivia inched away as he approached. She felt the coal scuttle pressing against her leg and realized she could not go farther in that direction. She wondered if she could speak the words he wanted loudly enough to be heard above the noise below them. He'd apparently thought the same and dismissed it because he was shaking his head.

"You haven't asked what I want," he said pleasantly.

Olivia didn't answer. To say that she already knew was to give something of herself away. He did not deserve even so little as that from her.

He beckoned her with a finger. "Come. Come closer. Would you make me pursue you into the corner?"

His question reminded her of the direction in which she was going. She changed course and sidled toward the bed. He could make what he liked of it but there was some avenue of escape by choosing that heading.

Olivia continued to twist the towel between her fingers.

"So you are for the bed after all," he said, noting her move to the side. "That is agreeable."

"You must leave." Olivia's voice was firmer now. "Lord Breckenridge will—"

"Not mind," he said.

It was his mistake to suppose that she believed him, and Olivia did nothing to correct his assumption. She was judging the distance remaining between them instead. She required something a bit shorter than what existed now. With that in mind, she held her ground when he took one more step toward her.

Like a mongoose to his cobra, Olivia struck with feral speed. With a flick of her wrist she snapped the damp towel at his head, catching him at the corner of his eye. He roared in pain and clamped one hand over the injured eye and used his other hand to flail at her. Olivia reared back, avoiding his half-blind groping, and twisted the towel in midair. She snapped it again, this time at the bulge in his trousers that he had taken no pains to hide.

This second application of the linen made him yowl. It also angered him beyond reason. Olivia had a glimpse of his red and watering eye as he dropped his hand away from it and lunged for her. She threw herself sideways across the bed. The flanking tables were knocked about, but only one teetered enough to fall. Unfortunately, it was the one that held the lighted candelabra. Two of the candles were extinguished as they fell, but the third landed on the bed where the flame immediately began licking at a lace pillow sham.

Neither Olivia nor her attacker noticed.

Still holding the towel, Olivia came to her feet on the opposite side of the bed. She feinted toward the door and when he did the same, she ran to the window. She had just time enough to throw it open and make a cry for help before she was caught by the waist and roughly hauled back inside. The back of her head collided hard with the sash and for a moment her vision was filled with bright light.

Griffin's glance was drawn to the ceiling of the card room by a distinctive thud. He shook his head, permitting himself a moment to wonder what Olivia was about before returning his attention to the play at the table. He'd made it a rule not to join any games in his own establishment. Suspicion of his play would invariably become a factor if he won and his pockets would suffer if he did not. The better course was to oversee the games and make certain they were fairly played. He had no desire for his hell to secure a reputation for supporting cardsharps and their marks.

It was not quite six months ago that the Allworthy cousins had taken liberties with the cards at this very table and nearly begat an incident with the French ambassador's son. On that occasion Mr. Restell Gardner had been present to manage the situation and keep it from spilling over into scandal.

The thought of Gardner set Griffin to wondering what had become of him. He hadn't seen him for some time, though he supposed that was to be expected given his relatively newly married state. One edge of Griffin's mouth lifted in a mildly amused smile. It wasn't as if Gardner could ask his wife to accompany him to the hell. Again.

Griffin schooled his features as he moved around the table slowly, taking in the hands that he was allowed to see without giving away what he thought of them. When he caught sight of a furtive movement just outside the entrance to the card room, he was careful not to frown and send some signal that had nothing at all to do with the game. He nodded politely to the players and excused himself just as Wick came into view again. The lad was not trying to attract his attention but appeared to be wanting Foster's eye. The footman was staring straight ahead, unaware of the gyrations that were being employed to garner his notice.

Bloody hell.

Griffin stepped into the hallway, snatched Wick by his collar, and carried the boy away from the patrons mingling outside the card room to servants' stairs at the end of the corridor. The boy did not struggle, but he did keep his hands tightly over his ears as if he expected Griffin to give them a good boxing.

"Explain," Griffin said, setting him down.

Wick, still with his hands over his ears, launched into an explanation that was delivered so hurriedly that Griffin could not follow it. At the conclusion, the lad tried to make a run around him and dash up the stairs. Griffin hauled him back and kept him in place with one hand on each of the boy's bony shoulders. It was the child's distress that kept Griffin from launching into a lecture that included all of the reasons why Wick was not permitted to move among the patrons.

"Again, if you please. This time with some respect for the cadence of proper speech."

On the second telling Griffin caught words like *help* and *Miss Cole* and *gentleman villain*. There was no making sense of it, but at the end Griffin gave Wick his head and let him charge up the stairs.

Unlike the floor below, this short hall was deserted, and Griffin could hear sounds coming from Olivia Cole's bedchamber that had been undetectable in the card room.

And . . . Oh, dear God above—was that smoke he smelled?

Wick came upon the door a beat before Griffin and rattled the knob. When the door didn't open he beat his fists against it. Griffin reached around him and tried the knob himself, calling out for Olivia at the same time. When she didn't respond, he pounded the heel of his hand against the door.

"Miss Cole!" Griffin rapped the wood hard. "Miss *Cole!*" He put a restraining hand on Wick's efforts. "Find Truss. Tell him to bring the key. Hurry!" Griffin punctuated the order by throwing his shoulder into the door. Except for compression of his own muscle and bone, there was no give. Griffin ignored the pain and rammed it again. The door held and he went back to pounding. "Miss Cole!" Dammit! "*Olivia!*"

Olivia couldn't move. She was pinned by the weight of the man on top of her. Over his shoulder she could see small flames spreading slowly across the pillow sham, fed by the draft from the open window. She tried to make him understand there was danger here, but he merely pressed a forearm across her throat and she was silenced. Every frantic look she cast in the direction of the fire, he seemed to interpret as merely an effort on her part to avoid looking at him.

His features, the ones she had briefly thought as handsomely molded, were twisted in a rage so profound that he was deaf and blind to everything at the periphery of his senses. She was not merely the center of what he saw. She was all that he saw.

He yanked at her shift. When the narrow blue ribbon sewn into the scooped neckline thwarted his attempt to rend the material, he shoved his hand under it. He groped for her breast, then finding it, squeezed with a viciousness that brought tears to Olivia's eyes and the air rushing from her lungs. She tried to draw another breath, but his forearm lay too heavily across her throat. It seemed he was pressing harder now. She pushed at his shoulders and tried to turn on her side to break his hold. It took only moments for her to understand he would not be moved.

Her hands fell back to the floor. If she did not panic, if she did not exhaust herself, she knew he would need the hand on her breast or the arm across her throat to assist him in what was ultimately his intent. If he killed her first it would be because there was madness in his rage, not because it had been his aim to do so at the outset. He might kill her afterward, to silence her, but it was just as likely that they would die together, consumed by the flames that were now twisting and leaping across the bed.

Olivia sucked in a deep lungful of air as the pressure on her throat was lifted. She coughed hard, breathing in the first acrid eddies of smoke to reach her. She managed to gasp a warning between the choking breaths. "The bed!"

"So you do want it," he fairly growled in her ear. "And comfort besides." He mashed his mouth against hers.

She blinked. He had completely misunderstood. She tasted blood on her lip as he ground his mouth on hers and felt him separating her robe at her thighs. He lifted his hips slightly as he grabbed fistfuls of her shift and raised it to her hips. She tried to keep her legs together, but he jammed a knee between them. She beat her heels on his calves and at the back of his thighs as he fumbled with the flies of his trousers. At her sides her fingers scrabbled on the floor, searching . . . searching . . .

* * *

Griffin pressed his ear to the door, trying in vain to hear something above the sound of his own harsh breathing. Frustrated, he kicked at it. Once. Then again. Bloody hell. Where was Wick? Where was Truss? Where was the *goddamn* key?

Olivia's fingertips found the edge of the towel that had been wrested from her hands. She tugged on it, first finding a finger's worth, then a handful. She whipped it across the back of his neck and found the opposite tail with her free hand. Beyond his shoulder she could see tiny tongues of fire lapping up the bedcover and applied all of her resolve to this last effort.

Before he could guess what she was about, she quickly crossed the tails of the towel and exchanged them in her hands so that she could pull them as tightly as her strength would allow.

The immediate effect was to make him release his cock so he could try to break her hold. When he grasped her wrists and pushed he only succeeded in tightening the noose she'd fashioned. He clawed at the linen towel, his eyes bulging, but could not get even so much as a fingernail between his skin and the damp fabric.

Olivia applied steady pressure. The muscles in her arms and across her back trembled with the strain required to sustain it. From the hallway she heard someone call her name again. When she'd heard it before she'd had no voice to cry out. Now she hadn't any strength to spare for the effort.

His face was ruddy, but no less so than hers. Olivia's temples throbbed as the hot blood of exertion collected in her head. Her knuckles were nearly as white as the towel she was gripping. There was a similar whiteness at his neck where his skin was pulled taut by the linen garrote.

He was able to heave himself up but not able to dislodge her hold. The space he created, though, gave her the freedom to move out from under him. The towel twisted on his neck as she shifted to one side. When his arms gave way he collapsed face down on the floor, and as quick as that she was on his back, holding the tails of the linen like reins on a horse that she meant to bring to an abrupt halt.

It might have been hearing her name yet again that gave her pause. It could also have been the heat at her back that finally stayed her hands. She gave it no thought at the time. She simply released both ends of the towel and stood, but not without first pressing one knee hard into his spine as she did so.

His groan satisfied her that he was alive, but also made her wary.

Olivia grabbed the towel as she leapt away from him, afraid he would recover the strength to pull her down again. Her attention was drawn to the door as it shuddered hard in the frame.

"Olivia! For God's sake. . . . *Olivia!*"

She spun on her heels and ran toward the sound of that voice. It was Breckenridge. She met his pounding by placing the flat of one hand against the door panel. Throwing the towel over her shoulder, she twisted the knob with her other hand. When nothing happened she remembered all the reasons that was so.

Glancing back, she saw that not only was her attacker beginning to stir, but the fire was slipping over the edge of the bed. "I can't get the key! Go! Go away! Get everyone out!"

She was not at all certain she was heard. She slapped the door and yelled the one word she hoped would garner his full attention.

"*Fire!*"

Chapter Four

Olivia didn't wait to learn if Breckenridge understood her. The fire at her back was skipping its way across one of the small area rugs. She turned and ran for the bathing room.

The pitcher and bowl on the washstand were the handiest items to easily fill with water. Once she'd dipped them into the tub she found the bowl was too awkward to carry. She let it drop to the bottom of the tub and hurried back into the bedroom with the pitcher. She aimed her first throw at the fringes of the fire, hoping to keep it from spreading. There was little enough time to judge the success of her action, but the thought she carried back into the bathing room along with the empty pitcher was that her best effort might count for nothing.

Olivia filled the pitcher again, set it down, then yanked the towel from around her neck and took off her robe. She pushed both items under the water until they were sodden before she dragged them out and took them and the pitcher back to the fire.

She tossed the water from the pitcher first, once again at the periphery of the fire, then she used her wet robe to smother a circle of the flames on the bed. Using the wet towel, she beat at the fingers of fire crawling over the edge of the mattress and frame.

Olivia had no sense of the passage of time. What she knew was her own labored breathing and the acrid scent of smoke, ash, and wet, charred wood filling her lungs. Her arms ached, heavier it seemed than the things she was carrying. Each trip added weight to the struggle.

When she got too close to the fire, flames licked at the damp hem of her shift or singed her hair. When she stood back, her efforts merely fanned the flames. If she tried to make her way too quickly, she found herself slipping on the slick puddles that dotted the hardwood floor. If she forced herself to slow down, it seemed that the fire was racing.

She finally fell into a rhythm that she completed by rote: dip, lift, haul, toss, return. There was variation only if she used the wet robe and towel to beat the flames or the pitcher to throw water on them, but even these actions she alternated in a way that made them appear part of her pattern.

In just such a manner she completed trip after trip, holding out for the fire's unconditional surrender.

Griffin and Truss found her sitting on the apron of the fireplace, her knees drawn almost to the point of her chin, her back resting against the green-veined marble jamb. She clutched each end of a twisted, dripping towel in her fists while the bulk of the linen was wrapped just below her knees, holding them in the tight fold she'd created.

Griffin gently opened Olivia's fingers and removed the wet towel from her hand. There was little of it that wasn't blackened, but the small white patch he found he applied to the streak of soot bisecting her cheek like his own scar. He noticed that she retracted a bit from his touch, but he took it as a good sign that she was aware of his presence.

When he'd first come through the door, Truss on his heels, he wasn't at all certain that that was the case. She hadn't given the slightest indication that she knew she wasn't alone any longer. It struck Griffin as unnatural, even otherworldly, that she hadn't turned her head toward their entrance. She sat, still as stone, as she did now, staring straight ahead at the wisps of smoke and steam still rising in curling ribbons from her bed.

Tears welled at the edge of her lower lashes, though whether they were prompted by some emotion or merely a consequence of the pungent irritants in the air, Griffin could not determine. The towel was useless here. He withdrew a handkerchief and pressed it into her hand. A tear slipped free as she lowered her gaze to the handkerchief. She stared at it a long moment, almost as if she were trying to reason its purpose, then she offered a brief, watery smile and raised it to her eyes.

Griffin used that opportunity to glance over his shoulder at Truss. The butler was stamping out smoldering patches on one of the rugs with all the high-stepping vigor of a fair colleen at her first dance. Griffin's brief grin turned grimace as he surveyed the damage to the room. At a glance he could see that in every way it could have been much, much worse. Close to the bed, the flocked wallpaper was streaked with water and soot. The bedcovers had supported a great deal of the fire, and he could see that not only were parts of the mattress burned, they might be burning still.

"Cease your jig, Truss," Griffin said, rising from his crouch beside Olivia. "Help me get this mattress out of doors. I think we can roll it sufficiently small that we can push it out the window."

Truss stumbled a bit as he brought himself up short. Recovering himself and his dignity, he grabbed one corner of the mattress and began lifting it toward the foot of the bed, smoldering bedcovers and all. Griffin quickly took up the opposite side and helped him. They hefted the bedroll to their shoulders and carried it to the open window.

It required effort, but a bit of cursing seemed to grease the opening, and they pushed it through. Griffin put his head out to make certain it cleared the small porch roof. It bounced, unfolded, then hung on the lip for several long moments before it fell in a cascade of snow, smoke, and feathers.

Griffin retreated from the cold and biting air and shut the window. He instructed Truss to carefully look around and make certain there were no other potential fires, then he returned to Olivia's side.

She lifted her head but made no attempt to stand. Her frown caused a thin black crease to form between her eyebrows. "Is he . . . ? He was moving when . . ." She craned her neck, trying to look around and over the frame of the empty bed. "I thought he would help, but he never . . ."

Griffin registered Olivia's confusion but not the reason for it. His dark eyes caught hers, held them. "He? Do you mean Truss?"

Olivia shook her head. "No. The other. Lying on the floor."

"What are you talking about?" It was then that he remembered something Wick had said: *gentleman villain.* "*Who* are you talking about?"

"I don't know. That is, I don't know his name."

Griffin did not try to make sense of what she was saying. There were other matters that required his attention first, not the least of which was Olivia's own condition. Her teeth clicked in the pauses between words and her body had begun to tremble violently as though she might actually shake off the cold. Her damp shift clung to her like a second skin, one that was not a whit warmer than the first. It was no surprise that she remained curled like a hedgehog in the one place in the room that offered a modicum of heat.

Griffin opened up the armoire, saw nothing that would serve, and removed his frock coat instead. He drew it tightly across Olivia's shoulders before grasping her wrists and lifting her to her feet. There was some slight resistance on her part, but he had no patience for learning the cause of it. When he saw she was unsteady at a stand, he simply lifted her.

"Put your arms around my neck," Griffin told her. "And stop squirming. I'm not going to—" He stopped because he realized her spastic movements weren't in aid of getting away from him. She was simply shivering that hard. "I'm taking her to my room, Truss. If Wick and Mason were successful in getting everyone out of the house, tell the staff to herd them back in. Serve them all drinks at my expense. That should engage them again. I saw Priestly at the tables. An explanation to him will be enough to calm the waters. He will see to it."

"How shall I phrase it, my lord?"

"Carefully." Depending upon Truss to show proper discretion, Griffin exited the room.

The lack of a maid frustrated Griffin's efforts to attend Olivia. He considered and dismissed the idea of requesting one of his female guests to assist him. The fewer people who knew that she'd come close to burning his establishment to the ground, the better. He did not yet know the cause of it, so allowing someone else to put their own construction upon events did not strike him as a wise decision.

After setting Olivia down on his bed, he gave her one of his nightshirts and went in search of towels. When he returned with an armful she was still sitting on the edge of the bed, heels hooked on the frame, trying to find the opening of the shirt.

Griffin set most of the towels near the fireplace to warm them and carried two to the bed. He used one to briskly dry her damp hair and the other to rub some heat into her feet and calves. His movements were impersonal but his manner was not without sympathy. He told her what he was going to do before he did it, offering her every opportunity to help herself.

Olivia let him remove his frock coat from her shoulders then draw his nightshirt down over her head. She reached under the fabric and tugged on her own nightgown, shimmying out of it as it was replaced by the infinitely warmer linen.

When he pulled back the bedcovers she crawled under them without any urging.

Griffin put his frock coat back on. It smelled of smoke now, he noted. He picked up the towels and her ruined shift and tossed all of it into his dressing room for Mason to deal with. The towels that had been warmed by the fire he rolled into linen logs and tucked them under the covers next to Olivia's body. She thanked him as she turned her cheek into the one he placed beside her pillow.

Griffin rang for a servant before he drew a chair to the bedside and sat down. Warm, healthy color was just beginning to return to Olivia's cheeks by the time his summons was answered. He asked for a report regarding the well-being of his patrons and was satisfied to learn that the excitement of the moment had subsided. The generous application of alcohol had dampened their enthusiasm for questions but not for gaming. Such comments that his absence aroused were met by assurances that he would soon return to tables. Griffin did not say whether that was likely or not, but he appreciated the footman's attention to this detail.

He requested a pot of tea for Olivia and a whiskey for himself before he dismissed the servant. When he turned back to Olivia, he found that she was watching him. There was a certain wariness in her eyes that made him question himself.

"Did I hurt you?" he asked.

She shook her head.

"Do you think I mean to?"

Olivia didn't respond.

Griffin's lower lip thrust forward as he released a puff of air. "I see," he said, taking her silence as answer. "I did not realize I had given you cause to think so ill of me."

Olivia's voice was little more than a whisper. The back of her throat ached with the effects of the smoke and repressed tears. "He told me you knew," she said. "That you knew he was there . . . in my room. I didn't believe him . . . but you're acting as if—"

"As if I don't understand," he said, interrupting her. "Except I am no actor. I *don't* understand. Who is *he*?"

"I don't know."

"Then you comprehend my confusion."

Under the covers, Olivia drew her knees up as she sought to contain her body heat. That her posture was also defensive was a point she did not care to contemplate. "He is one of your guests. A gamer."

"Describe him."

She closed her eyes. "A bit taller than I am. A year, perhaps two, on either side of my own twenty-four years. Fastidious in his dress. Pale yellow hair. A sweet, almost shy smile. Blue eyes. They were . . . cold." She shivered slightly and her eyes flew open. Breckenridge was watching her closely. She avoided his gaze and stared at a point past his shoulder. "He was slight of build, but strong. Athletic, I think, one would say. Perhaps someone who pursues gentlemanly activities like sparring or fencing."

"He might be any of a great many gentlemen who come here of an evening. Is there nothing else? Something that distinguishes him?"

"Something like a scar, you mean?" Olivia wished she might pull the covers over her head as soon as the words left her mouth. She may as well have added: *Like yours?*

Griffin drew a forefinger along the length of his scar. One corner of his mouth lifted in a wry smile. "Does he?" he asked.

She shook her head.

He let his hand fall. "More's the pity."

His ease with this conversation gave Olivia pause. "You don't believe me," she said. "You don't believe that someone came to my room."

"I didn't say that."

"Aren't you thinking it?"

He shrugged as if what he was thinking was unimportant. "What I know is that no one was in your room when I arrived, and no gentleman pushed past me to get to the door."

"Then he escaped through the window."

"Without you seeing him?"

"I was occupied."

"Of course you were. Putting out the fire. I've not forgotten." He sat back in his chair; his head tilted to one side so he could catch her eye again. This time he was able to hold it. "How did it start exactly?"

"Does it matter? You are not doubting there was a fire, are you?"

"It's no good trying to be defiant. You haven't the strength for it." He reached for the folded blanket at the foot of the bed and snapped it open over her. "There. Better? You are not yet warm enough, I think. Should I add a hot brick or two?"

She shook her head.

"Tell me about the fire," he said again. "What happened?"

"I'm not certain. I didn't see it begin. I suppose it was when the table toppled."

Griffin remembered the thud he'd heard. Had it been that? "Go on. How did it fall?"

"I must have knocked it over when I threw myself across the bed." She observed his raised eyebrow. "To get away from him. He was backing me into a corner. I could think of nothing else to do. I thought if I could get to the window, I could make my own escape. It's odd that I didn't think he might take the same route out."

"Yes," he said. "Odd."

"In the morning—when there's light—you'll be able to see that I'm telling the truth. You'll see where he dropped to the roof below and then to the yard."

Griffin thought of the mattress hitting the roof, then the ground. There wasn't likely to be a sign left of Olivia's gentleman. He could not be encouraging, but he offered, "I'll look at first light." She seemed satisfied with that, closing her eyes briefly. "Wick said there was someone," he told her. "A gentleman villain, I believe, were the words he used, so you see, Olivia, I don't discount what you're telling me. I'm simply trying to make sense of it."

She felt the prick of tears and blinked rapidly. "He had a key," she said. "He showed it to me. How did he come by a key to my room?"

The same question occurred to Griffin, and he had no answer at the ready. "Did you think I'd given it to him?"

She shook her head. "No. Not at all." She hesitated and answered truthfully, "Not then."

"But later," he prompted her gently. "But later you did."

"Only when I thought you—"

He didn't allow her to finish. "When you thought I was merely acting as if I didn't understand. Damned by my ignorance, I suppose. Tell me, what do you think now?"

"The same as I did in the beginning: that you didn't invite him to attend me, nor even turn your back so that he might do it with your tacit approval."

"That's right." Leaning forward, Griffin rested his forearms just above his bent knees. His regard was steady, unflinching. "Will you know him?"

Olivia nodded. "If I see him, yes. But I do not wish to see him, my lord. In fact, I wish I might never see him again."

"I understand."

"No, you don't. You cannot possibly understand."

"Perhaps not," he allowed. "But if it occurs that your paths cross, you must come to me."

She said nothing.

"Olivia. I will have your promise."

"And if I give it? What do you mean to do?"

This time it was Griffin who made no reply.

"There is nothing for you to do," she said. "I am not your

responsibility. In truth, I am little better than your prisoner. You are in no position to defend my honor." She shifted, sliding an arm under her pillow to lift her head a few inches. "I would have your promise, though. I would have you swear not to tell my brother."

"He has the right to defend your honor."

"That is supposing I have any, which I do not."

Griffin wondered what he might say to that rather singular announcement. He settled on, "You judge yourself too harshly, I think."

"You know little enough about me to stand on that opinion. Promise me that you will not speak of this to Alastair. You have seen for yourself that he may be provoked to act recklessly."

"It seems a cowardly tact. He'd have reason to challenge me for failing to protect you."

"He'd *think* he had reason. I think he does not. What happened, happened to me. It is my story to tell, no one else's. I beg you to honor that."

Griffin plowed his fingers through his hair as he considered what she wanted. "You are not entirely persuasive, but you are persistent. I collect I will have no peace on the matter."

"You will deserve none."

Needing to think, and requiring some movement to facilitate that process, Griffin pushed to his feet. His action was abrupt—and in retrospect, threatening—and he glimpsed wariness in Olivia's eyes as he towered over her. He stepped back, nudging the chair out of the way. "Pardon me. It was not my intent to give you fear of me."

"I'm not afraid of you."

He turned before she could see the small smile that kicked up one corner of his mouth and did not argue the point. She deserved a measure of pride when so much had already been taken from her. He added wood at the fire and waited until it was a proper blaze before he addressed her again.

"You have my word, Miss Cole. I won't speak of this night's work to your brother."

"Thank you."

"I don't know that my decision deserves thanks. You might regret wresting that promise from me."

"It is difficult to imagine. After all, I can tell him myself if I judge it is the proper thing to do."

Griffin conceded her point, although he did not make too much of it. The tea and whiskey arrived, drawing his attention until it was served and the footman had departed. Olivia, he noted, was looking more the thing now that she was sitting up in bed. The footman had arranged a veritable throne of pillows for her warmth and comfort, and she fostered the impression of royal privilege with the grave dignity of her expression, in spite of the fact that her face and throat were still streaked with soot and his nightshirt was likely to swallow her whole.

Olivia held her cup and saucer carefully in one hand as she raised the other to allow her sleeve to slide down her arm. After transferring the cup, she did the same with the other arm. A bit of tea sloshed onto the saucer when Griffin suddenly appeared on the periphery of her vision and sat on the edge of the bed. Before she knew what he was about, he'd set his drink aside and was neatly rolling up the sleeves of the nightshirt.

"Better?" he asked, retrieving his drink.

Olivia managed to hum her approval. She quickly raised her teacup to her lips to hide the fact that not a single word could be pushed past the lump in her throat. She sipped, swallowed, and felt the ache ease. For all the defenses she had in place, she had never been able to guard herself against an unexpected kindness.

Griffin removed himself from the bed and returned to his

chair. He held his whiskey between his palms and stretched his legs so the toes of his boots were just under the edge of the bed.

Olivia was struck again by the impression of weariness. It was masked to some degree by his casual posture, but it resided there just beneath his skin, a peculiar tension that held him together even as it stole his strength. He had the look in his dark eyes of someone who rarely rested even when he slept, perhaps most especially when he slept. It was not her place to ask after him, so she tucked the thought away for examination later and continued to sip her tea.

"I should like to hear the whole of what happened in your room," Griffin said. "If you are prepared to tell me, that is."

Olivia appreciated that he framed it so carefully but wondered if she truly had the right to refuse. She caught the glimmer of his smile as he waited patiently for her response. How was it that he seemed to know what she was thinking?

She indulged in a deep breath and released it slowly. "He did not rape me, if that's what you want to know."

"You are telling me what did *not* happen. I'd hoped you'd be able to tell me what did. How was it that Wick came to know that you were in danger, for instance?"

"I was able to reach the window. I threw it open and managed to get my head out before I was dragged back. I think I screamed. I must have, else Wick would have had no cause to raise the alarm. I certainly didn't know he was in the yard."

"Sent out on the cook's errand, I believe. It was difficult to make out most of what he was telling me. Excitement did not lend itself to clarity of his expression."

Olivia could well imagine. "Poor Wick."

It was her perfect sincerity that made Griffin cock his head to one side and study her in this new light.

"You are staring," she said.

"Am I?"

"You are. Have I a smut on my nose?"

Laughter rumbled deep in his chest. "On your nose. Your cheeks. A crease of it on your brow." Because she held the cup and saucer she hadn't the means to hide her face behind her hands. Taking pity on her, though not necessarily because he regretted pointing out the blackened state of her complexion, Griffin relieved her of her tea before she upended the cup. He set her drink and his aside, then disappeared into his dressing room.

"Stop rubbing," he said upon his return. "You're making it worse. Hold this." He placed a basin of water in her lap and soaked a flannel in it. "I'm sorry, but this will be cold." He wrung out the flannel as he hitched his hip on the edge of the bed and turned to her. "Close your eyes."

She blinked several times before she obeyed, then the damp flannel was against her cheek. She could feel the gentle pressure of his fingers on the other side of it, washing her face like velvet.

"Go on," he said. "Tell me the rest of it."

It took her a moment to realize he meant that she should go on with her story. It seemed oddly intimate, uncomfortably so, yet there was ease here, too, because he'd seen to it that her eyes were closed.

Griffin prompted her. "You were telling me that he pulled you back into the room after you called for help."

"Yes. I hit my head on the sash hard enough to see a flash of . . ." She frowned slightly. "No, I don't suppose it was that hard after all. I think what I saw was the fire."

Griffin put his fingers at the back of her head and probed gently. He found a bump. Even a gingerly exploration caused her to wince. "Hard enough."

She waited until his hand dropped away before she spoke again. "He . . . he pulled me down. The towel I'd been using to dry my hair was on the floor where I'd dropped it. I thought there might be some use for it. There were no other weapons at the ready."

"No, I don't imagine there were." Griffin applied the cloth to her left cheek. "So did it prove helpful?"

"After a fashion . . . That is . . . It is difficult to . . ." Her voice trailed off as she considered the words in her own mind. There was no bow she could put on the thing to make it pretty. She'd almost strangled a man. That was the truth she could tell him, but it was the truth that he would hear that troubled her more. The truth that she felt not a whit of remorse. "I don't think I want to say."

"Very well. You don't have to."

Olivia felt compelled to offer something in its place. "The noise you made at the door distracted him."

"Is that right?"

She ignored the thread of skepticism in his voice and nodded. "And . . . and I was able to throw him off." It was not a complete lie. "I ran to the door, but you couldn't open it from your side either, and I was afraid he might take me down again if I tried to take the key from him."

"A perfectly reasonable fear," said Griffin. Acid churned in his stomach.

"Was it? I felt the coward."

Griffin dropped the flannel in the basin and placed two fingers under Olivia's chin, lifting it. "Look at me, Olivia."

She knew herself to be compelled by the softly spoken command. She opened her eyes and found herself mirrored in the dark reflection of his own.

"You beat out a fire that might have consumed every one of us. That is not the act of a coward."

"It was easier to fight it than him."

A smile tugged at one corner of Griffin's mouth. "Sometimes it does not matter which enemy you choose to fight. What matters is that you fought. It is my opinion that you acquitted yourself admirably against both." He watched her stir uneasily, though whether she was discomfited by his praise or his proximity he didn't know. He drew back and removed the basin from her lap. The water was gray with the sooty residue from her face. He tilted the bowl a bit, drawing her attention to it. "You haven't a smut left."

She smiled faintly and made to touch her cheek. He caught her wrist when it was halfway to her face and shook his head. Olivia examined her hand and saw that his good work would have been for nothing if she'd touched any part of her face. When he cast his eyes at the basin, she obligingly dipped her hands in the water.

"It seems that a bath was wasted on me this evening," she said as he cleaned her fingers.

"What do you mean?"

"The lads prepared a bath for me tonight, though I suppose Truss or Mr. Mason supported the idea of it. I fear I am dirtier now than I was before my first soaking. Still, it was a bit of good luck to have so much water nearby." She glanced at him. "How did you imagine I was able to put out the fire?"

"I didn't imagine. It was almost entirely out by the time Truss and I entered. It didn't occur to me to wonder how you'd done it. I'm afraid I was more concerned that you survived it."

She nodded. "The £1,000. Yes, it's understandable that you would want to protect Alastair's marker."

"Bloody hell," he said feelingly. "My concern had nothing to do with the debt." He finished wiping down her palms with brisk, almost agitated swipes, then stood and carried the basin back to the dressing room.

"You'll sleep here this evening," he said when he returned. He staved off her protest by lifting a hand. "There really is no other room available. I will stay in my study, of course. Did you have any supper?"

"No, but—"

"I'll send Foster with it. I have to see to my other guests. My *paying* guests, I suppose you'd say."

Olivia had quite a lot she'd like to say, but she was ignored when she called out to him. She knew better than to suppose he hadn't heard her. Her voice was still hoarse and husky from the effects of the smoke, but she'd seen the slight hesitation in his step and did not mistake the cause of it.

She'd poked at a tender spot and he'd dismissed her because of it.

It was gone three when the last of the patrons were finally steered from the gaming hell. Footmen cleared the rooms of empty glasses and sneaked a sip now and again from the ones that weren't quite so empty. Wick and Beetle swept the floors and kept an eye out for stray coins. The drinks cabinet was refilled, the wine cellar locked, and the tables cleared of the detritus of gaming: ashes, snuff, unclaimed markers, dice, and cards. It fell to Mr. Truss to sort through the cards to make sure none had been marked. Each time he found one with a suspicious crease on the corner, he tossed it, then made up new decks to be used the following evening.

As was his habit at the end of each evening, Griffin carried the money box to his study. While his staff worked to set the hell to rights, he counted the night's earnings and recorded it in his account book, separating the income into columns based on the origin of the revenue. The roulette wheel did well for him most nights, and this one was no exception. His earnings for vingt-et-un were steady, a fact that he found interesting as Mrs. Christie was no longer a presence at the table. She always managed to draw in players, so he had expected to see less income once he released her from his protection. That this was not the case merely underscored the other damning revelations about her involvement in his business.

The competitive card games between players, either as individuals or partners, brought him no money. The drink that these players consumed, though, brought him a great deal, and it was not unusual for a player who'd had a good run of luck to leave some of his winnings on the table for the house. He noticed that that particular column showed a marked increase, as it had every evening since Mrs. Christie's departure. He'd been right to suspect that she regularly helped herself to the winnings when she'd cleared the tables. She'd also been pleased to accept a modest percentage of the winnings she gave him each night. Alys Christie had taken her share, then taken it again. The figures he recorded now were sufficient to prove her cheating to his satisfaction.

Griffin closed his eyes briefly, rubbing them with a thumb and forefinger. He stifled a yawn and the figures in the ledger blurred. He shook off the fatigue and added the columns again. When he arrived at the same sum three times over, he replaced his quill, stoppered the inkwell, and sat back in his chair waiting for the page to dry before he closed the book.

He was all for his bed.

That was when he remembered that Olivia Cole was sleeping in it.

He had several thoughts concerning that turn of events, none of them particularly gallant or charitable.

Bloody hell.

Griffin glanced at the chaise longue situated at an angle between two walls of books. He never used it, but it filled the space nicely and served to hold the overflow of books that always seemed to be present in the room. He'd have to clear it before he could lie down.

He rubbed his eyes again. The mere thought of moving those books wearied him. When he considered that he would have to retrieve linens and blankets from the hall cupboard and nightclothes from his own bedchamber, he wondered if he might just be able to sleep in his chair.

It was the possibility that he might wake her that settled him on the matter. He could send Mason or even Truss to get what he needed, but the same end concerned him. He could not imagine that she would have no questions. Mason and

Truss could not answer them, and he was of no mind to do so at this hour.

In truth, there was little enough to tell her, and Griffin allowed that perhaps his internal argument was simply in aid of avoiding her. That insight, if accurate, did not set particularly well with him as he'd always believed it was in his nature to go at a thing head on.

He'd done just that with his staff, gathering them in small groups at different times so the hell's routine and service would not be interrupted and his own absence would not be remarked upon. He asked them about the keys—which were primarily in Truss's care but not inaccessible to others—and had them account for their use throughout the evening. The most valuable keys—those to the wine cellar, liquor cabinets, meat locker, silver drawers, and linen cupboards—were all kept on a ring that Truss carried with him. The keys to other rooms were seldom used and hung on pegs in the servants' hall. If it was determined that there was a need to lock a particular room, then Truss added that key to his ring or delegated responsibility for it.

It was no surprise to discover the key that turned Olivia's lock was missing from its peg.

No single key opened everything, but there existed one key that opened many of the doors to the bedchambers. Truss held this key as well and was able to produce it when called upon to open Olivia's door.

Sitting back in his chair, his eyes partially closed as he stared at the fire, Griffin could recall far too easily the emotion that had roiled through him as he'd tried to gain entry to her room: guilt, frustration, fear. He felt some measure of all those things now as a picture of Olivia Cole, her long, slim frame curled defensively against the fireplace, formed in his mind. Much of her braid had come undone and strands of fiery ginger hair close to her face were already dry and curling. It was not possible for a moment to distinguish those flickering tendrils from the flames mere inches from her. She'd seemed oblivious to her proximity to the fire, or perhaps it was merely that she craved its warmth, but Griffin remembered thinking that with a single spark she would ignite like a candlewick.

Her complexion had been as pale as salt. The effect was to make her eyes burn more brilliantly than was their usual cool green cast. It seemed to him that she weighed next to nothing when he lifted her, though part of him conceded it was the strength of his own fear that made carrying her feel effortless.

He'd made discreet inquiries of some of his better-known patrons, asking offhandedly about a gentleman who might have been among them earlier. He owed the young Corinthian two quid, he told them, but had neglected to make careful note of the man's name. He moved among his guests, pausing to pose his question, offering the same brief description that Olivia had offered him, knowing all the while that it was unlikely to bear fruit. With the help of the footmen, he tried to create a list of patrons who had come on their own and those who had come as part of a larger party. It was a doomed exercise. There simply was no way of knowing with reasonable certainty who came and went. The order that he'd given to evacuate the building worked against him as it was impossible to know how many guests departed after being herded outside.

Foster thought he'd seen a gentleman such as Griffin described, but it turned out he was thinking of Mr. Pennyweather, whom another footman had seen gallantly escorting his lady friend from the hell when the alarm was called.

Wick had only seen the villain at the window. To the boy, the gentleman was more shadow than substance. He could confirm the presence of such a person in Olivia's room, but he couldn't offer a detail that might lead to identification.

Griffin was forced to admit he might never learn the name

of Olivia's attacker, and nothing about that outcome pleased him. It was yet another complication in his increasingly complicated life.

On impulse, he strode to the bookshelves, removed three particular volumes, and checked for the presence of his pistol case. Still not satisfied, he took it from the shelf, opened it, and examined the weapons. He'd been tempted to fire one tonight. The pistol ball would have made short work of Olivia's lock, but the fear of firing into her gave him a long enough pause that Truss was able to appear with the key. He closed the lid and returned the case to its hiding place. He knew some hell owners kept their weapons close at hand, even carried them on their person like highwaymen were wont to do. Griffin had never seen the necessity of it.

Still, he thought, putting the books in their place, a bit of practice with them was not out of the question. Afternoons came to his mind as just the right time for that sort of activity.

When Griffin sat back at his desk, he opened the concealed drawer and drew out Alastair Cole's marker. He read it again, wondering once more at the young man's intention in offering his sister in place of a ring. *A gem rarer than the one I wear* . . . Did he value her so little, or so much?

. . . show her more care than the disdain you showed for my bauble.

Griffin could not help but think that it was Alastair who had shown disdain for his sister, yet there was no denying that Olivia had not railed against her fate. What was it she'd said to him? Oh, yes. *I have no honor.*

What was he to make of that?

She will reward you in ways you cannot imagine.

Griffin came close to crumpling the marker then. He'd seen to her comfort, her health, and the improvement of her mind. She'd rewarded him by setting his hell ablaze and forcing him to contemplate carrying a pistol.

Alastair Cole was right. It was an end he could not have imagined.

Mason entered Breckenridge's study with a very light tread, loath to disturb his employer if he had finally found sleep. True, it was well past the time when Breckenridge would usually rise, but Mason was aware of how little rest the viscount had enjoyed since the attack on Olivia Cole. It was not simply that Breckenridge hadn't been able to avail himself of his own bed, it was that he'd refused the comfort of one in any of the rooms on the floor above. He did not explain his reasoning, though Mason surmised it was because he did not want to be too far removed from Miss Cole. It seemed to the valet that even when Breckenridge was mingling with his patrons there was some part of him always alert to any disturbance above stairs. Last evening the viscount had been moved to investigate a thud that had turned out to be nothing more than a book dropping to the floor.

It was Mason's opinion that his employer's attentiveness was, if not quite unnatural, then extraordinary.

Griffin felt no compulsion to sit up or open his eyes as the door clicked into place behind his valet. He recognized the stealthy movement as the one Mason employed when he was reluctant to disturb, as though the consequence of every step must needs be weighed.

He managed not to sigh his annoyance. "What is it?"

"The seamstress just left."

"And?"

"Miss Cole has asked if she might speak with you."

"The garments do not suit her?"

"No, I believe they suit her admirably."

"She finds them insufficient then."

"I doubt that is the case."

"I don't care for her thanks, Mason. You may tell her that."

The valet cleared his throat uncomfortably. "I'm not certain that . . ." He did not continue, his voice trailing off as Breckenridge deigned to open one eye and spear him with a disbelieving glance. "Never say she means to refuse the gift."

Mason simply shifted his weight from one polished boot to the other.

Griffin cursed under his breath as he pushed his legs over the side of the chaise and sat up. He consulted his fob watch. "My frock coat, Mason. You may show Miss Cole in on the half hour." That would allow him time enough to collect himself, though perhaps a more apt description would have been to prepare for battle.

Olivia demonstrated none of the cautious deliberation that marked Mason's entry just twelve minutes earlier. She stepped up to his desk, planting herself opposite Breckenridge, and came directly to the point.

"I cannot accept the wardrobe," she said. "You cannot insist that I should."

"What a patently wrong-headed thing to say. I can, and I do." He looked her up and down. She was wearing a heavy, blood red velvet robe that he recognized as one of the garments that had been delivered only this morning. The color did not flatter her complexion, but the sleeves and hem had already been let out to accommodate her long-limbed figure. He observed that she'd rather ruthlessly closed the robe all the way to her throat and tightly belted the braided cord at her waist, though whether this was in preservation of her modesty or an act of self-abuse he was not prepared to say.

"That robe was among the things that were sent to your room, was it not?"

"Yes."

"And it seems you have accepted it, so how can you say otherwise?"

"I haven't accepted it. It's been forced upon me. All my clothes were removed."

"I believe it was the consensus of Truss and Mason that they were hopelessly damaged by the smoke."

"It doesn't matter. They were *my* clothes. You had no right." Willing herself not to cry, Olivia shook her head and bit hard into her lower lip. The pain did not keep her chin from quivering. "We will never be able to repay the debt if you mean to increase it at every turn."

"Increase it? How? I wasn't aware that I had."

"Not aware?" He could not be so obtuse? "First it was the new outer garments so that I might take my daily walk. Mr. Mason refused to return my pelisse, bonnet, and gloves."

"Did he?"

"You know he did. He would not do so unless instructed by you."

Unperturbed, Griffin allowed, "You could be right."

"There is also the matter of my meals."

"Are they not satisfactory?"

"I am referring to their cost. And the books. I shouldn't wonder that you mean to exact a lending fee."

"I shouldn't wonder."

"And I must account for damage to my room. The fire was not my fault, but neither was it yours. I know repairs are already under way."

"They certainly are." He had good reason to know that the carpenters hammered while he tried to sleep. The hours for the craftsmen were not at all compatible with the hours he kept.

"The cost must be considerable," she said.

Griffin pressed his steepled fingers under his chin. He knew himself to be both curious and amused, though was careful to let neither show. Carefully neutral, he said, "Let us say it is not inconsiderable."

Olivia's mouth flattened. He made a distinction so subtle as to be unimportant. She pressed on, determined to make him see reason. "And now you present me with a wardrobe that I did not ask for and do not want and include the services of a seamstress to made certain every garment fits."

"There would be no point, don't you agree, to present you with clothes that you cannot possibly wear."

"The point is I cannot wear them at all."

"Why? Was Mrs. McCutcheon unable to make the alterations? My sisters are not generally wrong about matters of fashion. They have all spoken favorably of her skills. Kate and Juliet in particular frequent her shop."

"You know she is perfectly satisfactory."

"Then did you fail to cooperate with her?"

"No, of course not. She was merely acting on your directive, and as you were not disposed to see me earlier to put a stop to the nonsense, I allowed myself to be pinned and poked and prodded."

Griffin detected his valet's fine hand in managing to bring the thing about. Mason had most certainly steered Olivia away from confronting him at the outset, giving Mrs. Mc-Cutcheon ample time to apply her talents to tailoring the wardrobe.

"Are the clothes in any way unsatisfactory?" asked Griffin.

"Only in that they are unwanted."

Griffin's hands dropped to the arms of his chair. "We are at something of an impasse, I believe. I have decided that you shall have them."

"Did you not hear me say that we cannot afford them?"

"We? You've said that before. You do not owe me a farthing."

Olivia was not deceived by his apparent largesse. "And if Alastair does not return?"

"Have you changed your mind? Do you think that's likely now?" He held up one hand to stave off her reply. "Don't trouble yourself to answer that. If you deny it, I don't know that I would believe you. It is better that we just wait and see what tomorrow brings. And the day after that. And so on."

"His debt is also mine," she said softly. "That is the way of things between us." She imagined it was precisely what her brother was counting on.

Griffin could find no reason to question her sincerity, only her wisdom. Accepting responsibility for her brother's foibles was foolish beyond measure. He shook his head, a barely perceptible movement that he masked further by tunneling his fingers through his hair.

"The clothes are a gift," he said at last. "There was never any intention on my part to add their cost to what is owed me. Rest easy and have joy of them."

Realizing that she was being summarily dismissed, Olivia required a moment to collect herself, then a moment longer to collect her thoughts. "Is it a surfeit of arrogance that leaves you with no room for compassion?" She lifted one hand, palm out, in a gesture that mirrored his earlier one. "No, don't favor me with a reply. If you deny it, I don't know that I will believe you."

She pivoted on slippered feet, giving him her very cold shoulder, and started toward the door. It occurred to her that he might be moved to call her back but before she could consider how she might respond to that entreaty he was blocking her path. She fairly vibrated in place as she drew up short to keep from stumbling into him. Pressure built in her chest until she realized she was holding her breath. She let it out slowly.

It was Griffin who took a step back, though not a step aside. He made no attempt to reach for her. "You are not easily intimidated," he said.

"Do you think so? I am not at all certain that's true."

"You hold your ground."

"I make a small footprint. It is little enough to hold on to."

His faint smile was edged with regret. "I have bullied you. Forgive me." Now he stepped aside. "Won't you sit down?"

Olivia hesitated.

"Please?"

She shook her head, afraid that she might finally give in to tears.

"Very well," he said. "Naturally you are free to go."

She did not mistake his meaning. She was free to go as far as her room. Her feet, though, remained rooted to the floor.

Griffin took advantage of her immobility to press his argument regarding the wardrobe. "I would have you accept the clothes, Miss Cole, as a favor to me. Someone should have use of them."

"It seems I cannot make you understand," she said. "They are gowns and dresses made for another woman, one who is not little more than a prisoner here."

Griffin's dark eyes took on a vaguely bitter cast. "As it happens, Miss Cole, they were made for my wife, but you will not be surprised to learn that she shared some part of your opinion. She was fond of pointing out that marriage to me was its own kind of prison."

Chapter Five

The passage of the following sennight without any word from Alastair helped Olivia arrive at the realization that she would have to make her own way. She tried not to think of his absence in terms of its finality. Even the most fleeting thought that he might have met a very bad end had the power to bring her to her knees. It was the same when she considered that he meant to abandon her. She knew a depth of such despair that it incapacitated her, and the hollowness of that feeling added to her fear.

Alastair's failure to present himself had other explanations that Olivia preferred to entertain. At the forefront of these was that Sir Hadrien had refused to advance Alastair's allowance. Olivia reminded herself that this turn did not mean her brother would not return, but merely that she could expect he would be a very long time coming.

It would be as it had been. She'd managed to live on her wits—and not much else—once before. There had been no expectation then that she would be rescued; indeed, she had never thought of her life in terms of captivity. It was as it was. She managed each day as she had each yesterday, and if she allowed herself to think that something might be different on the morrow, it was just in those moments before she slept and only in the early days when she still believed she could order her dreams.

Olivia knelt on the cushioned window bench in Brecken-ridge's bedroom with her palms pressed to the glass. Looking down her nose at Putnam Lane in only the most literal sense, she could easily count the number of pedestrians at this time of morning. A mere hour earlier, when Mason had escorted her to the park, there'd been almost no one about. She'd had occasion on some of her walks to spy late-night revelers fi-nally stumble from the hells or glimpse gentlemen in the act of straightening their frock coats and flies as they departed the brothels. Mason invariably steered her away from these sights, although Olivia suspected it was done as much in aid of preserving his own dignity as it was in acknowledgment of her sensibilities.

She so appreciated the effort he made on her behalf that she did not disabuse him of the notion that she possessed any finer feelings. She simply accepted his direction and allowed him to lead on.

Olivia smiled as she watched a pair of women emerge from the townhouse opposite her. Linking arms, they lightly de-scended the steps. They both wore wide-brimmed bonnets that hid their faces, one decorated with an assortment of plump fruit and the other with colorfully dyed ostrich feath-ers. These adornments bounced and swayed in lively accom-paniment to their movements. In tandem, the women seemed to sense they were being watched. Uncertain of how well they could see her, Olivia nevertheless retained her smile as they looked up. It was difficult to know whether they were startled by her presence at the window. Their faces were so brightly painted that their expressions were lost to her. She ventured a wave and knew herself to be ridiculously pleased when they responded in kind.

The communication was brief. The women were about other business that encouraged them not to tarry. Olivia watched them hurry away and entertained herself wondering where they were going. It seemed likely that with their particular tastes and devotion to fashion, they were leaving Putnam Lane to frequent the shops of their favorite dressmakers and milliners.

She envied them their freedom, though not their destination. This last week she had spent interminable hours being fitted for all the clothes she had never wanted. There had been no easy surrender on her part, but she didn't suppose that mattered. In the end, she'd given in, and that's what she imagined that Breckenridge would remember.

It was of no consequence to her that the clothes were castoffs. Discovering that they had belonged to his lordship's wife was of less account to her than discovering he had a wife. Still, her refusal to accept them was predicated on the fact that she'd had her own clothes but apparently no rights regarding their retention or disposal.

Breckenridge had ordered all of her garments—with the exception of her outerwear—returned to her. Her initial pleasure faded when she realized that although every article had been laundered, the acrid scent of smoke lingered on all of them. The odor could not be masked with soap or fragrance. It had worked its way into the warp and weft of the fabric and would not be removed.

Olivia might have stubbornly insisted on wearing them anyway if not for the fact that the mere act of breathing in the presence of the clothes prompted an unpleasant visceral response. Coupled with the memories that flooded her, she finally admitted that keeping them might soothe her wounded pride, but would give her no peace.

She offered no explanation to Mason when she told him that she'd reconsidered her decision not to accept Breckenridge's offering. The valet ventured no comment nor gave any hint of his own feelings on the matter. He simply nodded and went about the business of making it so.

It was a bit galling that Mrs. McCutcheon arrived that very afternoon with several pieces nearly completed in their alterations. Olivia surmised from this that Breckenridge had never believed there would be any other outcome than that she would fall in with his wishes. She could no longer even accuse him of high-handedness, not when he'd put the choice before her. How difficult, she wondered, had it been for him to do that?

Olivia shifted on the bench so that she was no longer kneeling. She pushed an embroidered pillow behind her back and leaned against the alcove wall. The fullness of her gown fell over her legs. Folds of pink India muslin slipped over the side of the bench and left her ankles and feet exposed. She wiggled her toes and felt her pale pink silk stockings stretch with the movement. She wished that she might not take pleasure from wearing anything so fine, but it was like asking her not to appreciate sunshine on her face or the sound of a child's laughter.

Mrs. McCutcheon had transformed Lady Breckenridge's wardrobe by repositioning the waistline to its natural level, adding fullness to the sleeves, rounding the bodices, and moving the ornamentation to the hemline. The fabrics she had to work with were of the best quality: Chinese silk, satin, cambric, soft muslin, brushed velvet, and tulle. There were cloth-covered and mother-of-pearl buttons instead of flat copper hooks and eyes. There were dresses for day, for evening, for walking, and for taking a turn in a carriage. Every gown was lined in cotton or sarcenet or silesia. She had undergarments of the finest batiste: chemises, petticoats, drawers, and shifts. There were slippers and hose to match her gowns, half-boots to be worn on walks, ribbons for her hair, and cashmere shawls with fringe that brushed her skin with such delicacy that she'd heard herself sigh with the contentment of it.

If she could believe Breckenridge, she was not beholden to him for any of it. Still, her own conscience was not so easily cleared of its sense of obligation. It made her vaguely uneasy that he had asked for nothing in exchange, and she could not shake the notion that he kept a mental ledger of every favor he extended her, whether or not she was pleased to accept it.

She lifted the book she'd been reading from the narrow sill but did not open it. Breckenridge had passed on to her a Gothic novel that she was almost certain could not have come from his own library. It had kept her up well past midnight so that now she used the back of her hand to stifle a yawn.

The hell was quiet if one discounted the occasional banging and rumble of deep male voices coming from the carpenters and painters working in her former room. She had yet to be invited to see their progress, but she believed they must be nearing the end of their work and that very soon she would be permitted to return. It was not that Breckenridge's bedchamber was inherently uncomfortable, only that she was made uncomfortable because she had displaced him.

Listening between hammer blows and the barking of orders, Olivia strained to hear the sounds of stirring from Breckenridge's study. Sometimes she could hear him moving about, especially if he was in what she thought of as one of his dark moods. On those occasions she could make out his heavier tread in the hall and feel the shudder of his door when he closed it. If he drank there might follow the sound of breaking glass or a series of thumps as stacks of books were toppled to the floor. She imagined that neither was caused by carelessness.

Griffin Wright-Jones, the honorable Viscount Breckenridge, would have taken deliberate aim.

Olivia knew him to be far quieter in the morning. If he rose before Mason arrived, which he did more often than not, she heard him throw open the window to his study and call down to the street urchins that had gathered below to fetch him a paper. He tossed coins for the purchase and later, once he had the *Gazette* in hand, he tossed a few extra for their trouble. She suspected more than one family had a bit of meat for their stew because of Breckenridge's charity. After the completion of this ritual, she heard very little until a footman delivered his breakfast and Mason came to assist with the routines of preparing for the day. By then it was almost always the beginning of the afternoon.

He often left then, though Olivia could only suppose where he went. The case that was frequently secured under his arm made her think he was depositing the hell's income, though going it alone seemed fraught with risk. If the weather was clear and not too cold, he walked. Sometimes Foster or Truss would leave the hell to wave a hack to the doorstep. She had never seen him take a carriage, although she knew from Beetle that he had one at his disposal. "A most splendid equipage," the kitchen lad had named it, and Olivia was inclined to believe him.

As often as she was discomfited by the knowledge that she spent each day and night almost entirely in Breckenridge's suite, she also knew that she would miss this view of Putnam Lane and her proximity to his lordship's study once she was removed from it.

Wanting to embrace the view now, Olivia turned to glance out the window again. None of the street children had arrived to mark their territory at the front of the hell. It seemed they knew better than to come upon the place too soon of a morning and risk waking Breckenridge earlier than was his habit. No doubt there were unpleasant consequences to be had for that.

Olivia did not know what they were, but the time had come to find out.

Griffin threw a forearm across his eyes and groaned softly as the series of sharp raps at the doors penetrated his consciousness. It seemed to him that he had fallen asleep only a few short hours ago. With his free hand he groped for the watch he'd placed on the floor beside the chaise. He flicked his wrist to swing the gold chain so the watch landed in his palm. There was nothing wrong with the timekeeper in his head, he realized. He *had* fallen asleep only a few short hours ago.

Mason would have already let himself in, so Griffin knew it was not his valet on the other side of the door. Similarly, any of his staff believing they had a message so urgent that they must wake him would also have entered by now. Griffin was very much afraid that he knew who was demanding entry.

He sat up and rolled his neck from side to side. His robe was lying at the foot of the chaise. He shrugged into it as he stood and loosely fastened the belt while he crossed the room.

Olivia Cole was indeed on the other side of the door. He made a brief study of her rather defiant posture, standing as she was with her fist raised at the level of her angled chin, and decided that not even she could manage to hold the high ground wearing a muslin day dress the color of a blush.

"You did not bring coffee." He closed the door in her face.

Olivia blinked. She let her fist drop to her side and for a moment did nothing save for stare at the door. *You did not bring coffee.* That curt observation might easily be construed as an invitation, at least to her way of thinking. He could have ordered her away, and he hadn't done so. That meant she might gain admission if she traded in the correct currency.

The second time she announced herself at the door she was brusquely given permission to enter.

"It took you considerable time to return," Griffin said. He pointed to the space beside him on the chaise and indicated she should set the tray there. One eyebrow lifted when he saw she'd only brought a single cup and saucer. "You don't care for coffee?"

"It seemed presumptuous of me to assume you meant for me to join you."

He snorted. "You would do well not to speak of presumption when you've taken the liberty to wake me at this unholy hour."

Olivia accepted the chastisement without comment. She watched him pour the coffee, add cream but ignore the sugar, then lift the cup to his lips. He paused, breathing in the fragrance of the brew before he sipped. There was something oddly intimate about witnessing his unguarded pleasure. She found herself discomfited and looked away.

"The kitchen staff must have been surprised to see you," he said idly between sips. "Please. Sit. I have no wish to advance this crick in my neck by staring up at you."

Olivia glanced around and chose the chair closest to the fireplace. She looked at him for permission to turn it in his direction. At his slight nod, she used her knee against the arm to nudge it around before she perched on the edge of the cushion. To keep her hands from fidgeting in the folds of her dress, she clasped them together in her lap.

She did not fail to notice that Breckenridge hadn't taken advantage of her absence to dress. Extending him the benefit of the doubt, she supposed he couldn't have been certain that she would return. Perhaps he had even tried to go back to sleep. He was still wearing his nightshirt, robe, and leather slippers. His chestnut hair was disheveled, his eyes heavily lidded, and there was a pillow crease in his right cheek that was a near perfect match to the scar in his left. She tried to imagine the circumstances in which she would not find him to be inordinately beautiful, and could not.

"I hope you do not mean for me to carry the conversation," he said finally, breaking the silence. "My opening gambit was to ask you about your foray to the kitchen. You have yet to answer."

Olivia squeezed her hands together. "The kitchen. Yes. I remember. Actually, no one was there when I arrived. I supposed Cook had returned to bed after preparing my breakfast, and I was reminded how much my presence disrupts the routine you've established here. It's why I've come actually. I believe I can put that to rights."

"I cannot permit you to leave."

"You are too suspicious. I was not going to suggest it."

He *was* suspicious, but also more than a little intrigued. "Go on, though I should tell you that while your coffee is as excellent as any served in the clubs, I am not in favor of you regularly going to the kitchen."

"Then you would not permit me to work there."

"Good Lord, no."

"I confess that is a relief." She'd had her fill of kitchens and as a rule avoided the one in her own home unless called there by Mrs. Beck to settle a dispute. "My excellent coffee aside, it's not the kitchen where I can be most useful to you."

"Really?"

"Do not mistake my meaning, Lord Breckenridge. You would not find me an agreeable companion in bed, either."

"You are too straightforward in your speech, I think, but don't assume you know the bent of my mind, Miss Cole. I recently relieved myself of a mistress. I am not looking for another."

She flushed. "Forgive me. I didn't mean to—"

He waved aside her apology. "In what way useful, then?"

"It would be better if I might demonstrate."

"By all means."

Olivia stood. Her eyes darted about the room in search of a particular item she'd seen in his study. It seemed it either had been buried under something else or actually put away. It was difficult to believe the latter, so she began a more thorough search, carefully picking her way among the stacks of ledgers and papers and occasionally turning something over to examine what lay beneath.

Wary, Griffin followed her movements over the rim of his cup as he drank his coffee. "Has the demonstration begun?" In response to her slightly annoyed, over-the-shoulder glance, Griffin shrugged. "It is a perfectly sensible question."

He chose a triangle of buttered toast from the tray she'd

brought and bit into it. There was no good reason that this piece of toast should taste better than what Cook prepared of a morning, yet it was undeniably true. Griffin brushed a crumb from the lapel of his velvet robe and chose another triangle.

"Perhaps if you were to tell me what you are looking for," he said. "I can freely admit you are making me uneasy with your poking around."

It was when she turned to respond that she spied the object of her search on the floor just under the head of the chaise. "Of course," she said, more to herself than him. "You were playing with them. I did not think of that."

She skirted a table and dropped to her knees beside the chaise, ignoring the exaggerated lift of his dark eyebrows. Careful not to brush his leg as she patted the floor just behind him, her fingers finally curled around the deck of cards. Smiling beatifically, she held them up.

Griffin felt his insides twist. He found the radiance of her expression was actually difficult to look upon. Ignoring most of what he saw and all of what he felt, he offered a wry observation, "Triumph such as you are now wont to show is generally reserved for coming upon the source of the Nile or being carried on a litter into the city you've just conquered."

He saw her smile falter and was both regretful and glad of it. "Card tricks?" he asked. "Is that what you mean to show me?"

Still stinging from his comment, Olivia made to rise with a measure of dignity. "Perhaps later. When you might be more inclined to appreciate them." She pointed to the nearby table. "May I?"

"Of course." He started to set his cup down in preparation of helping her, but she waved him away.

Olivia pulled the cherrywood table toward the chaise. It was not the proper size or shape for what she wanted to demonstrate, but she would make do. She stood on the opposite side of the table and began shuffling the cards.

It took her a few moments to find her rhythm. The cards

were well used, slightly thick because of it, with corners that snagged and faces that did not easily slide against one another. She was also badly out of practice. Twice the cards fluttered from her hands, making her feel gauche and clumsy.

Griffin's cup hovered halfway between his lap and his mouth as he gave over all of his attention to Olivia Cole. Her long, elegantly tapered fingers moved and manipulated with a speed and deftness that his eyes could not easily follow. Even when some of the cards escaped her hands, she shoveled them up with the remainder of the deck in a fashion so smooth as to give the impression the initial fumbling was deliberate.

He put his cup aside and leaned forward. She tapped the deck on the table, squaring it off, then fanned it open, first with the back of the cards showing, then again with the pips and faces turned up. She did this several times, flipping the cards back and forth with a flick of her wrist.

When she paused, he glanced up and caught her frowning. "What is it?" he asked.

"Will you look under the chaise? The four of hearts and the queen of clubs are missing from this deck."

He did not inquire as to how she could possibly know that—she'd neither sorted nor counted the cards—but when he felt around under the chaise his fingertips caught the edges of two cards. He picked them up and laid them face up on the table. The four of hearts and the queen of clubs.

"You purposely left them behind when you picked up the rest of the deck," he said.

Olivia drew the two cards toward her and slipped them into the deck. "You know I didn't examine the cards when they were under the chaise. I couldn't see them properly." She handed him the deck. "Take as few or as many as you like." She turned her back and waited.

Griffin removed one card and slipped it under the tray at

his side without looking at it. He slid the deck toward her again. "All right."

Olivia pivoted, picked up the cards, and resumed shuffling. They stuck occasionally, and she had to adjust the pressure of her hands and fingers to compensate. She spread the cards in a perfect arch on the table, flipped them once, flipped them back, and gathered them up again.

"The six of spades," she said.

Griffin lifted one edge of the tray and slipped the card free. He glanced at it before pushing it across the table toward her. "The six of spades."

A smile tugged at the corner of her mouth. "Did you suppose that if you examined it beforehand you might give it away? I should very much like to see what expression of yours hints at the six of spades."

He scowled at her.

"Really? I confess I would have mistaken that for one of the knaves. A diamond, mayhap, or a heart."

"Amusing," he said in a tone that communicated the opposite.

Olivia tried to school her smile but it would not be tempered. It was only when she realized that she was enjoying herself that it faded. Her hands grew clumsy again and she lost several cards. She flinched, turning her head and raising one shoulder a fraction, then dropped a small curtsy and offered an apology for her awkward handling of the cards.

"Why did you do that?" Griffin asked.

"Do what?" She attended to her shuffling and did not look at him.

"Make that bow and apologize."

"Did I?" Olivia divided the deck and nimbly worked the halves between her fingers, passing them back and forth between her hands. "I didn't realize."

"Yes, when you dropped the cards." He inclined his head to one side to try to catch her eye and was left with the impression she was purposely ignoring him. "Just after you drew back."

"I couldn't say," she told him. "I don't recall doing it."

Griffin chose not to press. He knew what he had seen and did not question the accuracy of his perception. She had anticipated a blow. That was the only reason people started in the manner she had. The lift of her shoulder was instinctive, a protection against a strike that was aimed at a more vulnerable point, perhaps her chin or cheek.

He returned his attention to her manipulation of the cards. She was remarkably smooth given the dog-eared condition of the deck she was using. There was rarely a hesitation; her initial stiffness was gone. She now was able to look away from her hands and still complete the cutting and turning of the cards without mishap. She had the sort of dexterity that would have enabled her to force any card on him that she desired. What she did, however, was slide the deck forward and ask him to make a cut.

Olivia took back the deck and laid out thirteen cards in two rows, ace through king, all of them spades. In the first row the ace was on her left, the six on the right. The seven of spades lay at the head, perpendicular to the two rows, and the remaining six cards, the eight through the king, had a one-to-one correspondence with the cards in the first row.

"That is the layout of a faro table," Griffin said.

"It is. I assume you have one in your hell."

"Of course."

"With a spade suit like this glued to the table?"

"Painted, actually. It is a very fine table. Antique, and in excellent condition."

Olivia nodded. She'd expected nothing less. "Without a traditional table here, we'll have to pretend these cards are permanently fixed."

"Very well."

"Would you like to make a wager?" She drew the remainder

of the deck to her and looked around for something that might be used as a marker.

Griffin picked up one of the toast triangles and tore it in half. He placed one half on the three of spades and ate the other.

Olivia chuckled. "It is an unusual token, but one supposes that as owner you are able to establish the house rules."

"Precisely."

Olivia paused a moment, waiting to see if Breckenridge wanted to rethink his wager or add another. When he simply resumed drinking his coffee, she said, "All bets are down." She turned over the top card on the remaining deck. It was a five of hearts. "The house wins on all bets placed on the five." Sighing, she feigned disappointment that he'd placed his wager elsewhere. "I should have liked to eat the winnings."

"Then you would be stealing from the house," he reminded her.

"A most excellent point." She placed the losing card on her right and turned over the next card, a seven of diamonds. "The house pays on all wagers on the seven. It appears you do not win either. Do you wish to make another wager or allow your toast to stand on the three?"

"I'll allow it to stand."

"As you wish. All bets are placed." The next card she turned over—the losing card—was a three of clubs. As the suit in faro was unimportant to the play, it only mattered that the card was a three. "The house wins on all wagers placed on the three. Oh dear, that means you've forfeited your toast."

"How fortunate for me that I am also the house," Griffin said, picking up the bite-sized piece and dropping it in his mouth. He made a show of enjoying it, too. "Did you force the three so the house would win?"

Olivia took exception to that. The entire line of her body stiffened. "You are asking if I cheated, and the answer is no."

"But you could."

She simply stared at him.

"But you could," he repeated. He picked up his last piece of toast and divided it. This time he made a wager with each half, placing one on the queen and the other in the space above and between the nine and ten, thus splitting that bet. "The next card you draw is the winning card for the punter. I want to win on the queen."

Olivia's mouth flattened. She wondered that she had allowed herself to expect something different from him. Her disappointment was sincerely felt, but when she reflected on it, she realized she was more disappointed in herself for lowering her guard than in Breckenridge for taking advantage.

"On the queen," she said without inflection, looking away. She covered the deck briefly with her palm while she idly stretched and contracted the fingers of her other hand. Lifting her palm, she tapped the deck once with a forefinger then turned over the top card. The queen of diamonds was displayed. "Punter wins on the queen."

Griffin whistled softly. "You can indeed." He picked up the piece of toast and set it back on the tray. "The house wins on the next turn. Since I split the bet, you can do it with either the nine or the ten."

"You do not even make it challenging," she said coolly. "Choose which card you wish me to show you, the nine or the ten."

"The nine."

With no enthusiasm for the task, Olivia laid her palm over the deck again while she absently fiddled with the sleeve of her gown. Out of view her thumbnail fanned the corner of the stack of cards. She lifted her hand.

"Wait," Griffin ordered. He reached across the table and did what no player would be permitted to do during a turn at faro: He revealed the top card himself. "A four," he said.

"So it is."

"You weren't able to do it that time."

"That's the card you lifted," she said.

"It was on top."

"Perhaps it was when you reached for it, but when I choose the top card, it looks like this." She turned it over and displayed the nine of hearts.

"God's truth, but you're adept at it." Griffin's tone was all admiration as he sat back and rubbed his chin with his knuckles. "You told me you possessed no happy talents."

"Obviously we define that differently." She swept her hand across the table, gathering all the cards, including the faro layout, then set the deck in front of him. "You appear to have an understanding of my usefulness. I should like to begin as soon as possible, tonight if you will. I imagine it will require some time for me to acclimate myself to the routine everyone else in the hell abides by, but I shall endeavor to do so as quickly as possible."

Taking a short breath, Olivia went on quickly before Breckenridge could insert a comment. "While I remain hopeful that my brother will return soon, I recognize that I must also be practical. I have expenses and no means of meeting them. There are debts I must repay, and I am depending on you to appreciate that. If you will not allow me to leave, then it remains that I have to find some manner of supporting myself here. You would not deny me that opportunity, would you?"

Griffin poured a second cup of coffee. This time he ignored sugar *and* cream. "I find myself staring up at you again."

Olivia dropped to the wing chair behind her, resuming her perched posture as Breckenridge rubbed the back of his neck. He let his hand fall away, sipped his coffee, and made a disagreeable face. "You take cream," she said. "You forgot the cream."

He grunted softly, added cream, and tasted the coffee a second time. The crease between his eyebrows softened. "You said quite a lot," he told her. "Shall I begin anywhere or is there some particular you would like addressed first?"

Olivia felt as if her chest were being squeezed. If he was going to allow her to work at his faro table, he would have just said so. She prepared herself to hear his objections and prayed she would not humiliate herself by showing the depth of her distress. "Begin where you like," she said, and was glad of the confidence in her voice.

"Tell me about these expenses you say you have. What are they?"

"I have a home in Jericho Mews," she said. "Or rather, I live with Alastair there. Or did." Impatient with herself, she blew out a puff of air. "The household staff needs to be paid. So does the greengrocer. Mr. Fox will not extend any more credit for meat if I do not pay the bill in full this time. Even in my absence there are things that must be done. The servants—and there aren't so many of them as you have—need to eat. I cannot simply ignore them because I'm here."

"Your brother does not seem to share your finely honed sense of duty, else he would be seeing to their wages, their needs, and your honor."

"If he were able to do anything differently, he would."

Griffin noted that what she offered was neither a defense nor an indictment. It was, in truth, a simple statement of fact. "I could arrange for you to close up the house and let the servants go."

Olivia could not help herself. She recoiled. "No!" When he stared her down under arched eyebrows she remembered herself. "No," she said, this time with considerably less heat. "It would not be a simple matter for the staff to find other employment, and I . . . I like the house and would not want to see it empty."

"Then your brother owns it?"

She shook her head. "You cannot recoup the debt he owes by taking it from him. He rents it."

"So there is rent to pay as well. You did not mention that.

Now I understand why you do not want it empty. You would lose it."

"Yes."

"I begin to see why your brother wanted you here. It seems he meant for you to have a place to live when he took himself off."

Olivia did not try to deny it. She was no longer certain that Breckenridge was wrong.

"What are you proposing again?" he asked.

"That you permit me to work for you."

"That's not possible."

"Of course it's possible. I showed you that I know faro. I can deal vingt-et-un also, and I know when the house must stand or take another card."

"I'm quite sure you do, but I run honest games here, and you, my dear Olivia, are a most excellent cheat."

Confused, she asked, "If you have no use for the skill, then why did you insist on knowing if I could force the cards?"

"Because it intrigues." He shrugged. "And entertains. You are perhaps the best I have ever seen."

"I thought you wanted me to cheat, else I wouldn't have shown you."

"Yes, well, now you know I do not, and it is your misfortune to be so very good at it that I could not possibly trust you. You may not credit it, but my reputation, such as it is, is important to me. For all that I am something of a pariah in certain fashionable circles, in the underworld of gaming hells, I am credited to offer a fair deal. However one wishes to interpret that phrase, it remains true. I expect the same in return, and that is known as well, particularly by those who've crossed me."

"Like Alastair."

"Exactly like Alastair."

"I have no intention of crossing you, my lord."

"Don't you? Again, I say, how will I know? I was looking

for your sleight of hand and could not see it. You will amaze my patrons as you did me, then you will make them wary. Whether or not you cheat is almost beside the point. If they suspect you are, they will not play."

"You're wrong," she said quietly, but with conviction. "Though I don't suppose you will give me the opportunity to prove it."

"Just so." Griffin took another sip of his coffee. "Is your brother so skilled?"

"I believe the answer to that is he owes you £1,000."

"You have me there," he admitted. "Does he know about your talent?"

"We've never discussed it."

"No? Why not?"

"It did not seem prudent."

"You mean he would have wanted you to teach him."

Olivia's hands tightened in her lap. "I suppose that's what I meant."

"How is it you learned and he didn't?"

This was the question she'd been dreading. He'd been circling around it long enough to make her dizzy from the anticipation of it. She didn't know until the words were out of her mouth that she would tell him the truth. "Alastair and I were not raised in the same home."

Griffin had suspected as much. "He lived with Sir Hadrien?"

"Yes. And his mother."

So Olivia and Alastair were half siblings. He'd wondered. "And you lived . . . ?"

"Here and there."

"That is rather less than specific."

"Forgive me, my lord, but you are not entitled to more." He was not deterred. "With your mother?"

Olivia said nothing.

"It is not the worst of all things to be a bastard," he said.

Her eyes darkened, and before she thought better of it, she said, "You know this from experience, I collect."

Griffin sucked in a breath. He was not accustomed to being spoken to in such a fashion, even when he deserved it, and he supposed he deserved it now. "I spoke out of turn. I am not a bastard."

"And neither am I. The truth is more prosaic. My mother died in childbirth and my father remarried."

There was much more, of that Griffin had no doubt, but because he could not justify his interest, most especially to himself, he asked for no other particulars. He addressed the problem of her home and staff instead. "Let us agree that you will compose a letter to your housekeeper expressing your need to be away some weeks longer. You will include sufficient funds to pay your servants and your outstanding bills."

"I haven't such funds."

"I'm well aware. That is why I shall make them available to you. Your housekeeper? Is she trustworthy?"

"Yes. She will carry out my wishes."

"Good. You will give me an accounting of what you need and I shall arrange it. I will want to see the letter, naturally."

"Naturally," she said dully.

"Come, there is no cause for you to act defeated. You cannot seriously have supposed I would permit you to work the faro table when I do not even employ a single female on my staff. It is dangerous, as you have good reason to know." He could not imagine that she needed to be reminded of the assault.

"This is different."

"How so?"

"I would be engaged in my work in front of you. It does you no credit if I cannot not be safe with you in the same room."

God's truth, but there was some logic to her argument, although he wondered if she had any sense that he might pose the greatest danger to her. He'd meant what he'd said about not wanting another mistress, but he was not entirely opposed to a less formal arrangement, one that brought her around at his whim, not hers. He had been thinking of it of late, unable to ignore the fact that she was sleeping in his bed—without him.

The carnal thoughts were not easily dismissed, and in truth he had not put forth much effort to do so. Olivia Cole was appealing in an otherworldly fashion. Her ginger hair would not be tamed by combs or braids and the wildness of it made him think she had walked through fire. It was a vision supported by the fact that she had survived one.

Her eyes, with their faintly exotic slant and emerald coloring, invariably aroused his interest. On most occasions she offered a direct, even impudent, stare that he appreciated simply for its novelty. When she avoided his gaze, it was not because she was shy of a sudden, but because she was unable to shutter strong emotion. She hid it behind long lashes as she glanced off to one side, an expression that might easily be misconstrued as demure, but was in fact a response to fear.

It was difficult to know with any degree of certainty what made Olivia Cole afraid. She'd remained clear-eyed and level-headed facing her attacker and didn't panic when fire began to consume the room. She'd been willing to incur his displeasure by not only leaving her room this morning, but presenting herself at his door. If he had to advance a theory, Griffin would say that the thing she feared most was herself.

That also intrigued, drawing him in when perhaps the wiser course would be to increase his distance.

He finished his coffee, set the cup aside, and rolled the stiffness from his shoulders. Too many more nights on the chaise, he decided, and self-preservation would dictate that he present himself at her door.

"You are in expectation of a reply," he said, studying her, "as if I might be inclined to change my mind. I am not so inclined. When your brother's debt is finally settled to my satisfaction you will thank me that I did not permit you in the gaming rooms. You have some sort of society to which you will return. Your life will proceed more smoothly if it is not rumored that you were once the faro dealer at Breckenridge's hell."

"You know nothing about my society. It is not a consideration."

Griffin thought he might throw up his hands in frustration. What kept them at his side was a suspicion that they might find their way to her throat. "You are relentless, Miss Cole."

She actually smiled.

"There is no reason you should be so full of yourself. It was not a compliment." He watched her school her expression but did not imagine for a moment that she was chastened. "You are Sir Hadrien Cole's daughter. I have not forgotten that, even if you have."

Olivia was quiet a long moment in which her stare did not waver. "You have it wrong, my lord. It is Sir Hadrien that has forgotten."

It was rare that Griffin found himself at a loss, but he knew that feeling now. Her voice did not hint at sadness; her eyes did not hint at pain. It was in the stillness of her posture, in the way she seemed to draw into herself that he sensed her self-protective isolation. Lonely, perhaps, almost certainly alone, she imposed distance without retreating and effectively, eloquently, told him she would say no more on the subject.

"Why is it so important to you?" he asked at last. "I've told you that I will see to your house and your staff and your creditors. What is it that I don't understand that makes you want to do this thing?"

Olivia responded with a question of her own. "Do you believe women can desire to act honorably, that they have a duty to account for their own debts?"

"You do not want to hear my opinion of women and honor and duty."

"That is a kind of answer, isn't it? You would not be looking for an explanation if I were a man; honoring a debt would be your expectation. You have satisfied yourself that I am no more than my brother's marker, and it is not only you, but Alastair, too, who sees me in such a manner. If I go on as I have, it is how I will come to see myself." She glanced at her hands, shook her head. "A marker. Can you imagine? Not flesh and blood, but currency. It is too lowering."

Even for me. She did not add the words, but they flitted through her mind. Afraid they would make her sound pitiable, she held them back.

Griffin regarded her with a certain amount of skepticism. "I cannot decide if you are sincere or well rehearsed."

She shrugged. "It doesn't matter. It is honest."

"You are correct," he said, inclining his head to salute her. "It doesn't matter. My mind is unchanged."

The hell was particularly crowded this evening, Griffin noted. He was aware that Mrs. Christie's absence had led to some speculation among his regular patrons. There were wagers in the betting books as to when she would reappear. Griffin did not discourage the activity, though he suggested adding a column that permitted bettors to mark their wagers as *when hell freezes*. This led to further speculation that perhaps a blizzard was in the offing.

It was a harmless enough activity and aside from that one comment, he remained quiet on the matter of his former mistress. He'd learned that she was frequenting some of the competing clubs—Johnny Crocker's most often—but this did not concern him. In spite of the acrimony of their parting, he wished her well, and if she did deign to visit his hell again, he knew it would happen only when she had captured the attention and the arm of someone she considered his rival.

It would not be enough for Alys Christie that she was doing well. She would want to know that he was not.

"Lady Rivendale," Griffin said, lifting the hand she extended to him and bringing it to his lips. "You are looking particularly fine this evening. It occurs to me that you will be the very devil to beat at the tables."

She smiled warmly and shed a decade off her fifty plus years. "I hope you are right, Breckenridge. I have it in my mind to win a perfectly vulgar sum of money tonight."

Griffin chuckled. "What is your game so that I might show you to your table?"

"Conquian." A gentleman some ten years her senior appeared at her side, a drink in either hand. She lifted the glass of wine meant for her. "Do you know Mr. Warner?"

"I have not had the pleasure." He made a slight bow. "Welcome to my club."

Before Mr. Warner could make a reply, Lady Rivendale offered a distinctly masculine snort. "Pray, Breckenridge, do not puff the thing up. It is a hell, a fine one to be sure, but still a hell. I shall be most disappointed to learn I've convinced Mr. Warner to provide escort to a respectable establishment. He has been to those. Tell me that you have not found religion. It would be too depressing."

Griffin laughed heartily, as much at the hapless Mr. Warner's expression of alarm as the countess's eccentricity. "It is still very much a hell," he assured her, and was rewarded by another of her merry smiles. She was in every way a beautiful woman, more so because of the energy with which she embraced life. He'd heard remark once that she'd earned the lines that fanned out from the corners of her eyes and mouth, so why would she hide them? Did a general hide his medals? Griffin had decided it was an excellent position from which to view one's life, and he admired her for it.

"We had a bit of a dustup last week and a row between the punters at faro only two nights ago."

"It has been a mannerly squeeze, then," her ladyship said, disheartened.

"Do not fear. I promise, if no one begins a brawl this evening, I will start the thing myself. Shall I show Mr. Warner the rear exit in the event you have need of a hasty escape once the fists fly?"

"I can find it, not that I would. A brawl is just the sort of entertainment I crave." She took Mr. Warner by the elbow. "Come along. Do not mind us. We are having you on a bit. Drink up and you will see that it is so or that it doesn't matter. The conquian table is in the next room. I am quite certain they will make room for us."

Griffin turned to watch her go, smiling encouragingly at Mr. Warner as the gentleman glanced back over his shoulder, uneasiness stamped on his countenance. If Mr. Warner proved himself a trepid escort, Griffin had no doubt he'd seen the last of the man. Lady Rivendale did not suffer the faint of heart.

Griffin moved among the patrons with an ease that belied the fact that his thoughts were otherwise occupied. He spoke to some, listened to few, and nodded politely when anyone caught his eye. He made a round of every table, caught tidbits of gossip, and showed a trio of high-stepping gentlemen to the door when he saw them produce their opium pipes. For a time after he'd bought the establishment he had tolerated the opium smokers while he was ridding the hell of its prostitutes. It was not unusual for someone to challenge his rule, and he did not employ his staff to purposely seek out the violators and eject them, but when it was blatantly done the guests were asked to leave or were removed.

No matter what aspect of the business engaged his attention, Griffin found he had gray matter enough to spare for the problem of Olivia Cole.

And she was a problem.

Until this morning her requests had been rather benign. He'd been very aware of the small ways in which she elicited the cooperation of his staff, and he'd made no move to interfere, but she hadn't asked for the wardrobe he'd provided, and she hadn't put the idea of a bath in anyone's mind. If she remained in the hell much longer, they would all be tripping over themselves doing for her.

The fact that she was not at all helpless was no sort of deterrent. He . . . no, all of them . . . had been seized by an urge to protect her. He was fighting it. His staff, even the occasionally severe and skeptical Mason, had never thought to resist.

Olivia Cole was such a presence in his mind that when he turned to the faro table to watch the play, he immediately dismissed what his eyes revealed as a flight of fancy. It was not possible that it was she standing in the banker's position at the table, smiling rather winsomely, slowly shuffling a new deck and monitoring the placement of the bets. Moreover, it was not possible that she had defied him.

"All wagers are down."

It was the voice, *her* voice, that made the incomprehensible suddenly quite certain.

Chapter Six

Olivia had a book open in her lap but had given up trying to read it. Her attention kept wandering each time she heard the echo of a footfall from the hall and stairway. It was difficult to imagine that Breckenridge would allow her defiance to pass without a confrontation. That he had not forcibly removed her from the faro table spoke to his ability to let a thing rest while he considered what course of action to take. It was not that he was patient, but that he was cunning. She was almost sick with the anticipation of his appearance at her door, though she could admit that it was no more than she deserved for disregarding his authority.

Olivia's nerves grew more taut as the hell quieted. The diminished activity on the floor below her room was a sure sign that the servants were nearing the completion of their tasks. She had fled the faro table immediately after paying out the last of the winnings to the punters and passing the hell's share to Breckenridge. Although he'd thanked her politely, she knew it was for the benefit of the patrons lingering around her table. There was naught but scorn in the dark, chilly glance he reserved exclusively for her.

When the knock at the door finally came, she still started with enough force to dislodge the book. She bent to pick it up only to have it slip from her nerveless fingers as Breckenridge entered.

"I thought we agreed you would keep the door locked," he said, closing it behind him.

Olivia retrieved the book and placed it on a side table. As she made to rise, Breckenridge came to stand in front of her chair. She was forced by his proximity to lower herself once again and tilt her head back to look up at him. He was not going to be sympathetic to the crick in her neck as she had been to his.

"The patrons are gone," she said. "There is no one here that means me harm." She regarded him steadily. "Is there?"

He leaned forward and braced his arms on either side of her chair. The fact that she didn't cower only served to incense him. "You are neither stupid nor naive. You know bloody well that I want to put my hands on you, and your apparent belief that I am, at my core, unwilling to do so is unwarranted. With very little more in the way of provocation I could be moved to turn you over my knee."

Olivia's breath hitched as her lips parted. Blood roared so loudly in her ears that she could not hear a single one of her scattered thoughts.

"Nothing to say?" he asked. "Good. I will assume that means I've persuaded you." He straightened but did not give quarter. His gaze slid over her, registering for the first time that she had not readied for bed and was still wearing the clothes she'd worn to the gaming room. There was but one conclusion he could draw from that. "You were expecting me."

"It seemed likely that you would want to discuss my decision to act in opposition to your wishes."

"You do not even pretend it was something other than defiance."

"I judged that it would make you angrier. Was I wrong?"

A muscle worked in Griffin's cheek, briefly whitening his scar. "No," he said finally. "You were not wrong." He took a small step backward and jerked his chin at her. "Take off that ridiculous turban. What possessed you to wear it in the first place?"

"A desire for anonymity," she said as she carefully unwound the pink silk shawl she'd fashioned into a headdress. "My hair is a rather singular color."

It was, but Griffin did not support the observation. "So your reputation is more important to you than you would have me believe."

"No, but I understand that preserving it seems to be important to you." She folded the shawl and laid it on her lap. "I darkened my eyebrows and lashes also."

He'd noticed. "And painted your cheeks and your mouth. Go wash it off."

Flushing slightly, Olivia rose to her feet. She ducked her head slightly as she slipped sideways to get past him.

Griffin brought her up short, gripping her elbow. He put a finger under her chin, lifting it, and his eyes narrowed on her right cheek just beneath the corner of her eye. "The beauty patch as well."

Olivia forced herself not to run. When she returned from scrubbing her face, Breckenridge was lounging comfortably in the chair she'd occupied. He merely pointed to the window bench, clearly expecting that she would comply. Recalling his threat, she did.

"You attracted a great deal of attention this evening," Griffin said. "I don't know that the faro table has ever had gentlemen three deep at every station."

"It did seem they were eager to play."

"They were eager to spend time in your company."

"Then they are very foolish."

"Perhaps."

She had expected Breckenridge's unequivocal agreement, so his less certain response surprised her. He was still studying her, though not as intently or coldly as he'd done earlier, but with more speculative interest. Not knowing what to make of that, she remained quiet, waiting for him to direct the conversation.

"I counted the winnings from the faro table," he said. "Will you venture to guess what the house took in this evening?"

"I cannot speak for all of your profits. At my table I think it was just shy of six hundred quid."

One of Griffin's eyebrows kicked up. He did not imagine for a moment that her guess was lucky. "Five hundred ninety-three pounds exactly, but I think you knew that."

She shrugged.

"Do you know what the punters won?"

"Some two percent less. Those are the odds in favor of the house in an honest game. It was an honest game, my lord. I did not employ sleight of hand or any trickery by distraction."

Griffin had watched the players' losses carefully and knew she hadn't skewed the odds in his favor. "That was my obser-vation also," he said. "In regard to the sleight of hand, at least. Your presence was distraction enough for the players, I think, to support the fact the hell's winnings were in excess of three percent." He held up a hand to stay her protest. "I am not ac-cusing you of cheating, merely of being a distraction. I don't suppose that if I were to poll the gentlemen I would discover that any of them minded. Some of their lady friends, though, were made unhappy by the competition for their attention."

When she seemed startled by this last, Griffin shook his head. "Come now. You were able to calculate the winnings within a hairsbreadth of dead-on accuracy, but failed to notice that more than one woman was cheerfully contemplating your demise? That is hard to credit."

"You may believe what you like. I can only say that my own attention was all for the play at hand. You will perhaps understand that the wagers and winning were substantially more important to me than the petty dramas staged by some of your female guests. Pray, what did I have to fear from any of the women when your place at the head of the murder queue was already secured?"

Griffin's smile became marginally less derisive. "And you should be glad of it, for I would do the thing quickly. Those women—all of them—would pluck out your heart with tweezers."

She blanched, her hand coming up as if she could ward off such an attack.

"Just so," he said, watching her narrowly. The urge was upon him to laugh, and he was hard-pressed not to give in to it. To make certain that he did not, he put another matter before her. "Did you see him tonight?"

The shift in subject was so abrupt that for a moment Olivia did not follow. When she realized what Breckenridge was asking, she let her hand fall to her lap. Her color did not return. "My attacker? No. I didn't see him."

"So your attention was not *all* for the wagers and winnings." When she offered no contradiction, he went on. "It was dangerous, what you did. Had you given the least thought to what you might do if you saw him again?"

Olivia shook her head. "I didn't, but it occurs to me now that I should arm myself with a pair of tweezers."

Griffin was not amused. "He might return at any time. You have to consider that. A public accusation would harm you more than him, unless, of course, it is your intention to force me to call him out."

"Put it from your mind. I will neither confront him publicly nor have blood drawn on my account."

Curious now, Griffin asked, "Is there some doubt in your mind as to the outcome of pistols at twenty paces?"

"There is always doubt, my lord, and you would be foolish to suppose that you could never be the loser of such a confrontation. You might slip as you turn to face him, or you might be possessed by a sneeze at the very moment you take aim. Your weapon might misfire. He might count off eight paces to your ten and shoot before you. His physician may be superior to your own. All things being equal, he may simply be luckier than you that morning. If your pride smarts because I entertain doubts that you would be the victor, then you are most desperately in need of a restraining hand."

"A surfeit of pride makes one vulnerable, is that it?"

"Yes."

"Very well," he said. His pride was not engaged, but he did not tell her this. What she had described were the risks, some more probable than others, that a dispassionate gentleman weighed before issuing a challenge. "Consider that you have duly restrained me. Now, what of your pride?"

"Mine?"

"Certainly yours. Is it not pride that prompted you to disobey me? You have determined that you must settle your own debts, attend to your household staff, and rescue your brother from his folly. What is pushing you toward those ends if it is not pride?"

"A finely honed sense of responsibility."

"That you take pride in."

Olivia pressed her lips together, not to bite back her reply but because she had none.

Griffin pushed his point home gently. "Can you not admit that you might benefit from a restraining hand?"

She had no liking for her own words being turned on her. "Your hand, my lord? I think not. It is not my best interests you have in mind, but your own."

"You think I'm influenced only by the debt that's owed me?"

"I think it cannot be discounted. I am nothing to you beyond it."

But you could be. He did not say it aloud nor give any indication that the thought had been occurring to him with irritating frequency. "Then let us speak of my interests, shall we?"

"If you like."

"At the risk of encouraging such action as you took this

evening, I can still allow that you have demonstrated an error in my thinking. None among my patrons this evening doubted that you were dealing a fair game. There are likely those who would not have cared and considered it a reasonable price for the time spent close to you."

Griffin's mouth twitched as Olivia snorted in a most unladylike fashion. "I doubt even a sound like that would have cleared the table."

"You are being ridiculous."

"No, unfortunately I am not. You skillfully fended their questions this evening and remained wholly professional in your attention to the game. Still, if you are to continue dealing faro, there will be more inquiries and you will have to say something more than 'place your wagers' and 'all bets are down.' Even your rather appealing smile will wear on their nerves if you do not throw them a bone from time to time."

"Not my bones," she said stiffly.

"A figure of speech, nothing more."

"What are you proposing? That you will allow me to deal at the table again?"

"In the event that we can arrive at certain satisfactory arrangements, yes."

Olivia was immediately suspicious. "What sort of arrangements?"

"You are far too transparent in the leanings of your mind. Truly, is the thought of bedding me so distasteful that you would abandon that finely honed sense of responsibility you say you possess to avoid just that end? I can tell you, it is not at all flattering to my person."

"Yet you persist in your belief that your attentions should be flattering to mine."

His dark eyes narrowed a fraction and pinned her where she sat before he gave up the pretense of outrage. A shout of laughter would not be suppressed. "Bloody hell, but it is that tongue of yours that is finely honed. How you managed to comport yourself with such decorum at the faro table is a fascination to me. I shouldn't wonder that you bloodied your own mouth each time you stayed your tongue. Your admirers were not subtle in making their feelings known."

"Perhaps it is that I am not averse to their attentions."

Griffin chuckled, not so easily taken in. "Have a care, Olivia, else I will be moved to take up that challenge." He observed her prepare to take exception to what he'd said, then suddenly think better of it. "Yes," he said. "It was indeed the challenge of a practiced flirt, though in your case I will allow that you most likely stumbled into it. You are curiously direct in some regards and in other ways almost painfully artless. I cannot make sense of it, and I don't suppose that asking you for an explanation will give me one."

He shrugged. "It is of no matter. I enjoy a puzzle." This confession did not seem to ease her mind, thus prompting his most diabolical smile. He thought he probably should not be enjoying himself quite so much, though how he had finally come to this pass was something of a puzzle itself. The threat to beat her may have been mostly an idle one, but he *had* contemplated turning her over his knee. Now he was amused by her and contemplating an arrangement that might serve them both.

Griffin decided that the sequence of events did not bear scrutiny. "Allow me to suggest the conditions by which you might deal faro in my establishment tomorrow night."

"I am listening."

"I insist upon your identity being protected. Your estrangement from Sir Hadrien is not sufficient to suppose that he will not cause me considerable inconvenience if you are harmed while in my care. That includes damage to your reputation and, by the connection of family, to his own. He may not cause trouble for me because he cares about you; he may do it because he decides I have caused trouble for him."

"You are afraid of him."

Griffin did not answer immediately, carefully considering

his reply. "I believe I would admit it if it were so," he told her. "The truth is more complicated than that. I am afraid of what he might cost me. He is an influential man, your father, and given to standing on the moral high ground. It is why I do not believe your brother will be successful in bending him to advance an allowance misspent on gaming and lady birds. The length of Mr. Cole's absence seems to bear me out."

"Very well, I concede that our father is not the sort of man one crosses lightly. What is to be done?"

"Changing your appearance is the obvious solution. I will have Mason purchase a wig for you. Several, in fact, of varying styles. Auburn, I think. Different than your coloring but not so dramatic that your eyebrows and lashes must be painted as darkly as you did this evening. You will apply color to cheeks and mouth but with a lighter touch than you used. If you look like a whore, you will be treated like one."

Olivia glanced down at her hands. "They did not treat me like one tonight."

"I imagine because they thought you were my whore."

"Oh."

"A consequence of being nearly attached to your side. There was most definitely a line drawn that no one crossed."

"I did not draw it."

"I did. Do not suppose you could have managed so well without me. You might have cut a few to ribbons with the sharp edge of your tongue, but there always would have been someone advancing. I believe I mentioned they were three deep."

He had, and so they had been. "Your mistress used to stand at the tables. I heard someone remark on it."

"She is my former mistress, and she didn't deal. Her mere presence at a table encouraged betting."

"Then she was a practiced flirt."

"Precisely."

"You were not moved to stand by her all evening."

"Mrs. Christie knew what she was about. It is clear to me that you do not—at least not entirely."

"So you will stand post while I deal the cards."

"No." He sighed. "I must move about the rooms, but you can rest easy that someone will be observing you. At the first sign of trouble, they will come and get me."

The thought of constant observation did not make her easy in the least. "It is not in my mind to cheat you."

"And it is not in my mind to allow you to be tempted. Nevertheless, the trouble I was speaking of is a gentleman's unwelcome advance that puts you at the center of a brawl. Someone will be moved to proposition you and someone else will be moved to speak up on your behalf. I will have to eject half my patrons if I cannot put a period to the thing quickly." His mouth twisted in a bit of a smile as he thought of Lady Rivendale hoping for some pugilistic entertainment. "Although there would be those willing to step aside so they might wager on the outcome."

"So I will wear a wig and some modest paint and you will see to it that nothing untoward occurs. Is there anything else that must be done?"

"You must have another name, of course. I noticed tonight that you did not offer one."

"I thought mystery served."

"One night, perhaps. You cannot go on in such a fashion else some enterprising rascal will set his mind on the truth and have at it."

"Then what do you propose?"

"You do not wish to choose a name yourself?"

"No."

He regarded her with consideration, lingering on her splendid green eyes. "Emerald, I think. Miss Emerald Hepplewhite."

Olivia pursed her lips. "Oh, very well, if you are going to be silly about it, I shall be Ann Shepard."

"Ann Shepard. Just like that?"

"My nanny." She was unaware that a shadow crossed her face. "Do not concern yourself. She is long dead now. A vague memory even to me, though I wish it were not so. I called her Honey, a childish corruption of Nanny, I suppose." Olivia shook her head slightly, her slender smile a bit winsome. "Or perhaps it is only that I thought she was sweet." The smile disappeared. "They did not like her, though, and she was sent packing. I recall that well enough."

Griffin did not ask Olivia to identify who "they" were. He slipped this morsel of information into the pocket of his mind that he'd constructed exclusively for all things Olivia Cole. It still had very little in the way of content.

"So, shall I call you Ann or Honey?"

"You may call me Miss Shepard."

He nodded, tempering his smile. "You should think of a story for yourself, some tasty bits of information that you may drop from time to time to calm your suitors."

"Is that really necessary? They are at the table because they want to win at faro."

She seemed to genuinely believe that. "Humor me then. I don't care what you say to them, but you should be prepared to say something."

"Where I live, for instance, and how I came to be dealing faro at your hell. Are those the sort of things I can expect to be asked?"

"I imagine. How will you answer such posers?"

"I suppose I shall have to put the speculation to rest and make it clear that I have replaced Mrs. Christie in your life."

"Yes, that will end the speculation," he said dryly.

"Really, my lord, if there is another more suitable explanation, I am unaware of it." She raised an eyebrow as he shifted in his chair. "Have I discomfited you? You have only to recall that you were the one to suggest it."

"I do not believe I suggested it precisely. I merely pointed out that the gentlemen playing faro were likely to have believed as much."

"What is that if not a suggestion? I certainly hadn't thought of it. I supposed they believed you were protecting your investment. Not me, I mean, but the money in the bank. In any event, it is Honey Shepard who will be your mistress, not Olivia Cole."

"Honey. I can't say that I particularly like that. It makes my teeth ache."

"Then it is good that you shall only address me as Miss Shepard."

"Ann is a fine name."

"Perhaps I will give you leave to use it on occasion."

Griffin chose once again not to press as they both knew he would call her anything he pleased. He stood instead. "I will speak to Mason in the morning about the wigs. It might be necessary to add more gowns to your wardrobe. A few items of jewelry, too. As my mistress, it will be expected." He saw her frown. "Do not worry. I shan't allow you to keep the pieces."

She nodded, relieved. He could not precisely force her to wear them. "You have said nothing about my wages."

He smiled. Olivia Cole did not disappoint. "I was thinking that a percentage of the winnings at your table would be in order. Say, half of one percent."

"How much do you usually draw in at the faro table?"

"Four hundred quid."

"And I brought you six hundred."

"Five hundred ninety-three."

"Of course. Five hundred ninety-three. And you would give me—"

"Three pounds," he said. "I rounded up. I am prepared to be generous."

"That is in no way generous. Five percent."

"One."

"Four," she countered.

"One and one-half."

Olivia shook her head. "Two percent."

"Done." It was a perfectly outrageous sum that he was promising her, but he reasoned it was far less than Mrs. Christie had been regularly stealing from him. "You have made a good bargain."

"Five percent would have been a good bargain," she said. "Two percent is only what is fair."

Griffin chuckled. He inclined his head, saluting her. "I should take my leave before I am persuaded to offer you three."

The faro table was crowded, just as he'd known it would be. Griffin had been wandering in and out of the room where Olivia was working since the hell opened its doors, and he'd never seen less than a dozen young bucks vying for a place at the table. As soon as one of them lost enough to force a move, another slipped into the vacated seat. If she simply managed to bring in the house at only a one percent profit, he estimated that the winnings would well exceed what she'd accomplished the previous evening.

He observed that her gown would not have been out of place at the theatre or a ball. If her dress lent her a certain elegance, then she lent it grace. The movement of her arms was fluid, her deft touch with the cards something to behold. She was a confection perfectly suited to a tray of iced tea cakes in a celestial blue satin gown with an overlay of tulle. The rounded bodice left her shoulders bare and her fine skin reflected the play of candlelight from the wall sconces. Her auburn wig fit her head snugly and was curled in a fall of clever ringlets that lightly brushed her neck whenever she turned. The hair was dressed with copper combs and seeded with pearls, the latter matching the pearls sewn in the bodice of her gown.

Her throat was bare and Griffin thought he should correct that oversight soon. She would wear pearls well, but he thought of her eyes and decided that an emerald would also do.

Her white elbow-length gloves were her most exquisite accessory. Although they fit her as well as her own skin, even she could not manipulate the cards with satin-covered fingertips. He was the one who had removed them and instructed Mason to cut the fabric back to her knuckles so her beautifully tapered fingers were free to do their very best work.

On impulse, after he'd helped her slip back into the gloves, he had lifted her hands to his lips and kissed those bare knuckles, watching her as he did so. Except for the soft parting of her lips, there had been no reaction that he could discern. No surprise. No tender fury. No resignation. She'd simply waited for him to be done, eased her hands from his light grasp, and brushed past him to make her way to the gaming rooms.

It might have been lowering if his heart had been attached to the gesture, but it was not that organ blinding him to good judgment. The blood pooling in his groin was a reliable indication of where the impulse had been born.

Griffin smiled politely in response to a tip of the head by one of the patrons, then moved to Foster's side to prevent being pulled into a conversation for which he had little interest and even less time. The footman stood at attention at his post just inside the doorway. As Griffin had instructed on the day of his hiring, his eyes constantly roamed the room, alert to the shifts in the crowd and the first inklings of untoward behavior.

"What is your view, Foster?" Griffin asked. "Is she able to handle them?"

"As deftly as the cards, my lord."

Griffin's gaze drifted to the faro table, then past it. "What have you observed about their interest?"

"Respectful. She draws them in but keeps them at a distance.

Not one among them has seemed to mind. Johnny Crocker played at her table for a while."

"Was he now?" That the rival hell owner deigned to step outside his own establishment was hardly the usual thing. "He didn't ask for me?"

"No. Came in and went straightaway to the faro table. I stood close by, just to make certain he didn't trouble her."

Griffin wasn't certain what to make of Crocker's interest, though he supposed it was possible that word had already spread regarding his new faro dealer. Perhaps Crocker wanted to estimate the potential damage to his own profits. "You'll let me know if he returns, won't you?"

"Immediately."

"Good man." He stepped away. "I'm going downstairs to observe the play at vingt-et-un."

"Very good."

Griffin chatted with several of his regular patrons in the hall and on the stairs before he reached another of the hell's gaming parlors. The dealer for twenty-one was Drummond, another of his household staff with multiple duties, though in Drummond's case it was generally acknowledged that he was a much better dealer than he was a footman. Truss tended to assign him the tasks that could not possibly be mismanaged.

Griffin watched the game for a while, congratulated Mr. Harvey's good run of luck and better skill, then moved on to roulette. The wheel was not favoring any one patron this evening and Griffin realized his own attention was wandering. When a quartet of young bucks, all turned out in matching scarlet waistcoats, spilled through the entrance, Griffin backed away from the table to watch them. Clearly from the volume of their speech and the color of their waistcoats, they were bent on making themselves a spectacle.

As soon as he saw they had fixed themselves on reaching the stairs, Griffin moved as quickly as the press of patrons around him would allow. He was familiar with their set, though not these four in particular, and found them to be essentially harmless and easily managed without incident as long as they were not too far gone in their cups. It was difficult to know at a glance how foxed they were. Their high spirits could be attributed to their anticipation of adventure, the relief of arriving at Putnam Lane unscathed, or the natural self defense of young men playing at something outside their experience. Perhaps their exuberance was rooted in all three, but Griffin suspected it was strongly supported by several rounds of hard drink.

He knew a moment's unease as they rushed the stairs before him. He followed at a more seemly pace, unwilling to call attention to them beyond what they had called to themselves.

Olivia gave no outward sign that she was aware of the rowdy and slightly ribald laughter that was drifting in from the hallway. She turned over the top card on the deck in front of her. "House pays on four."

She smiled at the collective groan that rose from the punters. Only one among them had a marker resting on the four. Showing sympathy for the losers, she paid out even money to the winning player and allowed all of them time to decide on their next wager.

"All wagers are down," she said. She hardly heard the words herself as successive waves of deep male laughter rolled into the room. Heads turned toward the full tide of sound, but Olivia remained attentive to the game. She showed the top card. "House wins on seven."

After listening to some good-natured protests from the losers, Olivia briskly collected all four of the markers resting on the seven of spades. It was a splendid return for the house. While new wagers were being set, she glanced up to see four gentlemen advancing toward her. She knew a moment's alarm at the rate of their approach, afraid their momentum would push the tide of gentlemen upon her.

"Bets down, please," she said to allow for some last bit of maneuvering and second guessing. When the last hand was withdrawn, she nodded. "All bets are down."

There was some jostling for position at the rear of the crush around the table. "Gentlemen. Have a care, else the markers will shift, and we will never sort out the winners from the losers." Even as she said it, the table was bumped and three markers slid off the painted cards into other positions. Olivia stepped back from the table and permitted the punters to re-arrange their wagers.

"Gentlemen," she said again, this time with a pointed look in the direction of the disturbance. "There is room enough for everyone to participate."

"I am in love," one of the newcomers declared as he craned his neck for a better view. "She has the voice of an angel."

"And wings," another said. "I swear she has wings."

Olivia refrained from rolling her eyes and offered an apolo-getic smile to those players who were waiting for her to turn a card. "The house will pay on the queen."

"Did she say play on the queen?" This query prompted a new wave of laughter. "I should like to play on the queen."

One of his friends pushed him forward, forcing a split be-tween a pair of gentlemen who'd been waiting patiently for their opportunity to move closer to the table. They drew them-selves up rigidly and in tandem closed ranks, shouldering the dandy back. He put his hands on their shoulders and launched himself upward for a better glimpse of the angel queen.

Olivia quickly paid the winners and proceeded with a new round of wagers. She was eager to move the game along before chaos took over and her winnings were lost to the re-placement of broken furniture and glassware.

The quartet did not allow themselves to be easily dismissed, but they settled down long enough to pass their wagers forward and follow the turn of the cards at a distance that kept everyone's fists at their sides. Thankful that they retained some measure of self-preservation, Olivia simply ignored their banal observations about her ethereal countenance and regal bearing. Drink had left them without wit or imagination.

"My lord," Olivia said softly, acknowledging Breckenridge stepping up to her side. She had been aware of his presence in the room from the outset. He'd closely followed the gentlemen in but hung back to observe their forward push and what would become of it. Several times she thought he would take them up by their collars and yank them out of the room, but when she glanced in his direction he seemed perfectly at his ease, merely mindful of the mingling of his guests.

Griffin placed a proprietary hand at the small of Olivia's back. He felt her stiffen under his palm. It lasted but a moment, then she relaxed, though he suspected it was accomplished with effort. "Finish this round," he said, "then Foster will spell you."

It occurred to her to protest, but she thought better of it. The punters were watching her closely, hoping she'd make some excuse to stay. She would not pit Breckenridge against them. Without missing a beat, she quickened the rhythm of an already fast-paced game, cheerfully encouraging the players to keep up with her. The wagers came and went furiously, with punters calling out, groaning, and shouting by turns depending on the card that Olivia pulled from the deck. It required only a few minutes for the table to be cleared.

Olivia let herself be led away on Breckenridge's arm. Her four newest admirers turned as one, their expressions thoroughly pitiful as they realized they would have no chance with her. She was almost past them when one of them stepped away from the group and tilted his head to make a better study of her.

Olivia held Breckenridge back and boldly turned to face him. "You wish to have an unobstructed view, perhaps?"

He blinked and shook his head. A lock of sandy hair fell forward over his high brow.

"Make another observation, then?"

His eyes narrowed, but the strain of so much concentration in light of the alcohol he'd consumed made them cross. For a moment he was unsteady on his feet. "You remind me of—"

"An angel," she said. "Yes, I know."

"No. It is just that you—"

"Possess the stately air of a queen. I heard you. I heard all of you. Now, you will excuse me." She smiled politely, coolly, and turned away, dismissing him as she squeezed lightly on Breckenridge's elbow.

Griffin escorted her to the stairs. "Go on," he said. "I'll join you shortly."

Olivia hesitated. "They're harmless, my lord."

"Griffin."

"What?"

"My name is Griffin. We are intimates, remember?"

"Pretending to be intimates," she said under her breath. Over his shoulder, she smiled at a couple passing them on their way to the gaming room. "Pretending, my lord. It is not the same as actually being intimates."

"I am quite aware."

The way he said it, a bit darkly and edged with a certain roughness, made Olivia feel winded of a sudden.

"Say it," he said, watching her closely.

She shook her head. "There's no one around."

He placed one hand on the banister and the other on her shoulder. "Humor me."

"You are too often humored, I think. Denial will improve the strength of your character."

"Astute and priggish. I cannot imagine that you will remain my mistress for long."

Olivia pursed her lips.

Griffin laughed. "Oh, very well. Run along." He removed his hands and stepped back, still chuckling as he watched her climb, haughty and stiff-spined, to the top of the stairs.

Olivia made straight for the window bench as soon as she

reached her room. She peered down at the street, angling for the best view. She did not have to wait long. In spite of her assurance that the gentlemen meant no harm, she saw all four of them summarily run off. They nearly tripped over one another in their haste to reach the street, though she was confident their intoxicated state also contributed to their clumsiness.

They took to the center of the cobbled street, dodging hansom cabs, private carriages, and ladies openly plying their trade. These near brushes with mishaps of every variety seemed to amuse them, for they laughed uproariously and continued on the wayward path they'd set, scattering only after one of them became violently ill.

Olivia recognized the gentleman bent over at the waist, spilling guts and drink into the street, as the sandy-haired fellow who had tried to peer beneath her paint and place her face. She could not summon any sympathy for his plight.

She turned away from the window and arranged herself comfortably on the bench awaiting Breckenridge's return.

Griffin knocked politely but didn't allow himself to be delayed by waiting for Olivia's response to enter. She rose from the window seat immediately. He held out a hand. "A moment if you will," he told her. "There is no hurry."

"That is because you will take your winnings regardless of who is dealing faro. I only collect my share if I am at the table."

"You are without doubt the most single-minded female of my acquaintance."

"You flatter me."

"Naturally you would see it in that light." He pointed to the bench. "Sit. I promise you this will not take long, and you have been standing since we opened the doors."

She sat but was compelled to add, "I am no hothouse flower."

Griffin hitched his hip on the arm of a wing chair. "Neither am I," he said, "but notice that I am enjoying a moment's respite as well." He paused, considering how best to approach her. She seemed to appreciate straightforwardness. "How is it that the blond fellow knows you?"

"Pardon?"

Griffin felt certain that her polite response was merely a tactic to permit her to gather her wits. He'd spoken clearly; it was not the words she misunderstood. Still, for form's sake, he repeated the question.

"I don't understand. Did he say he did?"

"I believe he was attempting to say just that when you interrupted him—twice."

"I remember the conversation differently. He compared me to an angel and a queen. It is a tiresome compliment men are wont to give when they are in their cups. Harmless enough, just as they were. You did not have to throw them out. I could have managed them."

Griffin realized that she had given him several openings by which he might distract himself from his purpose. He was as admiring of her talent for diversion as he was frustrated by it. "He compared you to neither of those things, although his friends had done so earlier. Once he moved closer to the table he watched you most attentively."

"Did he? I'm afraid I was otherwise occupied." She frowned. "You could not know that anyway. You were standing beside the doorway. His back was to you."

Griffin was ridiculously pleased that she had noticed he was even in the room. She was, as she'd said, otherwise occupied. "He moved to the side. I saw enough to be convinced he was studying you."

Amused, she said, "Perhaps he is an artist and will return with a request to paint me for the ages."

"I believe he was trying to place your face, not contemplating painting it."

"Well, that is disappointing."

Griffin was not humored. "He knows you," he said flatly.

"You're wrong."

"He simply does not know how he knows you."

"I've never seen him before."

"That may be true, but it doesn't mean he hasn't seen you."

"Are you doubting me? You said it may be true, as if I were lying."

"I doubt everyone. It was not meant to be critical of your character. I regret if I offended you."

Olivia found the apology perfunctory, accompanied as it was by a careless shrug. "I don't know him," she said again.

Griffin believed she was still being evasive. "They have never been to my establishment before."

She frowned slightly. "I'm not certain what that has to do with anything."

"It is merely an observation. I believe word of you at the table has already spread."

"Why would anyone make mention of it? Do gentlemen really have so little of import to discuss?"

"They must have their amusements." He shrugged. "At the moment, you seem to be one of them."

Olivia offered him a tight smile. "It is no source of pleasure to me."

"I didn't think it was. I mention it so that you will tread carefully. Foster tells me that Johnny Crocker played at your table tonight. A path would have been cleared for him. He's of a formidable size."

She thought back. "I recall such a gentleman. He was circumspect in his wagers. Hardly said a word. His interest was in my hands, not in my face."

"He was observing whether or not you were cheating. He's good at it himself, so I imagine he wanted to see if there was competition."

"He played fairly and so did I."

"Good. There'd have been a row otherwise. He has his own establishment and wouldn't mind acquiring mine, not that I'd let him. I've heard Mrs. Christie's name coupled with his."

Olivia hardly knew what to say to that, so she offered nothing.

Griffin regarded her a long moment. "You don't know Crocker, do you?"

She sighed. "You are considerably troubled by this notion that I am known to others or that they are known to me. I hardly recognize my own reflection, so why you think anyone saw through this painted face to my own makes no sense. It is far more likely that in the case of the foxed gentleman, he saw nothing more than was presented to him and was trying to put a name to a whore he once enjoyed."

Griffin laid his arm across the back of the wing chair. "Have you been such a whore, Olivia?"

The directness of his question startled her to silence. He posed it with a matter-of-factness that he might have used to inquire if she had ever been to the theatre or if her preference was for scones over honey cakes. "I suppose I deserve to have the question put to me," she said quietly. "I have given you reason enough to suspect it." She drew in a short breath and released it slowly. "As you doubt everyone, I don't know that it makes the least difference what I tell you, but no, I have not been a whore."

"Are there those who would say differently?"

She smiled, but there was no humor in it. "Aren't there always?"

Griffin had reason to know the truth of it. "If Alastair hadn't offered you as his marker, what would you have done?"

"You mean how would I have paid the staff, the creditors, and managed the house in his absence?"

"That is precisely what I mean."

"I don't know. That's as honest an answer as I can give you. I've thought about it often enough, but I can't say that I ever arrived at a satisfactory solution. You must have realized it. I can pretend that you are keeping me here, yet we both know I need to be kept. I haven't tried to bolt, have I?"

"I'd bring you back," he said.

"You would, and I'd let you." The admission shamed her. She looked away, annoyed by the tears that surfaced with so little to provoke them. She made a quick swipe at her eyes and bit down hard on the inside of her lower lip. Pain was a balm for thornier emotions.

Olivia didn't know when Breckenridge had come to stand in front of her, but he was suddenly there. Quiet. Attentive. Waiting. She glanced up, blinked, and forced composure into what could easily have been a watery smile. An arched eyebrow served as a question.

Griffin leaned forward, slipped his palms under Olivia's elbows, and lifted. She came to her feet easily, without resistance, and stood inches from him, her head still raised but her smile faltering at the edges.

"We are of a kind, you and I," Griffin said quietly. "I think you know it's true."

Then he bent his head and laid his mouth over hers. There was very little pressure in the kiss, just a touch, a tender brush. Sweetness and solace. He offered only as much as he thought she could accept and was uncertain from the beginning if she could accept any of it. Her lips trembled under his, and her breath came lightly, then not at all.

His hands slid from her elbows to the small of her back. He resisted the urge to pull her closer and let her find her own way into the shelter of his embrace. She edged closer, her mouth parting. He changed the slant of his mouth, licked her lower lip with the damp edge of his tongue. The breath she'd been holding was released on the faintest of sighs.

He caught the scent of lavender on her skin and the taste of mint on her mouth. The fragrance made him think peculiarly of innocence—the taste of things fresh and unsullied. He deserved neither, he thought, and took a measure of comfort that neither were being offered to him. His imagination supported what he craved, but the reality was merely lavender and mint.

Olivia raised her hands, then let them fall back to her side. She hadn't quite known what she wanted to do with them. Touching him, her fingers on his shoulders, at the back of his neck, drifting into the curling ends of his dark hair, all of it seemed too much, or possibly it was that it wouldn't have been enough.

His kiss made her remember emptiness and longing. It made her think of what she could have in the moment but would always be denied in the forever. In spite of that, or perhaps because of it, the kiss stirred her.

Warmth became heat; desire displaced comfort. She wondered why she was no longer afraid, why standing in the circle of his arms should make her abandon good sense and caution.

He smelled faintly of tobacco and tasted of brandy. She thought of things certain and solid. He held her loosely, but she could have leaned back against the clasp of his hands and he would not have let her fall. It was the very security of the embrace that allowed her to soar, to feel what was unimaginable only minutes ago.

She did not deserve it, she thought, and took a measure of comfort that she had not asked for it, that he could not know what he'd given her. Her imagination supported what she craved, but reality was tobacco and brandy and a pair of hands at the curve of her back.

The kiss deepened, held.

Then it was over.

They drew up simultaneously. He lifted his head; she lowered hers. Still feeling the stamp of the kiss on their lips, they stared at each other.

Griffin spoke first, his voice thick and husky. "That was unexpected."

"Yes."

"I've wanted to . . . from the first."

Olivia was not prepared to be quite so honest. She simply nodded and let him make of it what he would.

Griffin blew out a breath, ran his fingers through his hair. "What do you—"

She didn't allow him to finish. "It shouldn't happen again."

"Are you certain?"

She wasn't, but Olivia didn't think she could show weakness. "Yes. You're married."

He didn't react. "Did you think I'd forgotten?"

"I think perhaps it is of no consequence to you."

"You couldn't be more wrong." He breathed in deeply, released it slowly. Resigned, he said, "But I comprehend that you have no reason to believe me."

Olivia waited, but he offered no explanation to persuade her differently. She admired him for that, because what explanation could there be that would suffice? "Excuse me," she said, ducking quickly around him. "I need to return to the faro table."

Griffin caught her scent again as she brushed past him. Closing his eyes, he let her go.

Chapter Seven

Over the course of the next ten days, Olivia found herself returning again and again to the moments before, during, and after the kiss. When she was of a mood to recall the thing fondly, she felt a measure of heat uncurl inside her until her cheeks flushed and there was an unmistakable tug of something both pleasurable and needy deep inside her womb. When the memory came unbidden, as it invariably did in the presence of his lordship, Olivia soured, her mouth becoming flat and uninviting, her jaw tightening so that it ached well into the evening. That Griffin seemed to know what she was thinking in those moments—and appeared amused by it— merely put her further out of sorts.

On occasion she brought the thing to mind because she wondered what she might have done differently. She told herself that such reflection was necessary to learn how such an end might be avoided, but too often she found herself contemplating an end in which she didn't turn her back on him.

Her humor was not improved for it.

Olivia rose from her bed and padded softly into the bathing room. A full week ago, she'd finally been able to return to the room she'd begun to think of as her own. The quiet suited her; the view from the window did not. She missed the rascals gathering on the street below Griffin's room and the glimpses she'd had of the prostitutes in their finery. The activity at the back of the house was limited to wagons lumbering down the alley, tradesmen and tinkers approaching the rear entrance, and servants carrying out slops.

She could no longer hear Griffin moving about. If she was being strictly honest with herself—and she was inclined to be—Olivia could admit that she missed this proof that he was nearby most of all.

She was uncomfortable with the realization that she'd come to depend on him, though she could not define the precise nature of that dependency. It was the shelter, of course, but not that alone, and the opportunity to earn a wage, though not only that. They had established a tentative peace, a somewhat guarded mutual respect, and a conversational manner that was frequently all thrust and parry. He often knew the bent of her mind, while she found his impenetrable except on those rare occasions when he wanted it to be otherwise.

Olivia did not discount the protection she was afforded because she was residing in the gaming hell. Breckenridge's hell. She found it peculiar that he wanted to safeguard her reputation when she had none worthy of such an effort. That she'd been able to defend herself against an intruder had left him singularly unimpressed. He seemed to embrace the notion that it should fall to him to repel all boarders, although he was not inclined to unduly restrain himself from advancing.

Still, she felt safe when she knew he was about, safer yet when he was near. The irony was not lost to her, and the taste of it was bittersweet.

When Olivia came out of her reverie, she was staring at her reflection and chewing lightly on her upper lip. Mocking herself, she wrinkled her nose and stuck her tongue out, then picked up her hairbrush and made a determined, ruthless pass through her flaming tangles.

It was her habit of late to eat in the kitchen with the staff, so when Beetle arrived carrying her breakfast she was immediately wary. When he informed her that Lord Breckenridge had taken his leave of them earlier and expected to be gone for several days, Olivia had to remind herself not to kill the messenger. No doubt Beetle had pulled the short straw when the servants were debating who should tell her. She took pity on the hapless lad and did not allow him to give her the remainder of the disappointing news, relating it to him instead.

"He means that I should stay here until he returns, I suppose," she said. "In my room."

Beetle stared at his shoes and nodded.

"Where did he go?"

"Don't rightly know."

"Does anyone?"

He glanced up, shrugged, then ducked his head again. "Mr. Mason, I expect, but he won't tell you. He doesn't tell anyone."

"And who will oversee the operation of the hell in his lordship's absence?"

"Mr. Gardner. He's a right 'un, sure enough. And knows a thing or two about gaming. Heard tell of him nabbing a cheat once, right here in this house, so he's a trustworthy bloke."

Olivia could not recall that she'd ever heard Gardner's name. She'd been formally introduced to very few of Breckenridge's acquaintants while she dealt faro, and only, it seemed, when not doing so would have raised more questions than it settled. And while he appeared at his ease presenting her as Miss Ann Shepard and called her Honey with feigned affection, she suspected none of it set well with him.

"Mr. Gardner," Olivia repeated. "Very well, I shall endeavor to make the best of it."

Beetle looked up, grinned. "You're a right 'un, too, miss, and that's a fact." Then he scurried off.

During Griffin's absence Olivia cast her line a number of times hoping to learn his whereabouts. Mason mostly ignored her attempts, except for the occasion when he pointed out in rather dry tones that she was fishing in a poorly stocked lake. Truss seemed to be genuinely ignorant of Griffin's destination, and what she managed to reel in from the rest of the staff was merely supposition.

Of Mr. Gardner, she saw nothing. That was disappointing because she imagined that the person Griffin most trusted to manage the hell would be likely to know things she was not privy to, though equally likely, she supposed philosophically, not to share any of them with her.

Her days took on the sameness that they'd had at the beginning. She read, walked, ate, and slept with little deviation from the routine. She worried about Alastair, about her home at Jericho Mews, about how long it would take her to repay the debt and what she would do once she saw the thing done.

She thought she'd known the answer to this last at one time, but she was no longer as certain of it. There were worse places to live than Putnam Lane and worse things to be than one lord's mistress.

Someone stumbling hard on the stairs caused a vibration to shudder through the house. Curious, she went into the hall to investigate and more clearly heard the sounds of a scuffle. The hell was hours yet from opening its doors to the rich and the rabble, but she could not fathom that any of the servants were exchanging blows. Even allowing for the high spirits of Wick and Beetle it was difficult to imagine.

Prepared to put a period to the fisticuffs, Olivia ran to the top of the stairs. She was glad for the support of the banister when she got there.

Her brother had finally come for her, although from the white-knuckled hold Griffin had on Alastair's throat, it appeared he was returning most reluctantly.

Olivia charged down the steps and wedged herself between the combatants. Several of the servants were already clustered at the foot of the stairs in anticipation of being called to lend assistance. Griffin, however, required none. It was her brother who was going to die.

"Release him," Olivia said, pulling on Griffin's hand. She tried to slip a finger under his palm. "You're choking him. He cannot breathe! Can't you see? He cannot breathe."

"There is nothing wrong with my eyesight," Griffin said. There was only a hint of strain in his voice. "Show your sister you can breathe, Mr. Cole."

Alastair sucked in a wheezing, labored breath.

"There. You see? Your brother can breathe."

Olivia gripped Griffin's thumb and pulled on it. "Let him go, my lord." Squeezed as she was between the two men, her own words sounded breathless. "Please."

Over the top of Olivia's head, Griffin made certain Alastair saw his displeasure and took note that what he would do was for Olivia, not for him. "As you wish." He released Alastair and stepped back against the rail, then gestured that they should precede him up the stairs. Olivia offered her shoulder to her brother, who looked as if he might simply slide down the wall. Griffin watched them go, then after he was certain the staff dispersed, he followed.

"My study," Griffin said when Olivia would have turned her brother toward her room.

She nodded jerkily and pointed out the room to Alastair, quite forgetting that he'd had occasion to visit it before. Once inside, she indicated the chaise and nudged her brother in that direction when his feet took root just beyond the threshold.

"May I pour him a whiskey?" she asked Griffin.

"No liquor," he said flatly. "I am not convinced he is yet sober. You may ring for whatever else you like."

Olivia glanced back at Alastair. She'd not smelled alcohol on his clothes or breath, but he sat like a man nursing a sore head, his shoulders hunched almost to the level of his ears.

"I cleaned him up," Griffin said, divining her thoughts.

Frowning, Olivia pulled the cord. She waited by the door

for the footman while Griffin crossed the room to his desk. He hitched one hip at the front rather than taking up his chair. Olivia noticed his attention was all for Alastair and that her brother had yet to look up. She wondered that she did not feel at all sorry for him.

The footman arrived and she asked for a pot of tea. The silver tray, the china cups, the detail to pouring, all of it would lend an air of civility to whatever was to come. At least Olivia hoped it was so. She was not certain that Griffin could be moved a second time to release Alastair from his throttling grip.

Olivia went to the foot of the chaise but did not sit. Alastair, she noted, did not look at her. Neither man said anything, waiting, it seemed, for her to end the silence.

"You are uninjured?" she asked her brother.

Alastair kept his head down, the weight of it supported by his hands. He nodded, though it was an effort to do so.

"You look as if you might be ill. Shall I fetch a pail?"

Alastair merely grunted softly.

"That is an Aubusson rug beneath your feet, Alastair." She did not mention that she had reason to know because she'd been sick on the very edge of that rug. "His lordship is likely to have some affection for the thing. We already know he has none for you."

"I'm all of a piece," he said.

"Then you will do me the favor of sitting up. If there is an explanation, I should like to see your face as you make it."

Alastair straightened. He jerked his chin in Breckenridge's direction. "Apply to him for an explanation."

The corners of Olivia's mouth sagged with disappointment. "Would you embarrass yourself further, Alastair? Would you embarrass me? I am entitled to hear something from you, am I not? You might begin, for example, with why his lordship had you by the throat."

"It is obvious by now, is it not? I did not want to see you again. I was trying to avoid just this end."

Griffin was more than a little surprised by Alastair Cole's capitulation. For all that he made a querulous offering, it was nonetheless a confession. Of course, Griffin thought, he may have well given in as easily beneath Olivia's take-no-prisoners gaze. He folded his arms over his chest and waited for her next volley, prepared to enjoy himself at Alastair's expense. Instead, Olivia lobbed it at him.

"You are too smug by half, my lord. It is not in the least attractive."

"So I have been given to understand." He made no attempt to temper the smile she'd correctly observed as smug. "It is perhaps unfortunate in this instance that I am not a vain man."

Olivia's mouth flattened in disapproval, but she returned her attention to her brother. "Where have you been, Alastair?"

"You must know that I went to see our father. Didn't Lord Breckenridge show you my note?"

"I read it. You didn't mention Sir Hadrien. I think you meant for me to make that assumption."

"I wrote that I was going to apply for an advance on my allowance. Pray, to what other person might I have gone?"

"Your mother, I imagine, though I did not consider it at the time."

Twin coins of color appeared in Alastair's cheeks. "No. She would not have been sympathetic."

"Was Father?"

Alastair's eyes darted away, then slowly returned to Olivia's. He lifted his chin slightly. "No," he said. "Under the circumstances, he was not at all inclined to help me."

Olivia closed her eyes, momentarily light-headed with the fullness of the difficulty facing her. She reminded herself that nothing had truly changed. Hadn't she been facing this very thing before his arrival? She had tried so hard not to hope that he might relieve her of the burden, but her disappointment was so profound that she realized some part of her had dared to imagine a different outcome.

When she opened her eyes, she saw Griffin stirring on the edge of the desk as if he was about to make a move to assist her. To prevent him from coming to her aid, she retreated a few steps until the back of her knees came in contact with a chair, then she sat. Alastair's face was in full profile, every one of his features drawn down at the edges. If he noticed her distress, he was too full of self-pity to lend support.

"It is not unexpected," she said quietly. "You must have known that Sir Hadrien was unlikely to be persuaded."

He shrugged. "There was nothing for it but to ask."

"Of course. It was the simplest solution." She continued to regard his wretched profile and willed her heart neither to soften nor break. "You have been gone a very long time, Alastair. Did Father invite you to stay?"

"He did. Mother also."

"I see."

Alastair's head swiveled sideways. "I didn't, Olivia. I couldn't. Two days, that was all I stayed. I journeyed back to London that quickly."

"But not as far as Putnam Lane," she said. "Where did you go? Where did his lordship find you?"

Alastair's gaze slipped away again. He said nothing.

"Where did he find you?" she repeated. Because her brother could not, or would not, answer, she turned to Griffin. "My lord?"

"Jericho Mews," Griffin said quietly.

Olivia thought it was fortunate that she'd chosen to sit. She pressed her palms to her midriff. It was as if she'd been pummeled. The ache was that real. "You returned home?" she asked her brother. "Is that true?"

"Only now and again. The rest of the time I stayed . . ."

When Alastair's voice trailed off, Olivia looked again to Griffin for an answer.

"With his mistress. It is what made him difficult to locate."

Olivia nodded, swallowed. "I didn't realize you'd been looking for him. How long? From the beginning?"

Griffin did not answer immediately. He considered lying, but decided that she deserved to know the truth. If she was courageous enough to ask the question, then only one answer served. "Since your second evening at the faro table."

"My second evening? I don't under—" Then she did. Griffin's search was not prompted by her dealing faro. He was moved to look for her brother because of the kiss they'd shared that same night. "I think you flatter yourself overmuch, my lord. Nothing would have ever come of it."

Griffin's half-smile teased with its mockery. "I do not flatter myself that I am anything save determined. You underestimate me, Miss Cole."

Alastair's eyes darted from Olivia to Breckenridge and could make no sense of what passed between them. Clearly, it was a matter to which neither wanted to make him privy. He latched on to the part he could comprehend. "You were dealing faro, Olivia? You?"

Still regarding Griffin, Olivia answered Alastair's query absently, "A game or two, now and again."

"Now and again?" Alastair snapped to attention, wearing indignation like a regimental uniform. He jutted his chin in Breckenridge's direction. "You permitted my sister to stand at the gaming table and deal faro?"

Griffin shrugged as if the matter were of no consequence. "It was faro or vingt-et-un. I determined that faro was the better choice."

Alastair shot to his feet and took a step forward before Breckenridge's arched eyebrow stopped him in his tracks.

"You wish to say something?" asked Griffin. "Issue a challenge, perhaps?"

"I . . . um, I . . . No, that is . . . no."

Olivia pressed the fingertips of her right hand to her temple and massaged the ache that was building there. "Sit down,

Alastair," she said quietly. "Be glad of his lordship's perverse sense of humor, else you would find yourself counting off ten paces at dawn."

Without conscious intent, Alastair's hand went to his throat. He sat. The smattering of freckles across his cheeks and the bridge of his nose were more pronounced against the paleness of his complexion. "You should not have been dealing faro," he said. "What Father says about you—"

Pained, Olivia cut him off. "Perhaps not. But you were not here to make your argument, were you?"

Griffin was careful not to show the least expression as Alastair's neck seemed to shrink inside the stiff points of his collar. It was entirely possible that Olivia's brother would seek refuge inside his frock coat like a turtle ducking into its shell. He cast his glance in Olivia's direction, saw her stricken countenance, and followed the direction of her gaze to Alastair's naked right hand.

Olivia's voice was hardly more than a whisper, thick with disappointment and heavy with the ache of unshed tears. "Oh, Alastair. What have you done with the ring?"

He was immediately defensive and not a little petulant. "Done? Why should you think I have done anything?"

Olivia merely stared at him.

"Stolen," he said, deflating slightly. "It was stolen from me."

Olivia found it was possible to feel sorry for her brother. She asked Griffin, "Might I have some moments alone with Alastair, my lord?"

Griffin looked from one to the other, hesitating only briefly before he nodded. "Of course. I will wait outside."

Olivia had not imagined he would give over his study to them, but that she and Alastair would make their way to her room. Her lips parted in advance of her protest, but his rather kind, compassionate smile kept her silent. That, too, was unexpected.

When he was gone, she stood and moved once more to

the foot of the chaise. Alastair, as a matter of course, made room for her beside him. "Did you mean to simply leave me here?" Alastair was long in replying, which she supposed was its own sort of answer. "I see."

He shook his head. "No. You shouldn't think it was ever my intention, Olivia. Not at the outset." He darted her a sideways look. "But after Father refused me, and as the days passed with no turn of fortune that would have helped me make good on my losses, I reasoned my way into believing you were better served in Breckenridge's care than in mine. I have not done well by you, sister. I do not imagine that will change."

"How can you say that? You have been my savior, Alastair. You rescued me."

"You must stop saying that. You cannot know how I wish it were true, but you have always been willing to give me too much credit, and I have been too willing to accept it." He stopped her protest by laying one hand over hers and turning in to her. "I am not yet the man you would like to believe I am. That is why I am invariably a disappointment to you. No, do not say it isn't so. Hear me out, Olivia. I know differently because I am a disappointment to myself as well.

"I have not had much success at managing my obligations since I left university. London presents one temptation after another, and you have seen for yourself that I am ever drawn to take another bite of the apple."

"You are young yet. You should have as many bites of the apple as you wish without having the burden of a sister who has no place in your society. It has been too—"

"It has been my failure," he said quietly, squeezing her hand. "Mine. Not yours. I look at you now and I find myself moved to make all manner of promises that I will see to your welfare and keep you safe. I would mean every word right up to the moment that I was distracted by the turn of a card or the turn of an ankle. You are my elder by only three years as the calendar would have it, but we both know who protects whom in this odd bargain we've struck."

Olivia swiped impatiently at the tears that welled in her eyes. "I am neither as clever nor as resourceful as you would have yourself believe. It simply makes you feel better to think so."

"I had not considered that, but perhaps you are right. That should give you pause, Olivia. You would do well not to depend upon me."

"I understand." And she did. Alastair was asking to be relieved of the responsibility of her. She slid her hand out from under his. "I regret making things difficult between you and Sir Hadrien."

"Do not even think it. It was perhaps my finest moment, standing toe to toe and telling him that I would have you in my life."

She could not manage the careless smile she'd hoped for. Her mouth trembled at the edges. "And now you will not."

"Oh, Olivia." He made to reach for her, but she avoided his arms. He could not blame her. "I have no right to offer you comfort."

Olivia stood and moved quickly to the window. Turning away from her brother, she hugged herself. A shiver went through her in spite of it. Her bones felt brittle, aching with cold. Splinters of ice embedded themselves in her chest, crystalized around her heart. If she exhaled deeply she thought she might see frost on her breath. The whole of her was frozen with fear. She could not think, could not act, could not move.

Aloneness crushed her.

Olivia did not know how long she stood there staring blindly, dry-eyed, onto Putnam Lane. She was unaware of any movement behind her, never heard any exchange of words. Insensible to her surroundings, made numb by the cold that gripped her, she did not startle when arms slipped around her from behind. She remained perfectly rigid as a pair of hands were clasped and pressed to her midriff. There was a disturbance against the crown of her hair, but she took no notice of it, and when something nudged her heels she stayed her ground.

Griffin held her, though not as he imagined he might. She stood leaning slightly toward the window, as exquisitely lovely in her still, proud pose as a ship's figurehead. And like that masterfully carved piece, she was impossible to cradle, impossible to mold.

He whispered her name, touched his chin to her hair. She did not pull away but neither did she turn her head. He tried to imagine what she was thinking and could not. She seemed wholly unaware of his presence.

"Come with me, Olivia," he said against her ear. "Come away."

When she didn't move, Griffin twisted his head and regarded her in profile. Her eyes remained open but unblinking. There was no indication that she'd heard him, so deeply had she drawn into herself.

Abandoning caution, Griffin released Olivia only in order to lift her. She did not settle easily in his arms, and when he urged her to put her arms around his neck her fingertips fluttered once, then were still. He moved swiftly to take her away, crossing the study easily with his long-legged stride. He had to wrestle with the door handle to exit and narrowly missed stumbling into Foster carrying the tea service. Directing the footman to follow him, he took Olivia to her room and laid her on the bed.

"Set the tray down," he ordered. "Then send someone immediately for Dr. Pettibone."

"Of course. And Mr. Cole? Shall I have him—"

"If he cares about his life in any measure, he is already gone."

Nodding once, Foster quit the room.

Griffin tugged at the bedcovers, pulling them out from under Olivia so that they might be drawn up. She curled like a babe as he tucked the blankets around her. He brushed back curling strands of hair that had fallen across her cheek and felt the unnatural coolness of her skin. He left her side long enough to pour a few fingers of tea into a cup.

"Here," he said, sitting beside her. "Drink." Griffin realized he was perhaps too optimistic that she would respond to this order when she hadn't to any that had come before. He carefully slid one arm under her back and lifted, then pressed the teacup against her lower lip and tilted it ever so slightly. He watched her mouth purse and recognized the suckling response of an infant. She sipped each time he tipped the cup, and it wasn't long before she'd taken all of it.

Griffin set the cup aside and lowered her once again to the mattress. Her eyelids fluttered, then closed. Her damp lips parted a fraction; her breathing eased. He arranged the covers again, smoothing them across her turned shoulder.

It occurred to him that he could easily be moved to thrash her brother within an inch of his life. He would take a certain pleasure in it, too, landing the blows with forethought, aiming for those places that would cause pain but not immediately lay him out. The kidneys. The ballocks. The soft spot below the heart and between the ribs. And when Alastair Cole was weaving on his feet, Griffin imagined delivering the final blow to the younger man's other soft spot, driving his nose sharply between his eyes and into his brain.

Yes, that would be satisfying.

In contrast to his violent thoughts, the fingers that touched Olivia's cheek were infinitely gentle. There was a hint of warmth where there'd been none before, a bit of rosy color where she'd been almost as white as the pillow beneath her.

He recalled his first glimpse of her standing at the foot of the staircase. The black velvet bonnet had shielded her glorious hair and shaded her eyes until she lifted her face in his direction. There hadn't been the least fear in them. He remembered that, remembered thinking that she was unnaturally composed.

She should have run, and now he supposed he understood more completely why she hadn't.

Even then there'd been some part of her that suspected she had nowhere to go.

All of her protests to the contrary had been for form's sake. She had been too proud then to admit, even to herself, that she truly had no place to return to. When she climbed the stairs to his study, it was because she believed she owed it to her brother. If she'd known with certainty that Alastair would abandon her, she still would have made the climb.

Duty prompted her first steps. Desperation kept her going.

Griffin eased himself off the bed, careful not to jostle her. He removed himself to the wing chair by the fireplace and waited for Pettibone's arrival.

Olivia came to wakefulness slowly and much against her will. It was no gentle thaw that she experienced, no gradual melting of her frozen self. What she felt was an ice pick driving deeply, relentlessly, chipping away at her thoughts, then her feelings, and finally her senses, until she lay bare and a bit bloody.

She winced, whimpered, tried to shield herself from the hammering point of the pick, and still it found her.

"Olivia." Her name came to her as though carried over a great distance. A weight settled on her shoulder. There was warmth there also. She shook a little with it. "Olivia."

She looked through the veil of her eyelashes first and recognized it was Griffin at her side. It was his voice then, his hand on her shoulder. When he shook her again, she cast off the last dregs of sleep and opened her eyes.

"Go away."

It was relief that provoked Griffin's smile. "Not just yet," he said, humoring her. "Dr. Pettibone is here."

Olivia turned her head and saw the physician standing near the foot of the bed. She frowned. "Has he come for me? Why?"

"He has come for me." When she lifted an eyebrow, he added, "Because I want him to examine you."

"You persist in the belief that you are amusing. You are not."

Griffin glanced over his shoulder when Pettibone chuckled. "She is returning to form. It is perhaps best not to encourage her overmuch."

The physician was wholly unrepentant. "Encouragement is precisely what she needs."

"What do you know?" He returned his attention to Olivia. "Pettibone still bleeds his patients."

A smile edged Olivia's lips. "Go," she said. "Leave us."

Griffin found her hand, squeezed. "She thinks she will have her way with you, Pettibone. Encourage her if you must, but, pray, do not indulge her."

Olivia waited until Griffin was gone before she pushed herself upright and gave the physician her wary, narrow-eyed regard. "You and I will deal well together if you remain where you are. I will also take it as the greatest favor if you never open your little black satchel."

Pettibone made no promises. "I suppose that depends on what you tell me, but have a care, Miss Cole, for I have been known to recognize a lie." He lifted his medical bag, dangling it as the proverbial carrot, and said pointedly, "I will take it as the greatest favor if you do not prevaricate."

Griffin had a drink waiting for Pettibone when the physician came to make his report. "Well?" he asked. "What is your verdict?"

Pettibone set his bag down and accepted the tumbler of whiskey. He sipped, sighed with pleasure. Among all his patients, Breckenridge had the finest stores of liquor and was the most free with it.

"Verdict?" he asked. "You mistake me for a judge mayhap."

"Most days I mistake you for a doctor. Give over, Petti-bone. How is she?"

"Composed. Cautious. Afraid. She would never admit to the last, of course, but neither can she fully conceal it. Nothing was to be gained by pressing that observation, so I did not. She is correct, though, Breckenridge. There is nothing I can do for her. Laudanum might help herself sleep restfully, but it will not change her circumstances. She wonders what your intentions are toward her brother."

"Her brother? Did she never once wonder what my intentions are toward her?"

"She did not mention it, no. Have you intentions?"

"I would not speak of them to you, now would I?"

Pettibone shrugged, sipped his whiskey.

"What does she imagine I will do to Mr. Cole?"

"I don't know. She did not elaborate."

"That is too bad. I would welcome ideas. At the moment, I am all for thrashing him."

"A pedestrian solution. I expected better."

"It is all in the execution, Pettibone. I could make it last a very long time and hardly bloody my knuckles."

Impressed, Pettibone raised his glass in salute. "There is no reason she should know."

"No reason at all."

"He really left her in your hands?"

"So it appears. As I told you earlier, he only returned because I insisted."

"She seemed to think it was because you threatened him."

"That would be another way to characterize it."

"And at one point you physically restrained him."

"She observed only one," Griffin said, and let it end at that. "Did you leave her with another vial of laudanum?"

"She had enough left from my previous visit."

Griffin nodded, not surprised. "I thought she might. There is nothing physically wrong with her, then."

"Not a thing."

"She was so cold."

Pettibone nodded. "You were right to send for me."

"You will always say that. You enjoy my whiskey."

"Guilty." He made the pronouncement in judge-like tones. In a less stentorian fashion, he went on. "The manner in which you described finding her after her brother left, well, it put me in mind of some of the soldiers I had occasion to observe in the aftermath of battle. What they had seen, or heard, or learned, created a disturbance so profound that they could no longer communicate. They lay like the dead, often staring out at nothing the rest of us could see. I do not know where Miss Cole's imaginings took her, but it was not a journey, nor a destination, for the faint of heart."

"What is to be done?"

"You mentioned intentions toward her, I believe."

"Yes."

"May I assume they include caring for her?"

"Yes."

"Then that is what is to be done."

Griffin nodded, sighed. "It frequently troubles me that I pay you for such advice."

Griffin quietly let himself into Olivia's room. His caution was unnecessary. She was sitting at the table, playing solitaire. Wisps of steam rose faintly from the cup of tea near her elbow. Three fingers of toast lay on a plate beside the cup, one with evidence that a bite had been taken from the crusty end. Crumbs littered the plate, giving him hope that the toast had once numbered four fingers.

"Winning?" he asked. He noticed that his voice had not

startled her, proof that she'd sensed his presence even though he knew his entry had been silent.

Olivia shrugged and did not look up. "When I cheat."

"Doesn't that belittle the achievement?"

"It is solitaire, my lord. Just now, I merely want to win."

He understood the need. "You are feeling more the thing?"

"I was never unwell."

Griffin did not argue the point. It was a matter of perspective, he supposed. "May I join you?"

"You already have."

Because there was no other chair in the room similar to the one in which she sat, Griffin drew the wing chair closer to the table, turned it sideways, and perched on the arm. He stretched his legs diagonally under the table and folded his arms comfortably across his chest.

She glanced up as she gathered the cards. "You have nothing you wish to say?"

"Not just at the moment, no."

Olivia considered and accepted it. She shuffled, laid the cards out, then began to play. She made her moves quickly, seeing the whole of the game at once and recalling what cards would be turned over as she went through the deck three cards at a time.

"Your hands are lovely," he said.

Whatever she had expected he might say, it wasn't that. "I chew my nails sometimes."

"I've noticed."

Of course he had. He noticed everything. She continued playing.

"I've noticed, too, that you cannot accept a compliment."

"How kind you are to say so."

Griffin chuckled. "My point exactly. You embrace what you perceive as criticism and throw off compliments as if they were hair shirts."

"It is a peculiarity, I admit, and one that is unlikely to

change." She saw she had come to the last of her plays. If she was to continue, she would have to cheat, and it was simply too lowering to do so in front of Griffin. She found she did not want to win as badly as that. Sighing, she drew in the cards and began again.

Griffin watched her in silence a while longer. When he judged her receptive to matters of import, he said, "You are welcome to remain here, Olivia. I do not have it in my mind to turn you out."

Her eyes on the cards, she nodded.

Suspicious of her easy acceptance, he said, "You have heard the like before, I collect."

"Yes."

"And what happened?"

"I was turned out." She shrugged. "Do not imagine that I think you are lying. I know you are sincere. It is my experience that everyone is sincere until they are . . . not. Whether it is changed by circumstance or condition, I have reason to know that what is in one's mind on any given day may be quite different on another. I fully appreciate that it is not a promise, and I thank you for not phrasing it as one. *That* I would not believe."

He had meant it as a promise, though. Now, knowing how little faith she had in such things, he could not speak of it. "Do you wish to stay?" he said instead.

"Yes." There was no hesitation in her answer; she paused only in the reflection of it. Her fingers lay still on top of the card she meant to turn over. "What will you require of me?"

"Does it matter?"

It was perfectly humiliating to admit that it did not. "No," she said finally.

"Then let us not discuss it now."

"All right." She turned over a ten of diamonds and made her play on the jack of spades.

Her compliance, perversely, did not cheer him in the least.

He was rather more alarmed by it. "Pettibone informed me that you wondered what is to become of your brother."

She smiled, though there was no joy in it. "I don't believe my question was as philosophical as you have made it out to be. I think I know what will become of Alastair. I only wondered what will become of him at your hands."

"He'll live."

"I hope so. He can never repay his debt if you kill him."

"His debt? Bloody hell, Olivia, I care no more than this"— he flicked a card from one of her stacks—"for his debt. Do you think I don't know that I have the better of the bargain in you than his £1,000?"

"Then he's settled with you."

Griffin ground his teeth until a muscle jumped in his cheek. He forced himself to relax, work out his jaw. He blew out a breath. "Yes. Something like that, though I would not go so far as to say that all is settled."

"He sold me, did he not?"

"Christ." The muscle jumped again. It was uncomfortably close to the truth. He ran a hand through his hair. "It may be his view, but it is not mine. There is no bill of sale."

"There is Alastair's marker."

"Already returned to him," Griffin said. Thrust in his face, he could have said. He wished now that he would have forced her brother to chew and swallow the damnable thing.

"So I am yours."

"If you like."

Olivia did not reply. She fingered the card he'd flicked away earlier and returned it to the proper stack. "Did you know his ring was stolen before I asked him about it?"

"Yes. He mentioned it on the way here."

"Did you believe him?"

"I suspect it was not an entire untruth."

Her eyes darted to his face. "You are generally more forthright."

"I think it is safe to assume he lost it in a card game, most likely a crooked one, if my sources are to be credited." Before she asked about his sources, he told her. "Misters Fairley and Varah. You will remember them, I think."

"Indeed. So they assist in matters other than the removal of women from their homes. How enterprising they are."

"On occasion. They observed your brother on successive nights at Crocker's club, deep in his cups and light in his pockets. I did not know then that he was in London, so their intelligence was appreciated. Do you recall that I told you about Crocker? He operates one of the lowest circles of Dante's hell. It was most unwise of Alastair to set any money down there, particularly unwise that it should have been at faro. Crocker's dealer uses a box."

She had yet another reason to shake her head sadly at Alastair's judgment. "A good player knows when a box has been rigged."

"Perhaps. I am quite certain you would. I've watched you track every card played, so I know you are entirely capable of seeing the deception, but your brother was already in desperate straits and unlikely to have been watching much beyond his own dwindling reserves."

Olivia slowly turned over three cards and made her play while her mind was otherwise engaged. "If Alastair was desperate, it wasn't because he wanted to honor the debt he owed you. He already had determined that he would not return for me."

Griffin could not fault her conclusion. "That seems to be the hard truth," he said quietly.

She was oddly grateful that he did not pretend it was otherwise.

"Your eight of spades plays on the nine of hearts."

"What?"

He pointed out the move she was going to miss if she turned the cards again.

"Oh. Thank you." She made the play, then continued as if

there had been no interruption. "How did Alastair take the ring back from you? You told me you'd put it in your desk. That little drawer where you drew out his marker, it would be a secret from most people, wouldn't it?"

Griffin rose and stabbed at the fire, then added more coals. "I have always wondered that you did not ask. It caused me to consider that you already knew." When her head came up sharply, he was glad of it. For a moment the glazed look of defeat vanished from her eyes as she prepared to take umbrage with his assumption. He put up one hand to forestall her. "It was a reasonable conclusion, and you know it. Your brother's marker was so outrageous that what was I to think except that you were party to his suggestion?"

It was difficult to remain offended when she could not fault his logic. "You might have asked," she said mildly. "Though I don't suppose you would have had cause to believe me."

"It did not seem so at the time." Griffin returned to his perch on the arm of the chair. Before he settled completely, he reached across the table and made a play for her that she was in danger of missing.

"That is annoying," she said.

"Yes, I know." He was unrepentant. "My sisters have said the same when they are at cards. I cannot help myself." When he leaned forward again, she lightly slapped his hand away. He grinned, mostly because she did not look at all abashed. He sat back, folded his arms, and was largely content watching her.

"You have not answered my question," she reminded him after a time. "The ring. How did Alastair take it from you?"

"He didn't. Not precisely. He had an accomplice."

"An accomplice? One of your own staff?" Even as she put the question to him, she knew the answer lay elsewhere. He had the loyalty of everyone who worked for him, and more than one servant had been moved to remark that he was a generous employer. Olivia could not conceive that Alastair had been able to persuade one among them to come to his aid. But if not a servant, then who?

Watching her, Griffin knew the precise moment Olivia hit upon the answer. Her eyes widened beneath raised eyebrows; her hands ceased to turn the cards. She stared at him, looking to him for confirmation of her thoughts before she gave them voice. He nodded once.

"Mrs. Christie?" She breathed the name more than said it and, conscious of insult, still posed it as a question.

"Certainly, Mrs. Christie."

"You have always known?"

"I have always suspected. I *knew* when I said as much to her and she did not deny it. She wanted me to know but did not possess the courage to say as much aloud. I broke off our arrangement, but in her mind she has had the last word."

A small vertical crease appeared between Olivia's eyebrows. "It seems you had a complicated arrangement."

He shrugged. "Perhaps it was. It was straightforward at the outset, at least to my way of thinking. Such entanglements as there were, were of her making. I did not encourage them."

He would believe that, Olivia thought, and she felt something akin to pity for Mrs. Christie. She could imagine that Griffin's former mistress had allowed herself to hope; therein were born the entanglements. "A woman scorned," she said softly, more to herself than to Griffin.

"One motivation, certainly," said Griffin.

"But you hadn't yet ended your arrangement."

"No, but she was entirely capable of seeing the road ahead. She may have known before I did that we would part ways soon. It is very much like her to plan for such an end."

"But to help Alastair . . ." Olivia could not quite grasp the sense of it beyond Mrs. Christie's desire for revenge.

"You are his sister," Griffin said gently. "His older sister, in fact. The truth does not come so easily when we fail to see our loved ones as someone outside their relationship to us."

Olivia blinked as the import of his observation was borne home to her. "They were lovers?"

He smiled because she was so clearly astonished. "You knew there was a woman."

"Yes, but . . ." She shook her head. "But Mrs. Christie? It is beyond my comprehension."

"Judging by the attention your brother received here—from women, I might add, who were clearly attached to their gentlemen escorts—I can attest to the fact that his face and figure were much admired."

Olivia waved that aside. "I am very aware that Alastair is possessed of a handsome face and figure, my lord, and for that matter, a handsome income as well, but he is not you."

Griffin found himself the object of Olivia's frank study. It was never easy being on the receiving end of such regard, which was why he often was the one initiating it. He suffered it for several long moments before he was struck by the humor of it.

"Have a care, Olivia, else I will think you mean to flatter me."

"Of course you will think that. You are ever hopeful. Still, at the risk of encouraging you, I must underscore my point that Alastair is not so well favored as you, financially or in any other way."

It was then that Griffin was compelled to point out what she'd allowed herself to forget. "He is also not married."

Chapter Eight

Olivia lay awake long after the house quieted. The candle at her bedside had flickered out sometime earlier, and it was the fire's meager light that stretched across the floor toward her. She had participated in the closing rituals that put the hell to bed for the night and prepared it for the following day's business. Until this evening, Griffin had never permitted her to have any role or responsibilities after the patrons departed. It was not that he assigned her any particular tasks tonight, but that he didn't stop her from taking part. She'd felt his eyes on her on at least two separate occasions, but he never interfered, and when he removed the money boxes from the gaming rooms and took them to his study, he did not insist she accompany him.

She was both glad of it and confused by it.

Olivia turned on her side and burrowed deeper into the bedcovers. She wondered if Mrs. Christie had ever known such disconcertion in her dealings with Griffin. If she had, it might have been reason enough to seek out Alastair. He was infinitely less complicated, though Olivia supposed that was as much because of his youth as his predilection for making the easy choices. Her brother's naïveté might have been appealing to a woman weary of another man's suspicious nature.

Alastair's heirloom ring had likely garnered Mrs. Christie's interest at the outset; his connection to Sir Hadrien had probably sustained it. The woman's sense of being wronged by Griffin went a long way to keeping her at Alastair's side and quite possibly provoked her to help him steal back his ring.

Olivia wondered if Mrs. Christie had been the first to propose the theft or if perhaps Alastair had put the idea before her. It rarely occurred to Alastair to guard his tongue. If he had a thought, he was pleased to speak it aloud, though most often it was simply to turn over an idea in his mind. Olivia recalled being disconcerted by her brother's conversational asides until she realized he wasn't really speaking to her. Mrs. Christie may not have understood that much of what tripped so easily from Alastair's tongue was meant to be ignored.

Still, it was Alastair who was the author of the marker. She could not put the responsibility for that on Mrs. Christie's shoulders.

All the rest, though, fell to her. She was the one who would have known Griffin was not wearing the ring, the one privy to the drawer where he'd hidden it, the one with ease of access to the hell and the freedom to move through its halls and rooms without calling attention to herself.

Mrs. Christie must be well pleased that the consequences of her theft were so far reaching. She had not only retaliated against his lordship in fine style, but she had relieved her new protector of his most onerous burden. All in all, it was a good piece of work if one shared her eye-for-an-eye sense of justice.

Olivia did not.

Wearily, she lifted her head just enough to plump the pillow under her. If she could not settle her mind, sleep would never come. It did not seem to matter that she was tired almost beyond bearing—she was still seized by a restlessness that made it impossible to find comfort in her own skin. She wished that she might throw it off as easily as her bedclothes or shed it like her nightgown.

When long minutes passed and she realized she would not sleep, Olivia finally surrendered, tossing the blankets aside and scrambling out of bed. She shrugged into her robe just as her teeth began to chatter and danced a bit on the cold floor until she found her slippers. She paused in front of the fireplace, taking advantage of its meager heat before she dashed out of the room.

Olivia did not think better of her flight until she arrived at Griffin's door. She stared at it, gently tested its handle, then paced off a dozen steps on either side of it before she determined there was nothing for it but that she should go forward.

"Did you mean to be stealthy?" Griffin asked as Olivia backed herself into his room. "If so, you are sadly out of it."

Olivia jumped and spun. She squealed. The high-pitched sound was altogether unfamiliar to her, and she clamped one hand over her mouth so neither of them would have to hear it again.

Griffin touched one palm to his ear. "That was unpleasant."

"You scared me to death."

"Obviously not."

She glared at him, hoping the expression was not lost in the dimly lighted room. In the manner of an accusation, she asked, "Why are you still awake?"

Griffin's eyebrows rose in tandem. "Because I am not asleep?" He lifted the book resting on his lap. "I find reading requires a conscious mind, though apparently not the writing of it." He closed the book and laid it aside. "This work is wholly impenetrable."

Curious, Olivia approached the bedside table and lifted the leather-bound book before he could pull it back. Laughter stuttered from her lips. "Why, it is a Gothic novel. You, my lord, are a fraud. It could not be a more straightforward tale, and the writing is elegant in its precision."

Griffin knew himself to be vaguely abashed. He held out his hand for the book. "A guilty pleasure," he said, reaching out to snatch it from her. When he laid it down this time, he purposely set it on his other side. "I have not failed to notice that you are not sleeping either. As it seems unlikely that you came here to discuss literature, and as you were bent on slipping into my room without announcing yourself, it would perhaps be prudent to explain yourself at this juncture."

"I was going to wake you," she said somewhat defensively.

"I should hope so." He adjusted a pillow at the small of his back and rested his head against the polished walnut headboard. "It is disconcerting to think you meant to smother me in my sleep."

Olivia blinked. "I would not—oh, you are teasing. I didn't realize . . ." She took a steadying breath, pressed her palms flat against her thighs. "There was no discussion of what you will require of me. When we did not speak of it earlier, it did not occur to me that we would not speak of it at all."

"Is it so important that we speak of it now?"

"Yes. I think it is." Otherwise she would never sleep, although she knew better than to tell him that. "You will have some terms, I collect, and I should like to know what they are."

"I did not put them to paper, Olivia." He moved his legs to one side and made room for her on the edge of the bed. "Sit down. Come. You have already bearded the lion."

Olivia sat. She folded her hands in her lap and stared straight ahead, giving him only her profile limned in candlelight.

"I suppose you wish I'd been sleeping," he said.

She nodded.

"Could I have expected you to crawl into my bed? Mayhap wind your arms around me? Your knees at the back of mine? It is not an unpleasant way to be awakened. Is that what you meant to do?"

"Yes."

Griffin gave her full marks for not dissembling. "Why?"

"To have done with it."

He chuckled low in his throat. "Pray, do not spare my feelings."

She glanced at him, unapologetic but mildly embarrassed that she had been so forthright. "I was unaware any of your feelings were engaged. If that is the case, I will choose my words more carefully."

He shook his head. "I hope you will not. Candor is an admirable quality and not practiced nearly often enough. I recall you telling me on the occasion of our first meeting that you are not a romantic."

Had she? "I find it odd that you remember."

"I remember a great many things from that interview. You also informed me that while you were not by inclination a romantic, you held out the hope that others might be."

"Fodder for poets and dreamers, else what would they have to hang their hats on?"

Griffin studied her profile. Its unlined purity was in complete contrast to her rather jaded perspective. "Have you ever been in love?"

"No." Then, because he said he appreciated her candor, she turned to him a second time and pinned him with an inquiring glance. "Have you?"

He did not answer immediately, not because he was searching for the proper response, but because he was trying to decide if he would give her any response at all. What loyalty did he owe his wife? What explanation did he owe Olivia? "Yes," he said. "Once. And briefly."

She regarded him steadily, satisfied with his answer. He did not have the look of a gentleman eager to reacquaint himself with that thorny emotion. "Perhaps we will suit, you and I."

"It's occurred to me also."

Olivia nodded, looked away. "Will you want me to undress?"

"Eventually." Griffin leaned forward and unclasped her

hands, drawing one into his. "But I suspect you will be cold if you do so outside of the covers. Your hands are already like ice." He tugged so gently that she could have mistaken it for her own movement toward him. With his free hand he raised the bedclothes. "Come. You will find it considerably warmer on this side of the blankets."

Olivia used the toe of one foot to remove the slipper on the other. When the second slipper dropped to the floor, she slid in beside him and unbelted her robe. He helped her out of it, tossing it at the foot of the bed, but he did not draw her down as she expected he would. He gave her part of his pillow instead, and she supported herself against the headboard just as he did. Her shoulder lay against his upper arm; his fingers remained laced in hers.

"Are you breathing?" he asked. "You do not sound as if you are breathing."

She sipped the air. "I am now. Thank you."

He smiled. He realized of a sudden that he appreciated her company. "If you wish, we can sit for a time. I cannot think of a single reason that we should rush our fences." He gave her hand a squeeze, laughter lurking at the back of his throat. "Other than your earnest desire to—how did you describe it?—yes, to have done with it."

"You are enjoying yourself, aren't you?"

Borrowing her words, he said, "I am now. Thank you."

Olivia closed her eyes. His thumb was making a pass across the back of her hand. She tried to think about only that, but her head throbbed anyway. She rubbed the bridge of her nose and the crease between her eyebrows with her forefinger. "I hope you do not always mean to be so agreeable," she said quietly. "It will be better if you are not too kind."

He wished he didn't understand what she meant, but he did. "All right." Out of the corner of his eye he watched her massage her brow right up to her hairline. He released her hand, and giving her no choice in the matter, brought her head against the curve of his shoulder and fit his arm around her. Several long minutes passed before Griffin felt most of the tension seep out of her. He nudged his chin in her hair. The stubble of his beard rasped pleasantly against her scalp.

It was Olivia who finally broke the silence, not because it was uncomfortable, but because it was not. "What would you be doing if I weren't here?"

"Wishing you were." He could tell she didn't like that response. "Too amiable? Very well. I would be reading. One or two chapters more, I suspect, then I would have put the book down and slept."

"Oh. That is good, then. I didn't know. I thought you might come to my room. It is better this way."

"Why?"

"It doesn't matter." She needed to know there was a place she could call her own, a place of refuge, of sanctuary. "It cannot be important to you."

"I beg to differ, but I won't press—unless you think that I am being too agreeable, in which event I will subject you to the tortures of the Inquisition."

"Do you know such things?"

He nodded. "I am partial to the rack."

"Really."

"Mmm." He kissed the top of her head and breathed in the lavender scent in her hair. She stirred a little in his arms, and he sensed tension pulling her taut once again. Kisses, then, were torture as well, it seemed. "The iron maiden. Shackles. Hammer and tongs."

"Impressive."

"Modesty prevents me from agreeing." He imagined she must have smiled. She nestled a bit, finding a more comfortable position for herself against his side. When she turned in to him, her knee nudged his. Her cheek pressed his shoulder just below the line of his collarbone. If she lifted her face, her lips might brush his jaw or find the underside of his chin. She didn't move again, though, and after a few moments he realized she wouldn't.

Olivia had fallen asleep.

Griffin waited until her breathing took on the steady rhythm of deep slumber before he eased her into a prone position. Because she was rather limpet-like in her attachment to his side, he eased himself down as well, pausing only to reach across her and pinch off the candlewick. He drew the covers over them and pulled a pillow closer to support his head. Olivia seemed to prefer to be supported by him, and while Griffin did not mind in the least, he wondered at her reaction when she learned they were not yet done with it.

Curiously perverse creature that she was, he imagined her relief would be short-lived.

Olivia stretched and pressed herself against the heat at her back. It seemed to her that she might have smiled, but it might have only been that she wanted to. A delicious sort of lethargy had sapped her strength, made her liquid. She drifted. There was no sound, no light. The current slowly turned her, then she became the current. Flowing. Rippling. Slipping effortlessly into the void.

She came up with a violent start. Fear wrenched a cry from the back of her throat. Her fingertips scrabbled along the edge of the covers to throw them off, and she kicked out in the same frantic movement. She was all elbows and knees, flailing between the sheets, digging her heels and head so deeply into the mattress that her back arced like an electrical current between two poles.

Griffin caught her just as she would have slipped over the edge of the bed and hauled her flush to his side. She was breathing hard in short, arrhythmic gasps that did little to fill her lungs and nothing at all to calm her. Her fingers curled in the linen of his nightshirt like talons, and when he tried to dislodge her she snarled at him.

"Olivia!" Her knee came up hard. Griffin tucked and took the considerable force of the blow on his hip. "Bloody hell, woman!" He shackled her wrists and tore her fingers loose from his clothing. She was panting, struggling. Firelight revealed her bared teeth and wildness in her eyes. Griffin wrestled Olivia onto her back and pinned her wrists above her head, a feat requiring no little force. He used one of his legs to trap both of hers but not without effort and almost being unmanned a second time.

He swore under his breath as she bucked and twisted and nearly succeeded in dislodging him. It did not seem possible that any woman could be possessed of such strength, but to experience it at the hands of this particular woman, with her willow frame and grave, graceful air, was in every way astonishing.

Afraid of hurting her, Griffin held fast and waited until she wore herself out. Come morning, she would bear the marks of his restraint. He imagined a bracelet of blue bruises around her wrists and perhaps a pale, purple medallion near her throat where he'd first pushed her back with the heel of his hand.

"Olivia," he said again, his tone more weary than gentle. "Olivia."

He was not prepared for her sudden collapse. It was not that she was merely still, but that she was boneless. The tension that had pulled her taut and defined her fight simply vanished. Suspicious, he eased his grip on one of her wrists, raised it, then let go. Her hand dropped like a stone. The same thing happened when he lifted and released her other wrist.

She had been asleep?

Griffin rolled away from her and lighted a candle at the bedside. He held the candlestick over her, letting the light wash over her face. Her eyes were closed, the long lashes looking like shadows just below them. Her lips were slightly parted, but her breathing was easy. Her complexion was smooth; for once she looked much younger than her four and twenty years. He saw peace here, the serenity she was denied when she was awake, and sometimes, it seemed now, even when she slept.

With infinite care, he drew her arms to her side again and rearranged the tangle of blankets over her when he witnessed her involuntary shiver.

He wondered what she might remember upon waking, if anything at all. What demons drove her to such violence? She was hardly more than a slip of a female, yet she had demonstrated a fierceness that set him back on his heels and gave him no choice in his manner of dealing with her. She had proven she was wholly capable of hurting him, even if she was hardly responsible for it.

Griffin set the candlestick aside but did not extinguish the flame. He lay on his side, his head propped on an elbow while he observed the gentle rise and fall of her breast. So easy was her sleep now that he could almost be convinced he was the one who'd had the nightmare.

He brushed away the tangle of hair that had been swept across her throat during the battle. His gaze narrowed on the crescent mark peeking out above the neckline of her shift. He gently turned back the fabric and saw the ruddy proof of his instinctive self-defense. He laid his fingertips against the stamp made by the heel of his hand and felt the heat of her skin and the faint pulse of her heart.

Without quite knowing he meant to do it, Griffin bent his head and placed his lips against the bruise. His fingertips slid over her shift, grazing her breast, then the slope of her ribcage. His palm came to rest lightly on her abdomen. He raised his head, but not before his mouth found the sweet curve of her neck.

That she was in his bed at all was something of a mystery

to him. She was wrong in believing he required her there as compensation for keeping her. His failing was in not correcting her assumption. The words had come to his lips several times, but he'd left them unspoken. He wanted her here, had for weeks now, perhaps from the moment she'd accepted his first challenge, but he wouldn't have forced himself on her, or even narrowed her choices so that she would accept him as the devil she knew.

What he'd done, though, upon reflection was perhaps no better. Allowing her to act on her assumption gave him what he wanted and placed the whole of the responsibility on her. There was no cause for pride there.

"What manner of things have you seen?" he whispered. He expected no response and received none. She did not stir except to draw another breath.

Griffin did not remove his hand from the flat of her belly as he dropped his elbow and lay his head against the pillow. He moved closer, turning her gently on her side, and fit himself against the curve of her body. His thighs supported the back of hers; his groin cradled her bottom. In this manner, he slept at last.

A slender chink in the drapes allowed the first hint of dawn to enter the room. Olivia lay on her side and watched the beam of light stretch itself slowly across the floor. It didn't matter that all across London people were beginning to rise and set about their work for the day. Here on Putnam Lane it was for all intents and purposes still the middle of the night.

She felt the pleasant blossom of warmth from Griffin's palm against her midriff. She didn't mind that he held her in such a way, tucked against his body as though he were sheltering her. It was only a harmless fancy if she did not allow herself to make too much of it, and the hot and rigid press of his cock against her bottom kept her from doing so. If his lordship was thinking at all, sheltering her was not what he had in his mind.

Olivia drew up her shift to bare her thighs and backside, then rubbed herself slowly against him. She heard his breathing hitch. His hips jerked, thrust toward her. She reached behind her and yanked on his nightshirt, pulling it up roughly so when she settled back a second time it was her flesh on his flesh. He moved against her, sliding, grinding. Olivia clamped her teeth together, her jaw as rigid as his cock, and grasped him in her hand. She was breathing through her nose now, nostrils slightly flared, the set of her features strained by determination, not lust.

She raised her upper leg and slid it over his, widening the space between her thighs to ease his entry. She pressed back and guided him, then bit down hard on her bottom lip as his hips jerked again and he pushed those first few inches into her. Behind her, he made a sound somewhere between a groan and a curse.

So he was awake now, if he hadn't been before.

Olivia forced herself to relax as she waited for him to move deeper. She'd expected he would begin to rut, especially now that he was conscious of being at least partially inside her. When he didn't, she tried to find a better seat against him. He stopped her, palming her hips so tightly she couldn't move.

"Would you have me rape you?" he hissed against her ear. "Christ, but you do not want this. You're not ready."

Not knowing what he meant, she squeezed her eyes shut, whimpered, and tasted blood on her lip.

"Be still!" She had only hunched her shoulders and ducked her head as though to prepare for a blow, but even this small movement shifted her body against his in a way that was pure torment. "For God's sake," he whispered a bit less harshly, "don't move."

She was tight, achingly so, but she was also as dry as a spent well. For all that she had provoked him to just this end, she was unprepared for it. She could barely accommodate his entry and not without pain, yet she would have him take her anyway.

"If we are to have done with it," he said quietly, "then it will be in a manner of my choosing. Do you understand?"

She didn't, but she nodded her head because he seemed to expect her agreement.

He gritted his teeth. "Can you not be still? You might have simply said 'yes.'"

"Yes."

"Better." His jaw relaxed, but only a fraction. "Sweet Jesus, I do not know if I can do this." Grunting softly, he pushed at her hips and withdrew. He ignored her sharp intake of breath and brought her buttocks solid against him again, as close to her as he could be without being inside her, and held her like that until he felt he'd gained a modicum of control.

He found the bunched hem of her shift and began raising it. She didn't help him, but neither did she resist. Once he had it over her head, he tossed it to the floor, then slipped his hands under the blankets and laid them flat against her skin, splaying his fingers on either side of her waist. He lowered his head and pressed his mouth to the bare curve of her shoulder. His lips slid along her collarbone as he turned her, and when she came to rest on her back, he suckled at her throat.

She seemed to have no difficulty keeping still now.

Griffin raised himself up and looked down into her face. Her modest smile might not have seemed forced if any part of it had touched her eyes. Shaking his head slowly, he placed his fingertips on her cheek and traced the fine-boned arch all the way to her hairline.

Curious, he asked, "What has been your experience here?"

"Here?"

"With a man."

"I'm not a virgin."

"That's not what I'm asking."

"Then I don't understand."

No, he thought, she probably didn't. "What did he want from you?" he asked.

"He?"

Griffin did not like to think what that meant, but he persevered. "They, then. What did *they* want from you?"

"They did not want to talk."

"I'm sure they did not," he said, "but it is not quite an answer to my question, is it?"

"They liked me to be quiet," she told him. "That is mostly what they wanted. It was becoming, they said, that I should be quiet."

"Christ."

She simply stared at him, waiting for him to continue in whatever manner he chose. She remembered clearly that it was what he required from her.

"What else?" he asked.

"They liked me to undress before I came to bed." She shrugged a bit uneasily. "Sometimes they helped me. Sometimes they watched."

That, at least, he could understand. "Was there nothing else?"

"No." She did not, would not, speak of the hot, labored breathing or the heavy hand that was sometimes clamped over her mouth when she was unable to be becomingly quiet. Of her own volition she did not tell him these things. What she *could* not speak of was the agony of waiting to be called forward, to be held for examination, the perfect dread of failure to please and its consequences. "No," she repeated on a thread of sound. "There was nothing else."

Griffin remained silent for a long moment, weighing what she'd said against what he'd already learned at her hands. "Were you willing?" he asked.

It was true that she'd gone easily that first time, led by her greed as blindly, even eagerly, as a beggar in want of a few coppers. That was what he was asking, she thought, and how she would answer him. He did not want to know that she'd never gone without a struggle after that, even if she was the only one to observe it. So often the struggle happened only inside her.

"I was willing," she said.

"And now?"

"I came to your bed, did I not? That speaks to willingness."

Griffin wasn't at all certain that it did. "You will have to convince me." He saw the edges of her mouth turn down and knew that she didn't understand. "Never mind. I'll know the truth of it soon enough."

Lowering his mouth to hers, he teased her lips open with the edge of his tongue. He nibbled, feasted, sucked. He angled his mouth differently, tasted her again. He drew a sound from the back of her throat and savored it as he did the kiss. He set his teeth against the cord in her neck and sipped on her flesh. Come full light, there would be a mark upon her skin here to match those at her wrist and breast. The difference, though, would be in the intent with which they were made. He'd held her wrists to restrain her, but he suckled at her neck to restrain himself.

His mouth was hot across her skin, but it had nothing in common with the other mouths she had known, the other heat that had scalded her. What Griffin was doing to her was drawing her out, not forcing her inside. Olivia was not certain she wanted to be so exposed. She could have stripped away her shift earlier and stood before him and not have been as naked as she felt now.

She'd thought if she came to his bed she might seize the moment and have ownership of what would happen between them. *In a manner of my choosing*. Those should have been the words she'd spoken. Instead, he had said them and she had agreed.

Olivia surrendered another sound, almost unrecognizable

as something that could have come from her, and she was frightened by it. She bit into her lower lip as his mouth closed over her breast. The flick of his tongue across her nipple was unexpected. Her flesh beaded as if she were inviting him to roll it between his lips. It required only a hint of pressure before her skin flushed with heat.

She thrust her fingers into his thick hair. She meant to tug on it, pull him away, yet what she did was lace her hands at the back of his head and cradle him so he would not move too quickly.

She needn't have worried. His tongue laved her aureole, licking, darting, treating himself and her to the hot suck of his mouth. She didn't recognize pleasure for what it was at first. The intensity was so sweetly sharp that what she felt was akin to pain. Pain was familiar. She could have embraced pain and kept her silence. What Griffin was doing to her made unbecoming sounds whistle through her teeth and rasp noisily from the back of her throat.

He never once urged her to be quiet.

His mouth gave attention to her other breast, and she held him there for a time, arching once to present more of herself to him and wondering with that small part of her that still had presence of mind if she might be struck down for it.

The covers shifted across his back as he slipped lower. Her hands unthreaded and fell to his shoulders. She plucked at the linen fabric of his nightshirt, wanting nothing so much as to feel his skin against her palms.

He reared up, shook off the covers, and yanked his nightshirt over his head. It tangled in his arms and he swore, fighting with it, and that was when he heard the most surprising sound from Olivia.

Her laughter.

It was small. And strangled. It was also unmistakable.

Griffin came out from under the nightshirt and stared at her. She smiled a bit unevenly, clearly embarrassed, then lifted her hands and helped him remove the shirt. She was the one who flung it away. It sailed over the side of the bed, and before it touched the floor, she'd flung her arms around his neck and held on.

His kiss was hard with need. He was impatient. Hungry. She was glad of it because it matched something inside of her—a need, an impatience, a hunger that was wholly unfamiliar to her. She was depending upon him to show her the way, and if she became afraid, to make her feel less so.

She met his kiss, reveled in it. Her arms circled his back as he moved over her. His fingers had tunneled into her hair. She felt the press of them against her scalp. He was devouring her mouth with his own. Their tongues circled, retreated, circled again. They separated to gulp air and when they came together a second time, he was planting kisses on her cheeks, her jaw, and over her closed eyes.

She fought him a little, but only so that she might lay claim to some part of his countenance. She kissed the corners of his mouth, rubbed her lips against the stubble of his beard, and traced the thin line of his scar with the tip of her tongue. She liked hearing his breath come unevenly and the sensation of his heart stuttering.

His skin was smooth, his shoulders taut. The muscles of his back shifted and bunched under her fingertips. She had never held a man in such a way before, never as a partner, an equal. The curling of desire was uncomfortable. Foreign. For a moment she felt a little sick with it, then it passed as he cupped her bottom and lifted her. Just then she could think of nothing save the heaviness of him pressing against her.

He split her thighs. She raised her knees and dug her heels into the mattress. She sucked in a breath, waiting for him to pull back just enough to make his first thrust. She closed her eyes. She could bear this, she thought. With this man, she could make herself bear it.

"Olivia." He said her name softly, drawing her out of her

self-imposed darkness. "Look at me. It's Griffin. Do you know that?"

She nodded. "Griffin."

He was absurdly pleased she'd said his name. Not Breckenridge. Not my lord. He kissed her lightly on the lips, surprising them both with the gentleness of it, then he lifted his hips and slowly pushed into her.

She was better able to accommodate his entry this time. She was damp, if not wet. He measured his thrust carefully, feeling his way by watching her eyes. The centers of them darkened, widened, then remained that way, a perfect onyx stone set within an emerald. Once he was seated, he held himself still. Her lower lip was faintly swollen. His kisses were not entirely responsible for that. She was pressing her teeth into it now, chewing on it. He stared at her, shaking his head slightly, and waited for her to release it before he began to move.

He willed himself to go slowly, take infinite care with her. Whatever she had known before him, it wasn't care. Her lashes fluttered but never entirely lay still. She watched him from beneath her shaded eyes, her head tilted back. The exposed, slender stem of her neck beckoned him. He kissed the hollow of her throat, tasted her skin along her bladed shoulder.

Her fingers tripped lightly down his back, riding the ridge of his spine. When he rocked, she held on.

"Lift for me," he whispered. When she did, he thrust more deeply, and then she was working with him, rising to meet his stroke, not merely holding, but participating. He knew the moment she felt the first twinge of pleasure, saw it when the twin creases of concentration disappeared between her eyebrows, heard it when her breath caught.

He wanted more for her than a hint of what might be, but his own crisis was nearing. He held back as long as he was able, feeling the strain of denial across the taut muscles in his back. His skin no longer fit him but seemed to have shrunk against his bones. When she raised a hand and touched his face, he imagined he might cut her with the sharpness of his cheek.

Her fingertips grazed his jaw, a faltering siren's smile edged her swollen mouth, and it was then that his body betrayed him. He ground against her one more time before his strokes came quick and shallow and a shudder took possession of his whipcord-lean frame.

Olivia skimmed the surface of pleasure; Griffin knew the depths of it.

He arched, stretching his coiled muscles as she seemed to contract around him. Her arms. Her legs. Even her mouth closed over him. There, where she held him most intimately, she was especially tight, and he was helpless to withdraw even if he had wanted to. He emptied himself into her.

Olivia expected that he would collapse against her, and she would have to accept the full weight of him. She tensed, preparing herself, then he surprised her again by lowering himself to his elbows and only sheltering her with his body.

He kissed her on the mouth, slowly, deeply, nudging her lips apart, tickling them with his teeth and tongue. It was the sweetly lazy kiss of a sated man, but it was outside Olivia's experience. When he drew back, she stared at him, wondering what was required of her now.

Griffin sighed, made regretful by what he saw in her face. He smoothed the worry lines across her brow with his fingertips. "There is nothing you must do," he told her. "Save sleep, if you like."

He watched her nod and felt her relax a fraction, though her eyes remained alert and mildly wary. Easing out of her, Griffin rolled to one side and lay on his back. He placed a forearm across his eyes and allowed himself a moment to bask in the lethargy that came after such intense pleasure. Almost immediately he felt her stir beside him. Without lifting his arm, he asked, "What are you doing?"

"Looking for my nightgown." Unaware of his scowl, she continued patting down the covers in search of the article. When she didn't find it, she slid to the edge of the bed and groped outside the covers along the floor.

"Why do you need it?"

The question seemed absurd to her, the answer obvious. "I am naked."

With his free hand, Griffin found the curve of her hip under the bedclothes and laid his hand there. "So you are, as am I. I fail to see that it presents a problem."

Olivia sat up, dragging the blankets with her. She noticed that her movement did not dislodge his hand. The shaft of rosy dawn light that slipped between the drapes was sufficient for her to look about. She spied her shift on the floor, most of it bunched under the bed. Conscious of Griffin's hand, she managed to slip one leg out of bed, snag the gown with the toe of her foot, and kick it high enough to snatch it out of the air.

"Impressive," Griffin said dryly.

Olivia glanced over at him, but his forearm was once more in place like a blindfold. As soon as she began to raise the shift to slip it over her head, she felt his hand leave her hip. It snaked outside the covers and was presented to her palm up like a platter.

"Give it to me."

"I did not perform the acrobatics for your amusement," she said. "It was all in aid of recovering my gown."

"I'm quite sure it was. Nevertheless, give it to me."

That he expected she would surrender it so easily galled her. That she did so, galled her more.

He pitched the nightgown over his side of the bed, well outside her reach, then he put out his palm again. "Your robe, also."

She had hoped he'd forgotten it. It lay bunched at the foot of the bed where he had tossed it after helping her out of it. She did a little flutter kick under the covers and managed to make the robe jump in her direction. When it was close enough, she caught it with her fingertips and dragged it toward her and passed it directly on to him.

With his forearm still in place, he did precisely the same thing with it as he'd done with her nightgown. "Come," he said, patting the space beside him. "Lie down."

Olivia was not so quick to obey this time. "You said I might sleep if I wished."

"Of course."

"But I prefer to do so in my own bed."

"That presents a bit of a dilemma, don't you think?" Now he lifted his arm just enough to give her the benefit of his darkly wry look. "Since I prefer that you do so here."

Unhappy, and too weary to shield it from him, she asked gravely, "Am I to have no say?"

Griffin would not allow himself to be swayed by what he glimpsed in her face. She did not need to be alone just now, no matter that it was her preference. He knew the look of someone bent on tormenting herself with second thoughts and recriminations. He'd seen it often enough in his own reflection. "You have had your say, have you not? And I have had mine. It is a disagreement, but given the fact that I have already confiscated your gown and your robe, I think it will be settled in my favor. Now, lie down, close your eyes, and appreciate your own victory."

"My victory?" She burrowed under the covers, though not in the space just beside him. Turning on her side, she drew up her knees protectively. "What nonsense."

Griffin finally let his arm fall away from his eyes and cast her a sideways glance. "If you will but recall, it was you who wanted to have done with it. And so we are."

She was glad for the relative darkness that concealed the heat in her cheeks. Still, she heard herself remark with considerable coolness, "It was you who put forth the terms, I believe."

"So that a small measure of dignity might be preserved."

Olivia flushed more deeply, remembering how she'd grasped his cock and parted her thighs for him. He must be referring to his own dignity because she'd already proved she had none.

Griffin reached for her, laying his fingertips across her cheek. Her skin was warm. "You're blushing."

She flinched, trying to escape his touch. He was already too often plucking the thoughts from her head; she did not appreciate him testing the waters by touching her face.

Griffin withdrew his hand but only reluctantly. He would have liked to drag his thumb across her lower lip. He turned fully to face her and punched the pillow under his head to find the most comfortable incline. Once he'd settled back and his eyes could rest on her again, he found himself moved by the sorrow of her expression. "What is it, Olivia?"

Afraid she might weep, she sucked in her bottom lip and shook her head.

"Will you tell me nothing?"

This time when she shook her head, she was able to offer a brief, watery smile.

"Poor Olivia," he said gently. "It has all been rather too much, has it not? Or perhaps in some manner, not nearly enough."

Confused now, the space between her eyebrows bore twin creases. He posed a riddle she could not hope to answer. "I don't know what you mean."

That did not astonish. "You gave a great deal and received nothing in return."

Olivia recalled the sweet, swift pleasure that had slipped under her skin and made every part of her tingle. Just thinking about the sensation brought it flooding back. "Hardly nothing," she whispered. Her eyes darted away from his as she pressed her legs together. She could still feel him there, inside her. Involuntarily, she contracted as though to hold him, and her eyes closed briefly as an echo of pleasure shivered through her.

Watching her, Griffin felt a powerful surge of lust. He pressed his hands into fists to keep from pulling her to him. He did not trust himself to take her with the regard she deserved, not when his blood was hot and his cock was once again at a full stand. What he wanted was her and his own satisfaction. They were irrevocably joined in his mind, one with the other. Neither alone.

"You should sleep," he said when he could trust his voice.

Olivia nodded, but when Griffin turned over, giving her his back, she simply stared at him. She had been so certain he wouldn't leave her alone, and yet that seemed to be precisely his intent. What purpose, then, was served by remaining in his bed?

She had only begun to ease herself out from under the covers when his rough, rumbling voice came to her.

"Don't do it."

Olivia fell asleep entertaining the rather odd notion that Griffin Wright-Jones possessed eyes at the back of his head.

Griffin tossed a few coins onto the street and watched the children scatter before he drew back from the window. It was a cold morning, with a brisk wind, and he'd already let too much it into the room. When he glanced at the bed only the ginger crown of Olivia's head was visible outside the covers.

He snapped open the paper young Fitz had thrown up to him. The boy had a good arm, and given a chance at a proper education would make a fine bowler. Fitz, though, like all of his friends, was unlikely to ever walk the cobbled paths at Hambrick Hall, Eton, or Harrow. The one time Griffin had suggested such a thing to the boy's whore-mother, she'd accused him of being a pederast. Apparently she could not fathom his interest in her child as being other than the most perverse.

It had been his last attempt at social reform.

He sat at the table, opened the *Gazette,* and lowered it just enough that from time to time he could observe the shifting lump in his bed that was Olivia Cole. It was considerably fortunate that she was not in need of social reform. He'd already proven by making her his mistress that he hadn't the least notion of how to go about it.

He began to read, starting with the news out of the parliament, then to the murder du jour, a particularly nasty piece of work perpetrated against two prostitutes in a Holborn hovel. He turned to the editorial page before his appetite was completely disrupted. Folding the paper in quarters, he laid it down beside his plate and uncovered a platter of toast and bacon. He helped himself to both, poured some coffee, then set a soft-cooked egg in a cup and gave it a satisfying thwack with the bowl of his spoon.

He peeled back the shell and dipped a finger of toast in the warm, viscous yolk. "Was it the smell of the bacon or the coffee that roused you to wakefulness?"

Olivia peered at him over the top of the blankets. "It was the crushing blow you delivered to that egg."

Griffin tapped his left ear with his fingertip as he bit off one end of the toast. He chewed with obvious relish, swallowed, and then spoke. "I can't hear you if you don't speak up."

Olivia poked her chin above the covers. She didn't repeat herself because she didn't believe for a moment that he hadn't heard her. Her eyes fell greedily on the spread before him and her stomach actually growled. She caught his grin because he made no effort to suppress it. "You heard that easily enough," she said.

He shrugged. "I am more attuned to some sounds than others. Would you like something? You will notice that there is a place set for you."

So there was. She had only seen the food. "I need a moment."

"Have as many as you like."

"No, I mean, mmm, I need . . . *a moment*." She glanced

significantly toward his dressing room. "You've been awake longer than I have." Indeed, he looked rested and very much in his element. Although he still wore his nightshirt, he'd covered it with a loosely belted silk robe, the silver-blue color of a frozen lake. He'd had time to shave, wash the sleep from his eyes, and brush back his hair—though the effect of this last was mostly gone as he'd plowed it several times with his fingers. "Please?" she asked when he continued to regard her blankly. "A moment?"

God, but she was lovely. Sleep-tousled. Flushed. Wide, imploring eyes almost too big for her face. Griffin blinked. "You want privacy," he said flatly. "Of course. Make free with my dressing room."

His obtuseness compelled her to point out, "I want privacy to get to your dressing room."

He looked from the bed to the dressing room door and back to the bed again. Mrs. Christie would have been pleased to parade her particulars twice that far. It was borne home to him that he had not clearly seen any of Olivia's particulars, and the stubborn set of her features warned him that he would not see them now.

"Your nightgown and robe are beside you," he said, pointing. He reached for a rasher of bacon and his cup of coffee before he pushed away from the table and turned his chair to face the window. "Run. I cannot promise I will avert my head for more than a few seconds." Grinning, he heard her scrambling to throw off the covers and retrieve her clothes. There was a small, one-two thump as her feet dropped over the side of the bed. The rush of those same feet across the floor could only be described as a scamper.

Oh, but he was tempted. He held himself in check until he judged she had almost reached the door. Swiveling, he caught sight of a deliciously naked back and the upper curve of her bottom before she disappeared into his dressing room dragging most of the bed linens behind her.

"I peeked," he called to her.

Olivia poked her head out as she made a grab for the door handle. "You have no shame."

"I never said I did."

She blew upward, targeting a strand of fiery ginger hair that had fallen diagonally across her forehead and right eye. It fluttered to one side and revealed her determined gleam as she hitched the blankets around her and lunged for the door again. She might have closed it on this attempt if it hadn't been thwarted by her own trappings. Ignoring Griffin's chuckle, she yanked on the blankets blocking the door, sweeping them aside, and slammed the thing shut.

"Temper, temper." He thought she might have sworn at him, but the sound of it was muffled by the door and the fact that he was chewing on a crisp bit of bacon. He was glad she had recovered her wits. She would need them about her for what he had planned.

Breakfast first, though. It was only fair.

Chapter Nine

Griffin waited until Olivia finished her cup of hot cocoa and daintily dabbed at the faint chocolate outline that defined her upper lip before he bore her off to bed. He had never before experienced breakfast as foreplay but that was what it was. It occurred to him belatedly that he may have been the only one to realize it, because when he seized her by the arms and hauled her out of her chair she was struck dumb.

She recovered by the time he tossed her on the bed and followed her down with his own body. Her accents were charmingly outraged. "My lord! It is daylight."

He did not so much as glance toward the window where earlier he'd parted the drapes. "You cannot object to daylight. It is the natural order of things." He rubbed his lips against hers. "Night followed by day. As clever as it is simple." He kissed her, first attending to her bottom lip, then repositioning his mouth and giving equal attention to the upper one. Somewhere during the transition she'd stopped squirming and sighed a bit gently. He was pleased when her arms came around him, though he had liked the squirming well enough.

Her kisses tasted like sweet, warm cocoa. She surrendered them as one drugged—slowly, thickly, with infinite care. He decided then that she could have cocoa at every meal if she liked, but that he would insist that it be served at breakfast.

Olivia sensed the change in the shape of his mouth. She pushed at his shoulders so that he would raise his head. "You are smiling," she whispered once she could see him clearly. "Why are you smiling?"

"You cannot expect that I will enumerate all the reasons now." He bent his head and touched his lips to hers again, then drew up and kissed the tip of her pared nose, between her eyebrows, and finally the center of her forehead. When he lifted his head and looked down at her, he saw she would not be moved. His smile actually deepened.

"Oh, very well, you may have your secrets," she said as though she hadn't just been made breathless by the wicked curve of his lips. Her fingers threaded in his hair, tugged, and brought him to her mouth once again.

Olivia hadn't expected to want him. When he'd picked her up and carried her to his bed, she had thought of nothing save that she would be made to suffer his touch in the full light of day. It wasn't until he placed his mouth over hers that she reconciled to the fact that there had been no suffering the night before and there would be none now. She was yet undecided if that were necessarily good.

She'd been aware of his eyes on her while she ate. They often fell on her mouth, which made her think she had a crumb on her lips. That made her touch the tip of her tongue to the corner of her mouth, which had the effect of making his eyes narrow a fraction. Believing that her manners were not up to the standard he set for his table, she raised her serviette several times to remove the offending bit of toast and invariably came away with nothing on the linen. She'd run her tongue along her teeth then, thinking perhaps a bit of bacon was lodged between them. That had only made his eyes darken somewhat dangerously, and Olivia fully anticipated that she would be asked to remove herself. She used what was available to hide her mouth and raised her cup of hot cocoa and sipped it as delicately as she could from lips she pressed into a perfect bow.

It was then that he looked as if he might come across the table at her.

Of course he did, but not in the way she had imagined.

Now she was under him, though not exactly, because he kept himself from trapping her with the whole of his body and took most of his weight on one hip, thigh, and elbow. He had done the same last night, she remembered, and she'd thought it had been considerate of him even then. As impossible as it seemed, she felt sheltered, not suffocated.

Her fingers twisted in his hair. She was not certain what she might do with her hands that would please him, while he seemed to have no such reservations. His hands were very busy, had been since the moment he fell onto the bed, and everywhere he touched pleased her. She had not suspected it could be done.

How had she not known of the spot just behind her earlobe that was so sensitive to touch that her skin pebbled? Or that brushing the inside of her upper lip could make her breath hitch? She had lived inside her skin for four and twenty years and knew less about what made her body thrum than Griffin had discovered in one night and a morning.

She moaned softly, tried to bite it back, then moaned again when he bent to take her breast a second time. He'd actually grinned as he lowered his head, watching her all the while, well pleased it seemed as her body betrayed its need and rose in offering.

He suckled her through the cotton shift, changing the texture of the fabric as it became wet and slightly more abrasive. Her breast swelled, the nipple hardened. He tugged on it with his lips, and she felt cords of pleasure being pulled between her thighs. He was changing the texture of her there as well; she was already something more than damp.

Olivia tugged at his nightshirt, drawing it up at the shoulders. Curious about him, she walked her fingers down his back, then allowed them to glide sideways at his hip. The faint hollow intrigued her, but the taut curve of his buttocks was where her hand found a perfect fit. She heard him groan softly against her breast when she squeezed.

She had no time to relish this small proof of her power to move him because he was engaged in new exploration. His interest in her breasts was all about diversion. His fingertips had found an opening between her knees and were now sliding purposefully along her inner thigh. She slammed her legs closed, trapping his hand, but it did not serve her in the least. He contented himself with teasing her other breast and in time she felt her thighs simply ease apart with no urging from him.

She tensed again when his fingers reached most intimately between her legs, but that is where his foray stopped. He simply cupped her mons while his mouth released her nipple and moved upward, lingering at her neck, then her jaw, and finally coming to rest against her lips. He licked, parted them with his tongue, and drew a whimper from her as she felt heat stir in her belly.

Another diversion, she discovered, because his fingers were suddenly inside her, probing, sliding. She tore her mouth away from his, gasping, and pushed at his shoulder, but only to give herself something to brace as her body lifted in a perfect arch.

She thought she might actually scream as pleasure flung her upward, but she swallowed it along with the breath she was holding right up to the moment Griffin's thumb found the hard kernel of flesh between her damp lips and rubbed. That was when she simply came out of herself.

This was no prickly pleasure skimming the surface of her skin. What she felt began deep inside and radiated outward, spinning, sparking, turning what was a warm glow into heat and light of an intensity she had never known before, one she had not suspected existed.

Watching her, feeling her shudder, knowing he had finally given her the fullness of pleasure she had been denied last night, Griffin delayed his own satisfaction in favor of enjoying hers. Her eyelids dropped to half-mast, her kiss-swollen lips parted, a flush rose from the neckline of her gown to steal over her complexion. She stared at him, though the look was more vague than pointed, her dark eyes not quite focused on any particular feature. He smiled, bringing her attention to his mouth, then he lowered his head slowly and kissed her at his leisure.

When he drew back, their lips parted with a damp little sucking sound that made him chuckle but discomfited Olivia. He saw her distress and tempered his amusement, moving more to one side as her fingers worked somewhat nervously on rearranging the hem of her nightgown.

"I find you are unexpectedly modest," he said. "No matter. It is rather charming."

"It is not an affectation."

"I didn't think it was. The affectation is when you pretend otherwise." He tapped her lips with his forefinger when she would have objected. "It was not long ago that I asked you if you were a whore. You didn't blink or blush then. In fact, I recall precisely what you said. You—"

Olivia talked around the finger that was still lightly pressed to her lips. "I said I had given you enough reason to think it. Really, can I depend on you to echo our every conversation?"

"When it's pertinent, yes." He removed his forefinger to tap the tip of her nose.

She brushed his hand aside. "It is annoying, you know, to have to reflect upon one's words at a moment of your choosing."

"Quite possibly true, but there you have it. So why is it so important to you to pretend one thing when you are altogether something else?"

"Why does anyone?"

"I am not asking about anyone. I want to know why you do it."

She shrugged, looked away. "Fear, I imagine."

He considered that. "What are you afraid of?"

"You cannot expect I will answer that."

"I can, but I won't insist."

"You wouldn't answer it."

"I might."

Olivia took the bait he dangled and dared to ask the same question he'd put to her. "What are you afraid of?"

"Why you, of course, but I mean to overcome it."

What he did, Olivia realized when she could breathe evenly again, was overcome her.

The faro table was crowded with punters, and for the first time, Olivia was truly at her ease facing them. She hadn't realized how much anxiety she'd felt on every other occasion until she experienced the absence of it. Griffin, too, was less often at her side, though not by any means less attentive. He did not pass through her gaming room without taking surreptitious measure of the gentlemen surrounding her table and judging their potential threat to her.

The arrival of a half dozen students not long after midnight caused her some concern, but when their manner toward her hovered between respect and reverence she comprehended that Griffin had taken them in hand before they ever reached her table. She hardly knew whether to be offended or grateful for his interference and concluded that she was a bit of both.

"I would have dealt with them, you know," she told him after Mason had been sent in to spell her at the table.

Griffin slipped his arm in hers and led her toward the unoccupied stairs leading up to their private rooms. It was quieter here, just off the hallway where patrons mingled, drank, and laughed until they settled on another game of chance. At a halfway point, he drew her down on the step so they were neatly tucked between the wall and the banister.

"I prefer you only deal with the cards," he said, releasing her so that he might rest his elbows on the stair behind him. He stretched his legs casually at an incline and glanced sideways at her, giving her benefit of a charmingly sheepish grin. "If you'll forgive the wordplay."

"I suppose it is your experience to be forgiven all manner of things. It is your smile that puts others at a disadvantage."

"Really? And I'd so hoped it was my wit and the soundness of my arguments."

"Let us say you are not altogether foolish."

His grin actually deepened. "Pray, you must stop thinking so highly of me, else I am bound to disappoint you."

Olivia had an urge to poke him with her elbow. She restrained herself, but only just. "What nonsense you speak. What are we doing here?"

"Stealing a moment for ourselves."

"Oh." Olivia thought he might kiss her, and she wondered if she wanted him to, but he remained exactly as he was. She worried her bottom lip, trying to unravel his meaning as if he'd spoken in code. Did he expect that she would kiss him? "What does one do with a stolen moment?"

"Sometimes nothing at all."

She approved of that. To mimic his posture, as it seemed pertinent to doing nothing at all, Olivia set her elbows behind her and reclined at an angle parallel to Griffin's. "It's a fine idea."

"A fishing pole and a swiftly running stream would improve it."

She nodded, though she wasn't as convinced. "Do you have many opportunities to fish?"

"I did. Not so often now."

She waited, content with his silence, sensing that he might be moved to reflect if she did not speak too soon.

"The park at Wright Hall has such a stream. The water is clear and cool, and runs so quickly there is always a pleasant roar in one's ears. Sunlight slips through the trees overhead and turns every spray into a translucent rainbow and every droplet into a diamond. The trout leap like acrobats and tease like coquettes. The most experienced anglers are patient and appreciate the performance. Some find it spiritual."

"Did you?"

"There were times, yes."

"And now you are in London."

"I am."

This time her silence did not prompt him to speak. "I have never fished," she said. "Although I like smoked trout well enough, but perhaps that is not spiritual."

"It can be." He winked at her. "It is all in the preparation."

Olivia's smile was rather winsome. "I think I will try fishing someday."

"Then you will want to know that using feathers from a lady's bonnet to make your own flies is ill-advised."

"I imagine it depends on the lady's affection for the bonnet. Did it belong to one of your sisters?"

"My mother, and she had, in my opinion, an unnatural attachment to the thing."

"By 'an unnatural attachment,' I take it to mean she was actually wearing the bonnet when you plucked the feathers."

"You are clearly too clever for your own good." He rose to his feet, then took her hand in his and helped her up. He kissed her once, briefly, warmly, and released her before it became something more. With no parting word, he tripped lightly down the steps and turned the corner into the hall.

Olivia pressed the back of her fingers to her lips and stared after him. Not so very clever, she thought, not when she hadn't the least notion of how to maintain her balance in his presence.

She slept alone that night and for a full sennight after that. It occurred to her to return to his room without invitation, but she remained in her own because except for the occasional kiss at oddly chosen moments, Griffin Wright-Jones hardly seemed to know she was still under his roof.

He was a curiosity. Olivia found herself studying him, rather more intrigued that he had set her from him since their night of intimacy than simply relieved by it. In her presence he often seemed mildly distracted so that she was never quite certain he was listening. It emboldened her at times, and she tested him, allowing small pieces of herself to drop like crumbs to see if he would sweep them up. He didn't. Such things as she told him were never commented upon; indeed, he often chose some other conversational thread to pull and let such bits as she gave him simply lie there.

In spite of Olivia approaching him several times in regard to his requirements, he had never shared them. Relying on trial and error and her own sense of what would be helpful, she became more involved in the nightly activities of the hell. She examined the cards for wear and recommended when decks should be discarded. She collected fallen chips and coins and passed them on to Beetle and Wick, who became her devotees because of it. When she asked Mason if she might propose some changes to the distribution of liquor and wine, he suffered her suggestions without comment, but implemented the whole of it the next evening.

They all came to her after that. It was as flattering as it was unexpected, although the part of her that retained a survivor's skepticism suspected Griffin's encouragement, if not outright manipulation of his staff.

While she had no access to the financial ledgers, she never

doubted that Griffin was scrupulously fair in his dealings with her. It required little effort on her part to estimate her table's winnings and calculate her share based on the percentage they'd agreed upon. She was never wrong by more than a few pounds as Griffin's more detailed calculations proved night after night.

He'd wanted to know how she was able to do it, but she had no explanation for it, nor any explanation for how she kept an account of the cards she'd dealt. Griffin had pointed out, quite correctly, that she could make even more money at faro as a punter rather than a dealer, but she had no interest in gaming as a participant.

It had not escaped her notice that he did not make any wagers in his own establishment and as far as she was able to discover, made none anywhere else. The former, she understood. It was the latter that gave her pause, and when she asked him about it, his answer was a terse, "If I wish to give my money away, I will choose a charity."

In spite of the late hours she was keeping, she woke most mornings before many of the staff. It was her habit to go to the servants' hall to carry back her breakfast tray, though either Beetle or Wick would have been pleased to deliver it. She would have preferred to eat with the staff, but comprehended very well they would have been made uncomfortable by her presence. It would have been that way whether or not they knew she'd been a visitor to their employer's bed. They simply accorded her a certain respect because of how they perceived her station relative to their own.

She often thought she should direct them to inquire of her father. Sir Hadrien would have been delighted to inform them she was no better than she ought to be. He'd made certain of it.

Olivia had removed her wig and was attending to her hair with punishing brushstrokes when she heard a staccato rap at her door. Her heartbeat tripped over itself as she set down the brush, and she felt a tightening in her chest. She could not imagine that it was anyone save Griffin expecting entry at this late hour, and above all things, she did not want it to be him.

She picked up a damp flannel and began removing the rouge, powder, and beauty mark she had lightly applied before she went below stairs to meet patrons at the faro table. The rapping at the door began again, this time a bit more insistently. She sighed. He would not be moved until she answered and perhaps not even then.

Olivia put aside the flannel and carried the candlestick with her into the bedroom. "Who is it?" she asked.

Griffin supposed it was a sensible enough question, but in his present mood it irritated him. "Breckenridge."

Olivia opened the door a few inches. "My lord?"

He scowled at her. "Will you not invite me in?"

"I'd rather not, unless you insist, then of course you may come in." She leaned into the opening and sniffed. "Are you foxed?"

He fiddled with the intricate knot of his cravat and impatiently removed it. "Fletcher was foxed. I was his victim." Dangling the offending article of clothing between his thumb and forefinger, he took a step back and indicated she should join him in the hall.

Olivia was on firmer footing where she was, but she did not want him to know that. She slipped out, holding the candlestick in front of her. "What is it?"

"I cannot find my error."

"I beg your pardon."

"My error. I cannot find it."

"And you think I have it?" There was sufficient light for her to see a muscle jump in his cheek. "Very well, you cannot be amused at this juncture. That is too bad for both of us, I think." She raised the candle a fraction higher to better observe his face. Strain was evident in the set of his jaw and the twin creases between his eyebrows, but Olivia was unconvinced that his problem of the moment was responsible for the weary tension she saw in the tightness around his mouth. "You will have to tell me something more than you cannot find your error. The nature of it would be a good place to begin."

"I cannot reconcile the accounts."

Olivia thought she might not be able to suppress the bubble of nervous laughter that came immediately to her lips, but she managed to choke it back and discreetly covered her mouth as she cleared her throat. "Perhaps if you wait until morning and review your records in a more rested frame of mind."

"You are supposing I will be able to sleep. I assure you, I will not."

"Have you tried?"

"There is no point. You may as well come with me."

Light flickered as Olivia's fingers tightened around the candlestick. For better than a sennight she had slept alone, quieting her nerves in anticipation of this moment, and now that it was upon her what she mostly felt was a deeply abiding disappointment, though she couldn't have said with whom she was disappointed more. If she had guarded herself better against hope, would his churlishly issued invitation have hurt her heart?

Olivia stepped outside herself, disengaging from any feeling at all. Numbness masqueraded as serenity. "Yes. Of course I will go with you."

She allowed Griffin to take the candlestick from her nerveless fingers and fell in step beside him. Aware that she was drawing only shallow breaths, Olivia wasn't surprised she felt a little light-headed when they reached the door to his bedroom. She slowed her steps.

He didn't.

Olivia stared at his back, then lengthened her stride to catch up with him. "I thought—" She didn't—couldn't—finish that sentence.

"You wish to say something?" he asked, glancing sideways.

She shook her head. "It's not important." Every part of her that had been numb was now awash in prickly feeling. It was as if the seat of all emotion had fallen asleep and pins and needles were the consequence of waking.

Griffin indicated she should precede him into his study and gestured vaguely toward his desk. A large ledger of accounts lay open in front of his chair. "You may sit there."

Olivia greeted this direction with suspicion, darting a look from him to the chair and back to him again. "At your desk?"

"Naturally at my desk. It is unlikely that you can work more comfortably elsewhere. The ledger is unwieldy if it is not lying flat."

"You wish me to examine your account book?"

He frowned. "You are not usually a slow top. Of course that is what I wish. Did I not say I couldn't find my error?"

"You did." She picked her way around the stacked books and over the discarded, crumpled pieces of paper lying on the rug and managed to maintain her grave demeanor as she seated her-self. Easing into the chair with Griffin's scent and the contour of his body captured in the soft, gently worn leather was unex-pectedly like being wrapped in his arms. She had an urge to draw her legs under her and curl in the cradle he'd unwittingly made for her. It was perhaps fortunate, she thought, that he came to stand directly behind her shoulder, which had exactly the opposite comforting effect.

Olivia looked up at him. "You mean to watch over me?"

In every sense. Griffin did not say it aloud, simply nodding instead.

"Very well." She leaned forward to take a proper look at the chart of accounts. In very little time she was able to forget his presence altogether.

Olivia had always been aware of the profit at the faro table, but she'd had no knowledge of what the other games brought in each night. One of her eyebrows kicked up as she reviewed the columns devoted to vingt-et-un, roulette, dice, and the private card games. Everything was recorded neatly in Griffin's meticulous hand. Each page, every column, revealed the faint tracing of his dry quill as he'd checked and rechecked his work.

After Olivia had examined the income, she turned to the expenditures. Once again, she lifted an eyebrow. She clearly saw the costs of operating the hell: the wages of the staff, their board, the liquor bill, the outlay for repair and replacement, and a host of incidentals, many of them recorded in a kind of code that she could not make out.

She picked up a quill but did not dip it in an inkwell. Much as he had done earlier, she used it to make small, nearly invisible ticks next to various items. "You have receipts for all of this?" she asked, pointing to the line for repairs.

"In the box there."

Nodding absently, Olivia continued her examination. Griffin turned a good profit, she noted, though she could not quite make out where it went save for that portion that he turned back over to the establishment. She imagined that accounted for his indecipherable codes. It was not her place to question anything unrelated to why he was asking her to review his work. She did, however, venture an observation.

"You are singularly mistrustful."

Griffin stared down at her bent head. Her long cascade of fiery curls tempted him to disregard his judgment and sink his hands into the flames. That would only serve to frighten her, which was the very thing he had been bent on avoiding this last week. To have her name him singularly mistrustful was rather like the accusation of the pot to the kettle. He hadn't mistaken her reluctance to go with him, nor missed the way her steps faltered when they neared his bedchamber. She would have gone with him if he'd led her there, he knew that, but it wasn't the manner in which he wanted her to come to him. He had been trying to provoke her interest if she had but the wit to know it.

"Why do you say so?" he asked, curious.

Olivia tapped the point of her quill against the ledger. "Because you do all of this yourself when you are perfectly able to employ someone. That strikes me as mistrustful. You do not administer the affairs of your estate in such a fashion."

"How do you know?"

"Because you are always here. You must engage the services of a steward or a secretary, someone who oversees the rents and income of Wright Hall and your other properties. They would be sadly neglected otherwise, and it stretches the imagination to suppose you tend to your affairs here with such diligence while allowing every other thing to go begging." She lifted her head and caught her hair in one hand, sweeping it aside as she turned to look over her shoulder at him. A small vertical crease appeared between her eyebrows as she considered what she'd just said. "I don't suppose I can have it both ways, can I? If you are by nature mistrustful then it does not follow that you would allow anyone else to manage your other properties, not if you value them as—"

"Perhaps you are simply wrong," he said, interrupting.

Shaking her head, she turned a bit more in her chair and hit upon the truth she had not seen before. "This is your income, isn't it? The hell is almost the whole of it. You operate this establishment because it is the lifeblood for all that came before, the bastard child that supports the family's rank and privilege."

Griffin stepped back from the chair. His hands fell to his side. For a moment he did nothing save breathe, then his fingers curled into fists and he nodded once. "It is known to only a few," he said quietly. "You understand that it would . . ." His voice trailed away. He would not ask for her silence. She did not owe him that. He avoided her hand when she would have reached for him in spite of the fact that he had wanted nothing so much as her unsolicited touch since she'd left his bed. Her touch. Not her pity.

Unfolding his hands, Griffin walked to the fireplace and poked at the flames. He did not hear her cross the floor, only sensed her presence when she was standing just behind his right shoulder.

"How did it happen?" she asked.

He shrugged, his attention on the fire. "In the usual way of such things. A long line of heirs dedicated to living outside their means. Bad investments. Failure to respect the land or the needs of the tenant farms. Committing too little money to the property. Daughters requiring dowries. Sons acquiring gaming debts, Bon Street creditors, and mistresses." He set the poker in its stand. Words came then that were reluctantly given. "Sons acquiring wives who vowed for richer or poorer but could not accept that they must live in reduced circumstances."

"Your wife?" asked Olivia. "Was she such a one?"

"My mother, actually. My wife made other promises."

Olivia did not venture a second question regarding her ladyship. To do so felt extraordinarily self-serving. "Is your mother living?"

He shook his head. "She died seven years ago, only a few months after I came into possession of this hell. There are those who say my decision to operate the establishment contributed to her death, though they are kind enough to only whisper it my presence."

She wondered if he whispered the same to himself. It would not surprise her if he did. He was not the sort of man who shifted responsibility. "Mason told me your father died some ten years back."

"He did." Griffin glanced back at Olivia for the first time. "Did he tell you how?"

"No. He regretted his momentary lapse in protecting your privacy."

"He would, though unlike my financial circumstances, the manner of my father's death is widely known among the ton." He did not miss the shadow that crossed Olivia's features and wished he had not phrased it in a way that underscored her exclusion from that circle. "He was called out for cheating. I believe a great deal of brandy had been consumed and there was also the matter of a slight toward Lord Ashcroft's wife. Ashcroft took my father to task, swords instead of pistols, and skewered him in front of his seconds and the estimable Dr. Pettibone."

"Then your father's cheating was—"

"At cards," Griffin said flatly. "Although adultery has been mentioned in some versions of the story. It depends on the mood of the wags as to whether it arises in conversation."

"It cannot have been an easy time for you or your family."

Griffin was quiet, reflecting. "No, it was not."

Olivia regarded his strong profile bathed in firelight. His scar was not visible to her at the angle she observed him, but the tic in his cheek was. For all the blunt speech, he was not indifferent to his father's passing, nor his mother's for that matter. She inched closer but remembered that he had avoided her earlier and did not try to touch him now.

"How did you come to take possession of the hell?"

"I won it."

"Oh."

"At faro. Wright Hall was my marker. This Putnam Lane property was the owner's." His lips lifted in a humorless half smile. "Did you think I never made a wager?"

She shook her head. "You might have lost everything."

"I bet the turn."

Olivia could hardly believe what he was telling her. Betting the turn meant he'd wagered he could correctly call the order in which the last three cards of the deal would appear. "I repeat: you might have lost everything. You had only a one in six chance of calling the turn of those cards."

"It paid five to one."

"I know what it pays. Did you value your home and lands so little?"

"I wagered the house, not the lands. I was not entirely foolish, and Wright Hall was in a sad state at the time."

"Still . . ." She let her thoughts go unspoken, certain he'd heard a great many lectures and second guessing regarding what could have been his folly.

"I won," he reminded her, following the turn of her mind. "That counted for something, though no one was prepared for me to manage the hell, least of all my mother and my wife. But I saw the possibility of finally being done with the creditors, restoring Wright Hall to its former grandeur, and making all the properties prosperous again. Exposing my reputation to another layer of tarnish seemed little enough in the way of cost."

"Your accounts suggest that you have a successful business here."

"I do. I've beaten back most of the creditors. Wright Hall will always be the work of a lifetime as it should have been for my father and grandfather. As for the properties, they are producing income again, though not yet in a manner that will support all that must still be accomplished." Griffin turned entirely to face her. "There are always unexpected expenses, losses that cannot be recovered."

Olivia nodded a bit jerkily, embarrassed at the reminder of her role in both what was unexpected and unrecoverable.

"You take it all too much to heart," Griffin said, watching her. "I was speaking of neither the damage to your room nor your brother's debt. There is expense and loss that has little enough to do with this establishment. My sisters, all three of them, needed to make good marriages if they were to be properly protected. Arranging those was no simple matter, not when our father had died in such an ignominious fashion. My mother insisted that each one of them have generous settlements to avert suspicion from our true financial state. Some of the best properties were discreetly sold to provide for them, and I am only now in a position that I might be able to purchase them back."

"Do your sisters know?"

"I couldn't say. I've never told them, and they've never mentioned it to me. They do not approve of my activities here, if that is what you are asking."

Olivia supposed that it was. His isolation was not so dissimilar to hers. She had not realized that until now. It occurred to her that his sisters didn't want to know the true cost of their good marriages. If they suspected, they avoided confirmation by never asking the question directly. Olivia understood that. There were questions she was avoiding as well.

She distracted herself by looking back at the desk. Reconciling the accounts seemed more important just now. "I should return to my work. I have not yet examined the receipts." She turned to go and never knew that Griffin's hand had come within a hairsbreadth of restraining her.

She went through the receipts carefully, checking her figures against Griffin's. He was no longer hovering at her shoulder, but had cleared a space for himself on the edge of the desk and set a hip there while he observed her. Nothing she'd heard caused her to revise her opinion that he was mistrustful, but she better understood the reason for it.

Olivia returned the quill to its stand, stoppered the ink well, and sat back. She closed her eyes, rubbed them with her thumb and middle finger, and almost sighed at how good it felt to relieve the pressure building behind them.

"You're done?" he asked. "You found it?"

She nodded and pointed vaguely in the direction of the ledger. She heard Griffin slide it across the desk toward him. Opening her eyes a fraction while she massaged her temple, she said, "It is the easiest error to make and the most difficult to find. You simply transposed some numbers. Not once, but twice. It speaks to your diligence that it does not happen more often. These accounts are the sort of thing that should be done with a clear mind, not one that has been fogged by obscenely late hours, tobacco, perfume, and drink."

"There was very little drink," he offered mildly. "Which receipts were the problem?"

"The carpenter and cook's accounting of the greengrocer."

Griffin found both and compared their totals to what he had entered in his ledger. Although he never doubted Olivia was correct, he needed to observe the nature of the mistake for himself. Seeing it, he shook his head, impatient with himself for not finding it earlier. He chose a different quill than the one Olivia had used, dipped it in ink, and began making the corrections. "How is it that you know about charts of account?"

"I managed the household books for my brother."

Griffin shook his head, his smile gently mocking. "No, I don't think that explains the whole of it. The principles are the same, I'll grant you, but you followed the distribution easily enough and asked no questions. Your facility with numbers and your deft handling of the cards suggests to me that you are more than passingly familiar with the operation of an establishment such as this."

Olivia straightened and opened her eyes, alert and guarded now. "You must realize the absurdity of that. As you have pointed out on a number of occasions, I am the daughter of Sir Hadrien Cole. A man of his stature does not suffer his offspring, no matter how ill-favored they are, to be employed in that fashion."

"Assuming he learns of it, which I believe he did not." He paused in making corrections to tap Olivia's nose with the feathered tip of the quill in mild admonishment. "So which of my competitors did you work for? Dunlevy? Parsons? Never say it was Abernathy."

"I have no idea who those gentlemen are."

"Perhaps not, else you would know they are not gentlemen." Griffin resumed his calculations. "I will venture another guess and say that you were not dealing cards in any of the London hells. Bath? Bristol? Do they have hells in Bristol? It seems bloody unlikely."

"I wouldn't know. I have never been."

"You will have to give up your secrets eventually, Olivia."

"I have been honest with you."

His glance swiveled sideways. "I did not say you were less than honest, merely less than forthcoming."

Olivia considered that. The same might be said of him, but she elected not to point a finger in return. Instead, she surprised herself by inviting him to ask a question. "But only one," she said when his eyebrows rose and his eyes fairly gleamed with interest. "So think on that when you put your poser before me."

Griffin realized she'd effectively set him back on his heels. There was no one question that stood above the others, therefore he would have to review them all. He chuckled. "I should be used to the sharpness of your mind by now."

"Yes," she said. "You should."

And because she said it with the perfect proportions of seriousness and sauce, Griffin was moved to abandon his ledger, lean across the space that separated them, and drop a kiss on her slightly parted lips.

"What was that in aid of?" she asked when he drew back.

"Must there be a reason? Sometimes one simply wants to satisfy an impulse." He saw her frown, closed the ledger, and crossed his arms to regard her frankly. "Do you imagine we've done that already?"

She knew he was referring to their one night and morning together. It was the exact thought in her head as well. "I supposed that it must be so. You did not ask me to join you again."

"Again? I did not invite you to join me the first time."

That stung, but Olivia held her head up. "You did not send me away."

"No, I didn't, did I? Do you recall that you wanted to have done with it?"

Her words, held up to her once more. She released her breath slowly. "Naturally, I recall it."

"Can you not conceive that I might have wanted something more?"

"Something more? I allowed you to make free with me. If you want something else you must say it plainly, else how am I to know? I haven't your talent for reading minds."

Afraid he might pull her from his chair and shake her, Griffin stood and stepped away from the desk. "I want you to come to me of your own accord, not because you think it's some bloody requirement. When did I give you cause to think I held you in so little regard? I am not your brother, nor your father, nor apparently like any of the men of your acquaintance."

He saw her begin to shrink in her chair and reconsidered the last. Perhaps he was *exactly* like every other man she'd known. Bullying. Demanding. Selfish. He blew out a breath, disgusted with himself, and plowed his fingers through his disheveled hair. "That was unforgivable. I apologize."

Olivia's fingers remained firm on the chair's curved arms, pressed whitely against the leather. It kept her from shrinking farther into the chair, further into herself. She stared at him, dry-eyed, watchful.

Griffin was struck that she was seeing him through the eyes of a wounded child, one without hope, without spirit, and suddenly he knew the question he wanted her to answer. "Before you came to my room, Olivia, how old were you the last time you were in a man's bed?"

He thought she might flinch, but she was already too frozen to do that. Still, she answered him, though he had to strain to hear it.

"Twelve," she said. "I was twelve." Defiance covered the

wounds. "And though you did not ask, I will answer the companion question. I was six."

Griffin was the one who flinched.

Olivia heaved herself out of the chair. "You should have considered your question more carefully. There are some things that no one should know." She brushed past him and made a quiet, dignified exit.

Olivia woke with a head as thick as paste and thumping like a drum. Moaning softly, she pushed herself upright, though nothing was improved for it. She reached for the glass of water at her bedside and realized simultaneously that the thumping was not entirely in her head. She recognized Wick as the one industriously beating on her door. One could be forgiven for concluding there had been a general call to arms announced by Wellington himself.

He strode directly to the bed after she bid him enter. "His lordship requests your company at breakfast," he announced importantly. "He said I should tell you it would be a kindness to him."

Remembering how they parted, Olivia was uncertain if she wished to do him any kindness. Before she could decide, however, Wick was lining up her slippers and holding out her robe.

"He will have scones, miss. Cook made them fresh this morning. And he requested hot cocoa as well. That's to please you because he never drinks it when he's dining alone."

Griffin's strategy was obvious, but effective. Using Wick to deliver the message was probably his best tactic since Olivia did not like to think of sending the boy back to Griffin with her refusal. "Go," she said, waving him off. "Tell him I will be there shortly. Wait. Leave my robe. Thank you."

She joined Griffin a half hour later after performing her ablutions, braiding her hair, and choosing a simple hunter green day dress from her wardrobe. He was also dressed and looking very fine in a black frock coat and trousers, a pewter gray waistcoat, a startling white linen, and a precisely knotted neckcloth. He rose when she entered the bedroom suite and made a short bow. It was almost ridiculously formal, and it rather made her feel like weeping because he was trying so hard.

"Will you join me?" he asked when she hesitated just inside the doorway.

"Yes, of course." He held out a chair for her and eased her toward the table as she sat. "Thank you."

Griffin returned to his seat. "May I serve you?"

"Yes, if you like, but do not fill my plate. I haven't the appetite for it."

He wasn't surprised. Except for the transparent violet shadows beneath her eyes, her complexion was wan. It was obvious she had slept no better than he last night. He cut a warm scone in half, added a dollop of sweet butter, and placed it on her plate. He indicated the eggs, but she shook her head. He gave her a rasher of crisp bacon instead and poured a cup of cocoa for her.

It was only when she bit delicately into her bacon that he buttered the other half of the scone for himself. "I wonder if you will permit me to escort you on your daily walks. Mason will be devastated, of course, but I have had my fill of the green-eyed monster and wish to take a turn with you myself."

She blinked. Twice. She held the strip of bacon like a dart that she might toss at any moment.

Eyeing the bacon warily, Griffin continued. "I understand if you would prefer my valet's company. He has his faults, but prying into the affairs of others is not one of them."

Green-eyed monster? she wondered. He was *jealous* of Mason? He might have confessed to any number of failings more believable than that. But what if he'd meant it? "May I assume that you are done protecting my reputation?"

"At your peril. We can hardly put Miss Ann Shepard to rest, can we?" He paused a beat. "Honey."

"I so dislike the hairpieces," she said on a sigh.

Griffin had no liking for them either. Even confined in a braid, he preferred the natural, dramatic fire of her hair to the more conventionally colored wigs. "A necessary evil. There is still your father to consider."

Olivia understood much better now how Sir Hadrien could impede Griffin's financial recovery. Her father would do it, too, if her position in the hell became known publicly. All he had ever required of her was anonymity, and until she moved in with her brother, she'd never challenged him. "Very well," she said. "I am agreeable. Will you walk with me this morning?"

"I will. I shall have to inform Mason directly, but we can leave in—" He cocked his head toward the door, frowning at the interruption. "Go away."

Olivia hid her smile behind her hand when the door opened and Mason slipped through a narrow opening as though stealth would make his entry less disagreeable.

"It is Mr. Gardner, my lord," Mason said. "He begs a moment of your—"

The door opened wider. "Be clear, man, did you hear me beg? Do I look as if I'm begging?" Restell Gardner removed his hat and revealed a thatch of flaxen hair gilt with sunshine. He tore off his scarf, passed it and the hat to Mason, then removed his coat and gave it as well. "Tell him, Breckenridge, I do not—" He noticed Olivia for the first time. "Miss Cole. That is you, is it not? I did not realize you were here."

Olivia had never been introduced to Mr. Gardner during the brief time he managed the hell in Griffin's absence, so she was surprised that he not only recognized her, but knew her name. Griffin's trust in the gentleman must be absolute. "Mr. Gardner. It is a pleasure."

"It is not," said Griffin. "Not at all. What are you doing here at his ungodly hour?"

Restell Gardner strode into the room as Mason slipped out of it. He did not wait for Griffin to extend an invitation to sit, but dragged a chair over to the table and put himself in front of the platter of scrambled eggs. "May I? I have not yet been home, therefore I have not yet had my breakfast."

"By all means, help yourself. You have news, I take it. Finally."

"Finally? You wound me. I have been about your particular business only a fortnight and have concluded it far and away more satisfactorily than all of your hirelings before me."

"I didn't hire you. You are doing me a favor, remember?"

"As you will do for me." His eyes swiveled to Olivia, though the question in them was for Griffin.

"You may say whatever you've come to say in front of Miss Cole."

Restell Gardner's clear blue eyes went from questioning to speculative. "Very well, then," he said, lifting a forkful of eggs to his mouth. "It concerns Lady Breckenridge, of course. I have found her."

Chapter Ten

Mason accompanied Olivia on her late-morning walk, then again a few hours before the hell was opened for the patrons. He was unaware he'd been very close to being replaced as her walking companion. Olivia was glad Griffin had not gotten around to telling him. His countenance was visibly morose today, his mood leaning toward the same black humor as his employer's.

Olivia had politely excused herself upon hearing Mr. Gardner's news. She did not expect that Griffin would try to stop her, nor did he. For once he was not able to conceal every nuance of feeling. She observed surprise, but not shock; resignation, but no rejoicing. There was only an infinitesimal pause as he raised his cup of coffee to his lips, while she had not been able to breathe. It had been impossible to know what it all meant, and Griffin had not sought her out following Mr. Gardner's departure to explain. In fact, not long after his friend's exit, Griffin had also left and no one, not even Mason, knew when he might return.

Olivia prepared for dealing faro, though she was uncertain if Griffin would want her at the table if he weren't present. He might appreciate that she and his staff could operate the hell in his absence, or he might decide she had put herself in harm's way. As the time neared to open the doors and neither Griffin nor any of his trusted friends arrived to oversee the gaming, Olivia became aware that the staff was looking to her to make a decision.

Olivia had every confidence in their ability to manage the hell's tables; it was the hell's guests that concerned her. Who among them could assert calm, reason, and authority if the patrons proved difficult? It was not solely a matter of physicality. There were footmen hired specifically for their ability to escort unruly guests from the premises, but their particular skills were rarely on display because of Griffin's talent for defusing all manner of tense situations. She did not pretend she was possessed of that same talent, and even if she was, Olivia also recognized she would not be accorded the same respect.

Standing at the window of Griffin's study, Olivia could monitor the traffic as night settled on Putnam Lane. She was anticipating Griffin's last-minute arrival, but also trying to gauge how much income he would lose if they did not open. She watched a carriage slow in front of the hell and the driver make a nimble descent to assist the passengers. A gentleman alighted first, his manner somewhat stiff but thoroughly unobtrusive. Following him was a woman who could not help but call attention to herself with her expansive gestures and energetic stride. She wore a black velvet mantle trimmed in ermine and a hat sporting a veritable fountain of snow-white ostrich plumes. Her companion had to hurry to keep up with her as she swept up the stairs.

There could be no mistake as to her identity. Griffin had described her bearing, style, and every one of her eccentricities in amused and admiring detail. This woman was easily one of his favorite patrons, perhaps the one he liked above all others, and she was charging toward the front doors of the hell as if she meant to take no prisoners.

Olivia knew then that the Countess of Rivendale was the answer to the question that had been plaguing her.

It was shortly after midnight when Griffin's carriage turned the corner from Moorhead Street to Putnam Lane. He noted there was little in the way of pedestrian traffic. Those who were walking did so with their heads down and their gloved hands bunched into fists. An icy wind spiraled along the lane, lifting skirts and hats that were not anchored. Candlelight winked in all of the windows; red lanterns swung in most of the doorways.

Anyone with a modicum of sense and a few shillings to spare was already in one of the hells or hurrying purposefully toward one. February was always good for forcing the players indoors. It was unfortunate, but unavoidable, that his own establishment would not benefit from the reliably bitter north wind.

Griffin leapt from the carriage without assistance and dropped his head to butt the elements like every other passerby. His posture, his fatigue, and the distracting nature of his own thoughts conspired to keep him from noting the activity in his hell until he crossed the threshold and was confronted by the crush of guests in the entrance hall.

Mason's dour expression eased upon seeing his employer arrive unaccompanied. He squeezed through the crowd with a slight spring in his step and still managed to keep his dignity intact. He took Griffin's hat, gloves, and greatcoat. "You are well, my lord?"

"I have no idea. Do I look well?"

"Peaked. You look peaked."

Griffin drew his valet into a corner where a pair of large potted ferns shielded them from curious glances. "Explain this."

"You will find it is all in hand."

"That is not an explanation. Whose hand is it in, exactly?"

"That would be the countess."

"The countess?" Griffin's eyebrows rose toward his hairline. "Lady Rivendale? Never say you mean that—" He stopped because he saw it was quite clearly what Mason meant. "Whose idea was—" And he stopped again as the obvious answer occurred to him. "Where is she?"

"Her ladyship?"

Griffin set his jaw and waited.

Mason sniffed. "Miss Shepard is at her station." He was going to add that she was doing very well indeed, but Griffin was already pushing through the crush.

Lady Rivendale stepped into his path just as he entered the faro gaming room. Her interference was so smoothly made that he had to believe she'd placed herself near the door for just such a purpose.

"La! Breckenridge! What an excellent evening I am having!" She slipped her arm through his and steered him into the adjoining card room and away from the faro table. It was only necessary to tug a little, and she observed that he was good enough to give her his polite attention, though a glower might have been more apt for the situation. "Mr. Warner has shown a surprising facility for command tonight, and I can tell you I am thankful to learn of it. You will want to know that he has kept a keen eye on all activity at roulette and vingt-et-un while I have seen to the cards, dice, and faro, of course. Your patrons as a whole have been sadly well-mannered this evening, so there was cause to eject only two." She sighed heavily. "It's been a disappointment, really, that they should behave themselves. I cannot think when I will have opportunity to watch Mr. Warner act with such delicious authority."

"I will arrange it," Griffin said dryly, "if you will promise never to assume the managing of my hell again. Don't you have a nephew who is a duke or some such title that should give me pause?"

"Godson," she said. "And he is a viscount, like you, not a duke. A blessing, really, as Sherry is high enough in the instep to make even me uncomfortable. But you shouldn't worry that he will call you out. He does not do that sort of thing any longer. A messy business, I believe he finds it, and really, he indulges me when I embrace certain unconventional pastimes as I have tonight."

Griffin darted a glance through the doorway to the faro table. His view of Olivia was entirely obstructed by the gentlemen making their wagers. "It is gratifying to learn that I will not have to face Sheridan, but is there not another relation who might come to take up cudgels?"

The countess frowned. "You cannot mean the Earl of Ferrin."

"Ferrin. Yes. He's the one."

She laughed. The rich, hearty sound of it turned heads, but she gave this no notice. "Do not be such a noddy. Ferrin is the very last person you should fear. He is married to my dear Cybelline, but more importantly he is Mr. Restell Gardner's brother, and Mr. Gardner frequents this hell. I know it for a fact."

Griffin had an urge to pluck a feather from her ladyship's hat and go fly fishing. "I am in no way relieved that you are so well set in society. The wags will have it on the morrow that you were greeting my patrons and counting my profits. I should not be surprised that they will put you at the center of some row and credit you with tossing out the two gentlemen yourself."

"Oh, I hope not. Mr. Warner should have the credit there. A pair of your footmen were standing close to assist, but he didn't know that, and truly, he was everything Wellington in his uncompromising authority."

Everything Wellington? Griffin could not help himself. She'd managed to coax a smile from him, which he suspected had been her goal from the outset. "Thank you," he said quietly. Bending near her ear as though to whisper something, he lightly kissed her cheek.

"You're a scoundrel, Breckenridge," she said, flushing as prettily as a schoolgirl. "And I adore scoundrels. Go on. I know you want to speak to Miss Shepard." She caught the sleeve of his frock coat and held him fast another moment. "I hope you will be easy with her. She had your best interests uppermost in her clever mind, and naturally, I would not have agreed if I were not intrigued by the idea of managing an establishment such as this. Women have so few opportunities to make their mark in business, don't you think?"

"If we have that discussion, my lady, I will never get to Honey's side, and well you know it."

"Honey." Lady Rivendale pursed her lips disapprovingly. "That is on no account a name that should be attached to a woman with her acumen. Do you know what I would call her?"

Still smiling, though somewhat distractedly, Griffin took the bait. "Do tell."

"I would call her Olivia." The countess had the pleasure of seeing all of his attention return to her and his smile falter. She patted his cheek lightly. "A consequence of being so well set in society." With that parting shot, Lady Rivendale excused herself by calling out to one of her many acquaintances across the way.

Griffin stood in his fixed position a few moments longer, then turned slowly on his heel and took his leave of the gaming rooms for the sanctuary of his bedchamber.

Olivia saw him go but could not leave the table to follow. She had fully expected him to draw her to some private corner and have words with her, so his exit gave her pause. She played out two more full deals and was prepared to begin a third when she spied Mason's silver-threaded head above the others and called him over to take her place.

Griffin was lying on his bed when she found him. He had

removed his frock coat, loosened his cravat, and pulled off his boots, all of it accomplished on his way to the bed without benefit of his valet or the use of his dressing room. Olivia collected his leavings as she crossed the floor and carried them away for Mason to deal with later.

Griffin rested with one arm cradling his head and the other thrown across his eyes. He lifted the latter just enough to spy her activity. "What are you doing?"

"Helping Mr. Mason. He is spelling me at the table." She left the dressing room and came to his bedside. "Can I get you something? Refreshment? Beetle and Wick will draw you a bath, if you like. Everyone else is engaged at the moment."

"So I observed. A veritable beehive of activity. Odd, that, since I gave no instructions to open in my absence."

"And gave none to suggest we shouldn't." Olivia sensed he was spoiling for a quarrel and since her ground was shaky at best, she opted for delaying the inevitable. "You are weary, my lord, and unlikely to be at peak form to set forth your best argument. Why not allow me to provide for your comfort first? You will thank me in the morning when you are feeling more the thing."

"Your approach is novel, Olivia. I will give you that. I confess I've had no dinner, nor any appetite until now. Can you find something in the kitchen?"

"Of course." When she would have turned to go, Griffin's hand snaked out and captured her wrist. She glanced down at his fingers curled around hers, then at him. "Yes?"

"A bath would be most appreciated." When she nodded, he squeezed her hand once, then released it. "Thank you."

Olivia merely walked from the room, but in her heart she knew she was fleeing.

Griffin was most definitely feeling more the thing after a long soak to wash away the dust of the road and a repast of beef stew, applesauce, and warm, crusty bread. He read by the fire until he recognized the change in the activity on the floors below and heard Olivia's tread on the stairs. He stepped outside his room and indicated she should join him. He accepted the strongboxes as she came abreast of him, then stepped back and allowed her to precede him into his bed-chamber.

He opened the upholstered lid of the window bench and set the boxes inside.

"You don't want to make entries in your books this evening?" asked Olivia.

"No. That, too, can wait until morning."

"You are certain? Are you unwell?" The change in his routine troubled her, and his faint smile was not reassuring.

"Sit down, Olivia. I wish to speak to you."

Nodding a bit jerkily, she dropped onto the window bench when she backed into it. "Yes?"

Now that he had her full attention, Griffin was uncertain how he should begin. He had rehearsed some version of it during his return journey, but he hadn't taken into account how the carefully guarded expression in her own face would tie this tongue.

"You always knew I was married," he said, starting with the most obvious point. "I never pretended otherwise and never asked you to indulge in the same."

Olivia did not know if a response was called for, so she simply nodded.

"This morning—before Gardner arrived—I had it in my mind to tell you the whole of it. About my marriage, that is. It seems self-serving to say that now, after the fact, but it is the truth. I would have prefaced it with an apology, of course, and asked you how I might atone for my boorish behavior."

"You apologized last night," she said. "I imagined your atonement came this morning in the form of scones, hot cocoa, and your request to accompany me on my walk."

"Then you must raise your expectations, Olivia, for that was merely a prologue. You deserve more."

She could not think of a reason why he would believe that, but she did not say so. Better to bring him around to what he meant to say than devote time to why he meant to say it. "It is late, my lord, so if you would be so kind . . ." She set her hands in her lap and folded them together.

"Yes. Of course." Griffin looked around for a place he might sit, realized he would find none of them comfortable at present, and opted to remain on his feet. "You heard Gardner say that he found my wife. What you did not have occasion to know was that I have hired a dozen or so men over the years to locate her. The last word I had on where she might be came shortly before I met you. There was some reason to believe she was in Paris. On the intelligence I was given by the gentleman I'd hired, I decided to make the trip myself. She was not there, nor could I find evidence that she might have been."

He saw a shadow of concern cross her face but did not know the cause for it. "There is something you want to know?" he asked.

Still frowning slightly, she shook her head. "It is difficult to understand, I think, though I suppose you will come to it eventually."

"Come to what?"

"How she came to be lost."

"If you are imagining an abduction or some other manner of foul play as others are wont to believe, set your mind at rest. Lady Breckenridge is not lost as much as she is in hiding. She did not wish to be found and still may not know that it's finally happened. Gardner did not approach her, merely discovered her location. Whether she will be there when he returns for her is yet to be seen. If she learns of the inquiries on her behalf, she may go again."

Griffin watched Olivia listen to him with the whole of her body. She leaned forward, head inclined just a bit to the right while a small vertical crease deepened between her eyebrows. Her gaze was centered and focused, and her hands had unfolded and lay open in her lap. He was touched and humbled that she would honor him with all of her attention.

"It's been a little more than six years," he said. "Elaine's departure was not entirely unexpected. She threatened as much from time to time as the mood struck her. You will perhaps find it odd, or perhaps a measure of her contempt for me, but she never attempted to hide the fact that she had taken lovers—and there was a succession of them—although she was adept at concealing the truth of it from others. It was her care for her own reputation, and in a smaller measure, mine, that lulled me into believing she had decided there was some benefit to a marriage such as we had."

Griffin finally set himself, as was often his habit, on the arm of a wing chair. He stretched one leg to the side and rested his arm across the back. "We were friends once, or so I thought. That has been the most difficult thing to reconcile. Elaine is seven years my senior, a second cousin on my father's side, and was a frequent visitor to Wright Hall when I was growing up. As a child, I thought she was a magical creature, the queen of my sisters' fairy court. I adored her then and that did not change when I learned she was very much of the flesh. I cannot find it in myself to be ashamed of it."

"Nor should you," Olivia said gently.

Griffin steeled himself against Olivia's compassion and went on. "Elaine and I married six months after my father's death. It was a rather hastily planned affair. We were not yet through a year of mourning, and I was deeply engaged in learning the extent of my family's debts. I had my mother to consider, for she could not be convinced there was the least need for frugality, and then there were my sisters, who would have to make good marriages if they were to be properly cared for."

Olivia closed her eyes briefly so he would not be put off by the sympathy she could not help but feel. He had been a young man, not yet twenty at his father's death, and barely that as he exchanged vows with a woman who seemed bent on taking advantage of his adoration for her. "You learned your lady was carrying your child."

Nodding, Griffin slowly released a breath. "I had imagined that some day I would find the courage to propose, but I had no confidence that she would accept. She'd had proposals before and remained unmarried by choice. I thought she was admirably free spirited, a woman with an income large enough to support her somewhat disdainful opinion of men. Her refusal to yield to the expectations of society was more fascinating than troubling, a point of admiration rather than alarm."

Olivia almost smiled then. How he would have been drawn to this woman, convinced that her unconventional manner demonstrated strength of character, never suspecting it could conceal the lack of it. "Her parents did not press her to marry?"

"There is only her mother, a widow who never remarried. Again, not for lack of suitors and opportunity. She is a handsome woman with independent means in the same vein as Lady Rivendale but without that lady's lively humor and delicious appreciation for life."

Griffin pushed his fingers through his hair and offered a grin rife with self-mockery. "It all seems so clear in the retelling, doesn't it? You must wonder at my naïveté."

She shrugged. "Everyone is naive at nineteen. We only think we are not, and that is the cruel irony of it."

Griffin appreciated her generosity. He could have pointed out that *she* was not naive at nineteen, indeed, not at twelve, nor eight, nor six. "Elaine miscarried, but I think you suspected that. It occurred only a few weeks after the wedding. Sometimes I think how life would have been different if we had not rushed to marriage, but that is naturally a ridiculous use of time and gray matter."

And in every way a human response, she thought. "Do you believe the child was yours?"

He gave her full marks for not avoiding the question. She could be fearless in her own fashion. "I did at the time. I came to doubt the truth of it soon after. I said nothing to her about my suspicions, and I cannot say if that was a mistake or not. What I believe is that it would have changed nothing in the end. Elaine would have still engaged in her affairs, and I could have not kept her at my side. I do not know when I came to the realization that she could not help herself, but there you have it. I do not offer it in defense of her behavior. As fantastical as it seems, she was compelled to be with men. With any man. With many men. I did not think she knew I meant to divorce her, but it may have been what provoked her to leave when she did."

"How is it possible she could have disappeared so completely for so long?"

"I did not try to find her immediately. Indeed, I did not know for better than a week that she had fled. I was operating this establishment by then, a situation that I believe I've mentioned she found most disagreeable, and she was at Wright Hall. Word came from her own mother that she was gone. My mother-in-law made it clear in her missive where she believed the blame should be placed. The hell was an abomination to them, and the choice I made to take it in hand myself was viewed as a very public snub of the ton and a complete disregard for my role and responsibilities as viscount and head of my family. As this view was shared by my own mother and to a lesser extent by my sisters, there was some sympathy for Elaine."

Olivia imagined that was in no small part due to Griffin keeping his own counsel. "Were you ever tempted to tell them all of it?"

"Not my own family, no. It was—is—a private matter."

"Yet you are telling me."

"Yes."

She thought he would explain his reasons for it, then it occurred to her that he might have no explanation, that what he was finally giving into was a need to tell *someone.* Who better than a woman with so many dark secrets of her own? She would not judge, merely listen, and that was what he wanted from her. Still, it bound them in some way, and perhaps it was this that he wanted as well.

She watched Griffin slide into the wing chair and sprawl casually, wearily, across it. "How is it that your wife avoided whispers among the gentlemen and wags of the ton? Pray, do not say her discretion alone accounts for it. That is not possible. If she was as compelled to act in certain ways as you say, it would have become known."

Closing his eyes, Griffin pressed the bridge of his nose with his thumb and forefinger. His words, when they finally came, held all the heaviness of a man who knew defeat. "Like a bitch that does not soil her own den, my wife did not choose her lovers from the society in which she mingled. She took servants to her bed. The grooms. Gardeners. Footmen. We once attended a week-long entertainment hosted by one of her dearest friends, and she slipped away to raise her skirts for the coachman, then the second butler, and finally the steward. I made excuses for her absences. No one among the servants complained."

Olivia watched his hand fall to the arm of the chair and lie there limply. She caught his dark gaze and was struck by the weight of his grief. Absent from his recitation, from his tone, indeed, from his expression, was bitterness. There may have been a time he'd known that emotion, wrestled with it, but it was no longer his constant companion.

She lifted her arm and made to reach for him, caught herself, and returned her hand to her lap. He was so focused on her face that it did not seem to her that he was aware of the gesture, then his hand turned a few degrees and partially exposed his palm. His fingers spread, curled, beckoned her.

Olivia came to her feet slowly. She took one step toward him, paused, then took another. It required but two more to close the distance. Her fingers brushed the back of his, were caught, then entwined. She would have dropped to her knees in front of his chair, but he tugged her toward him at an angle that brought her onto his lap. She twisted slightly to spare him her weight, and she caught his uneven, mildly mocking grin as he took it upon himself anyway.

She sat very still, her hand linked in his, uncertain of what she should do. She had an urge to touch his face, so she did that, palming his cheek, tracing his scar, brushing his lower lip with her thumb and lingering at the corner of his beautifully sculpted mouth.

"You still grieve," she said quietly. "How you must have loved her."

"Once." He kissed the pad of her thumb before she drew it back. "Once, Olivia, she was my world. It was a long time ago, and only briefly. What I imagined she felt for me was just that, my imagination. I know now that she is incapable of any finer feeling. Sometimes she amused herself playing at being in love—or what she thought it must be—but her affairs never lasted long. She knew a great deal about lust, and nothing at all about love."

"It is all rather difficult to comprehend. You pity her, don't you?"

"I do now. I despised her for much longer than I ever loved her."

Olivia considered that. She was in no hurry to pose her question. The circle of his arm around her waist and the niche he made for her against his shoulder was a comfortable fit. "Then why have you made searching for her so important? It cannot be only for purposes of divorce. As distasteful as that end might be to you, it could be accomplished without her presence, couldn't it? It is she who broke her vows and abandoned the marriage."

Even as she was putting the question to him, she was aware that he was regarding her rather oddly. "What?" she asked. "Have I taken too great a liberty? Said something I ought not have?"

"You really don't know, do you?"

Olivia was perfectly at sea and did not take pains to conceal it. She simply stared at him, waiting.

"I was so certain that someone would have told you by now. Truss. Mason. The lads. Even the patrons could have whispered it in your presence. Most of them have heard the gossip."

"Then it is much, much older than a nine days' wonder, for I have never learned of it."

"So I see." His fingers gently tightened on hers. "After Elaine's disappearance became known, I was questioned quite thoroughly by the authorities. There are many people, Olivia, even after so much time has passed, who suspect me of murdering my wife."

She said nothing for a long moment, trying to take it in. How surpassingly singular that their lives should be touched by so much in the way of injury. The difference, though, was that he carried the burden of suspicion while she carried the burden of guilt. She could not say if one weighed more heavily than the other. She knew only there were days when she was crushed by it and could not fathom it would be so different for him.

"But you were here in London when Lady Breckenridge left," said Olivia. "Didn't you tell me that?"

"I did, and I was. And, yes, there were many who could support my presence here. Apparently, when one is a person of property and some influence, it is not enough to be firmly situated in one location while a murder is taking place in another. I could not very well deny that I had the means to engage in murder for hire."

"But where was the evidence that her ladyship was killed . . . or even dead? There can have been no body."

Griffin's smile was wry. "Now you are allowing logic to influence your argument. My mother-in-law was not so particular as that when she leveled her accusations and made her concerns public."

"But her daughter . . . Was she so unaware of her daughter's behavior that she would risk bringing it to light?"

"I will never believe she was unaware, but what she used to support her charge was the divorce, except in her version it was Elaine who desired it. I was named the adulterer."

"Were you?"

"By that time, yes. I was regularly visiting a young widow."

"Mrs. Christie?"

"Lord, no. My arrangement with Alys was made less than a year ago. The widow asked me not to return when it appeared her good name—and that of her late husband's—would become grist for the mill. I honored her wishes, of course, understood her concern completely. She had her own future to consider."

Olivia nodded absently. "It does not seem that adultery could have been all that your mother-in-law presented as her daughter's motive for divorcing you. It is too often done by men and many wives find it prudent to suffer in silence or seek their own pleasure."

"You are right. That is why Elaine's mother made so much of my decision to manage this establishment myself. While Elaine engaged in her particular vices with some discretion, I engaged in mine openly. I made no attempt to operate this gaming hell through agents as others of rank have done on occasion. At the outset of my ownership it was as much a brothel as a place to make wagers on any number of unsavory things. It was not so long ago that a parade of glassy-eyed opium eaters trudged regularly through the house. I might have allowed it to remain all of those things if Elaine had not taken herself off. I take no pride in admitting that the ugliness of this business appealed to me. It was there in my marriage, in my heart, how could I not be comfortable with it in every other aspect of my life?"

Griffin searched her face. This time it was he who brushed her cheek with the back of his knuckles. "You understand, don't you?"

She did not think she would be able to tell him. The words lodged in her throat along with the aching lump of unshed tears. "Too well," she said at last.

He nodded. "I knew. Somehow I knew I could say it to you. All of it." With little in the way of urging, her head came to rest at the curve of his neck and shoulder. "My desire to find Elaine is only selfish. I have come to care that much for my reputation in polite society that I would have the rumors finally put behind me. I will divorce her immediately upon her return, and then she may go wherever she wishes and with whomever she wants. Indeed, it is my fervent hope that she will go quickly."

"She might be different," Olivia said. "You are."

"Perhaps. My plans will not be changed by it."

"Perhaps." But she said it on a thread of sound, her lips merely moving around the word.

Griffin's cheek pressed against her hair. He drew back. "You are still wearing your wig, Honey."

She smiled faintly. It was difficult to know which one of them disliked the artifice more. "Naturally. I came here directly from the tables."

"Take it off."

Olivia did so, but when she would have removed herself from his lap to put it aside, Griffin plucked it from her hand and tossed it negligently toward the window seat. It came to rest like a furry lap dog on a plump, embroidered pillow. She tried to look disapproving of his carelessness, but her snort of laughter could not be mistaken for anything save what it was.

He watched for a moment, his eyes darkening as she combed her hair with her fingers. He took her by the wrist. "I'll do that."

Olivia wanted to close her eyes and simply surrender. His fingers did not so much sift through her hair as caress it. Her scalp tingled. He raised tiny bumps on her flesh. She was warm of a sudden, uncomfortably so between her thighs, yet her desire was to move closer to the source of the heat rather than draw back from it. She fought it until he simply caught her hair in his fist and used it to pull her inexorably toward him.

The kiss was long and deep and sweet. Their lips and tongues meant to savor, not merely taste. She would be joined to him, she thought, not in the obvious carnal way, though that too, but in the sense that he was a comfortable, comforting fit for her, as gentle to her skin as a kid glove, as easy around her heart as a velvet ribbon.

For once, the danger inherent in such a notion did not drive her away. She held fast to him, slipping her arms around his neck and pressing herself to him. She felt her breasts swell above the deep cut of her bodice. Her nipples rubbed against the soft fabric of her chemise. She felt him stir under her so the shape of the cradle he provided for her changed. Olivia did not mind; she was stirred as well.

His hands rested at the small of her back, but occasionally one would make a pass up her spine. Sometimes the other drifted lower, palming her bottom. Her dress was raised, though how it was accomplished she couldn't say. A mystery almost its equal was how she came to be straddling him, her knees pressed to the back of the chair on either side of his hips as though she had him in a vise.

Olivia's skirt billowed around them but her drawers lay on the floor. Her fine satin garters and silk stockings rubbed against his trousers, making a deliciously intimate sound like something she might whisper into his ear, or he into hers. Under cover of her gown and the spread of her petticoats, he opened the front closure on his trousers and drawers. She was lifted, then settled carefully on him. He watched her face, most especially her eyes. He watched her irises become more deeply emerald as the centers darkened; he watched her eyelids grow heavy until they could no longer sustain any look of surprise and held only contentment.

That look did not last. It could not. Not when he lifted her again and thrust into her. A small moan escaped her lips. He smiled, wanting more of it, wanting more of what must be done to make her surrender that sound.

Her hands rested on his shoulders. She pushed, yielded, took him again. She went about it slowly, rising, falling, her hips moving provocatively. Her gown rustled, the silk shivered. She rested once, or pretended to. It was all done as a tease, and she had not known until that moment she might be capable of teasing in such a manner. Her forehead came to rest against his. Her eyes closed. She felt his warm breath, felt the strain in every line of his body as he strove for control.

She leaned back enough to take in his face. He had not closed his eyes as she had, but had been watching her all the while. The intensity of his expression made her self-conscious, but when she started to glance away, he drew her back with a forefinger placed at one side of her chin.

"Do not make me forgo the pleasure I find in looking at you," he said. "What? Do you think I am flattering you? That you are surpassingly lovely has nothing at all to do with it. It is my selfish pleasure I'm speaking of, the pleasure of watching your eyes change color and knowing I had a small part in it. The flush that puts pink in your cheeks, whether in anger or passion, I know I provoked it in some measure. And when you see me, truly see me, it is as though you are able to look past what is flesh and blood and bone, and it seems your face reflects a certain affection for me. I would not have you deny me the pleasure of believing it might be so."

"It is," she whispered. "It is affection." And though she might be damned for it, neither could she deny it.

Griffin inched them toward the edge of the cushion. "Hold tightly." Almost before she knew what he was about he heaved them somewhat awkwardly out of the chair and carried her, still joined to him, to the bed. He took the brunt of the fall, turning at the last moment to back into the mattress before he collapsed and brought her down on top of him. Her gown floated around them and there was an infinitesimal beat in which her very breath was lost.

They stared at each other, startled by the force of their fall and the speed at which need and hunger reasserted themselves. The cadence of their laughter was both changed and charged by Olivia's whimper and Griffin's low growl. He eased her gown over her shoulders and loosened the ribbon that gathered the scooped neckline of her chemise. He cupped her breasts; his thumbs passed across the pebbled nipples. She leaned forward and he took one in his mouth, suckled her. Her honeyed walls contracted around him. His hips jerked. She stayed with him even then, no longer sensing his movement but anticipating it.

She felt his muscles tense, the skin tighten across his chest. The cord in his neck stood out as he strained under her. He wanted her to come with him, urged her to do so, but she wasn't ready, not quite, and she needed to see him lead the way.

He said her name, called it out, and then his body rippled under her as a wave of pleasure went through him. She kept moving, riding, and his hand stole beneath her gown and touched her in that place that was hot and hard and slippery with musk-scented dew. Her pleasure collided with his, and she shuddered with the strength of it just as he had.

Her hair fell forward as she bent her head and caught her

breath. He pushed his hands into it at her nape and dragged her toward him. Her mouth settled over his and they shared a long, wet, leisurely kiss.

When they finally parted and Olivia eased away from him, Griffin did not respond quickly enough to keep her from leaving the bed.

"I need a moment for myself," she said when he began to sit up. "I won't be long." She disappeared into his dressing room and closed the door behind her.

Good as her word, when she appeared minutes later, she was fresh faced and scrubbed pink. She also wore only her chemise. Griffin, for his part, had used the time to strip to his drawers and set a better fire in the hearth. He brushed off his hands and made certain she was all for their bed before he risked leaving her to attend to his own ablutions.

When he returned, Olivia threw back the covers just enough for him to slide into bed beside her. She was on her side facing him with one arm under her pillow to raise it at a comfortable angle. He blew out the candles on the nightstand before he settled in. She could just make out his profile and occasionally the gleam of his white teeth.

"Do you suppose my brother knew the rumor attached to you?" she asked.

"I tend to believe everyone does, so I am no judge. You didn't. Why do you ask?"

"Because if he knew, that means he gave me over to someone who was thought to be capable of murdering his wife. That does not speak well of him, does it?"

"Pray, you do not mean I should answer that. There are already so many things he's done that do not speak well of him."

Olivia drew up her knees. The fabric of her chemise stretched tautly across them. She opened her mouth to speak, said nothing, and closed it again.

"What is it, Olivia?"

How had he known? "Nothing."

He let the lie pass. She would tell him eventually; he believed that. Trust first, he thought. She could not give over herself without it, and in that way they were no different. "Go to sleep," he said.

Olivia had not thought she was so tired, but she yawned abruptly and realized she was only trying to deny it. She was asleep before she set her thoughts in order, snugly fitted to Griffin's body, extending to him all the confidence she could not during her waking hours.

The sweet lethargy in the aftermath of their lovemaking made Olivia's violent attack all the more unexpected. Griffin woke struggling to draw a breath. One twisted corner of the sheet was pulled taut around his throat, and it was Olivia who gripped it with a strength that defied his first effort to loosen it. He managed to slip two fingers between the sheet and his neck and give himself enough leverage to fill his lungs and grind out her name.

He could not make out her features clearly but his earlier experience made it unnecessary. He knew she was sleeping, that her eyes would be vacant and unfocused, that her profound terror would be masked by the strain of her struggle. He said her name again, less urgently this time as he felt her begin to weaken. Circling one of her wrists tightly, he pressed the pulse point as hard as he could until her fingers spasmed, then opened. He tore the sheet out of her hand, unwound it, and sucked in a deep breath.

He was not prepared for her second attack any better than he had been prepared for the first. He raised his forearm too late to block both of her hands. She sunk the fingernails of one hand into his chest and would have drawn blood if he hadn't slapped her away. As it was, he felt her nails scrape his skin sharply enough to raise welts. He used measured force to take her by the upper arms and push her onto her back.

She twisted, kicked, managed to make a few blows connect with his shin. She should have yelped in pain; instead, he was the one who grunted. He stayed her hammering toes by throwing one leg across hers, then pinned her arms down at the wrists. She fought on, but there were peaks and valleys in the struggle and each successive bout was weaker than the one before.

It was only when she finally lay still and her breathing quieted that Griffin determined he could safely release her. He touched her face, felt the heat in her cheeks and the beads of perspiration across her upper lip and brow. When he shifted his shoulder, firelight glanced across it and cast her features in a pale, golden glow. He saw her lick her lips.

Griffin rolled out of bed and padded to the dressing room where he poured a glass of water for her. He wet a flannel as well, wrung it out, and carried it and the water back to the bed. He debated the best approach, then decided to cool her flushed skin with the damp flannel first. She murmured something that might have been a protest as he gently wiped her brow, but she also turned her face to the cool relief he provided. He went on as he was, carefully placing it against her cheeks, her upper lip, and finally her throat.

When he was done, he slid one arm under her back and lifted her enough so she could take the water without choking. As soon as he pressed the rim of the glass to her lips she began to sip. It was when she stopped, coughed, and pushed his hand away that he knew she was awake at last.

"What are you doing?" she asked, suspiciously eyeing the glass in his hand. "Do you mean to drown me in my sleep?"

Griffin set the glass aside. "I think we can agree that tossing you in the Thames would be a more effective method." He crawled over her, straightened the covers, and made himself comfortable on what he thought of now as his side of the bed. "You had a nightmare."

"I did?"

"Mmm." He punched his pillow, set it against the head-board, and leaned back. "You don't remember?"

"I don't dream," she said. "I never do."

"Not true. What you don't seem to do is remember them."

Olivia was cold. She didn't know how Griffin could be sitting up in bed, his bare chest exposed above the turned-down blankets. She inched closer to the warmth that came from him and slipped her toes under his calf. He was in all ways better than a hot brick.

"Your feet are like icicles." In spite of that, he didn't try to escape them. He found her hands and gave them a quick rub. Her heartfelt sigh made him smile. "Do you recall even a little bit?"

Because she didn't, she closed her eyes to see if that would help bring the thing to mind. "No," she said, tilting her head up at him. "Not a thing. Did I speak, ask for water?"

"No. You were feverish, or at least it seemed so."

She placed the back of her hand against her forehead. "It appears to have passed, but perhaps it's why I am so chilled now."

Griffin decided to act as if she'd issued an invitation. He slipped under the covers and drew her against him. Her arm slid across his chest as her head fit neatly in the curve of his shoulder. Her knee rested on top of his thigh. "Better?" he asked. He smiled, satisfied, when she hummed her agreement. "Will you be able to sleep now?"

"I thought I was sleeping before."

"After a fashion, I suppose you were."

"I disturbed you. I'm sorry."

Seemingly of its own volition, Griffin's hand went to his throat. "Not so much," he said. "We'll talk in the morning." The thought that she might not let him live so long was more amusing than the opposite, though why that should be escaped him. He let his hand fall from his throat to her hair. He sifted through curling strands with his fingertips. "It must be the fire in your hair."

Olivia nodded sleepily, though she had no idea what he was talking about. Her head was muzzy, and it occurred to her that she might be dreaming now. She hoped she would recall it later, for the whole of it was very pleasant indeed.

She had planned to rise before him, but when she opened one heavily lidded eye, she saw Griffin was already sitting at the table enjoying his coffee and reading the paper. She'd slept through the children calling to him from the street and the thump of the paper against the window. Perhaps the morning ritual had been managed in silence, the urchins' aim truer than it usually was, but she doubted it. She'd slept as if drugged.

"Will you join me?" he asked, putting down the paper. "Or shall you take your breakfast in bed? There is a tray here for just that purpose."

Olivia thought she spied a certain gleam in Griffin's eye. She suspected he was confusing serving her in bed with servicing her in the same. More alert of a sudden, she pushed herself upright. "I'll join you." When a sly grin lifted one corner of his mouth and he chuckled, she knew she'd been right to assign him less than honorable motives. Still, she deliberately passed directly behind him on her way to the dressing room, then surprised him by sliding her arms around his neck and bussing him on the cheek. She was already dancing out of his reach by the time he recovered.

She joined him a few short minutes later wearing one of his warmer, brushed velvet robes. She'd rolled up the sleeves and wrapped it tightly with a belt, but the hem swept the floor with her every step.

"I must say, you improve the look of the thing." Griffin handed her the platter of eggs.

"Thank you, though I like it on you well enough." Taking the dish, she spooned herself a generous serving, added two sausage links, three fingers of toast, a small bowl of porridge, and a cup of tea with cream and sugar. She looked up just as she was prepared to tuck into her eggs and saw Griffin was regarding her with equal measures of amusement and disbelief. In defiance of his expression, she speared eggs and half a link of sausage with her fork and managed to put the whole of it in her mouth, then proceeded to talk around it. "I hope you do not mean to stare." She waggled her fork at his paper. "By all means, return to your reading."

Chuckling, he obliged her, though he was not above stealing the occasional glance, sometimes around the paper, sometimes over the top. Once, she caught him out and lobbed the crusty end of her toast at him. He was so surprised it was fortunate he did not capture it in his open mouth.

Olivia was still smiling when she raised her serviette and dabbed at her mouth for the final time. She pushed her plate away and announced that he could come out from behind his paper. "You were very kind to indulge me," she said. "If you had insisted upon watching me, I might well have choked."

And there was the segue he needed. "By curious coincidence, Olivia, I also wished to speak of choking . . ."

Chapter Eleven

Olivia did not ask to see the bruising around his throat to confirm what he told her. Griffin came slowly to the realization that her failure to challenge his story was not merely because she believed him, but because she believed she was capable of just such a thing. Not that she wasn't distressed by her behavior. There was no mistaking either her deeply felt embarrassment or her even deeper horror.

She remained at the table as long as she could, but he observed the slow drain of color from her face and knew it was only a matter of time before she fled. He didn't flinch when she jerked the chair out from under her with enough force to make it rock on its back legs and ran into the dressing room, holding her arms crossways in front of her stomach. In spite of her consideration in shoving the door shut behind her, he still heard the sounds of her being sick.

She emerged some ten minutes later, pale but composed. The table was cleared of everything save for the pot of tea and two dry triangles of toast. She sat at the table, her head bent, while Griffin finished his quiet discussion with the footman. She remained that way until the dressing room was tidied and all evidence of her abrupt illness was removed.

Griffin poured her a cup of tea and pushed it directly into her line of sight. "Here. Drink. You will feel more the thing."

She nodded, grasped the cup in both her hands, and raised it halfway to her lips. It hovered there, keeping her hands warm, but doing nothing at all to settle her nervous stomach. Griffin placed two fingers under the cup and lifted gently, giving her the momentum she could not seem to find for herself. She brought it to her mouth, sipped. While it did not make her feel more the thing immediately, it began to warm her from the inside.

"I am compelled to point out, Olivia, that I have come to no harm." Griffin nudged the plate of toast toward her. "Your reaction is altogether more than I could have reasonably predicted. Some modest embarrassment might be expected because the behavior is both curious and singular, but it is also clearly not within your control. Your response suggests that you not only hold yourself responsible but that you could command your nightmares to take a different course. If such a thing is possible, I have never heard of it. If you cannot accept that I do not blame you, then you can trust that I will never speak of it again."

Olivia lowered her cup and raised her head. She searched his face, looking for some sign of the condemnation he denied. It wasn't there. "You don't understand."

"That's right. I don't. But neither, I think, do you. I am not afraid of you, Olivia. I'm afraid for you. When you take so much upon yourself, I fear for you more, not less." He watched her lips part as though she meant to say something. This was followed by an almost imperceptible shake of her head, and he knew she was erring once again on the side of caution for herself and mistrust of him. "You had no idea, did you?"

Her eyes fell on her cup. "I have no recollection of attacking you," she said carefully.

"That's not quite an answer to the question I asked, is it?"

Olivia pressed her lips together as much in annoyance as to

keep herself from answering thoughtlessly. "There have been times that I've awakened to find the sheets twisted like ropes, the pillows stuffed between the mattress and the headboard, my feet at the wrong end of the bed. So, it's not true that I had no idea something was not right, but with no memory to support what happened I didn't . . ." She shrugged uneasily. "I just didn't know."

"Something like this has happened before. I had to restrain you. You never woke."

Olivia set her cup down and quickly placed her hands in her lap under the table before Griffin could see the tremors. "There were bruises. I didn't know . . . I thought . . ."

"You never asked."

She'd been afraid to. He would know that now. "It won't happen again."

"I'm not certain how you can say that."

Now she looked up at him, her eyes widening slightly. "Because I won't share your bed again."

"Well, now, there is where we disagree, because I am quite sure you will."

"That is a ridiculous notion. Would you take a viper to your bed?"

"I did. In point of fact, I married her. You, my dear Miss Cole, are not a viper."

Olivia's response was to reach across the small table and tug hard on the satin collar of his robe. The flesh at the side of his neck was rubbed raw. The mark she'd made did not completely ring his throat but it was not for lack of effort on her part. Her hand flew to her mouth, and the words she might have gasped were smothered.

Olivia dropped back into her chair slowly. "You don't know," she whispered from behind her hand. "You don't know, and I can't tell you."

Griffin casually straightened his collar and smoothed the lapel. "You can tell me anything, Olivia."

She shook her head. "You only think I can. It will be different—everything will be different—once you know."

Frustrated, but keeping it contained, Griffin sat back in his chair. "Perhaps, but for what you have already suffered at the hands of others, I wouldn't blink if you told me you'd done murder."

And as simply as that, he knew he'd tripped over some part of what she kept to herself. He knew it even before her head snapped up and the blood drained from her face. He was slow in reaching for her, and she managed to get away before he caught up to her and steered her away from the dressing room and back to the table. "You can have nothing left in your stomach to retch," he said quietly.

It was true, but the feeling did not pass easily. "You cannot imagine how it would please me to faint."

He moved his chair and sat beside her, then took her hands into his. He forced heat into them with a brisk massage. "Have you killed someone, Olivia?"

"I don't know." She removed her hands from his, fisted them, then splayed and stretched her fingertips. She stared at them, unable to meet his eyes. "I don't know. I think . . . I think I might have."

"Then you may as well say all of it. Asking Restell Gardner to discover the truth will put me in his debt for all eternity."

She risked a glance at him. "Is it so important that you know the details?"

"As opposed to knowing so little that I must sleep with one eye open the rest of my life? Because that is what I'm willing to do." He watched her, made certain she understood the implication. He meant for them to share a bed for a lifetime, and she would have to accustom herself to the idea. It was clear she did not expect it and had no idea how to respond. It was unlikely she even believed him. "Begin anywhere you wish," he said. "We will sort it out together."

Olivia drew in a calming breath and released it slowly. She

nodded once, then produced the first words haltingly. "His name was Rawlings. I heard him called that by the others . . . his friends, I mean, or at least I supposed they were his friends. There were five of them at the table. Two pints of ale. A tumbler of gin. Another of whiskey. Rawlings . . . he was the glass of port. I served the ale, gin, and port three times over. The whiskey only twice. I imagined they might be students. They were of an age with me at the time, most especially the two pints and the tumbler of gin."

Griffin listened carefully, trying not to give way to surprise and distract her from her tale. Had she just described herself as a tavern maid?

Olivia caught Griffin's eye, then found a point past his shoulder to set her gaze upon as she continued. "They were already in fine humor when they seated themselves near the hearth. I supposed it was because they had shared a flask on the coach. It was a bitterly cold evening, and every coach that stopped wanted accommodations for the passengers, whether or not they usually took respite there."

Not simply a tavern then, Griffin thought, but an inn on a well-traveled coach route. A place where she could be alone among many, a stranger to the guests if she wished, familiar and friendly if she wanted it otherwise.

"We had our fill of travelers that night and were trying to decide how many could be squeezed into a room. Some passengers had already agreed to three and four to a bed and negotiated a fair price. Others were less inclined to make allowances. The students whispered among themselves, drew broom straws, and made plans. I gave it little thought. With so many to look after, they attracted no more notice than the rest. One of them, the gin, I think, produced a deck of cards, and they played long after many of the guests retired for the night."

Olivia took a sip of tea. Her mouth had become dry of a sudden, the back of her throat uncomfortably tender. "They were not overly attentive toward me as I brought them drinks. There are comments that one expects, but I had had occasion to hear far worse than anything that was said to me that night. Even well into their cups they were most genial. As a whole their temperament was unexceptional."

"Rawlings?" asked Griffin.

Olivia's eyebrows drew together slightly. "It did not strike me as odd at the time, but later . . . afterward . . . I realized he'd contributed very little."

"And watched you overmuch."

"Perhaps. I don't know." She added tea to her cup but didn't drink. Instead she used the cup to warm her hands again. "I had a room of my own in the attic. It was small but entirely comfortable. Because every room was in such demand that night, I gave mine up to a pair of lady's maids. I was paid handsomely for the sacrifice by their employers and my own, so it was advantageous for me to go elsewhere. I agreed to make my bed in the carriage house, though that is rather too grand a name for the structure. It was more in the way of a stable but large enough to accommodate several coaches and all of the cattle."

"And the drivers, footmen, and tigers, I imagine."

"Well, yes. Naturally." She required a moment to register his disapproving tenor. "It is inappropriate for you to assume they presented the least danger to me. I knew most of them, as they frequently made stops in Royston. I could have expected any one of them to come to my aid."

"But they didn't. Or do I misunderstand the turn your story is about to take?"

"If you think they had any opportunity to assist me, then you most definitely misunderstand the situation. I never reached the carriage house. I left by the back door carrying a wool blanket and a lantern. I recall clutching my mantle to keep it from flapping around me. A woolen scarf covered the lower half of my face. The wind was fierce, howling. I had to lean into it to remain standing. Except for my small light, the yard was dark, and by the time I realized I was not alone, I was being pushed hard to the ground. The lantern spilled out of my hand and the light went out. I had no breath to call for help, not that I believe I would have been heard. I was among the very last to retire. The likelihood of waking someone was small, and the wind was banging the shutters against the stone."

Olivia's eyes found Griffin's. He was making no more judgments, simply listening instead. She could hold his gaze now, though why that should be she wasn't sure. What she had to tell him was more difficult, not less. "You might wonder, with the lantern extinguished, how I knew it was Rawlings," she said quietly. "But I—"

"The port," said Griffin. "You smelled port on his breath."

She nodded. "That is it exactly. Few others drank it that night. His height. The shape of his frame. It was not hard for me to determine that he was my attacker. He spoke very little. A few words to direct me, to tell me in most explicitly vulgar terms what he wanted me to do for him. I could not do it, Griffin. I couldn't. I fought back. He was hampered by the blanket that was caught between us, my heavy mantle, and my strength."

Griffin offered a gently wry smile. "I don't suppose he considered that carrying tray after tray weighted with drink made you as strong as most dock workers."

"No," she said. "I don't suppose he did."

"You used your scarf?"

She nodded. It was easier now that he was able to draw inferences from all that she'd told him. "He was so intent on his own attack that he failed to notice mine. I managed to unwind the scarf from my throat and loop it around his. I caught him high on his neck, just under his chin, and I pulled . . ." She returned her cup to its saucer and stared at it. "And pulled." The slight tremor was once again in her fingertips. The tea rippled. "I twisted the scarf and pulled for as long as I was able. . . ." Her voice drifted off. She held herself still and found composure. "They came then . . . all four of them. Gin. The whiskey. Both pints of ale. I never heard them above the sound of my own breathing. I don't know what drew them from their beds or what they saw. They tore Rawlings away from me, dragged him off into the night. He never protested, never struggled. Whiskey stayed behind long enough to make certain I could rise, then he hurried off to join the others. They went in one direction away from the inn. I went in another."

Griffin understood then that Olivia's dreams were not merely nightmares, but hauntings. She was visited by specters as she slept, every choice she made that evening came at her again, and she was helpless to make them any differently.

"Is it so important what I think, Olivia? Will it truly ease your doubts to know I think you acted as nature intended you should? The sort of peace you seek isn't conferred on you by others. It seems to me that we make that peace within ourselves." He shrugged lightly. "But even that is only my opinion."

"Have you ever done murder?"

"No, but defending oneself is not murder."

"Perhaps that is so among gentlemen. You have your peculiar rules. But I believe society will judge me differently."

"Rawlings's companions didn't. They took him away, not you. You don't know that he's dead by your hand. You don't know that he's dead at all."

"I know what I felt."

"Killing such as you described is not a thing done quickly," Griffin said. "His friends may have saved his life by coming upon you when they did."

Olivia could sit no longer. She rose and went to stand at the window. Across the way, the front door to the brothel opened and the pair of whores she knew only by their taste in outrageously adorned bonnets emerged. Hugging herself, she stepped back so they wouldn't see her when they looked up. "No better than I ought to be," she said softly. "No better at all."

Griffin turned in his chair. Olivia's back had a steel rod where most people had a spine. Nothing would come of taking the opposing view. He chose a different tack. "What happened afterward? Where did you go?"

"I fled. It seemed all that was possible for me to do, though running away surely damned me. I had a bit of money saved that I was able to take, and I made my way from one town to the next, found work now and again. I eventually took a coach to Cambridge. I knew my brother was there. Alastair set up a house for me there while he finished his studies."

As an explanation, it left much out. Griffin was far from satisfied. He continued to regard her stiffly set shoulders and spine. A few moments of silence was all that was required to prompt her to turn. Her chin was thrust a fraction forward as though she meant to challenge him. The slight quiver warned him she didn't have the strength for an interrogation. It was not what he wanted in any event.

"Alastair doesn't know," she said quietly. "I could never bring myself to tell him. Whatever you might think of him, you must know that he took a great deal upon himself when he offered me a place to stay. He did it knowing that our father would not look kindly upon him for it. Indeed, in the first round of sparring Sir Hadrien threatened to cut him out of his inheritance. He settled for reducing his quarterly allowance instead. Because I was at the source of the conflict, even his mother could not be prevailed upon to make up the difference."

Griffin's gaze remained on hers. "Do you blame yourself, Olivia, for Alastair's gaming? Come, be honest. Is there yet some part of you that holds yourself responsible? After all, if you had not sought him out, he would have his full allowance and no need to seek some manner of supplementing it. You were a financial burden to him, there's no denying the truth of that."

Olivia was reminded that Griffin understood too well the sharp turns her mind took. "My presence caused him difficulties," she said carefully. "And he made decisions as to how he would deal with them."

"So he did. You would do well to remember it. Far from being a burden, you were a convenience to him. Your presence gave him an easy excuse for gaming. In all likelihood, he would have taken it up regardless of his financial circumstances and lost sums in excess of whatever his father gave him. Many young men do; most survive the experience and come out wiser for it on the other end. I imagine your brother will too. What is required is time."

Olivia remained silent for a long moment. She was conscious of Griffin's study, the way his head tilted as he waited her out, but he advanced no pressure, only patience, and the ache she carried when she thought of her brother was eased because of it.

"I think you must be right," she said finally, softly. Her shoulders rose and fell on a small sigh as her breath came without any accompanying tightness. "I don't know when I should have come upon the truth of it myself."

"In time." A wry smile edged his lips. "I suspect you are rather more accustomed to accepting fault than assigning it to others."

"Perhaps."

Sensing her wariness, Griffin did not underscore the point. "Will you finish your tea, Olivia?" He leaned forward, touched the side of her cup. "It has not yet grown cold."

Olivia dragged her eyes away from his and glanced at the tea service and uneaten toast points. For once, the rumble in her stomach was pleasant, not ominous. A bit self-consciously, she pressed one hand to it, then returned to her chair.

"What did you mean about Mr. Gardner?" she asked.

The abrupt shift in subject tugged at Griffin's mental balance. "Pardon?"

"Earlier you said that asking Mr. Gardner for information about me would put you in his debt for all eternity. I wondered what you meant."

"Oh." He felt as if he were once again righted, though it was a narrow thing. "Gardner has a faculty for discovery, I suppose you'd call it. One can apply to him to set all manner of things right again."

"Such as finding Lady Breckenridge."

"Yes. That is one example."

"Why did you not ask for his help at the outset?"

"Because I have only recently learned of his peculiar talent. He does not seek out his clientele; indeed, he does not assist everyone who applies to him. Word of mouth brings people to his door, then he decides what he will do."

"And he agreed to help you."

"Yes."

"Now you are in his debt."

"Yes, and he trades in favors, not currency, so I have no idea when or how I might be asked to return it." Griffin did not miss Olivia's flash of disappointment. "There is something you would like to ask of him?"

"I'm not . . . that is, no . . . no, I don't think so." She shrugged. "In any event, what favor could he possibly gain from an association with me?"

"That is for him to decide." When she said nothing, he prompted gently. "Why don't you ask it of me? Perhaps it is something that does not require Gardner's extraordinary skills. Is it outside all possibility that I might be of service?"

His rather obvious cajolery raised her smile. "I cannot decide if you mean to be modest about your own talents or wounded that I did not apply to you first."

"Which approach will have the greater chance of disarming you? Tell me, and I shall refine it."

Olivia was not proof against his honesty. Her smile deepened as she shook her head. "I am disarmed. Completely. I do not thank you for it, nor for making me admit it."

It was only fair, Griffin thought. He should not be the only one without weapons at the ready. Suspecting that she would not believe him, he held his tongue and waited for her to name the service he might do for her.

"Do you recall the four gentlemen who came here together awhile back, all of them so deep in their cups that you were forced to show them the door?"

He did not require further clarification. "I do, indeed. There was one that—" He stopped, rubbed his chin with his knuckles. "Whiskey. Gin. Two pints of ale. Am I right?"

"I think so. It's been some years."

"And the one who spoke to you? Tried to place your face? Which one was he?"

"The whiskey. Or I believe he might have been."

"You could have told me then."

"No," she said. "I couldn't have. I denied the truth to myself."

Griffin understood well enough how that was done. "What is it you want?"

"As you said, peace of mind, I suppose. They know what happened afterward. I never have."

"If they meant to come forward, they would have by now. Years ago, in fact."

"I thought so, yes. I listened wherever I went, hoping to hear something as much as I dreaded the same. I could never learn what had become of Rawlings, but then I might have mistaken his name. I was too afraid to return, so I kept going. I believe what you said about defending myself . . . most of the time. It is what I did when I was confronted by the intruder in my room. It was as if Rawlings was given a second chance and I . . ." She fell silent, shaking her head. "There is guilt, though, that I left Rawlings to others and fled, and fear of what is still unknown."

Griffin understood her vulnerability. "How were you called when you were employed at the inn?"

"Livvy. Livvy Cole."

"Would they have learned it that night?"

"I don't know."

"Did you never think of taking another name? That you opposed the idea when I suggested it seems to fly in the face of common sense."

Olivia touched her fingers to her temple and pushed back a wayward strand of hair. "I suppose we see it differently."

"But when you were at the inn, weren't you hiding from your father?"

"In hiding? No. What a peculiar notion. It is truer that throughout my life he hid me away."

"How?"

"At school, of course. There are such things for girls, you know, if one's parents aren't inclined to employ a governess. As you have mentioned, my father likes to take a position on the moral high ground, so it should not surprise you that confession and repentance figured largely in my education."

Griffin's eyes narrowed as he considered what he knew about the schools available to young girls. If Sir Hadrien was determined to put his daughter away, then the school would be isolated and have little in the way of interference from the outside. "A convent school," he said, looking to Olivia for confirmation. "Confession and repentance. I'm right, aren't I? You were educated in a convent school."

"You are rather too proud for coming to it on your own when you only had to ask. Pride goeth before destruction, and a haughty spirit before a fall."

He could imagine that she had been required to learn and recite a great many proverbs. "How old were you when you were sent away?"

"Six."

He owed it to her, he thought, not to let pity creep into his expression. "And when you left?"

"Twelve."

Griffin nodded slowly. He knew what to make of the half dozen years between her sixth year and her twelfth. Only the most depraved mind could reconcile what she'd learned at the school as part and parcel of a young girl's education.

"You are thinking the whole of it must have been terrible," she said quietly. This time it was Olivia who slid her hand across the table and beckoned him with an open palm. He fit it in hers and her fingers closed around his. "It wasn't. Or if it was, I choose to remember it differently. There were kindnesses. I was well educated, sheltered, and fed. There were games. Giggling. Silly gossip. We had books and instruments. Some girls played; others sang. We had prayers, of course. You will not be shocked that there was an extraordinary amount of praying. Also lessons in deportment. In drawing and sewing and conversation. French and Italian were spoken. Latin, also. History. Geography. Penmanship. Poetry. There were riding and dancing lessons. We learned such things as to make us comfortable companions. There was no hardship in that, save for my own lack of interest in all but the books and conversation."

Her brief account was not so different from his own experiences at Hambrick Hall, but he would not have described the purpose of such things as to make him a comfortable companion. Had she realized even at so early an age that she was being prepared for something that was perhaps beyond the pale? He decided not to turn the conversation in that direction but asked instead, "What sort of student were you?"

"Can you not guess? A diligent one. Most desirous of pleasing. In the beginning it was to please my teachers, but in the end it was to please me. There was no way to avoid all punishment, but I was not called forward as frequently as others. A palm lashing was common. Canings were relatively rare. The punishment chair was the most feared."

"Punishment chair? What is that?"

"It was not used at your school?"

"Until you tell me what it is, I have no idea."

"It's simply a chair with the center of the seat removed. There were several of different heights so that as a girl grew taller there was always a chair sufficiently high enough to cause her feet to dangle just above the floor."

Griffin began to have a picture of it in his mind. "Her legs would have become numb," he said. "Swollen as well, I imagine."

"Yes, if she had to sit in it long."

"I should think twenty minutes would be long enough to get the desired effect. How long were girls required to sit?"

She shrugged. "Half an hour for minor infractions. An hour or more for the important ones."

A muscle jumped in Griffin's cheek. The line of his scar became pronounced. "No one could possibly stay on their feet after so long in the chair."

"Not easily, no. I imagine that's why they applied the strap when a girl faltered and fell. How long it took to rise from the floor depended on her strength of character and will."

Griffin wondered if his face was as cool and colorless as it felt. He was careful to speak quietly, certain she did not deserve to hear his thoughts at the volume he heard them in his own head. "Bloody hell, Olivia. Strength of character and will be damned. That is nonsense. You are describing an abomination. Torture, not punishment, and in no wise discipline."

She blinked. "It has never been done to you?"

"God, no. The dons, house masters, and proctors at Hambrick Hall were strict and embraced the efficacy of the rod, too much so for my tastes, but even they would shy from what you are telling me. Who stood over you while it was being done? The sisters?"

"No. Oh, no. They prayed for us. They could not . . . would not . . . no, the sisters had no part in that."

They had also deliberately turned their heads, but Griffin did not say so. "A priest, then. Was it a priest?"

"Sometimes." She could not be certain when she ceased to hold his hand and he began holding hers.

"Sometimes," he said softly. It meant there were other tormentors. "Olivia, who were the men that forced themselves on you?"

Olivia flinched a little, but he held her fast. She had wanted him to know that she had memories of light and laughter that were separate from the darker recollections and that she was shaped by both experiences, not one exclusive of the other. "I should not speak of them."

The childlike tenor of her voice startled them both, but it was Griffin who frowned. She had spoken the words as though she had learned them by rote and was now obliged to recite them.

As if testing the waters, she said them again. "I should not speak of them."

"Is that what you were told, Olivia?"

"I don't remember. It seems as if it must be, doesn't it?"

He squeezed her hand gently. "Perhaps it is something that one cannot come at directly. It's possible you never knew their names. What can you speak of?"

"Not all of us were chosen. The girls, I mean. I remember that. We were not all selected to go."

"To go where?"

"To wherever it was that we went." She drew her hand back and chose one of the cold toast points. "I was a child. I cannot say more than that. I don't know where I was or where I was taken. It was a very small world and was not made significantly larger by being taken beyond the convent walls."

"Did you go alone?"

"Alone. In pairs. Never more than three. I told you once that I went willingly that first time. Do you remember?"

"I remember."

"My greatest shame is that I wanted to be chosen. There were presents afterward. Sweets. Ribbons. Gloves. Lace. Pretty bonnets and slippers. I was envious of what I saw other girls receiving. I had nothing from home. No letters. No packages. I learned quickly that I should never expect to receive anything from my family, so when girls returned from their carriage rides and showed the gifts they'd been allowed to take, I wanted the same."

Griffin thought of his sisters. He imagined them elbowing one another out of the way, leaping across prostrate bodies to reach the waiting carriage first. They would have been eager, even greedy, and they would have been made to pay dearly, just as Olivia had been made to pay. But for the grace of God, there went Jenny, Kate, and Juliet. "You did nothing wrong."

"I know it, and yet it does not always seem so."

"That is because when you reflect upon it you think you had a choice. You didn't. Never once. Not even at the first."

Griffin's implacable features were softened by Olivia's tears. She knuckled them away impatiently. She required him to be uncompromising in the position he took and in the position he took it from. She wanted to be—needed to be—convinced. "How can you know?"

"You would know it as well but for the fact that it happened to you."

"I was called out to one of the carriages many times."

"Do you say that to punish yourself?"

"I say it so you will know what I am."

"I know what you are, Olivia, and it is not what you think they made you. You said you were not a whore, but I am no longer certain that you believe it."

"Their gifts paid for me."

"Their gifts paid for your silence. That is what they purchased. They could have had you for nothing."

Olivia simply stared at him. As often as she'd drawn back the curtain on her past, she had never seen it in such a light before.

Watching her, the left side of Griffin's mouth edged upward. He had managed to trip her up in the best possible way. He could see her taking in the view, examining it from this new perspective. Her splendid green eyes were narrowed just enough to sharpen her glance, and her mouth, her very tasty mouth, remained parted on an indrawn breath. A curling tendril of flame-red hair fell over her brow and dipped low enough to hook her lashes. She thrust her lower jaw forward and blew up, the action a mixture of irritation and impatience, and dislodged the curl. It settled at the corner of her eye and she allowed it to remain there.

"It makes an awful sort of sense when I hear you say it," she told him. "It makes me think that the time will come when I'll be able to speak of them."

"I would not be at all surprised."

Olivia prepared to choose another piece of toast and saw that her plate was empty. She could not recall that she'd eaten any of it. Similarly, her cup was drained.

"Hungry?" Griffin asked, divining her thoughts.

"Ravenous."

He stood. "Then attention must be paid."

Olivia did not anticipate that Griffin would want to accompany her on her walk. She was standing at the front door, fastening the frog closure on her mantle while she waited for Mason to reappear with his gloves in hand, when Griffin came down the stairs dressed for the out of doors. Her eyebrows rose in tandem. Too late she realized that her expression was not simply one of surprise but hinted at the fact that she found him indecently handsome to look upon. His quick half-grin made it clear that he'd had a hint of her thoughts and approved of the turn they'd taken.

Olivia pivoted, giving him her shoulder. He had a cheval glass in his bedchamber and therefore no need to view his reflection again in her eyes. She thought she heard him chuckle as he came abreast of her, but when she cast him a suspicious sideways glance he was perfectly stoic.

It was no good. She sighed. "You have the profile of a Roman god," she said, "and that is all I am prepared to say on the matter of your exceptionally fine countenance."

She was already on the lip of the second step by the time Griffin caught up with her, and this time she was quite certain he was laughing. A smile edged her mouth, deepened, and in another moment she joined him.

They walked to Moorhead Street, turned, separated briefly as they dodged a stack of crates that indicated a move to or away from the district, then made a diagonal crossing in the direction of the park. Griffin helped Olivia adjust her sable-trimmed hood as the wind kicked up and gave her the lee side of his body. Thus sheltered, she was able to speak without the accompaniment of chattering teeth, though she liked their companionable silence well enough. He was the one who finally breached it.

"I went to see my sisters yesterday," he said. "After I spoke to Gardner and we agreed that he would bring Elaine to London, I decided that calling upon my sisters was in order."

"To inform them?" asked Olivia.

"To warn them. They do not know the particulars of why my marriage collapsed, but they have supported me in their own way. That means they make free with such criticisms and advice as they believe will help me and form a protective phalanx about me when anyone outside the family is wont to do the same."

"I do not suppose they could demonstrate their great affection for you in any better manner."

"I suppose not, no."

"Nor you for them. You show considerable tolerance. What could very well be an annoyance becomes a source of amusement."

He smiled because she understood so completely. It astonished when one considered that she had so little experience with family herself, but she had neatly defined the workings of his. "Jenny was rather less disagreeable than Kate or Juliet upon hearing my news, but she is the one who will insist that they meet to strategize. Jenny favors strategy. Kate and Juliet have a tendency to simply charge into the fray, so she must save them from themselves. At least that is how she explains the fact that she has always been their leader."

"They sound formidable."

"Amazons. Brave men have been known to quiver in their presence." He drew Olivia closer as they stepped aside to make way for a nursemaid with two young children in tow. The children, rosy-cheeked and giggling, seemed oblivious to the elements, while their nurse walked with her head down and shoulders hunched, oblivious to everything else.

"Have you nieces and nephews?" Olivia asked when the trio moved on and they resumed walking.

"Five. Kate has twin girls; Juliet, a boy and an infant girl; and Jenny, another girl. I had not seen any of them since Mathilda's christening. She's Juliet's baby. It seemed like a good idea to spend time with them yesterday. With Elaine's arrival imminent, it is unclear when the opportunity will present itself again."

Olivia knew it was foolish to think they could not speak of his wife, but she was in a foolish frame of mind and wanted to enjoy it awhile longer, damn the consequences of dreaming while she walked, and please herself by stealing glances at the man who'd been her fierce and tender lover this night past.

She did not fail to notice that he had fallen silent also, and the cast of it was darker than her own. She let him have at the problem that set his mind to brooding so that she might indulge in her selfish, simple thoughts a few moments longer.

"I instructed Gardner to escort Elaine directly from Bath, where she has been residing, to the hell," Griffin said as they began their second circuit of the park. Like an army of foot soldiers waiting for inspection, the tall oaks stood at attention on either side of the promenade path. He gave them no heed, turning to gauge Olivia's reaction instead.

"Is that wise?" Aware of his regard, Olivia schooled her features and strove for a tone that was more neutral than indifferent. "She will not thank you for it."

"There is no arrangement I can make that will garner her approval. I am under no illusions that she will return willingly. I have prepared Gardner to anticipate the very worst sort of behavior from her."

Olivia could only imagine how lowering that must have been for him. She nodded jerkily, understanding. "Perhaps Mr. Gardner will not be tempted."

"Oh, I am quite certain he will be tempted, but more in the way of wanting to stuff her in a trunk and shove it from a bridge. Gardner has the good fortune to be firmly set in his marriage and deeply in love with his wife." He paused, frowning as an unpleasant thought occurred to him. "But then Ulysses had Penelope waiting for him when he succumbed to the call of the sirens."

Olivia laid her hand gently on his forearm. The restraint was not to stay his steps, but to stay his thoughts. "He will not return to Bath alone, will he?"

"No. I have some concerns for the men who accompany him, but he assures me none of them will be alone with her."

He looked down at her gloved hand, then at her. "You think I am making too much of it."

Her faint smile was gently chiding. "You alluded to Homer."

"I did, didn't I?" He sighed. "It was kind of you not to pick up a stick and beat me with it."

She let her hand fall away. "I was confident of your good sense returning." She rubbed the underside of her chin. The soft kid leather of her glove was like the caress of his fingers against her skin. "Lady Breckenridge's arrival presents me with the opportunity to take my leave. We should discuss that. I am not certain when—"

"Take your leave?" That brought him up short. He watched her walk on, then closed the distance quickly with a few long-legged strides. "What do you mean?"

"Are we discussing it?" asked Olivia. "I have the distinct impression you mean for us to have a row."

That observation had the effect of cooling Griffin's heels. "Do you imagine I want you leave?"

"No. The opposite, in fact, but I am hoping you will agree that this is not one of those times when you should have your way. I will be a distraction at best; at worst, a target for Lady Breckenridge and a shield for you. You can comprehend, I hope, that I have no wish to be any of those."

"Do you believe I hold you or myself in so little regard that I would use you as a shield?"

"Of course not. It is the sort of thing that happens in spite of one's intentions that it should be otherwise. I believe you will deal more fairly with your wife—and she with you—if I absent myself."

It was the reasonableness of her argument that undid him. It didn't matter that he had no liking for what she was propos-ing; he knew she was right. "I can set you up in a house," he said finally. "I should have made the offer earlier."

"It's all right. I wouldn't have accepted. In fact, I won't now."

"You mean to be difficult."

"I hadn't thought so, no. I was hoping we might reach a compromise."

Griffin had the sense that what she was calling a compromise was merely getting what she wanted all along. He was set on telling her so, but heard himself asking to hear it instead.

"I thought I would return to Jericho Mews."

"With your brother?"

"I doubt he is spending any more time there than he ever did. That is why it suits. Do you think he will not allow me to stay?"

"Temporarily? He will be pleased to have you. You will relieve him of all the responsibilities that have plagued him these last weeks: the staff quarrels, the budget, the creditors, the rent. Yes, he will most certainly welcome you."

"I intend to be his guest, not his mother."

Griffin shrugged. "I am not sure that matters. It is the sort of thing that happens in spite of one's intentions that it should be otherwise."

She recognized her own words being turned on her. "It seemed more pertinent when I was talking about you."

"It frequently does." His glance was wry. "This is what you want, Olivia? Jericho Mews?"

She caught the sleeve of his greatcoat and held on, raising her face to his when he felt the tug and turned. "No, it's not what I want, but it is right for now."

"Tell me what you want. Give me that at least."

Her hand slid upward from his sleeve and ruffled the capes on its climb to his shoulder. It did not linger there long, but came to rest at the left side of his face. Her thumb made a light tracing along the path of his scar and stopped at the corner of his mouth.

"I want to be with you," she said. "With you, not apart from you. I don't want a residence that is purchased for my shelter and your convenience. I don't want to wait upon you or your visits. Neither do I wish to serve at the whim of my brother, nor to be dependent upon him for my keep. You will have to think carefully about that before you invite me back to the hell. You will have to be certain that there is a place for me in your life." She stood on tiptoe and pressed her lips hard to his just once before she settled back on her heels. Her hand fell to her side, and she was gratified to see that she had surprised and alarmed him. "Don't mistake that I mean you must have me for your wife or not at all. That is not an arrangement that could possibly suit either one of us. I will accept a place in your life without marriage; in fact, I am certain I prefer it."

It was rather a lot to take in, especially when she'd muddled the thing by kissing him as if she'd been compelled to do so. The impression of her mouth on his remained even as she began walking away. Griffin glanced around, saw that while they were not alone in the park, no one else was giving them notice, and lunged forward to catch Olivia by the elbow. Her feet did not quite touch the ground as he half-carried, half-dragged her to the sheltered side of an enormous chestnut. He shackled her wrists in his hands and drew them as high as her shoulders, then urged her back against the trunk and followed with the press of his hard frame. There was time enough for her lips to part, but no time to draw a full breath.

His capture was complete when his mouth slanted across hers. Hungry as he was for the taste of her, he gave no quarter. His lips worked over hers, his tongue speared her mouth, followed the ridge of her teeth and the sensitive underside of her lip. He stole a soft moan from the back of her throat and savored it as another man might savor smuggled brandy. The fact that there were risks in the pursuit and possession made it all the more dear.

He drew back just enough to reposition his mouth. He nudged her lips at an angle, worried the bottom one between his teeth as she so often did, then ran the edge of his tongue across the tiny indentations he'd made.

Olivia was boneless, held up by his hands on her wrists, the trunk at her back, and the knee he thrust between her skirts. She might very well faint if he let her go; she might very well faint if he didn't.

His will was not a simple thing to ignore. It was like his kiss—coaxing, teasing, gentle and fierce by turns, insistent. He did not always get his way, but he knew what he wanted. Just now he wanted her.

He made her want him in return.

Even as Olivia thought it, she knew it wasn't quite right. He had not made her want him, he'd simply laid bare her need. She wanted him of her own volition, and her will was every bit as firm and fast as his own. It was equally difficult to ignore.

She wrestled free of his hands and threw her arms around his neck. Her hood fell back, exposing her hair first to the wind that came in small bursts around the tree trunk, then to his fingers. She lifted herself against him and wished that he could take her inside his coat, inside his skin if such a thing was possible.

His kiss was as rough as the bark at her back, but she returned it measure for measure, wanting him now in no other fashion than this. Her grip around his neck and back tightened.

Her eyes flew open when she felt the vibration of his groan against her mouth. She drew back so quickly that her head bumped the trunk. Careless of the thump to her own head, her eyes focused on his face first, then on the hold she had on him. "Did I hurt you?"

Griffin bent and touched his forehead to hers. "Not until this moment, and it's not because you have a lock on my neck." He eased her hands down. "Come. We can't remain here. Someone will see us. We should—"

He stopped because Olivia had shifted her head and was no longer gazing into his eyes. The point of her attention was somewhere past his right shoulder. Apparently they had already drawn attention. He straightened, turned to seek out the same view she had, and caught the young gentleman in the act of replacing his hat. His posture suggested he had recently doffed it, and the smirk on his lips suggested it had been done with a certain insolence. Griffin's eyes were drawn to the shock of fair hair cropped and curled close to his head.

He turned his head sharply toward Olivia. She was pale as salt. No other confirmation was required. Griffin took off at a run.

Chapter Twelve

Olivia wished she had never seen her attacker in the park. Had Griffin been able to run him to ground, there might have been some good come of the encounter. Griffin had not, however, and it changed the routine of everyone in the hell as a consequence. No one save her made noises about the inconvenience, and because no one paid her the least attention when she did, she learned how to set her jaw so that a muscle twitched in her cheek. It was a source of amusement to Griffin as he considered that her imitation of him not only hit the mark but was flattering besides.

Olivia was required to have two escorts when she left the hell and a pair of footmen standing post when she dealt faro. The gentleman villain—as Wick insisted upon calling him—was considered to be a reckless and dangerous rogue, one who might very well have already returned to the hell unnoticed. Griffin was convinced that it was not happenstance that put him in the park, but that he had been observing her for some time. Even if it wasn't true, everyone around Olivia agreed it was the safer course to act as if it was.

Olivia twirled a quill pen between her fingertips as she made mental calculations over an open ledger. She sat with her feet curled to one side, her kid slippers lying under the chair. She had yet to change into her nightclothes. Her only concession to the lateness of the hour and the completion of her duties in the gaming room was to remove her wig and paint before she sat down with the book of accounts.

Griffin reclined on the chaise in his study and watched her. It was a pleasure, really. She was capable of such fierce concentration that it changed the shape of her face. The space between her eyebrows puckered; the line of her mouth all but disappeared as she pressed her lips together. She used the feathered end of the quill to occasionally push back a fallen lock of hair or absently make a pass across her temple.

The skirt of her ice-blue gown spread over the chair like frosting. She wore a loosely knotted silk shawl about her shoulders. Her throat was bare, a condition he could not rectify because she would not accept jewelry from him and preferred not to wear those few pieces his wife left behind except when she was turning cards. An emerald, he thought, would be the obvious complement to her eyes and coloring, but something sapphire would work as well—something so deeply indigo that it would hint at violet in certain light. He watched her touch the quill to her throat, lightly tickle the hollow. That raised his smile. He had reason to know she was sensitive there. He'd made it a point to sip from that particular spot whenever he could, and she surrendered the tiniest of whimpers each time he did.

Griffin loosened his stock and unbuttoned his frock coat. He plowed four fingers through his hair. The heat that was in him now could not be explained by the roaring fire. He knew the source of it well enough: she was currently occupying his chair and amusing herself with a feather.

"I could make better use of that quill," he said.

Olivia looked up, blinked owlishly. "Oh, you're still here. I thought you'd gone."

She was so entirely guileless at times that he could not take offense. He pushed ravishment to the back of his mind and sat up. He removed his stock, folded it around his hand. "Are you almost finished?"

"Almost. One more column. Do you wish to see?"

"Perhaps when you're done. I trust you."

"I know you do, and it remains a puzzler. I can make a mistake the same as anyone."

"I don't doubt it, but you won't cheat me."

No, she wouldn't do that. She smiled at him, warmed by his confidence, and set herself once again to the task at hand. Still, she could not resist adding, "I'm much more likely to throttle you."

Griffin was glad he was only reaching for his whiskey, not drinking it. Surely he would have choked. As it was, a bit of the liquid sloshed over the edge of the crystal tumbler. "I cannot know whether to be alarmed that you mention it or relieved that you can find some humor in it."

"As it's been more than a fortnight since I attacked you, relief strikes me as a better response." She quickly added the numbers in the last column, checked to see that all was balanced, and pushed the book away. She returned the quill to its stand and stoppered the inkwell, then sat comfortably back in the leather chair. "Have you slept with one eye open?"

"No." Griffin sipped his whiskey. "I have not so much as peeked." He often fell to sleep after she did, but that was simply his way, not a precaution. She'd shared his bed the evening after he had given chase to the gentleman villain and slept as deeply and trustingly as an infant. He could not help but be encouraged by that. Nothing seemed as likely to push her toward a nightmare as sighting her attacker in the park.

He'd finally come to know the whole of how she'd defended herself against the villain. It had required some prodding on his part, a bit of insistence, but Olivia gave him all of it in the end, filling in those details that she'd left out on the first telling. Griffin had had to wrestle with his own rage, most of it rooted in what he remembered as his own helplessness. He hadn't been able to put her out of harm's way, and when it found her, he was the one who couldn't reach her. Nothing about that set well, but he'd held it in check because his anger served neither of them. He'd applied himself instead to appreciating her courage and cleverness and waited until he was alone to give in to the other.

He'd even snapped a few damp towels, finding them as viciously effective as she described.

"Would you like a glass of wine?" he asked. "Sherry?"

Olivia shook her head. "You expected Mr. Gardner would arrive today, didn't you?"

He had, but he hadn't realized she'd known. "Prickly, was I?"

Prickly was inadequate to describe the flashes of impatience she saw in him earlier. Never one to suffer fools for long, this evening they were not even given an audience. He did not move among his guests so much as prowl, and she saw him seek the view from the window in the card room on several occasions. "Yes," she said, tempering her smile. "Prickly."

He blew out a short breath, set his tumbler aside, and idly unwound the length of linen stock from his hand. "I calculated that enough time had passed for Gardner to make the journey to Bath and back again, though to be strictly honest, it's not the impending arrival of my wife that concerns me overmuch, but your departure." He regarded her carefully set expression. "I suspect you knew that, didn't you?"

Realizing that her effort to conceal it from him had been for naught, Olivia sighed. "It occurred, yes. You will not insist that I remain, will you?"

"Would you listen?" Tossing the stock to the foot of the chaise, he held up one hand, palm out. "Don't tell me. It is better if I can permit myself to believe that you would. In exchange for that kindness, I will not ask it of you."

Olivia gathered her hair at her nape and drew it forward

over her shoulder. She combed it with her fingers. "The villain will not find me at Jericho Mews. He knows less than nothing about me."

Griffin was not convinced of that, but he did not share his doubts with her. It seemed to him that by trailing after her when she left the hell, the gentleman villain must have learned something. "You will not be gone long. Elaine cannot remain here underfoot, nor do I believe she will want to. It is necessary only that she understand my intentions."

"Do those include parading her in front of the ton?"

"Parade? I will escort her. Once will be sufficient to prove that she is still among the living. I have no wish to shame her."

"Then be careful that you do not," Olivia said quietly. "You mean to divorce her. There will be censure enough in that."

"I assure you, the censure of the ton will not bruise her in the least."

Olivia's smile was gently chiding. "I was thinking of you."

He arched an eyebrow and regarded her curiously. "Have I given you cause to think I care for the good opinion of the ton?"

"Many times, but the one that is most relevant to this discussion is the length and breadth of your search for Lady Breckenridge. It is more than a matter of pride, though that would be reason enough for what you've done. It is also about your good name. That you operate this establishment is something that can be, and is, tolerated in some fashion. Society accepts a rascal now and again and is the better for it. A murderer is not a rascal, and the suspicion that you murdered your wife will always attach itself to your name unless you prove differently."

Griffin approached the desk and drew Olivia to her feet. He lifted her chin with the cup of his hand. "I prefer to believe I don't give a damn."

She nodded, met his gaze. "I know," she whispered. "It is the same for me."

* * *

Olivia returned to her brother's house in Jericho Mews the
following morning. She didn't have to explain why she was
choosing to leave just then. Griffin anticipated her departure
the moment he'd confirmed that his wife's arrival was imminent. For his own sake as much as hers, he did not accompany
her. Foster and Drummond, accompanied by the lads, made
the short journey from Putnam Lane to respectability in a
hansom cab that Griffin hired for her.

Mrs. Beck was glad to see her and even wept a little. This
show of emotion embarrassed the housekeeper enough that
she did nothing to stop Olivia's entourage from trudging
through the house in muddy shoes, trunks thumping in their
wake.

When the time came for them to leave, they were not easily
dismissed. Foster and Drummond pushed the boys forward a
few steps but barely budged themselves. Olivia held Griffin
responsible for that. Their discomfort at going without her
was palpable. They easily looked up and down the street a
half dozen times in search of the gentleman villain before
they were satisfied he had not dared to follow them.

Olivia stood outside her home until the cab disappeared.
Only then was she able to go to her room and begin unpack-
ing. She brought everything Griffin gave her, not because she
thought she would be gone so long, but because she did not
want Lady Breckenridge to stumble upon her altered castoffs.
No woman would appreciate that.

Alastair was not entirely welcoming, but neither did he
turn her out. He required some time to accustom himself to
the idea of her return, no matter how brief it was supposed
to be. To make amends for his initial lack of warmth, he offered to hire a maid for her since he'd released Molly Dillon
from the staff. Olivia thanked him for his generosity and politely refused it.

"I would rather that Father does not learn you are living here again," he said as they dined that evening.

"So he has restored your allowance. That is good." She took a small bite of the soused fish. Cooked in vinegar with onions and peppers, the fish had a pungent taste that did not agree with her, and she set her fork down to sip from her glass of wine. "I will go no farther than the park if you like, and at such times when it is unlikely to be crowded. That way you can be assured that no word will reach him from any quarter." She saw it made him uncomfortable to state that it was indeed his preference, but she would not carry his discomfort for him.

"I would prefer it. Mother is likely to hear you have returned first, and we know she is a tattle."

"So you say. I do not remember her well." Olivia regarded her brother over the rim of her glass. "Before I thrust myself into your life, Alastair, had you ever spared a thought for me?"

He shifted uneasily in his chair. "Yes. Yes, of course. You were a great mystery to me growing up. Mother sometimes spoke of you, just incidental comments that seemed to surprise her when she heard them aloud, as if the words had escaped. I wondered about it, but questions were not encouraged. She once tried to tell me that you died, but I never believed her. There was no vault in the mausoleum to account for it, and I was old enough by then to know when I wasn't being given the truth. I supposed that if she felt compelled to lie to me, no one else would be inclined to impart the truth."

"You never told me that."

"No, well, it is not the sort of thing I thought you'd ever want to know." He tilted his head to better take her measure. "I have almost no memory of living with you at Coleridge Park."

"That is not surprising. You were hardly more than an infant when I was sent away. I was uncertain you would even know who I was when I sought you out at university." Olivia had never forgotten who she was, but there had been a concerted effort at Coleridge Park to put her away. "You did know me, though, and never once hesitated to invite me in."

"I was curious," he said, "and possessed of a certain amount of guilt. I wish I could say I was generous, but you know now that I am not that man."

"Your honesty gives me hope that you will be some day."

"Ah," he said, flushing a little at the rightness of her words. "You know just where to drive the nail."

They ate in uneasy silence after that, but when she retired to the drawing room, he followed her. Olivia picked at the stitches of a tablecloth she'd begun to embroider months earlier and abandoned when Alastair had gone missing. It had not been an inspired effort from the beginning, merely a way of passing time, and now she undid her work and wondered what it would be like to tug at the threads of time in the same manner.

When Alastair turned away from poking at the fire he caught sight of his sister's gentle smile. "Are you in love with Breckenridge?"

Olivia's smile remained unchanged. She didn't glance up. "If I am, you will not be the first person I tell."

"You will probably find it strange, Olivia, but I like him. I know he does not return my regard, but it does not change my respect for him."

"You were enjoying the affections of his mistress while she was still under his protection. I think it is difficult for him to respect that." She lifted her head. "Have a care how you respond, Alastair. You gave me to him, remember."

"It wasn't like that. Or not precisely like that. I never meant that you should—"

Olivia stopped him with a look. "Let us not speak of it. I am content, and you did no more than our father before you." Perhaps it was the way of the Cole men to make whores of their women. She bit her tongue on this last thought and returned her attention to ripping the uneven stitches. "Are you still visiting Mrs. Christie?"

Here was a subject Alastair did not wish to pursue, yet he was startled into replying. "She is under my protection, yes."

"She is significantly older than you."

He shrugged. "Father approves. I told him about her. He cautioned me against losing my heart and making a mad, foolish, and wholly unsuitable proposal, but that was the extent of his concern."

"I'm sure it was."

"He is a practical man, Olivia, with sensibilities of entitlement. In his prime I imagine his lovers were legion."

Olivia jerked, pricked her finger. She turned her hand to keep from staining the tablecloth with blood and raised her finger to her lips. When Alastair inquired after her, she merely nodded to indicate she was fine even as memories best forgotten began to churn.

She'd bled the first time she'd been taken from the convent. Other times as well. Her hand shook with fear that she might bloody the tablecloth. They would make her scrub it clean, erase the evidence of her sin. Was she the sin? Was she the sacrifice? It had been an age since that particular memory had come to her, but no amount of time was too far in the past. Now, tasting blood on the tip of her finger, it was as if it were happening in this very moment. *Look at what you have done, my sweet girl. My own dearest child. Can you smell the blood?*

"Olivia?" Alastair left the fireplace and dropped to his haunches in front of her. "You are pale. I don't think—"

She pushed the tablecloth off her lap with such force that Alastair almost toppled backward when he tried to gather it up. She stood, stepped around him, and murmured her apologies before she fled the room as if she were about to be set upon by all the demons of hell.

* * *

"It was most peculiar," Alastair said, lying back to cradle his head in his palms. "I tried to speak to her later, but she would not open the door to me. I think she had been weeping."

Alys Christie made appropriate consoling noises. "Then she would not want you to see her in such a state. It does not matter that you are her brother. You are a man, and no woman is fond of being looked upon at such moments. Unless she cries prettily; that is altogether different. In that event, she does well to be seen as it can often be employed to her advantage." She walked her fingers down the center of his chest. His skin was pale and smooth and firm. Her nails left faint pink crescents wherever she pressed. She felt a surge of tenderness toward him and that pleased her. He was very young, she thought, but not entirely unschooled, and that pleased her as well. "Does your sister cry prettily?"

Alastair sucked in a breath as Mrs. Christie's fingers slipped under the drawstring of his drawers. She had the lightest touch when she teased him. He could feel his cock stirring. What had she asked him? "Prettily? No, I don't think so."

"Then ease your mind. There is nothing she expects from you." She turned a fraction more in to him and kissed him on the mouth while her hand slipped lower. "You were right to leave her. I cannot be sorry for it has brought you here."

He caught his breath again as her fingers wrapped around him. "Did you enjoy the theatre tonight?"

"I did." She took full advantage of his young body's resiliency and worked him quickly to a cockstand. "I missed you, though. I had to sit between Mr. Landis and Baron Collison's eldest son, who bathes as infrequently as his father if I am any judge."

Alastair caught her hand, interrupting her rhythm before she made him come in his drawers. "The play's the thing."

She laughed, kissed him again, and kept her hand still. "Has Breckenridge finished with her?" she asked with perfect indifference. "You have not said why she returned."

"Didn't I?" It still astonished him that he could speak at all in this woman's presence, but at the moment of his crisis he never knew what would spill from his lips. He recalled his father's caution, but it was difficult to keep it front and center when she was milking him dry. He eased his hand away from hers and did not discourage her when she threw a leg across both of his, rose up, and straddled him. "I thought I did." He groaned as she pressed on his fly with her palm just before she released him. He sprung erect, a fine soldier in want of inspection. She was thorough, as always. "Olivia returned because of Lady Breckenridge."

Mrs. Christie's cool smile edged closer to scorn. "Oh? She is only now learning that he is married? My, but she was an innocent. I had no idea." She lifted her hips and eased herself slowly onto him. He pulsed inside her. "I suppose she has come to understand he will not marry her. Dashed hopes." She drew her nightgown over her head and flung it away, then bent forward to kiss him. "What a pity."

Alastair murmured something incoherent against her mouth. It was only as she was sitting up again that he was able to give distinction to the words. "I don't know what hopes Olivia harbored, but it is Lady Breckenridge's return to London that sent her packing."

"Her return?" Mrs. Christie removed Alastair's hands from her breasts and set them firmly on her thighs. "Do you mean to say that he's found her? She's really alive?"

Alastair dug his heels into the mattress, seeking purchase so he could pump his hips. "Of course she's alive," he said between clenched teeth. "Why wouldn't she be?"

"Because everyone thinks she's dead. There are still a great many people who believe he murdered her." She thwarted his movement by seating herself more heavily on his groin and ignored the rush of air that left his lips.

Alastair felt beads of sweat form just below his hairline. He allowed that there were less pleasant tortures than the one he was experiencing now, but God's truth, he was praying for her to rotate her hips just so. "Everyone seems to be wrong," he said, appealing to her reason. "If it is rumor, it is certain to be a very old one. I've never heard of it."

"Not *that* old. Naturally, you would not know it. You only patronized his hell. You did not rub shoulders with Brecken-ridge's intimates."

The sharpness of her tone warned Alastair that he had offended her. Apparently using the word "old" had been enough to poke at her sensibilities. "I doubt his intimates are the ones wagging their tongues." He felt her thighs tighten as she pinched him between her knees. Her frustration was likely to take the breath from him, but Alastair was quite certain it would be worth it. He eased his hands out from under hers and cupped her hips. His fingertips pressed the smooth skin of her buttocks.

Alys stared down at him, more amused by his single-mindedness than aroused by it. She made herself tight around his erection and drew a small moan from his parted lips. When he urged her upward, she didn't resist his effort. She circled her hips. "Is this what you want, my darling boy?"

Alastair bucked under her in response, driving himself deeply into her even before she'd fully settled on him. He surprised a sweet moan from her. "Is this what you want?"

He was not such a boy after all. She rose and fell again, watching his eyes darken at the center and his skin flush. He was a beautiful young man, prideful as well. Already there were signs that she would not always be able to lead him around by his cock, but just now he gave himself over easily enough. She moaned again, this time as she let her head fall back. She drew her hands between her thighs, then higher across her belly until she cupped her breasts. The square cut emerald ring that she wore on her thumb glowed in the candlelight. Twenty-one diamond chips sparkled as she rubbed it over her budding nipple. She closed her eyes, confident that he was watching her, seeing the ring, and feeling all kinds of powerful as he drove himself hard into her.

Alys Christie permitted him to make himself proud.

Olivia frequently had breakfast in her room. Alastair, if he was in residence, did not rise until much later. In the afternoon, he made calls upon his friends or visited the clubs, and because there were deliveries from Bond Street, Olivia knew he also shopped. As she had no interest in the same, she walked daily in the park that was the centerpiece of Jericho Mews. Mrs. Beck was not always available to act as a companion, so there were mornings that she walked alone. Griffin would not have stood for it, but Alastair made no objection.

While her brother was often gone of an evening, he did take tea with her. It was in this manner that she was kept abreast of the activities in town, those that he attended as well as those he only read about in the *Gazette*. He had remarked on several occasions that there was no word of Lady Breckenridge's presence at any of the affairs that drew the notice of the paper. He'd also heard nothing whispered in any quarter that she'd returned to London, and while he no longer visited Breckenridge's hell, his friends had observed no change in the operation of the establishment save for the regrettable absence of Miss Ann Shepard, more familiarly known as Honey, at the faro table. This last was communicated to her in reproachful accents.

Olivia did not try to explain what she did not understand, and her resolute silence on the subject of Lady Breckenridge both irritated and impressed her brother, though she'd had no particular wish to do either.

She read in the drawing room where the light was better. Sometimes she applied herself to the tablecloth and accepted Alastair's critical observation that she took as many stitches out as she put in. She played card games with him when tedium would have otherwise strained their tempers, but resisted showing him all the clever tricks she'd been taught, afraid that he'd use them unwisely and make himself the target of a pistol ball.

Olivia avoided asking about the state of the household accounts. When Mrs. Beck sought her out with some concern, she resisted the urge to settle the matter and turned the housekeeper in Alastair's direction. It was obvious to her that he'd been managing his affairs in her absence. He might prefer to rely on her to attend to the details he found onerous, but preference was not the same as need. In truth, once again, she required more of him than he required of her.

Olivia pushed this last thought to the back of her mind and laid out a row of seven cards. She dealt from the deck, adding to the piles in a neat and orderly fashion. She did not often play solitaire, but she'd brought out the cards in anticipation of Alastair's return. The teapot and cups rested on the silver tray to her right, ready for service upon his arrival. She kept her hands busy to refrain from stealing a biscuit. He'd look at the tray, count the sweets, and know she'd pilfered one. His teasing would not be entirely kind.

Her head came up as she heard the front door open. She cocked it to one side at the sound of him stamping his feet to remove the wet from his boots. He had not let the day's steady drizzle stop him from leaving the house and was likely soaked through. It was easy to imagine him throwing off water droplets like a puppy, sending a cold spray into the far corners of the entrance hall.

Her faint smile faltered when he came through the door. He'd given over his hat, but Mrs. Beck was trailing after him trying to relieve him of his coat. His movements were uncharacteristically brusque and his eyes were grim. She started to rise but what she saw in his face had her sitting again. The cards slipped from her nerveless fingers.

Alastair pressed his coat into Mrs. Beck's hands and waved

her out of the room. Turning, he withdrew a folded copy of the *Gazette* from under his frock coat and advanced on Olivia. Complementing his impatient stride and bleak expression, the tone he took with her was severe.

"You will have to read it yourself, Olivia. You will not want to hear it from me." Using the folded edge of the paper, he pushed aside her cards. He opened the *Gazette* and placed it before her. "Page three."

Frowning, Olivia smoothed the paper with her palms. Her fingers, she noted, were trembling ever so slightly. Alastair was already walking away, turning his back to her at the fireplace as she carefully turned the page. Even without further direction from him, it took her only a moment to find.

The family of Elaine Ellen Wright-Jones, *nee* Stoppard, Viscountess Breckenridge announced her passing on 25 March, 1823.

Olivia's vision blurred. Individual letters floated in the tears that gathered at the rim of her eyes; the words bobbed like flotsam. She could only make out that the account, like the viscountess's life, was altogether too brief, and it was this brevity that struck at Olivia's heart.

"I should go to him," she said quietly. "It will be better if he doesn't have to send for me."

Alastair turned on his heel. His hands were clasped behind his back, warming them at the fire. "Go? Go where? Did you read the notice, Olivia?"

"I . . . um . . ." She glanced at it again, tried to concentrate.

"Never mind," said Alastair. "She's being interred at Wright Hall. Today. Breckenridge is not in London. He is not anywhere you can go, which is just as well if your intention is to fly to him. You will have to stay here awhile longer yet, though I cannot say it is agreeable. You forget yourself if you think he would welcome you at this time. He is certain to be surrounded by family. How do you explain yourself to them?"

How indeed? Olivia set her elbow on the table and her head in her hand. She rubbed her temple. A tear dripped from beneath her lowered lashes, and she dashed it away. "Where is the ring, Alastair?"

The non sequitur caught him unaware. He required a moment before answering. "What has that to do with anything?"

"It's the reason you set me in his path. But for your debt, but for the ring, I would have remained unknown to Breckenridge, and he to me. No explanations would be necessary. So, I will ask you again: where is the ring?"

"I told you." He jutted his chin defensively. "It was stolen. I was cheated of it, if you must know. At faro. Johnny Crocker uses a rigged box in his establishment."

"So I've heard." It was precisely as Griffin had told her. Still, it was gratifying to have it from Alastair. He owed her the truth, and she owed him a reminder that he was not without responsibility. "So you cannot get it back?"

Alastair thought of where the ring resided now. Mrs. Christie took particular delight wearing it when they were together. She'd managed to relieve Johnny Crocker of it in a game of whist where she proved herself the better cheat. "I could get it back," he said.

"Then do not ask me again how I will explain myself to his family when what explains your actions is no source of pride to me, nor, I hope, to you."

Feeling the sting of her words as a slap, Alastair sucked in a short breath. "Do you want the ring, Olivia? Is that it?"

"It doesn't belong to me," she said, trying to make him understand. "Until you pay your debt, it belongs to him. I want you to make it right, Alastair. Not for my sake, but for yours."

He frowned. "Why is this important now?"

"Because I am going back to him," she said. "And it's unlikely that you and I will have occasion to speak again. I should have said it before now, but now is when I've been moved to say it. I owe you something for taking me in when you did—both times. But I never owed you the whole of myself." She stood up, carefully gathered the cards, and let the newspaper lie. "Make it right, Alastair."

She was halfway across the room when he called to her. "Father said you'd land like a cat. And so you have. You're so bloody in love with him that you should thank me for what I've done."

Olivia faltered once, then walked on.

The doors of the hell were closed when she arrived. As it was well past nightfall, and the time when gentlemen and their lady escorts would normally be milling about the entrance hall and moving between the gaming rooms with a drink in their hands, Olivia waved to the hack driver to make certain he stayed while she tested the doors. They were not only closed, but locked and barred on the inside.

She'd had no one accompany her from Jericho Mews, and her trunks and valises were particularly vulnerable on the roof of the hired cab. A few passing gentlemen had slowed as they approached the steps to the hell. Aware of them, Olivia did not wish to call undue attention to herself. A woman alone on Putnam Lane at this hour was viewed in a very particular light, always red.

Olivia hurried down the steps, spoke briefly to the driver, then climbed back in. She breathed more easily when the gentlemen moved on, and the cab rolled forward. They circled the block and entered the alley from the cross street. Approaching from the rear, Olivia could see the servants' hall was lighted. Even as she threw open the door and made to step down from the cab, she saw Beetle carrying out a bucket of wash water. He was preparing to toss it, most of it in her direction, when he took notice of the hack, and finally of her.

"Miss Cole!" He dropped the bucket, clipping his toe, and hopped toward her on one foot. "Oh, but it's a pleasure to see you again, miss. What a time of it we've had. Missed you fierce. We all did." He finally stopped hopping and took stock of the valises as the driver hefted the first one down. "Here, I'll be getting that. Go on inside, let Mr. Truss know you're here, and just see if the others don't come running out to help." The second valise he caught almost pitched him to the ground, and Olivia hurried off before his eagerness to help knocked him unconscious.

She asked for her old room, but her things were deposited in Griffin's bedchamber. She didn't insist they be moved, which she suspected Truss was counting on. She had never kept more than a few items of clothing in Griffin's dressing room, but sometime during her absence the armoire she'd used had been moved here, and now stood ready to be filled.

She stared at it, wondering if Griffin had meant for it to be waiting for her, or whether his wife had used it. Had they shared the room while she was here? The bed? Olivia realized she didn't know whether Mr. Gardner had ever delivered Lady Breckenridge to the hell. It was not the sort of detail that was mentioned in the *Gazette*'s death notice.

Succumbed after a long illness.

Olivia had finally been able to make out those words. A long illness. Perhaps that was why there was no news of her returning to London or attending a single affair. If she had stayed at the hell, the secret had been closely guarded. If she had been cared for at Wright Hall, Griffin had not been at her side. He had never operated the hell from a distance.

Beetle and Wick appeared to help her unpack. Mostly they just sat on one of the trunks, beating a tattoo against the side with their heels, while she did the work. She could have asked them any one of the questions about Lady Breckenridge that occurred to her, but it felt like taking advantage and she let them chatter on about the things that were concerning to them.

Apparently Beetle's mother was getting married to a decent enough bloke who promised she was done whoring. Beetle was happy enough about the marriage but miserable at the thought of leaving Wick.

"It's a good thing you returned when you did, miss, else I might already be dragged off and have no chance to say farewell."

"Then I'm very glad I came. I'd want to say farewell also. I'll miss you, Beetle."

His cheeks flushed a bright pink and he ducked his head, but not before he showed her his shy, gap-toothed smile. "Go on with you, miss. What am I to you but underfoot most times?"

"Well, I've grown accustomed to you there," she said stoutly. She carefully withdrew an ivory cashmere shawl from one of the valises and refolded it so it would fit neatly in the chest of drawers. "Wick is certainly going to pine for you. All of the staff, I should think. His lordship as well, though you were never under his feet the way you were mine. Why is that, Beetle?"

Wick took a sharp jab at Beetle's ribs and answered for him. "It's on account that you smell better." He wiggled his eyebrows. "Like rose petals."

Olivia made a threatening gesture toward both boys, which only caused them to giggle. "It's lavender, not roses." She turned away before they could see she was smiling.

Beetle jumped down from the trunk to pick up one empty valise and scoot another toward her. "You're wrong about his lordship. Missing me, I mean. Oh, maybe just a little he will, seeing how I shined his boots all proper and Wick never got the knack of it, but he's got his own boy now, so that's good, though I don't suppose that one will have to polish boots."

Olivia straightened slowly as she lifted the valise. She did not set it on the seat of a chair as she'd meant to, but hugged it to herself instead. "His own boy? What do you mean by that?"

Beetle hopped back on the trunk, clutching the empty

valise much as Olivia was. "His son, miss. His lordship has himself a son."

Olivia sat in the wing chair in Griffin's study, a wool rug thrown over her legs. After a brief burst of spring-like weather, the turn in the skies was a disappointment. Rain hovered again, falling intermittently throughout the day. The chill was deep, almost impossible to dismiss, and sitting as close to the fire as she could reasonably do safely did not help overmuch.

She closed the book in her lap and tucked it between her hip and the arm of the damask-covered chair. Tipping her head back, she closed her eyes. It had been nearly a fortnight since she'd returned and still there was no word from Griffin. The hell remained closed night after night, during which Olivia slept restlessly, the incoherent but constant hum of voices and rattling traffic from the street serving to punctuate her sleep at odd moments. She'd awakened once with the sheets tangled but not twisted, hugging her pillow, but not throttling it. A dream then, she'd decided. No nightmare. No terror.

When Griffin returned she would tell him that she'd dreamed of him. It was probably true. She wanted it to be true.

The household staff was pleased to have her back, though they treated her with rather more deference than she wished. They hardly knew what to do with themselves with the doors closed each evening. It was inevitable that they turned to cards and dice and spun the roulette wheel themselves. Thus far, Wick and Mr. Truss had winnings exceeding everyone else, which meant a great many others were engaged in doing their chores. She'd had a turn trimming candles after making an incautious wager with Wick—and losing.

She heard the door open behind her but didn't turn. "Bring the tea here, Wick, and set it on the table. Have a care not to topple the books, or anything else. I cannot be certain I put it all in order the last time you stumbled and went head over bucket."

"Someone's guts will be garters if you didn't."

Olivia didn't move, didn't dare move. She let the whiskey-soft voice wash over her, settle in her hair, caress her face, slip under her skin. She felt him approach, but he remained behind her. She stayed just as she was, eyes closed, breathing in the scent of him. His fingers touched her hair, caressed her face, and slipped under the edge of her shawl to lay her skin bare.

She reached for him then, laid her hand over his. Just that, nothing more. Olivia welcomed him home.

Griffin required a few moments to collect himself before he could stand before her. Relief briefly shuttered the pain and weariness in his eyes. He removed the rug from her lap, took her hands, and lifted her to her feet. "I didn't bring tea."

"It's all right." She drank him in instead. His face was thinner than she remembered, more sculpted, the scar more noticeable. His hair was damp at the edges, darker than chestnut there, curling just above the collar of his frock coat. There was the faintest bluish tinge in the outline of his mouth, lingering evidence of the bone-chilling wet that had been his companion on his journey. Shadows marked the underside of his eyes, their color not so different from what she observed in the line of his lips.

Olivia removed her hands from his, stepped close enough to feel the chill coming from him, and unbuttoned his frock coat. She inched closer still, this time to bring her body flush to his, and slid her arms under his coat and around him. She rested her cheek against his shoulder, turned her face into his neck, and held on.

Griffin's chest heaved once, then his arms closed the circle at her back. "Christ, but I wanted you to be here. I was afraid . . . so afraid that you wouldn't come back." He turned his mouth toward her, pressed his lips to her forehead. "Your housekeeper said you'd gone," he whispered. "She didn't know where. I don't believe she would have told me if she'd known. I was wild for finding you; I think she was afraid of me."

"You went to Jericho Mews?"

"Mmm. It's where I thought you meant to stay. When she said you'd left . . . bloody hell, Olivia . . . I was going to make your brother account for it."

"Alastair didn't show me the door. I found it myself. I didn't want to wait for you there, not any longer." She tipped her head back and looked at him. "He brought me the notice of her ladyship's death. I pitied her, Griffin, but I was sorry for you."

"I know," he said gently. "I know." He brought her head back to the curve of his neck as a small tremor slipped through her slender frame. She wept softly, almost soundlessly, and when she was done he gave her one tail of his intricately tied stock to wipe her eyes. He glimpsed her watery smile as she did so. "I wished I could have told you myself." He shook his head, sighed. "If wishes were horses . . ."

"Do you think I didn't understand? I did. If you'd written, I don't believe I would have been able to stay away. Can you imagine?" Alastair's words came to the forefront of her mind. "How would you have explained me to your family?"

Griffin's arms tightened. He laid his cheek against her ginger hair. "What accounting could I give save the truth? I would have introduced them to the woman I love."

Olivia stayed upright because she was already leaning into him. "Is it truly so simple as that?"

"It is, for me. I cannot say what they will make of it." He nudged her hair. "Nor can I say how you will receive it. You are not going to be sick, are you?"

She smiled because he did not ask if she was going to faint. He knew her that well. "No, I am not going to be sick."

"Well, there is something to be said for that." Griffin did not anticipate a like reply and did not receive one. He was satisfied for now that she hadn't squirmed out of his arms and charged for the dressing room. He felt another tremor slip down the length of her back. No tears this time, but a reaction to the cold he'd brought into the room and pushed right up against her. She'd absorbed his chill while he'd taken her heat. It was, as so often was the case in his dealings with Olivia, an exchange in which every advantage was his.

Griffin set her from him long enough to remove his frock coat and settle her shawl evenly on her shoulders. He picked up the rug and set himself in the wing chair, then invited her to join him. "Do you think I'll break?" he asked when she lowered herself with so much care onto his lap. "You weigh as much as a thistle. Come, ease your legs over here. Let me cover you with this." He snapped the rug across her and tucked it around them both. "Here. What's this?" He found the book she'd been reading, held it up, examined it. "*Songs of Experience*. You like Blake's work?"

"It's very fierce, isn't it? Fearless, too. I admire that."

"Of course you do." He lowered the book over the side of the chair and let it drop to the floor. She settled comfortably against him, finding just the right niche for her shoulder, for her hip, and finally, for her head. "What news of the gentleman villain?" he asked.

"None at all. He never showed himself to me. I told you he would not find me at Jericho Mews."

"Just because he did not show himself, it doesn't follow that he wasn't there."

"He does not deserve so much of your attention. I am here, aren't I? And all of a piece. Enough has been said on that matter." She pressed two fingers to his lips to stay his objection, and she was not swayed when he caught her hand and kissed her knuckles. "Tell me the rest," she said in a tone that was both gentle and firm. "All of it. You will have no good sleep until you do, and you are already fair on your way to exhaustion."

He did not release her hand, but set it against his chest and covered it with his own. "She had consumption. Had been seen by doctors well over a year ago. In Italy first, then France. One of them recommended the hot springs at Bath. She returned to England, most reluctantly, I believe, as by her account she'd been engaged in a splendid liaison with the Comte Auguste DeRaine, and presumably all of his liveried servants."

"Griffin."

"I'm sorry. It's what she told me, what she wanted me to think. I don't know if it's true. DeRaine did not accompany her to Bath. There are similar springs in France that would have served as well. The comte may have sent her out." His chest rose and fell with his next deep breath. "It speaks to Gardner's wealth of contacts in every kind of society that he was able to find her. She had been in Bath less than three months, living as the widow Jeannine Aubert, though a more accurate description of her state would be that she was dying as that widow. Gardner did not learn that particular detail until he met her."

Griffin rolled his shoulders slightly, shedding some of the tension that was pulling his back taut. "Elaine used her own name—her maiden name—when booking passage, and she came through London. Gardner and his men followed that trail from inn to inn, found variations of the name, and traced the permutations until they led to the widow. I don't know if I'd have sent him after her if I'd been aware she was dying. I don't know if he would have gone. Faced with the choice of what to do when he came upon her, the truth of her condition obvious to his eyes, he tells me he simply explained why he was there and asked her if she would accompany him back to London."

"And she agreed," Olivia said softly. "How extraordinary."

"Extraordinary." His tone communicated it was none of that. "She had her reasons, Olivia. Atonement was not among them." He closed his eyes briefly against the press of the firelight. "God's truth, but I didn't know it would be so hard." He squeezed her hand, tilted his head, and regarded Olivia's calm, yet somehow expectant features. "There is a child. A boy. Hers, she says, and I cannot think why she would lie about that. Mine, she also says, but then why would she say otherwise when she wants legitimacy for him and for herself?"

"Are you so certain he is not yours?"

It was the directness of the question, the lack of surprise in her eyes, that let Griffin know Olivia had had some hint of what he'd found so difficult to say. "Someone told you."

"I've been here since the day you buried your wife, Griffin. It would have been impossible for me not to learn of it in all that time. Still, it was not revealed in a deliberate fashion. It was not even the thrust of the conversation, merely an aside. Impulsive, really."

"Beetle," said Griffin. "Or Wick. But I am wagering on Beetle."

"You'll get no name from me. Except for that once, no one talks about it in front of me, and I have not asked. It was your place to tell me, and so you have. Now, I want to know if you are certain he is not yours."

Griffin was a long time in answering. "No. No, I'm not."

And because she understood that had been the very hardest thing to say, Olivia cupped his face with her free hand and brought his dark, troubled eyes back to hers. "You do not like to recall that you were intimate with her after you had full knowledge of her adultery."

"Once," he said. "Only once." To his own ears he sounded like the veriest schoolboy offering that most ridiculous of defenses to the headmaster. He'd done better when he *had* been a schoolboy. "Bloody, bloody hell."

"He must be six or there about."

"Six in three months. June. The timing . . . Hell, it is not merely timing, but a precise calculation. I would not expect less from her. Whether it is his true birth date, I doubt if I will ever know. He says it is, but what else would she have taught him to say? There were documents, though. A record of his birth. It does not mean a great deal to me. According to Elaine, the physician attending her at the birth wrote it out. Perhaps it is a common practice in Italy. I don't know. Perhaps it is merely an invention, something done because she was always capable of taking the long view and thought there might be need for it some day."

"Does he look like you?"

"He looks like her."

"How is he called?"

"Nathaniel. He is Nathaniel Christopher Wright-Jones."

"I see." One corner of her mouth edged up in a sad parody of a smile. "Of course he would have your surname. Does it trouble you?"

"Trouble me? That is making much too little of what it does to me. If I denounce his mother, I shame the boy. If I accept him as my son, I have a bastard for my heir. If that is not being placed squarely between Scylla and Charybdis, then I cannot comprehend what is."

Olivia swept back a lock of hair that had fallen over his brow. "Homer again," she said, her smile tender. "But you have it exactly right."

Chapter Thirteen

Olivia could not recall that Griffin had ever slept before she did. The novelty of being awake after he'd found sleep gave rise to curiosity. Indulging herself, she raised her head on her elbow and studied his face. In the dim candlelight, the shadows beneath his eyes disappeared. Lines of fatigue lost their definition. He looked infinitely less weary than he had standing before her so short a time ago. The scar that bisected his cheek had the effect of raising one corner of his mouth, his beautiful mouth, just enough to lend the impression of a wry, yet somehow contented smile.

She wondered at his dreams, if he had any. He looked as if he embraced one now, something pleasant and darkly humorous. The thought of it raised her own smile, and she touched his cheek with the back of her knuckles and drew them down ever so lightly toward his jaw. He murmured something unintelligible; it was enough to make her withdraw her hand.

Carefully, she lifted the covers and slipped out of bed, glancing over her shoulder most of the time to see that he was not wakened. She drew on her robe and slippers, took the stub of the candle from the nightstand, and quietly exited.

Her curiosity extended well beyond Griffin's sleeping countenance. She turned in the direction of her former room, stood outside the door for several long minutes simply listening, then let herself in.

The child lay in the very center of the bed. He slept on his side, one thin arm lying outside the blankets, the other thrust under his pillow so his head was raised at an angle.

Olivia drew closer, raised the candle so its light fell over the dark, tousled hair and narrow face. She had questioned Griffin's decision to bring the boy to the hell; now she understood it. Features that were so careworn, so drawn even in sleep, had no place on the face of a child, and the child had no place anywhere but with the man who would be his father.

Did he look like his mother? Olivia wondered. Or could Griffin only see those features that set the child apart from the man?

Nathaniel Christopher Wright-Jones. The name was bigger than he was. He was slight of build, with bony joints, sharp cheekbones, and a small, pointed chin. In contrast, the hand she could see seemed too large an appendage for the frail delicacy of his wrist and arm. She imagined him moving about with the charming awkwardness of a pup, trying to negotiate walking and running with hands and feet that he hadn't grown into.

His lashes were long and dark, but just beneath them Olivia saw the same violet shadows that she'd seen beneath Griffin's. She lowered the candle, but these shadows were too deep and remained like bruises on his pale skin.

Motherless boy.

Olivia did not assume that what she saw on the child's face was evidence that he grieved. It was as likely evidence that he'd borne a weight much too heavy for his thin shoulders and for far too long. Perhaps it was evidence of both.

His legs twitched beneath the blankets, and he flopped abruptly onto his back. Olivia sucked in a breath as the left side of his face was made visible to her. The thin white scar bisecting his cheek was the twin to Griffin's own and no accident or coincidence could account for it. Olivia did not attempt to restrain herself. She leaned over the bed and extended her hand, traced the scar with the very tip of her finger, a touch so light that not even the baby-fine hairs on his face were disturbed.

She let herself out of the room as quietly as she'd entered. This time when she paused on the other side of the door it was to press the sleeve of her nightgown against her eyes and wait for the hot, salty tears to subside.

Olivia pushed herself upright in bed when the *Gazette* thumped against the window for the second time. Griffin continued to sleep like the dead beside her. Sighing, she rose, found a few coins at the bottom of her reticule, and jingled them in her palm as she went to the window. She unhooked the latch and pushed the window open, then leaned out and waved to the tribe of young ruffians below.

It took three tries, but the smallest among them gave her the pitch that she was finally able to catch. She slipped the paper under her arm, tossed the coins, and waited long enough to make certain the little fellow snagged something for his effort.

"Impressive."

Olivia pulled the window closed and turned. Griffin was sitting up, leaning against the headboard, and rubbing his bristled jawline with his knuckles. He cocked an eyebrow at her and offered her a sleepy half smile that made her heart trip over itself. She threw the newspaper hard at his head.

Griffin ducked, but late, so the corner caught him on the shoulder. "Bloody hell, Olivia." He unfolded the paper over the nightstand so that the pebbles the boys sometimes put in the creases to give it a bit of weight didn't drop, roll, and scatter to the floor. "What was that in aid of?"

"How did you come by your scar?"

He blinked, frowning. It was dawning comprehension that

flattened out his mouth and narrowed his eyes. He stopped knuckling his jaw. "Elaine laid open my cheek with her riding crop. We had been married three months, no more, and I'd just confronted her with my suspicion that she'd taken one of the footmen to our bed." He fingered the scar. "This was her response." His hand fell away and curled into a light fist at his side. "You've seen him, I take it."

Nodding, her complexion going a little pale at what he'd described, Olivia dropped to the window bench and clutched the edge of it on either side of her. "Last night. After you'd fallen asleep. I went to his room because I was curious. Why didn't you tell me?"

"Because I wanted benefit of your fresh opinion on it, uninfluenced by my own."

"How does he explain the scar?"

"He doesn't. He says very little. Gardner told me he spoke to no one save his mother on the journey from Bath and every inquiry was to her welfare and comfort. While she was being cared for here, in the same room he now occupies, I might add, he rarely left her side. A room was prepared for him above, but he would have none of it. He went there obediently when I insisted, but by morning he'd found his way back to her bed."

"She died here?"

"No. She wanted to return to Wright Hall, and as she and I both knew her stay there would be brief, I allowed it. There can be no doubt the last journey hastened her passing. I believe she was depending upon it. I cannot say whether the child blames me for allowing her to have her way. Sometimes I imagine it is accusation that I see in his eyes; sometimes what I see is nothing at all. The latter is far more concerning."

Olivia became aware of how tightly she was holding on to the bench. She eased open her fingers and let the blood flow again. "How did Lady Breckenridge explain the scar?"

322   *Jo Goodman*

"As the child's failure to defend himself properly during a fencing lesson."

"Bloody hell."

"Precisely."

Olivia shook her head, pinched the bridge of her nose as she thought. "He could not lift a sword, let alone wield it."

"That was my thought also."

Her hand dropped to her lap. "She did it to him, Griffin. Deliberately. She scarred her son. It was what I thought when I saw it, and nothing you've told me alters that opinion. I doubt there is anything that can be said that will cause me to believe otherwise."

"It is the same for me." He pushed a pillow behind his back. "After the services for Elaine, there were matters requiring my attention that of necessity meant I had to leave Wright Hall. I placed the boy in my sister Juliet's care as her son is of an age with him, and she had a nanny and tutor already in her household. When I returned for him she reported that he was obedient and mannerly to a fault, and largely silent. Thomas, Juliet's son, had no success in drawing him out, and my nephew is credited to be up to every trick."

"So you brought him here," she said. "I should not have questioned your judgment."

"Of course you should. His presence here cannot help but affect you."

"Except for my own experience with childhood, I know nothing about children."

"You know almost nothing about being a child," he said quietly. "And neither, I think, does he."

Olivia felt a sudden ache behind her eyes. She looked down quickly, blinking. The tears she held at bay settled in her throat. Swallowing hard, she took a steadying breath and waited for the pressure in her chest to ease.

"Olivia? Are you well?"

She glanced up, smiled ever so slightly. "It is only that your comprehension touches me. For myself, but for Nathaniel as well. You will call him that, won't you? Nathaniel. Not the child. The boy. Her son. It will be better, I think. For him, certainly, but for you also."

"Nat," he said. "I shall call him Nat, I expect. Nathaniel is too big for him."

Her smile deepened marginally. "It is, isn't it?" Another thought occurred to her that she knew she needed to give voice to. "He's not ill, is he? He's so slight. I wondered . . ."

"Dr. Pettibone's examined him. There appears to be no lung ailment. Elaine was slightly built, so perhaps that accounts for it. He does not eat a great deal, but I anticipate that will change in time." He raised his hand toward Olivia, beckoned her to come to him. "Have you rung for breakfast?"

Crossing the room, she shook her head. "I only just awakened myself. Shall I ring now?" She paused a step outside of his reach when she read the intent in his eyes. His appetite was for something other than the usual breakfast fare. Her eyebrow kicked up. "You cannot mean to ravish me again."

"Actually, I do."

Olivia's eyes followed his down to the faint rise in the blankets lying across his lap. She sighed. "That was awake before you were, if you must know."

He chuckled. "That is often the way of it."

Nothing was served, least of all her own appetites, by keeping him at arm's length. Olivia launched herself onto the bed, catching him unaware so that he was tipped sideways and she had the immediate upper hand. She pinned his wrists and shimmied under the blankets, a little breathless by the time she had him restrained to her satisfaction.

Griffin grinned up at her. The curling ends of Olivia's hair tickled his shoulder until she threw her head back and tossed it behind her. "You cannot mean to ravish me again."

"I do," she whispered, her eyes darkening. "I certainly do." She bent her head and brushed her lips against his. She nudged them open, tasted his upper lip with the tip of her tongue, then the lower one. She kissed the corner of his mouth, his jaw, then used her teeth to worry his earlobe.

Her breath was warm, humid, and Griffin felt his pulse quicken as she teased him with her lips, teeth, and tongue. She whispered something he could not quite make out, but what she said was infinitely less important just now than how she said it. How she said it raised ribbons of heat that twisted and curled under his skin.

He tried to catch her mouth when she lowered it a second time, but she darted away at the last moment and turned her attention to the cord in his neck and the underside of his jaw. Her breasts rubbed against his chest, pleasing her, but pleasing him more. She squirmed a bit, balancing the need to find a fit for herself against his frame with delicious discomfort each time she failed.

He snagged a breath, held it, as she traced the line of his collarbone with the damp edge of her tongue. She sipped his skin at the curve of his neck and shoulder just as he had done to her last evening, leaving her mark on him, taking possession.

He tentatively attempted to lift one of his hands, but she was having none of it and pressed his wrist back. He thought he let her, but he wasn't entirely certain that in an earnest battle that she might not emerge the victor. Certainly he'd have bruises for it, much less enjoyable in the making than the one she was giving him now.

"Do I amuse you?" she asked darkly, lifting her head so her mouth hovered a fraction above his. "You chuckled."

"Chuckled? You are mistaken. I would not." He cleared his throat, pushed back the laughter that threatened to reveal his lie, and suffered the thorough study she made of him. "A guilty man would confess, you know," he told her. "You are uncannily persuasive."

"I am merely looking at you."

"My point precisely."

She put her mouth to his, kissed him warmly. "You are kind to flatter me." She smiled, feeling the rumble of laughter in his chest tickle every one of her nerve endings. Rather than take him to task for it, she deepened the kiss.

Olivia made free with his body. She let his wrists go because holding them only hampered her search and discovery. She welcomed the contrasts between them, the broad plane of his hard chest to the more yielding softness of her own, the spread of his hand against her smaller one, the narrow line of his hip still capable of cradling her curves.

She indulged herself in the taste of him, the scent of him, and finally, the sound of him as he whispered her name in a way that spoke to his pleasure . . . and later, to hers.

The heat that came upon them made their clothing an irritant. They grappled with her belted robe and his drawers. He bunched yards of her nightgown in his fists as she reared up and released it again when she straddled him. He helped her take him into her, shifted his gaze from the point of their joining to her eyes, watched her and saw his own need and satisfaction reflected there.

She moved slowly at first, arching over him like a water nymph rising from the sea. He held her hips, pressed his fingers against her bottom, but let the rhythm, the pace, be what she wanted. She worked him slowly, but not for long. Frustration overtook her, need overcame her, and she surrendered all of herself to a tidal wave of selfish, primal pleasure.

And took him in her wake.

Neither of them spoke in the immediate aftermath. The tremors were too sweet to interrupt. They lay unmoving, waiting for their hearts to cease hammering. Griffin had one arm flung across his eyes, the other across Olivia's back. Her face was turned toward his neck, the rest of her lay flush against him. She could not find the wherewithal to push herself away and the arm lying heavily on her back like a paperweight made certain she stayed precisely as she was.

"God." Griffin made the low, guttural response with feeling. "Mmm."

"I am undone."

"Mmm."

"Did you crawl inside me?" he asked. "It seemed as if you did."

Olivia bit the side of his neck gently.

Griffin accepted her chastisement, stopped talking, and in moments was sleeping soundly.

Nat knew nothing about card games. He offered this information in the hope that it would persuade Miss Cole to seek other entertainments. She was not in the least put off by his ignorance, a turn of events that he found altogether disappointing. He was of a mind to remain in his room and play with his soldiers. He had enough for two armies now and intended to re-create the pivotal battle where Alexander met and defeated Darius, the great king of all Persia. He did not explain this to Miss Cole because it was his experience that women found such stories tedious. Battles and bloodshed did not appear to interest them.

It was incomprehensible.

"Shall I teach you Napoleon?" Olivia asked as she shuffled the cards. "Sometimes it is called écarté. Are you familiar?"

"Écarté," he said, dragging his eyes away from her hands as the cards flew back and forth between her fingers. "I know that word. It means far apart. Lonely."

"Just as Napoleon was on Elba and later, St. Helena, so it is all of a piece, isn't it?" She stopped shuffling and passed the deck to him for a cut. When he simply stared at her, she explained what he should do. "It is your choice. Most players prefer to cut. They all do if they are concerned that the dealer may be moved to cheat on the deal."

He glanced at the cards, then at her.

"I will not be offended if you make a cut. You have no reason at all to trust me."

He separated the deck carefully, choosing to make two almost equal piles, then restacked them opposite of his cut.

"Very good," said Olivia. She took up the cards and dealt them each three, then two. She explained the rules and object of the game. "It will become clearer after we play a few hands. As for the scoring, you and I should agree on what we'll use to make our payments. Have you any money?" At his frown, she shrugged. "No, I didn't think you would. It's of no matter. I brought a purse of farthings with me." She reached for the small leather bag she'd attached like a pocket to her morning dress and laid it on the table. "Go on. You open it and divide the coins between us. What you are able to win from me, you may keep, but what I am advancing you now must be returned. Do you understand?"

He nodded and divvied the coins with the same precision he'd used to cut the cards.

"If you bid that you can take all five tricks," Olivia explained, "that is called a nap. Upon succeeding, I will have to pay you ten. But if you fail to make your nap, then you must pay me five. Bid a Wellington, and it means you bid to take all five tricks but have to give me ten farthings if you fail. Bid a Blücher, and the payout is twenty for one of us." She paused, picking up her cards to examine them, then encouraged him to do the same. She stole a glance at him as he studied his cards. His small mouth was no longer set in the grim line that was his usual mien. Earnestness had caused his expression to take a different shape, and the point of his pink tongue peeked out from one corner of his lips. "You know who Wellington and Blücher are, don't you? I didn't think to explain."

"Waterloo," he said.

"I wonder if they know their names are now attached to a card game," Olivia said, "and if they're honored or find it lowering."

He did not venture an opinion about Olivia's musings, but said instead, "Wellington should pay more than a Blücher."

"Ah, an Englishman through and through, aren't you?" When he did not respond, she did not pursue and directed him to bid his hand. She was surprised, and not a little pleased, when he did so without hesitation. "I can do better than your three hearts, so let us see how you play out the deal."

He won four tricks handily, while she managed to take the last. She settled a farthing on him and watched a glimmer of a smile surface. Satisfied, Olivia showed him how to make the deal and the play continued.

"He won twenty-three farthings from me," she told Griffin at tea. "Can you imagine? And never played the game before. It was quite astonishing. I think he must possess a formidable intelligence."

Griffin chose a slim slice of pound cake from the tray and slid it onto his plate. "I cannot say anything about his intelligence. What I imagine is that you pushed some very good cards on him."

She made a face. "Oh, very well. In the beginning. Just to give him confidence to make a bid, and that has nothing at all to do with his cognitive powers. He still could have offered no bid, but he took the risk, and I found that reason enough to hope." She wagged her fork at him. "Have you visited him today?"

"No." A shade defensively, he added, "Other matters required my attention."

Olivia merely raised a brow and let him make of it what he would before she tucked into her own serving of pound cake.

"I intend to speak with him later." He took a bite of his cake, then washed it down with tea. "Did you find it awkward?"

"Conversing with him, you mean? A bit, yes. He was not so impolite as to ask me to leave him, but it is a certainty that he did not want me there. I am stubborn, though, and meant to have my way."

"It cost you twenty-three farthings."

She smiled, shrugged. "It is money well spent, in my opinion. He has kindly offered me an opportunity to win it back."

"Thus the lamb is led to slaughter," Griffin said, shaking his head. "I am all admiration."

"Thank you. It does seem as if it may go well." She regarded Griffin over the rim of her cup. "Did you have tin soldiers as a child?"

"Yes. A legion of them. Why?"

"There looked to be two or three score of the little men under Nat's bed. I saw them when I was sitting at the table. Were they a present from you?"

"No. I have never seen them. It is doubtful my nephew shared his own. Did you ask him about them?"

She shook her head.

Griffin shrugged. "He had a small trunk and several cases when he arrived from Bath. I suppose he could have brought them with him."

"Did you prize your legion?"

"Most definitely. I set up battlefields in my room, across my desk, on the bed, under it. Played at it for hours at a time. Boys do, you know."

"No. I didn't."

She was a cunning strategist, he thought, in the way she could arrive at her point by any route. His acknowledgment of her aim was something less than gracious. "Oh, very well, I suppose it presents an opportunity for young Nat and me to find common ground."

Olivia hid her smile behind her teacup. It was a beginning.

The hell was particularly crowded that night. Word of mouth in and around Putnam Lane was all that was necessary to fill the halls and gaming rooms. Patrons came as much to pay their respects to Griffin as they did to make their wagers. The betting books were opened, the faro table attracted gentlemen three deep, and the tables where cards were played had onlookers waiting for a turn in one of the chairs.

Griffin politely accepted the condolences of those regular patrons who were little more than acquaintances. Those who knew him better had already expressed their regrets in missives that arrived at Wright Hall soon after the announcement appeared in the *Gazette*. Tonight, they simply made certain they caught his eye and conveyed their concern for him.

Griffin could have done without any particular attention being paid to the passing of his wife. He made no attempt to follow any mourning customs, knowing the effort would be regarded as hypocritical in as many circles as the lack of the same was regarded as disrespectful. Rather than try to do right by a society that could not be satisfied, he elected to please himself.

He was wending his way in the direction of the faro table when a movement on the upper stairs caught his eye. Turning quickly, he spied Nat ducking back into the hallway. Griffin decided against going after the boy and waited to see if he would reappear as soon as he thought it was safe to do so. When he judged sufficient time had elapsed for Nat to have returned to his room, Griffin waited just a bit more and was rewarded when a shock of russet-colored hair showed itself at the top of the stairs, followed by a pair of equally dark eyes.

Those eyes widened with the realization of having been neatly caught out.

Griffin held up his forefinger in a gesture that could signify a great many things but in this case meant *stay*. He did not expect Nat to bolt, but neither was he prepared for the fear he saw in the child's eyes as he climbed closer. Because of that, he did not place his hand on Nat's shoulder when he directed him to return to his room, but fell into step at the boy's side instead.

Once they were inside the bedchamber, Griffin took up a chair so he was not towering over the child and motioned Nat toward the bed. Griffin chose not to be insulted when Nat responded rather too hastily.

Deciding to go at the matter directly, Griffin asked, "Do you think I mean to strike you?"

Nat blinked. His mouth was dry and his tongue cleaved to the roof. He tried to swallow but the lump in his throat was firmly in place and the sound that left his lips was an embarrassing gagging noise.

Regarding him warily, Griffin asked, "Are you going to be sick?" Nat's quick shake of the head was unconvincing. "I have some experience with this. Much to my regret." Griffin rose, went to the dressing room, and returned with the basin from the washstand. He set it on the bed beside Nat and went back to his chair.

"Perhaps it will be more productive for me to say some things rather than put questions to you." Griffin did not wait for any sort of response, only gauged that Nat was listening, and went on. "I flatter myself that I am not strictly bound by the conventions of society. It is not always a wise choice to fly in the face of what is expected, but it is *my* choice. If you do not comprehend what I've just said, it is of little matter. It is merely a preamble to what I will say now, and in time, I think, you will appreciate it.

"I do not hold to the notion that sparing the rod spoils the child. Whether that benefits you remains to be seen. You may be confident that I will not lift a hand against you nor take up a cane. You may also be confident that I will not permit you to show such willfulness that you endanger yourself or others. That is what you did this evening by placing yourself at the top of the stairs. I appreciate curiosity, but it is misplaced in this instance. You may ask questions about this establishment,

and you will receive answers, but you may not wander from
your room while there are patrons about."

Griffin's left eyebrow lifted a fraction while his gaze remained frank and assessing. It seemed to him the boy grasped
most of what he'd said well enough, but he had to be sure.
"Do you understand?"

Nat nodded. When that response appeared to have been
judged inadequate, he found enough spit had formed in his
mouth to permit him to speak. "Yes, sir. I understand."

"Good. Then perhaps you can tell me what it is you hoped
to learn by visiting the top of the stairs." As Nat was dressed
in his nightclothes, Griffin thought he could safely assume
the boy had not meant to leave the hell. Also, the servants'
stairs would have been more the route to take in that event.

Nat was not proof against the long, expectant silence that
followed. "I could not sleep for the noise."

"It is frequently noisy. A cup of warm milk at bedtime will
help you sleep. I will instruct Cook to make you a posset. You
might have rung for it yourself, yet the noise drew you out
of your room. How did you imagine that would help?"

Nat flushed a little and for the first time his eyes darted
away. He pressed his lips together until they all but disappeared.

"Did you wish to find Miss Cole?" asked Griffin. When
Nat offered up a single shoulder shrug, Griffin realized he'd
hit close to the mark. He tried again. "Were you looking for
me?" When the boy's head shot up and the most alarming
expression took shape on his face, Griffin realized his question
had missed the target entirely. "Very well. You were *not* looking for me. I can surmise that you were not in need of one of
the staff else you would have used the bell, so that brings us
round to Miss Cole again. As much as I appreciate the challenge to my gray matter, it would be ever so much better if you
would simply speak on your behalf."

Nat said nothing.

Griffin sighed. "As you wish. I will have the posset sent to your room. Drink it all." He stood. For the first time since entering the room, he felt awkward and uncertain of what should be done. "Nanny Pritchard used to tuck me in. When I was your age or thereabouts, I pretended I wanted none of it, but she managed the thing anyway. Do you . . ." He hesitated, wondering if Nat would make his own feelings known. He was encouraged when the boy neither blanched nor shied away and decided to save both of them from asking the question. Instead, he approached the bed and indicated that Nat should remove his slippers and robe. He took away the basin and held up the covers while the boy crawled under them, then made a neat cocoon around every part of him but his head.

"Good night." He tousled Nat's hair. The texture was fine and silky. "You may sit at breakfast with me and Miss Cole, if you like."

Nat stared up at him. "Do you mean it, sir?"

"Yes, of course. I find it less confusing if I say only what I mean. I am also appreciative when others do the same."

"Then I should like it, sir."

Griffin nodded. He was on the point of leaving the room when he caught a hint of Nat's small voice adding, "Above all things."

There was no breakfast room or family dining room in the hell. The rooms that had been intended for such use had long been turned over to gaming. So it was that Griffin, Olivia, and Nat took their breakfast in Griffin's study at a table carefully cleared for just that purpose.

Olivia watched with amusement as Nat's eyes darted about the room. The child was evidently impressed that so much in the way of clutter was tolerated. He had been gently warned upon his entry that he should not touch anything, and to his credit, his hands had not left his sides. He'd made one slow, but complete circuit of the room, gazing at the books with something like yearning in his face, making a cursory examination of the porcelain and jade figurines crowded together on the drinks cabinet, and finally pausing to study his own narrow face in the mirror above the mantel. Olivia did not think she would ever forget how he'd turned his head, just so, to better make out the line of his scar. Her own attention had darted to Griffin then, and she saw that he had been riveted by the very same.

"I imagine you are wondering how Lord Breckenridge finds anything," Olivia said. "It remains a mystery to everyone, including his lordship, but if he wants a particular item, he knows precisely where to go."

Nat bit off a piece of toast and chewed thoughtfully. "*The Castle of* . . ." He paused, his tongue working around a word he didn't know.

Griffin set his cup down and arched one eyebrow sharply. "*Otranto.* Is that what you're trying to say?"

"*Otranto.* Yes. That's the one."

"That is too easy." He pointed to the stack of books to the right of the chaise. "Third up from the bottom. It is not a particularly good representation of a Gothic novel, but it helps support the candelabra nicely."

"He is rather too confident," said Olivia, finding her voice after a moment's astonishment had left her without words. "I would not trust him. It is all right if you wish to look."

"No, that's where it is. I remember."

Olivia looked from Nat to Griffin. Her accusing glance took in both of them. "You arranged this. I have never heard of *The Castle of Otranto.*"

"Horace Walpole," they said as one, but Griffin was looking at Nat oddly while Nat was sinking his small teeth into a muffin the size of his fist.

Olivia excused herself from the table and went to the stack. Dropping gracefully to her haunches, her gray morning dress wreathing her like smoke, she counted three up from the floor and tilted her head to read the spine. "You are both unnatural."

She returned to the table and regarded Nat with an expression only marginally less surprised than Griffin's. "You have read the book?"

"Only the side of it."

Griffin found he could only shake his head. "He is a quick study, I think. What else did you observe, Nat? Can you tell me, for instance, where I might find *The Vicar of Wakefield*?"

Nat licked at the muffin crumbs above his lip as he applied considerable thought to this challenge. He closed his eyes, scanning the room in his mind's eye, and said slowly, "Bottom shelf. Left side. Between four and eight from the far end, I should think."

"Six, actually," said Griffin as Nat opened his eyes and looked at him expectantly. "Now, have you seen a deck of cards with a blue backing?"

"No, sir."

"That is too bad. Neither have I, and I was most particularly fond of them." He dipped the point of his toast into the yolk of his soft-boiled egg. "Miss Cole?"

"They are in your desk drawer. I put them away."

Griffin sent Nat a look that put them on the same side against the sole female in the room. "You see? She has put them away. It is an annoyance, but one that must be occasionally suffered if one wants—"

"Wants?" Olivia asked pointedly when Griffin suddenly fell silent. "Wants what, exactly?"

"Harmony," said Griffin, inspired to respond in this fashion by Olivia's look, as well as the tines of the fork she was pressing into his thigh. "There are certain advantages to harmony, Nat."

"Does it hurt, sir?"

"Harmony? Why, no, it is—" He stopped this time because

Nat was shaking his head. "Oh, you are referring to the fork in my leg."

"Yes, sir."

Olivia removed the fork and stabbed a thin slice of ham with it. "How did you know?" she asked Nat. "I am not always so easily caught out."

Nat was uncertain he could explain it. He'd seen it in their faces—one pained, but more as a pretense than fact, and one grim, but slyly so. There was also the matter of a missing fork and the hand that had held it, as well as the exchange they'd made in which no word passed between them. It was not easily explained when he understood almost none of it. He'd simply said what came to his mind.

"It just seemed you might be moved to take a poke at him," Nat said. "I think he meant to push you to it."

"Sometimes his lordship doesn't require a push. He just steps into it. I acquit him of cruel intent."

"You are too kind," Griffin said dryly. He glanced at Nat. "Miss Cole tells me you won twenty-three farthings from her yesterday."

"Yes, sir. It was her money."

Griffin considered that. "Yours now, though I understand what you mean. Would you like to have some money of your own? Like it enough to earn it?"

Surprised, Nat still did not hesitate. "Yes, sir."

"We had a boy here, a few years older than you. Beetle. Do you recall seeing him about?" When Nat shook his head, Griffin went on, remembering how the child had rarely left his mother's side. "He's gone now, moved away with his family. There are things he did for me that you could do."

"Griffin," Olivia said softly.

Griffin did not give any indication that he'd heard. "Everyone here does something, Nat, and earns a wage for it. What do you think of that?"

"Would I be a servant, then?"

"You would be Nathaniel Christopher, I believe. Nothing about working for sixpence a week makes you more or less than that. I will speak to Truss about what he can expect. You will have to make time for your studies, of course, and what you get by way of compensation there is a head full of peculiar things that someone else thinks you should know. As fine a memory as you possess, you will take to it admirably."

"I shall have a tutor?"

"As soon as I can secure the services of one. Later you will go to school, but not just now, I think. You've had a tutor before, haven't you?"

"Mother taught me."

Griffin tried to imagine it and failed. "Then she did well by you," he said vaguely.

"She did not know about battles, sir. History was tedious, she said."

"And you like it?"

"Yes. Very much. Comte DeRaine liked it also, and he had books and maps. Do you have maps, sir?"

"No, but that is easily rectified." Griffin might have imagined the smile that tugged at the boy's pinched mouth, but he was quite certain he did not mistake the wistfulness in his eyes. Satisfied, Griffin finished the last of his coffee. "Did I tell you, Miss Cole, that Nat left his room last evening?"

He had told her all about it, but she feigned ignorance. "You did not, my lord. What was that in aid of, Nat?"

Nat fought mightily to refrain from squirming. Beneath the table, he gently swung his legs. "The noise," he said. "It woke me."

A slightly different version, Griffin thought, than he'd heard the night before. He'd thought Nat hadn't been able to fall asleep. He said nothing, allowing Olivia the opportunity to learn what he had not been able.

"The voices from below rumble through the house,"

Olivia said. "Sometimes you can feel it when you're lying abed. Did you?"

Nat nodded.

"You probably didn't notice when you stayed before. I've been told you were very attentive to your mother." She regretted causing the flash of pain she saw in his eyes. "When I slept there, I could sometimes hear shouting from the street. It is hard to imagine anyone could be so loud, but there you have it. The hours on Putnam Lane are rather different than what you're accustomed to, I expect." She watched him closely, trying to divine what it was that she saw in him. There was a reserve in his demeanor, a sense that he was holding something tightly to his chest. She imagined herself lying in that bed again, alone, hearing and feeling every strange sound, and then she imagined herself at his age.

At not yet quite six.

"I was afraid," she said. "Deeply so. And I am ever so much older than you."

"You are a girl."

"True, though I am not certain that alone accounts for it. I know I didn't show your courage, because I stayed in bed with the covers pulled up around my head, while you went off on your own."

Nat's eyes dropped to his plate, and he bit his lip. He thrust out his chin, but it still wobbled.

Olivia felt very much like weeping herself. She didn't dare look at Griffin. If he was in any way sympathetic, she would most certainly cry, and if he wasn't, she would be provoked to stabbing him again.

"Tell us about the noise you heard," Griffin said. His tone was quiet and firm and did not invite refusal. He put his hand over Olivia's when she would have answered on Nat's behalf. "I think Miss Cole and I have mistaken the matter. You must set us right."

Nat nodded ever so slightly. His feet stopped swinging under the table.

Griffin and Olivia found themselves actually holding their breath.

"The window," he said.

Now Griffin and Olivia exchanged glances. They realized as one that Nat had not gone to find the source of the noise that had disturbed him, but fled from it.

"What sort of noise was it at the window?" asked Olivia. "Tapping? Scratching? Rattling?"

He nodded again.

"All of that?" asked Griffin.

"Yes, sir." Nat finally looked up, his features set as stoically as a Spartan's. "It was my mother come for me. She said she would come for me." The remains of his muffin crumbled between his fingers. "I do not want to go with her, sir."

Griffin stared at Nat. Throwing a few coins to the urchins every morning, sending Wick on an errand, exchanging words with Beetle as he handed over his boots, none of that prepared him for dealing with this child, or this child's fears. "It was the wind," he said. "Or a tree branch. Many things can cause noises such as you heard. It was not your mother."

Rather than mollifying the boy, Griffin saw Nat's large, dark eyes well with tears. Before he could speak and make right whatever he'd made wrong, he felt Olivia trod hard upon his toes. Relief far surpassed the pain.

"Of course you will not go with her," Olivia said. She gently removed the mangled muffin from between Nat's hands and used her serviette to briskly dust off his palms. "Lord Breckenridge will not allow it. It is his wish that you will remain here, and no one, not even your mother, can gainsay him. He will also not allow her to disturb your sleep, so you can be certain that when you hear a noise at your window, it is naught but one of nature's moody tricks."

Nat regarded her uncertainly.

"Look to his lordship, Nat, and see for yourself that what I'm telling you is true."

Nat's attention swung to Griffin. "Is it so, sir?"

The cast of Griffin's features was solemn. "It is." Griffin expected his word to be the end of it, but he watched Nat's eyes dart to Olivia again, this time settling on her hands, both of which were resting lightly on the tabletop. "You are perhaps looking to see if she has a fork in my side?"

Nat offered a guilty, watery smile.

Under the table, Olivia carefully removed her foot from Griffin's instep.

Griffin simply nodded to each of them in turn, affecting lordly condescension to indicate his satisfaction with the morning's work. He was pleasantly surprised when Olivia's hands and feet remained where they were, although he suspected her show of restraint was for Nathaniel.

The child's presence at their table was not without its benefits.

"There are no tree branches close enough to scratch at his window," Olivia said when she and Griffin were alone. "And no wind at all to speak of last night."

"I know. The same occurred to me." He closed the book of accounts, pushed it to one side, and leaned back in his chair. "Perhaps Truss and Wick can engage the boy . . . Nat, that is . . . in some activity so that I can have a look without alerting him. He will have no confidence at all in me if he thinks I am looking for evidence that it was his mother."

"I think we mistook the matter there. He is not grieving her absence as much as he is fearing her return."

Griffin pushed his fingers through his hair. "God's truth, but she was ever a piece of work. It is little wonder he was so attentive to her. How frightened she made him of her passing." Shaking his head, he blew out a large, noisy breath. "It does not bear thinking the kind of things she must have told him about me."

"Nat will come to his own opinion. He is as bright as a new penny and will only require time to put order to what he's been told and what he sees for himself."

"Time with me, you mean."

"You would not begrudge him that, would you?"

"Begrudge him? No. But that does not mean that I know what to do with him. You tried to caution me when I began to offer him an opportunity to earn a few coppers."

"And it was well done of you to ignore me. You did right by Nat, giving him a purpose and such dignity as a child can manage. You have a deft touch."

Griffin was not as certain. "Do you think he's my son?"

"I don't know. But I think it is the wrong question."

"Oh? What is the right one?"

"Do you want him to be?"

Frowning, Griffin rubbed the underside of his chin. "Bloody hell, Olivia, but you force me to look at a thing sideways."

She came around the desk, bent, and kissed his furrowed brow. "It is not a punishment," she said, chuckling. She tugged on his wrist. "Come, I want to see for myself what might have been at Nat's window. Set Truss and Wick on him so we may have done with it."

Nat obediently trotted after Wick when the older boy came for him and announced Truss had work for them below stairs. As soon as they disappeared from the hallway, Griffin and Olivia went to Nat's room.

Griffin pushed open the window. Foster was already in the yard, making a survey of the ground. He looked up when he heard Griffin call to him.

"Footprints all around, m'lord. Can't say whose they might

be or when they were made. There are an uncommon number of them at the corner. That doesn't seem right. Can't think what anyone's doing there."

Griffin eased himself out of the window and dropped a few feet to the porch roof. Olivia immediately thrust her head out the opening. He gave her a cautionary glance.

"I am not coming out," she told him with some asperity. "I am here to make certain you do not break your neck."

He did not inquire how she meant to do that. He stepped carefully on the steep incline of the porch roof, looking for evidence that someone else had recently done the same. He found it at the edge, two small dents where the gutter had been pushed in. Leaning over as far as he dared, he caught Foster's attention. "Look for a place where he might have set a ladder." He pointed to the approximate location on the ground. "There and there."

"Right you are. Just so. Two gouges, an inch or so deep." He bent, examined them more closely. "Made recently. No rainwater collecting in them."

"Where is our ladder, Foster?" The footman was already on his way to the outbuilding where such things were stored.

Griffin straightened and climbed the slope back to the window. By the time he reached it, Foster was emerging from the building.

"Looks to have been our ladder that was used," the footman announced.

Not surprised, Griffin merely nodded. He waved Foster back inside and turned to examine the window. Olivia pointed out the scrapings she had already seen.

"Someone was trying to get in," she said.

"Mmm. I thought we might put it down to a bluey-hunter, but that does not seem to be the case."

"Bluey-hunter?"

"A thief who steals lead from the tops of houses. It is common enough around here." Griffin checked the sturdiness of the window frame. It would hold, though nothing would stop a glass cutter. "I think we would do well to suspect it is the work of the gentleman villain."

Olivia helped him back inside, closed the window, and set the latch. "We will have to move Nat to another room."

"Of course. I will depend upon you to arrive at a suitable explanation."

Nodding absently, Olivia asked, "If it is the gentleman, do you suppose he came for Nat?"

Griffin cupped the side of Olivia's face. "You know that is unlikely, and while I appreciate your desire to protect him, I think we must apply ourselves to protecting you."

Chapter Fourteen

Olivia held her candle high and surveyed the floor so she might carefully pick her way through the battlefield. Nat had arranged his regiments so they flanked his bed, guarded his window and door, and stood fast on the edge of his night table. A single misstep would alert him to an intruder—or at least he thought so.

She had promised that she would look in on him, just as she had every night since he'd been moved to the room above the one she and Griffin shared. He'd made the move to his new room obediently, never questioning the necessity of it, but Olivia had seen the flash of alarm in his eyes and had offered her company to ease his fears. The first few evenings she'd stayed with him until he fell deeply asleep. By the fourth night, she was able to ease out of the room shortly after his eyelids began to droop. Now that almost a fortnight had passed, she left after he said his prayers.

The soldiers, though, remained alert to the slightest disturbance.

Olivia reached the bed and gently pulled back the blankets that were covering Nat's thickly thatched hair. She could make out the narrow furrows where he'd pushed his fingers through his hair in perfect imitation of what he'd seen Griffin do. Her throat grew thick with tender emotion, and she did not resist the urge to put her own imprint upon his tousled head.

Assured that all was well with him, Olivia stepped away from the bed—and onto the raised bayonet of a foot soldier. She was still cursing softly as she limped out of the room.

"A casualty of war?"

Startled, Olivia's head snapped up. She managed to hold on to her candle, but a fat droplet of hot wax slipped free and spread over her thumb.

Griffin caught her hand, steadied it, then removed the candlestick. "I am most sincerely sorry, Olivia. Are you burned?"

She pulled back her hand and blew on the wax until it was hard enough to peel away. "It is nothing," she said, showing him the pink blossom on her thumb. "But, really, Griffin, you have a way of simply . . . *appearing*. It is disconcerting."

"And you have a way of simply . . . *dis*appearing." He gave her a measuring look. "You said nothing about leaving the faro table."

"I told Mason."

"You did not tell me."

"I was looking in on Nat."

"You did not tell me."

Olivia sighed. It was no good telling him she thought the precaution excessive. He did not agree, and in this he would have his way. "I will endeavor to do better. It is not so simple a thing as you would like to believe. I am not accustomed to accounting for my whereabouts."

"You did just fine when you were confined to your room."

There was nothing subtle about the threat. "That is unfair, Griffin. I will not be put away." She held his level gaze and gave no quarter. She would not be moved, and she would not be threatened.

Griffin finally shook his head. "Bloody hell, Olivia, but you define obstinate."

"I do." She raised herself on tiptoes and kissed him on the mouth. His own jaw was stubbornly set and softened only marginally as she pressed the kiss. "You know something about defining it yourself," she whispered. She kissed him again, then set herself back on her heels. "Did you only come here in search of me?"

"You were half the reason."

"I thought that might be the way of it." She reached behind her and opened the door. "Have a look yourself and mind the troops."

She stepped aside and waited for him at the top of the stairs. He was gone for several minutes, longer than was strictly necessary to assure himself of the well-being of a sleeping boy. She imagined him standing at Nat's bedside much as she had, attending to his breathing, the gentle parting of his lips, looking for some trait in that narrow face that was familiar from the study of his own reflection. When he returned, she sidled close to him and slipped her arm in his. Giving him a light squeeze, she laid her head against his shoulder. "He makes furrows in his hair."

"Does he?"

Olivia didn't believe he'd never noticed, but she didn't challenge him. "Mmm. Like you."

"It doesn't signify."

"It doesn't have to. It's endearing."

Griffin thought about that. "He is rather more interesting than I supposed he might be."

Chuckling, Olivia straightened and began to pull him down the stairs. After the first few, he held her back. She looked up at him, saw the gravity of his expression. "What is it?"

"I was thinking about you."

"Me?"

He nodded. "When I was looking at Nat, I was thinking about you."

"I don't understand."

"You were his age, probably every bit as small and fragile as he, and someone looked at you and decided . . ." His voice trailed off as words failed him. He cupped the side of Olivia's face in his palm. "It is incomprehensible to me." What he glimpsed in her eyes told him it was the same for her. "Was there no one, Olivia? No one who stepped forward to offer protection?"

"There was." The memory raised a bittersweet smile. "Honey Shepard."

"Your nanny?"

"Yes. You look surprised."

"You were packed off to school. How could she have known what was happening?"

"She didn't. I have always imagined she thought I was well out of it there. It would have been a reasonable assumption."

Griffin frowned. The implication was that she had not been safe at Coleridge Park. "Well out of it?" he asked. "Or well away from it?"

"The latter, I suppose." Olivia shook her head as he would have posed another question. "This is no place for it, Griffin, and you should be very certain you want to know because there is nothing you can do as a consequence of it." She tugged lightly on her arm and was released, then pivoted on the step and hurried off.

Olivia lingered in the gaming rooms after the hell's patrons had taken their leave, completing her own duties with something less than her usual efficiency. It was only when she began to find reasons to be dissatisfied with the work of others that she realized what she was about. Griffin, also, would be aware of her delay and know the reason for it. She recalled how he'd tested her that first day, standing imperiously at the top of the stairs, pinning her back with that dark, remote glance of his, then walking away as if he were indifferent to what he saw.

It had been a pretense, but she hadn't known it. He was not indifferent then, and he was certainly not indifferent now.

And that made her fear for him.

She found him stretched out on their bed, his head cradled in his palms, his feet crossed casually at the ankle. He'd removed his frock coat and waist coat, loosened his cravat, and tugged at the tails of his shirt so it was bunched negligently about his waist. She imagined him in such a pose on a grassy bank, dappled by sunlight and disturbed by a light breeze. His fishing pole would be resting beside him, the hook merely dangling above a swiftly running stream. His face would be similarly set in contemplation, but the nature of his thoughts on that occasion would be far less troubling.

Griffin lifted his head a bit to acknowledge Olivia's entrance. His eyes followed her to the dressing room, then he closed them again as he heard the familiar sounds of her washing away her painted face and removing her auburn wig. He said nothing when she took longer than usual to make her ablutions and dress for bed. Some evenings he played the lady's maid for her, but tonight she did not ask for assistance and he offered none. It was not her way to avoid him for long, so he respected her unspoken wish to be permitted these private moments.

When she came to the bed, he held out his hand and invited her to sit. His occupation of the mattress on the diagonal gave her room enough on the edge. She turned sideways, drawing one leg up under her and supporting the other by hooking her heel on the frame. His thumb absently brushed the back of her hand.

"You are certain you want to know?" she asked quietly, picking up the thread of their earlier conversation.

Griffin nodded. "It will not change what I think of you, feel for you." He held her eyes. "You were a child, like Nat. Remember that when you suppose there was something you could have done. Think of him and know you were without weapons."

"I am not without weapons now," she said. "And neither are you. Promise me, Griffin. I would have your promise that you will take no action on my behalf."

He considered her words carefully, then his own. "As you wish."

Olivia took a deep breath and released it slowly. "Very well. I feel certain you understand more than you let on, but since you cannot yet know the whole of it, it is this: Sir Hadrien regularly came to my room at Coleridge Park. I do not know how old I was that first time. I am not even certain I recall it. He didn't hurt me, though, I am sure of that. What I have come to remember is there were many occasions that I was simply invited to crawl into his lap. That was pleasant enough, or it seemed so at one time. Later, I was invited to touch him. It was a game, the touching. Tickling. Squeezing. He touched me also, praised me warmly. Such a good girl. My own dearest girl. I might have invited him to touch me as well. I don't know. It is difficult to know now what was my idea and what was his. I know I wanted to please him. It was important to me. There was his wife, my stepmother. And Alastair. My family had changed and my place seemed secure only as long as I was in my father's lap."

"It was his idea, Olivia. All of it was his idea."

She shrugged lightly, unconvinced that it mattered. "I cannot say when Honey Shepard made her discovery or how long she might have held on to the secret before she approached my stepmother. You comprehend that so much happened out of my sight, out of my hearing. I suppose my sense of what must have occurred came to me over time, first in the convent school, and later still after I was sent to Miss Barnard's Academy in Crawley. They are a constant companion, those memories, but I try to keep them at my side so they do not creep up behind me or block my way."

Her gaze had drifted away from his, but now it returned. "Honey was dismissed. My stepmother's doing, I am sure. I don't suppose she thought she had any other choice. Knowing the nanny was in possession of such a secret, it would have been difficult to tolerate, so she removed her from the house. It was a great loss to me, but I had little time to accustom myself to her absence. In very short order, I was sent away."

Olivia fell silent. Griffin's hand anchored her, kept her from moving. Her heart hammered wildly, and she waited for it to calm. "You know what came to pass while I was at the convent school. I don't know how it was chosen, though I have always believed it was my father's doing. I told you I learned to expect nothing from my family while I was there. No visits. No gifts. That wasn't entirely . . ."

Griffin waited, watched her swallow hard. He kept his gaze steady, patient, but not urging her on. Finally, he finished what she could not. "He was one of them."

She nodded slowly, grateful that he could finish it. "After so long a time, you would think I'd be able to say the words. I cannot. What you said about them buying my silence, I suppose that is true. My father certainly did. I kept the secret, and he never tired of telling me how proud he was, just as if I had accomplished something important. I suppose that is how he thought of it, so perhaps it was not entirely a lie. I was not his only little girl. I knew that. But I also knew I was his favorite." She swiped at the tears that hovered on the rim of her lashes. "He gave me to them, Griffin. He sent me to them when it pleased him to do so. To sit at their table while they played cards, to deal for them as I'd been taught, perform on command, and later . . . as any one of them was struck by a fancy . . ." Olivia shuddered once, then was still. "I was a present on some occasions . . . his marker on others."

This last squeezed Griffin's heart. He could not help but think of his own role in re-creating the ugliest scenes of her childhood. It hardly mattered that he'd known none of it. Alastair, also. They'd opened a door to her past and pushed her through it.

He swore so softly it was hardly more than an expulsion of air. He would have pulled his hand from hers, but this time she was the one who held fast. It made him remember that he'd told her he was prepared to hear all of it, and now he knew the cost. The full weight of what he'd done bore down upon him.

"You didn't know," Olivia said.

"I'm not sure that should matter."

"Of course it does. I am no longer a child, Griffin, and I did not have to accept becoming Alastair's marker. Do you think I didn't realize I could have left this place? All of your words to the contrary, you would have allowed me to go. Alastair's life and reputation would not have been worth tuppence, but you wouldn't have made me account for his debt."

"I'm not certain that's true."

"And I'm certain it is. I was an inconvenience to you, one more item in your expense column. From the very first, you understood better than I that Alastair would likely leave me behind. You were prepared. I wasn't." Her mouth twisted in a wry smile. "You did not come to my room. I went to yours. There was no force, no coercion. You never asked it of me. Never once."

"Neither did I turn you away. I wanted you there, Olivia, and it served my own interests to have you come to me."

Olivia inched closer. She leaned forward and touched his lips with her own. "I didn't understand it then. Couldn't. You wanted something more than what I gave you that night. Credit both my extraordinary experience and my impover-ished imagination. I didn't know what could be." She kissed him again, sipped the breath from his mouth. "I'm learning, though. I'm learning that everything is possible."

Griffin abandoned his sprawl in favor of making room for Olivia beside him. He lifted himself on one elbow and laid his other arm across her midriff. "What happened at twelve?" he asked.

The abrupt shift made her frown. "Twelve? I was at the faro table then. You know that I—"

He stopped her by placing a finger to her lips. "Not twelve o'clock. Twelve years. Your twelfth year, to be precise. Why were you moved from the convent school to Miss Barnard's Academy?"

"My first course." She saw that he did not immediately understand that she was not speaking of her studies. "My first *monthly* course. I supposed then that it made me unattractive to them, and that was true after a fashion, but I came to understand later that the possibility of carrying a child was a risk they were not prepared to accept. There were no expectations of the carnal kind at Miss Barnard's. I continued my academic studies as if those carriage rides away from the convent had never happened."

"And then?"

She raised her hand and touched the side of his face. "You know," she said. "You always know when there is more." When she saw the observation would not turn him from his question, she continued. "And then it was time to leave. I had been prepared all along, you see, to take my place at some gentleman's side, or perhaps at the side of a succession of gentlemen. There certainly would have been a marriage arranged for me, but there would have been certain expectations in it that are not part of the vows one usually makes, and there also would have been expectations outside of it. That was all clearly explained to me. Better to make my own way, I thought. I demanded to be allowed to go."

"It is difficult to believe Sir Hadrien let you go easily."

"He didn't, but I have always credited my stepmother's touch in bringing the thing about. It is supposition only, gleaned from things my father said the last time he spoke to me. I barely remember her, never saw her again after I was sent away, and I have no illusions that whatever her objections might have been, they had little enough to do with me. She was protecting what was hers by marriage, most particularly her son. She wanted all ties to me severed—afraid, I think, that I might exercise some unsettling influence on Alastair. Though my father would never admit to any vulnerability, he feared exposure. I had no such power over him because he knew I would remain silent. The same wasn't true of my stepmother. In the end, I think he believed he had no choice but to do as I wanted."

Griffin caught her wrist. His thumb brushed back and forth across the fine blue-veined web on the underside. "Was there no compromise possible? My God, Olivia, to set out on your own . . . A young woman with no protection . . ." He fell silent as he realized how absurd his protest was. "I'm sorry. You never had benefit of anyone's protection, did you? Your confidence in your own resources was not misplaced."

"Sir Hadrien arranged a teaching post for me. I stayed a few months, long enough for him to suppose I was satisfied and would not be difficult, then I left. I went as far as my small savings would take me, then I found employment at an inn and disappeared into comfortable anonymity, greeting passengers, serving food and drink, making myself useful through industry. It is where I learned the rudiments of managing accounts. The facility I had with cards made me a favorite with the students traveling between university and town. The innkeeper and his wife were hard-working, pleasant folk, glad enough of my contribution to their enterprise that they looked after me."

"You are speaking of Mr. and Mrs. Romney."

Olivia's eyebrows drew together. Her eyes darkened as her

gaze narrowed. "I am, but I've never told you their names. What have you done, Griffin?"

"Spoken to them. No more than that. After Elaine died, I made a rather circuitous journey returning to London. It occurred to me that I might learn something about Mr. Rawlings."

"Without asking me?"

"Yes," he said simply. "I presumed you were yet at Jericho Mews. The hell would remain closed, and arrangements for Nat to stay with my sister were easily made. I seized the opportunity."

Olivia was slow to give up her annoyed expression. "Why am I only learning of it now?"

"Because I have not yet received confirmation of my suspicions. I could only do so much in the time available to me; the remainder I placed in Mr. Gardner's capable hands. I expect to hear something very soon."

"So you will owe him a second favor after all. I'm not certain that should have been your decision alone."

"You are overly concerned with this matter of a favor and a debt and have asked nothing about my suspicions."

Olivia's eyes darted away and she fell silent. Her throat was at once too dry and narrow to manage even a few words.

"What I did, Olivia, was in aid of seeing you free of this fear you harbor. Like your memories, it is also your constant companion. Do you think I don't know why you cannot say you love me?"

"Perhaps I don't."

"Look at me, and perhaps I'll believe you."

She did, but it was not a look she could sustain. "It signifies nothing," she said. "You may put whatever construction you like upon it, but it still has no meaning."

"So you say." Griffin caught her chin as she would have turned her head and levered her back using only his fingertip. "I do love you, Olivia, and that is not predicated on you returning the same feeling for me. I choose to believe you do, though I will not insist upon hearing it. If it has not come to you yet, I hold out hope that it will. Mayhap it will strike you suddenly, for no reason that you can name, and you will know with the same certainty I do that it has always been love, if not from the first, then from only a few moments past it. You could not have known it then, but looking back, you will wonder how it escaped your notice, or why it was so important to deny what so clearly fit, and in our case, was so clearly inevitable."

Now she stared at him, and because her throat closed again, she said nothing.

"Shall I tell you the rest of what you're afraid to hear?" If he hadn't been watching her closely, alert to the faintest change in her expression, he would have missed the slight parting of her lips and the soft, sibilant sound of her reply. "I could find no corroboration of your story, Olivia. No evidence that anyone ever died at the inn, no tales passed on about a murder on the grounds, no indication that there was ever an investigation related to a death by any authority."

Olivia struggled to sit up and realized that Griffin's arm about her waist now served to restrain her. Frustrated, she lay back and ground out, "It does not seem possible. When they lifted him away from me, he was so heavy. They struggled with his weight. I don't know how he could have lived."

"I don't know that he did."

"I don't understand."

"There was no death at the inn, but a Mr. Rollins—not Rawlings—was found hanged in his room at university. As best I could determine, the timing of his death connects closely to your departure from the inn."

"But how could you know that? I never said any—"

"The Romneys," he said, placing a finger to her lips when she would have protested. "You've spent these last years looking over your shoulder, Olivia, imagining the inevitability of being found out and alternately wondering if there was truly anything to be discovered."

He was right, but that did not make it easier to hear. "I don't understand about Mr. Rollins. He hanged himself?"

Griffin's reply to her question was a noncommittal murmur. "I did not learn about that from the Romneys. There would be no reason for them to know of it. I visited Cambridge and made inquiries. You said you thought all five of the travelers at your table were students. It seemed the place to go once I located your inn." He saw she was not entirely at ease with what he had done, but had little choice to accept it. "Your decision to go to Alastair while he was yet at university was not without risk. You must have known that. There was every chance you might have had an encounter with the students who came to your aid. Was that what you hoped would happen? You'd have had your answers then."

Olivia realized she honestly didn't know. "I'm not sure it was done of a purpose. At the time it seemed that Alastair could offer sanctuary, and I rarely ventured far from the residence he found for me. How curious it is, to think on it now, that I should have put myself in the very midst of a place where I might expect to find answers, then avoid every opportunity to look for them."

"Curious, yes, but then we are all pieces of work, are we not?"

"I suppose."

"There is another matter still to consider."

She sighed. "There can't be."

He gave her a wry grin. "You assumed that Rawlings and his friends fled that night, but I can tell you now it wasn't so. Rawlings never returned, but whiskey, gin, and two pints of ale were all present the following morning. If Rawlings's friends were able to explain his disappearance to the satisfaction of others, especially the Romneys, what then accounted for your absence?"

"What?"

"Consider this. You disappeared, Olivia. If there was no evidence that anything was amiss, then it would seem you vanished without cause. The Romneys would have been concerned. You imagined you were leaving behind a body, but I am telling you one was never found there. The good innkeeper and his wife would have wondered at your absence. You have said they cared for you. You left no note, no explanation. What reason might they have been given that would have satisfied everyone?"

Olivia's eyes widened slowly. "They believed I ran off with Mr. Rawlings."

"And there you have it." He tapped the tip of her nose with his finger. "I have never accused you of being a slow top."

"They told you?"

"It was not so straightforward a conversation as that. I may not possess Restell Gardner's experience in eliciting information, but I could appreciate there was need for circumspection. Mrs. Romney in particular was quite willing to talk about the trials of managing the inn. Finding good help being chief among them. You can imagine how it went from there. She mentioned one young woman of whom she was most particularly fond, but discovered her to be as lacking in good judgment as those who came and went before her. 'They meet a rascal,' she told me, 'posing as a gentleman who promises much in a fine, silky voice, and then they're gone without so much as a by-your-leave.'"

He waited as she took it all in. "It was your disappearance that was remarked on by the Romneys. They would not have recalled anything about the students who stopped at the inn so many years ago if your departure weren't fixed so clearly in their mind. It certainly gave me pause, Olivia. You also, apparently."

She nodded slowly. "I thought that when no one came for me quickly that the Romneys may have taken it upon themselves to protect me. It never occurred that there might be another reason for their silence." She searched Griffin's face. His expression held no urgency that she accept any of the things he'd told her. She was free to examine what he'd said, free to discredit or embrace all of it. He had no compelling need to convince or coerce her. It was enormously liberating and unlike anything in her experience.

"What is to be done now?"

"Nothing except wait on the confirmation that the man you thought was Rawlings is indeed the same gentleman found hanged at university. It ends there, Olivia. It must. For everyone."

She understood what he was saying. Whether the hanging was coerced, done by his own hand, or staged to hide evidence of a murder, the inquiry ended with the fact of his death. "The identity of this man, that is what Mr. Gardner is trying to establish?"

Griffin nodded. "He is engaged in a search of the London hells, looking for the foursome who appeared here. He has a description such as I was able to give him, and he expects to be successful. The four of them are bound by what happened that evening, and it makes them easier to find than if they'd scattered."

"You have done so much," she said softly. "Given so much." How had she not known? she wondered. How had she not known from the very first?

She lifted one hand and laid it along the side of his face. Her thumb made the lightest pass down his scar. "I do love you, you know."

His smile was gentle. "So you have come to it at last." He turned his head and caught the heart of her palm with his lips. He pressed his kiss, then folded her hand around it. "That is quite something indeed."

"It is good of you not to be smug." She felt as if what she held in her fist had substance. She settled it between her breasts. "It is disconcerting how often you are right about a thing."

"I am going to treasure you said that and keep it close for all the times I am wrong."

Olivia drew down his head and raised hers a fraction. "Will you have me now, Griffin? I think I should like that very much."

Their mouths closed that infinitesimal gap. Heat blossomed the exact moment their lips touched, and their need was mutual and immediate and powerful.

Olivia tore at his stock and linen until she had her hands splayed across his chest. Her fingers curled a fraction, and she lightly scored him with her nails. His flesh was warm and taut and responsive. He anticipated her touch, prepared for it, and sucked in a breath just as she would have dragged her hands across his flat belly. Her fingers dipped unerringly into the small space he gave between his abdomen and his trousers.

He groaned against her mouth as she clutched him. His fingers fumbled with the fastening to his fly. She released him long enough to deftly manage the thing herself, then took him in hand once again. He was hot and hard and thick in her fist. She could feel the coursing of his blood, the steady pulse that matched the one in his throat and was set to the beat of his heart.

Griffin caught her hand and held it still. "Not yet. Not just yet. I want . . . God, Olivia . . . you can't . . ." He covered her mouth hard with his as she squeezed her fingers ever so slightly. He throbbed heavily in her fist. He pushed his tongue deep in her mouth, ground his mouth against hers, then ground his hips equally hard.

Olivia arched, pushed herself against him, dug one heel into the mattress for purchase, and all but slipped under his skin. There was a brief struggle, and for a time they were equally matched, but she lost ground gradually as he drugged her with long, slow, deep kisses that left her boneless and pinioned under him.

She looked up at him, her darkening eyes vaguely unfocused,

her lips swollen and damp. Her wrists were caught in his hands and held in place on either side of her head. Odd, but she did not feel as if she'd lost, and the gradual appearance of her slightly wicked siren's smile underscored her satisfaction with the turn-about in their play.

Griffin gave her wrists a little shake that only had the effect of deepening her smile. "You are maddening," he said, his throat tight of a sudden. "And I thank God every day for it."

That pleased her, for she hadn't the least idea how she might go about being anything else. The knowledge that he wouldn't ask it endeared him to her, and she thanked him in her own way. To the extent that she could move under him, she did so. The press of his body on hers made it provocative in the ex-treme. "You will not make me wait overlong, will you?"

"I should," he whispered. "But it will kill me." He bent his head, kissed her again, ran the edge of his tongue under her upper lip and sipped. He made a feast of her mouth, then placed kisses at the corner of it. He dipped his head and found the curve of her neck and shoulder. His teeth caught her skin, bit down gently, worried it, then laved it as though licking a wound. Her whimper, the hitch in her breathing, provoked him to do more of the same.

He released her wrists, but only because he needed his hands to open her robe. He fairly dragged it off her body, then applied himself to the problem of her nightgown.

The thin, delicate batiste was a modest barrier at best. Grif-fin made damp circles at the tip of her breast. The pink aure-ole was visible through the fabric. The nipple rose like a bud. He took it between his lips and sucked.

Olivia's fingers plowed through his hair, folded, and held fast. Slender ribbons of heat curled in her belly. She closed her eyes, squeezed them, really, and felt nothing so much as the rhythmic tug of his mouth on her breast. She arched, wanting more, still more, and he frustrated her by moving his attention to her other breast and beginning again.

Her hands slipped out of his hair and found his shoulders. When he lifted his head, she tore at her gown herself and made a knot of the ribbon that closed the neckline. He had the nerve to laugh, though the sound of it was so darkly wicked that she was aroused by it rather than offended.

"Let me," he said, pushing her hands aside. His fingers were only marginally more skillful than hers, but the frustration of the exercise merely added to the heat. He spread the material wide, laying her breasts bare to the glow of the candlelight and the gleam in his eye. "Touch yourself."

Olivia's mouth parted, but no sound emerged. The tip of her tongue appeared, and she licked her lips.

"Go on," he whispered. "Touch yourself."

She lifted one hand, quite uncertain it was done of her own volition, and slid it gently across her right breast. The budding nipple caught in the vee between her index and middle finger. The touch of her own hand excited her. The sight of it excited him more. She closed her fingers gently around the nipple and tugged and knew a corresponding tug in her womb. He pushed himself against her then, rubbed his cock in the cleft of her thighs.

Her fingertips grazed her flesh, circled her breast, and finally cupped the underside and offered herself up to his mouth. She bit into her own lip when he took it, suppressing all but a mewling cry at the back of her throat.

He imagined the taste of a sugared rose, the petal softness, the sweetness of dew. He felt the break in her breathing, the change in the tension of her slender frame. Her head was pressed back into the pillow, her chin lifted and her neck arched. Her throat worked convulsively.

He thrust against her, the sheer folds of her nightgown taking the place of a virginal barrier. She was as deliciously frustrated by it as she was aroused. He gave her the hot suck of his mouth again, and this time he tore the shudder from her body and a cry from her throat.

He made neither of them wait now as he lifted just enough to yank at the hem of her nightgown. She scrabbled at it with as much purpose as he until it was bunched at her hips. Her thighs parted, knees lifted, and she cried out a second time as he pushed himself into her.

Olivia's hands slipped under his drawers and palmed his buttocks. He was seated in so deeply that she knew nothing but the heavy fullness of him pressing against her. He was still now, as she was also, and they held themselves in just that manner until their breathing calmed.

"Go on," she said, nodding faintly. "You should not be made to wait, either." And to make certain he did not, she contracted around him, squeezing as she'd done earlier with her fist. This was far more complete, infinitely more intimate.

Not proof against her heat or her urging, Griffin began to move. In moments his need outstripped his calm, and he rocked them both to the edge of crisis and then beyond it.

Olivia was aware of Nat's grave regard across the small table that separated them at breakfast. Griffin was still soundly asleep on the floor below, but Olivia did not think his absence had anything to do with Nat's curious study of her. The child was absently fingering one of the tin soldiers that he'd placed around the butter dish, and as the soldier had his bayonet aggressively thrust forward, she wondered if it was the same fellow who'd stabbed her foot the night before.

"What is it, Nat?" she asked. "Have I grown horns, a third eye? I am no stranger to your table, so what is it that has caught your attention this morning?"

He stopped fiddling with the soldier but didn't reach for his spoon. His porridge had already grown cold. He shrugged.

"Nat," she cajoled gently. "You may say anything. Do I have crumbs on my chin? A cocoa mustache?"

A smile came and went as he shook his head. "You look that same," he said, "but different."

"Do I?" As an explanation it was not in any way precise, yet Olivia thought she knew precisely what he meant. For her, though, it went more deeply than appearance. She'd awakened this morning the same, yet different. Her reflection in the mirror above the washstand had revealed nothing to her, but the boy across from her was perhaps more accurate than a looking glass. "I might be different," she said. "It's a different day, after all."

He tipped his head to one side, nodded, and began swinging his legs under the table as he picked up his spoon. "Your face is soft."

"Oh." Olivia took a bite of toast. "How is it usually?"

Nat used his spoon like a shovel and dug a hole in his porridge. "Just different. Awake."

There was an apt description. She'd gotten very little in the way of rest in what was left of the night. Every time Griffin reached for her she went to him eagerly, and when he swore he would never be able to move again, she was pleased to show him how wildly wrong he was. She supposed she did look soft and sleepy, though having a yet-to-be six-year-old child remark upon it was disconcerting.

"Did you come to my room last night?" Nat asked.

Olivia was grateful for the change of subject. "I did. I was attacked by one of your infantry. Quite possibly that soldier with the bayonet. What battle were you planning?"

"Marathon."

"I don't recall that the ancient Greeks had bayonets."

"Spears. They had spears."

"Of course." If Nat could imagine his floor defined the plains of Marathon, then he certainly could imagine spears. "Lord Breckenridge came to see you also. Did you know that?"

He nodded. "He scattered a great many of my men about, but he left something for me."

"He did?"

Nat stopped swinging his legs and stood his spoon upright in his porridge. "Would you like to see?"

"I would, yes." How like Griffin to never mention it. She watched Nat scoot down from his chair and quickly cross the room to his bedside. He reached under his pillow and drew out a small velvet bag that fit neatly into the palm of his hand. He carried it back to the table and placed it beside Olivia's plate. "Perhaps you should open it," she said. "I shouldn't like to be speared a second time."

He thought that was amusing. "It's not a soldier."

"It isn't?"

Nat shook his head. He spread the drawstring and opened the bag, then tipped it so the contents spilled into his open hand. "I hope you will not tell him that I should have liked a soldier better. I would not have him think me ungrateful."

Olivia stared at the square-cut emerald set in its bed of twenty-one diamond chips. She touched the ring with the tip of her forefinger, nudging it a bit across Nat's open palm.

He misunderstood her wariness and offered the sage observation that it would not bite her.

Olivia was not as certain. "I've seen this ring before," she said. "That you have it seems quite odd to me."

Nat bristled. "I didn't steal it."

"I didn't think you did," she said gently. "How do you know it was his lordship who gave it to you?"

"Who else could it have been?"

Who else indeed. She did not answer Nat, but she was certain it had not been Griffin who'd clumsily crossed Marathon last night. "Will you be terribly disappointed to learn that a mistake's been made? I think perhaps this ring was meant for someone else. I shouldn't be at all surprised if there is not a velvet bag just like this somewhere in his lordship's room with a splendid major general inside."

"Do you think so?"

Olivia smiled at the hopefulness of his expression. "I feel certain of it. May I take the ring?"

"Oh, yes. Have a care, it's a weighty thing."

Once again, Nat had put his finger on it exactly.

It was Foster that Olivia entrusted with the task of finding the perfectly turned-out major general. She settled enough money on him to buy Wellington's entire army but made the major general the first order of business. She also gave him the velvet bag to place the commander in.

She watched him hurry along Putnam Lane until he turned the corner at Moorhead Street before she returned to the house. Somehow she must have imparted the importance of the mission because she could not recall the footman striding so purposefully in any direction.

Olivia found Griffin in the dressing room. He was toweling his hair dry and droplets of water scattered as he shook himself. Mason was setting out his clothes and trying to avoid the spray.

"Will you leave us, Mason?"

The valet hesitated, but not for long. Griffin's head came out from under his towel and looked from Mason to Olivia and back again. He did not bother to grant permission as his valet was already excusing himself. "If you are going to make a habit of directing Mason in his duties, you really should marry me."

"What nonsense. What does one have to do with the other?"

"Not a thing, I suspect, but after your declaration of last evening, I find myself compelled to put the matter of our unmarried state before you."

"Our unmarried state suits me."

"Yes, well, we are at odds there." He tightened the hitch of the towel around his waist. "I am hoping to change that."

Olivia set her mouth in a disapproving line and handed Griffin his robe. She waited until he put it on before she took the ring from her pocket and thrust it forward, displayed in the palm of her hand.

Griffin stared at it, then at her. He cocked one eyebrow. "Is it your brother's ring?"

"The very same. Go on. Take it."

He plucked it from her palm and made a cursory examination. When he would have returned it, he saw she'd already dropped her hand to her side. Uncomfortable with the idea of putting it on his own finger, he slipped it into the pocket of his robe. "How did you come by it?"

"Nat gave it to me at breakfast. He thinks you put it under his pillow last night."

Now both of Griffin's eyebrows lifted to attention. "Why would he suppose that—" He stopped as the possibilities presented themselves. "You think your brother was here?"

"If there is another explanation, I should like to hear it."

"He lost the ring, remember? At Johnny Crocker's hell. In a rigged game."

"Yes, but when I stayed with Alastair, I asked him about the ring and whether or not he thought he could get it back. He said he could."

"But why would he?"

"Because he needed to. It is a matter of self-respect."

"That is a seed you planted and nurtured, not something that came to him on his own."

"You had some part in it also."

"How is that?"

"Alastair likes you. More to the point, he respects you. And, pray, do not say it is my imagining that makes it so. He told me. That he returned the ring speaks more to your influence than mine."

Griffin snorted lightly. "He is yet a child. Nat has more in the way of good sense than your brother."

Olivia did not disagree, nor did she feel obliged to defend Alastair for form's sake. "However it came about, you now have the ring. The debt is well and truly settled."

"It was settled already, Olivia. When your brother left you in my care, it was settled, and God's truth, but I got the better part of it." He pointed toward the bedchamber. "Join me at the table. I've yet to have a cup of coffee or a bite of toast."

Olivia led the way out. She poured his cup for him before she sat and slathered strawberry jam on his toast while he drank. She nudged the plate forward until it rested directly in front of him. "If there is more you wish to say about the ring," she said, sitting back, "I am most desirous of hearing it."

Griffin took a large bite of toast and rather a longer time to chew it than was strictly necessary. "That was something a wife might do, you know. Pouring my coffee and spreading the jam."

"Really? It seems to me it is most capably done by a nanny."

Griffin's mouth twitched. He raised his cup in a vague salute, conceding the point. His argument had not been well conceived, and he appreciated that she had not stated the obvious, namely that his wife had never once attended him at breakfast. He washed down the toast with coffee, then set his cup in its saucer and regarded Olivia frankly.

"I heard some time ago that Mrs. Christie came into possession of the ring. She is known to frequent Crocker's establishment and may have entertained the notion that he would make her his partner. He is completely untrustworthy, of course, but then, so is she. I imagine on this occasion, she was able to get the best of him."

"Then she won it back for Alastair. He's still with her, is he not?"

"I have not heard differently, though I do not go out of my way to learn such things. As to whether she won the ring for him, I would not place a wager there. One rarely goes wrong depending upon Mrs. Christie, first and foremost, to look after herself. It is not beyond reasonable to suppose that she has come to some understanding with your brother and another with Mr. Crocker. She does not move from one situation without making arrangements for the next."

"I wish you'd told me."

"Perhaps I should have, but we both seemed to have put this matter of the ring behind us. I never wanted it, Olivia. Not for myself. I'd hoped possession would ensure your brother paid his debt, nothing more." Griffin found the ring in his pocket and set it on the table. He nudged it with his fingertip, turning it round. "Have you wondered at all how your brother was able to enter?"

She hadn't. Now she did. "A key?"

"Most certainly. And that could have only come from Mrs. Christie. She would have had access to them at one time."

"You think she still has keys in her possession."

"It seems likely. Truss is particular about locking the doors. Everyone on Putnam Lane does the same. The hells are too vulnerable otherwise."

"So he stole the ring from her, and the key, and came here. I am not certain I take your point."

Griffin stopped turning the ring. It wobbled, then was still. "Someone else once had possession of a key," he said. "You cannot have forgotten that."

Olivia blinked. "The gentleman villain."

"The very same. I thought—we all did—that he lifted the key from the peg in the servants' hall. Guests do not normally venture below, but we believed he could have done so unnoticed because almost all of the staff is engaged in the gaming rooms. The presence of this ring makes me suspect he had the key to your room when he entered the hell that night."

She frowned. "Are you saying that the villain is responsible for the return of the ring?"

"No. Not at all."

"Then Mrs. Christie."

Griffin flicked the ring so it skittered and spun across the table toward Olivia, the emerald and diamonds flashing. "For returning this? Hardly."

Olivia stared at the ring for a long moment before picking it up. She turned it over in her hand thoughtfully, then, on impulse, slipped it on her thumb. She looked up at Griffin.

"Yes?" he asked, knowing full well that she'd worked it out for herself. Her eyes flashed much as the emerald had.

"You think Mrs. Christie sent the villain."

"You have it exactly."

"But why?"

"As to that," he said, taking her hand, "we shall have to ask."

Chapter Fifteen

Alastair ducked. The black lacquered jewelry box Alys Christie flung at his head sailed over it instead and thudded hard against the wall. The hinged lid remained intact until the box dropped to the floor. Alastair glanced at it but not for long. The damaged treasure chest and all of its spilled booty were much less concerning than the tortoiseshell hairbrush Mrs. Christie prepared to launch at him next.

He feinted left, then right, and took a glancing blow off his shoulder. Her aim was true. He was merely a bit lighter and quicker on his feet.

A second hairbrush, this time one with a heavy silver backing, thumped against the door as he spun sideways. She'd meant for it to slam into his chest.

He took a step toward her, hands extended slightly to ward off the next missile. "Alys."

It was his cajoling tone that further incensed her. Never taking her eyes from him, she blindly slapped the top of her vanity until her fingers found something useful. She gripped her handheld mirror with the ferocity of a warrior and raised it just above her shoulder. This time she did not let it fly immediately.

"You had no right!" Her nostrils flared as she sucked in a

breath. Her normally pale complexion was flushed with angry color. "That ring was mine. Mine!"

Alastair's raised eyebrow emphasized his skepticism. "Really? You were able to convince yourself of it?"

Her hold on the mirror did not falter, but he had captured her attention in a manner that stayed her hand. "What do you mean I was able to convince myself? You were there. So were dozens of witnesses. I won the thing from Johnny Crocker, and that makes it mine."

"I lost it in a rigged game. You not only encouraged me to make that wager, you knew the dealer's box was set against the players. Crocker runs an honest game only when it serves him, and there is probably no one as knowledgeable on that count as you. He took the ring from me so you could take it from him. I know very well that you are in league. It has always been about the ring, though I was slow to see it. You coveted it from the first. Looking back on the occasion of our introduction, it was the ring that brought you to my side, the ring that you admired."

"Your accusation has no substance."

He stood a bit straighter, more confident now, no longer feeling at a youthful disadvantage. There was a hint of disdain in his cool green eyes. "I notice you do not deny it."

"What would be the point? You will believe what you will." She lowered the mirror a fraction. "Have a care, though, not to put your assumptions about. You will not like the consequences."

"As it happens, your threat aside, I have no intention of sharing what you did with anyone. You are known to be the grasping, cunning one, so hearing that you managed another coup will hardly surprise the masses. I, on the other hand, do not wish to be reminded of my own colossal folly." He tipped his head to one side as he considered her, his smile only mildly contemptuous. "I cannot regret our association, Mrs.

Christie, but if you throw that mirror at me, I will consider that you have ended it."

She did not lower the mirror, but neither did she pitch it at him. He looked as if he might be inclined to pitch it back . . . or paddle her with it. This last was an intriguing thought, though she was quite certain she would like it only in the abstract. The humiliating reality was not to be borne.

"So you have come into your own now, is that what you would have me believe?"

"Come into my own? I haven't any idea what you mean."

"I am speaking of your transformation, of course. From rascal to self-righteous prig. You are ruined, I fear." She dropped her hand to her side and lightly tapped the mirror against her leg. "Your sister has ruined you." The slip of a smile she offered did not touch her cool blue eyes. "But then, you have ruined her. Perhaps it is only fair."

Alastair's jaw worked and at his side his hand clenched and unclenched. "You would do well not to mention Olivia."

"Why? Am I not fit to speak her name? Olivia. O-li-vi-a." She held her ground when Alastair took a step forward. He was still too far away to strike her, but the intent was there. "She's proved to be no better than she ought, wouldn't you say? Isn't that what your father told you? The truth will out. I cannot decide if you meant to prove him wrong by throwing her in Breckenridge's path, or hoped to prove him right. Either way, you were well rid of her, and isn't that what you desired above all else?"

"You should stop talking now, Alys."

"Have I made you uncomfortable?" Her sly smile deepened a fraction. "I recall very well that you were weary of her presence. You told me she regarded you with such disapproval that you could not bear to be in the same room with her."

Had he said that? Alastair wondered. He'd been cross with Olivia, so he probably had. "I believe I made too much of it. She was concerned for my welfare."

"Hers also. How easily you forget that. She was an albatross, you told me."

"I feel fairly certain I never called her such."

"A weight, then. A burden of significant proportion. That is what you would have had me believe. And you wanted rid of the responsibility for her. She took much more than she gave, do you recall saying that? Her presence in your home forced you to live in reduced circumstances, set you outside your father's good graces, and made your mother critical of you at every turn. You had no liking for any of it."

Alastair flushed, but he accepted the words she threw back at him because he remembered very well that they had once been his own. His deep shame made him mute.

"You wagered recklessly, Alastair, and you lost. You *were* lost. You did not apply to your sister for help after Breckenridge relieved you of your ring. You came to me. How sad you were. Pathetic, really. And I took pity on you, helped you get it back. Two birds with one stone, because you never objected to shedding yourself of your responsibilities to Olivia at the same time."

Alastair stiffened as this last dart hit center, but he found his voice. "It was wrong of me, Alys. Olivia stood for me as I was never able to stand for her. She didn't hesitate; that's what Breckenridge told me when he dragged me off to face her. I was so cowardly that I fought him to avoid her."

He judged that Mrs. Christie had settled herself enough that he could turn his back on her. He went to the drinks cabinet in the adjoining sitting room and poured himself two fingers of scotch. When he looked up, raising his glass, he saw that she had followed him. "Would you like one?"

She shook her head. "You walked away from me."

"So I did. Trading barbs such as we have made me thirsty." He regarded her over the rim of his crystal tumbler. She had left the mirror in her bedroom, but it only made her marginally less dangerous. "I take it you are not yet finished."

"I'm not, no. And I don't need your permission to continue, so, pray, do not insult me by giving it."

He merely sipped his drink.

Alys thrust her chin forward. "I never thought Breckenridge would accept her as your marker. I thought his mistrust of women ran too deep for that. A miscalculation on my part, and a serious one as it turned out. He kept her and put me out."

"Do not delude yourself, Alys. He would have put you out anyway. Your association was nearly at an end, else you would not have looked me over so carefully."

She did not deny it. "It is about choice. Mine, not his. Your sister provoked him to do it."

"That is hardly likely. It is fairer to blame me. Did you not tell me Breckenridge suspected your fine hand in helping me take back the ring?"

"A suspicion only." Alys shrugged. "I could have persuaded him to see it differently. Olivia's presence made him unreasonable."

Alastair recognized the futility of argument. This time when he made no reply it was of a purpose.

"I want the ring back," Alys said.

"So you have said. You will have to apply to Breckenridge for it, though that supposes he actually knows he has it."

"What do you mean?"

"I did not precisely place the thing in his hand. Ever the coward, I suppose. Neither did I return it to his desk where it might sit unnoticed for weeks. I put it in his son's room."

Mrs. Christie's breath hissed between her teeth. "He hasn't recognized the brat. The betting books favor the child being his wife's bastard."

"Be sure to tell him that when you ask for the ring."

She ignored that. "What possessed you?"

"I told you. Cowardice."

"Madness is more like it."

Recalling that he'd nearly broken his neck stumbling over the infantry, Alastair was inclined to agree. "I'll claim the ring when I can pay the debt. It is what I should have done at the outset."

"Sir Hadrien will not be pleased to learn what's become of it."

"I don't suppose he will, but he's a practical man and will accept it is better lost to the viscount than to you."

Mrs. Christie did not hesitate. She closed the distance between them and laid her hand hard across Alastair Cole's cheek. She watched his eyes water with the sting of her slap, but he made no move to retaliate. Desirous of goading him further, she raised her hand again. This time he caught her by the wrist.

"I am not opposed to striking a woman," he said. "But that is not what you had in mind, is it, Alys? Do you think I don't know what you want?"

"The ring," she whispered. "I want the ring."

"And a proposal to go with it, I'm thinking." He bent his head and placed his mouth near her ear. He could feel her tremble. With anger. With lust. "What I mean to propose is of a decidedly different nature."

"All bets are down." Olivia scanned the table to memorize the placing of the wagers. Occasionally there was a gentleman who tested her with a bit of sleight of hand. Most efforts were clumsy, and she caught them right off. Sometimes, though, the effort was good enough to be worthy of her observation, and she tracked their cheating through several games before she settled with them privately.

Tonight she was intrigued by the deft play of a pair of gentlemen who looked as if they might be, if not brothers, then cousins. They were most excellent at diversion and delivery. One would draw attention, while the other dropped a chip—

usually concealed in his palm or cuff—on the card that would match Olivia's draw from the deck. They did not do it on every turn, but often enough that they were winning well in advance of the odds that they should do so.

She wasn't particularly insulted that they tried their hand at it at her table. The mental diligence she applied to watching their antics kept her from entertaining thoughts of those things over which she had no control—the matter of Mrs. Christie and the gentleman villain being chief among them.

Griffin had called upon Mrs. Christie several times in the last two weeks and never found her at home. On his last visit, he'd been frustrated enough by the housekeeper's protests and vague accounts regarding her mistress's whereabouts that he'd made his own inspection of the property.

And discovered for himself that Mrs. Christie was indeed gone from home.

Thwarted, Griffin sent Misters Fairley and Varah, who once again were beholding to him for the forgiveness of certain debts, to bring Alastair around to the hell. That worthy was also gone from town, a situation Olivia found disturbing when it coincided with Mrs. Christie's absence.

That her brother may have eloped to Gretna or conceived the notion that he might actually introduce his mistress to their father made Olivia's stomach churn. She doubted her brother understood the complete folly of either of those actions. She'd hoped that by returning the ring, Alastair had meant to reconcile not only his debt with Griffin, but his relationship with her, yet she'd written to him twice and had no reply to either overture.

Olivia drew herself sharply to the present and looked over the table. Her inattention had been mere seconds, but she'd nearly missed the chip drop that put a wager on the ten. The card she'd turned over by rote was naturally a ten spot.

Smiling warmly, as if nothing untoward had just occurred, Olivia paid out the winnings. She caught Mason's eye and indicated that she would need to be spelled soon. He began to make his way to the table by walking the perimeter of the room.

Olivia was so intent on completing the game and escorting the cheats to a private corner for a dressing down, that she missed the faint stir among the patrons as a new player was admitted to the room. It was only when there was a parting of gentlemen around her table that her attention was drawn to the cause of it.

Sir Hadrien Cole stood directly in her line of sight.

Olivia's fingers closed more tightly over the cards she held, but she didn't flinch. Her father regarded her without expression. She had forgotten how terribly difficult it was to keep her chin up and her eyes level when he looked on her in such a fashion. It was not a look that placed her beneath him, nor one that showed the least curiosity. She was nothing in his eyes. Nothing.

And the knowledge chilled her.

"Miss Shepard?" His voice had a deep, resonating timbre that was at odds with his slender, narrow frame. He stood taller than many of the men around him but could have slipped like a shadow among them. His eyes were not merely gray, but the cool, darker color of pewter, and an exact match for the hair at his temples. Those eyes were rather too closely set on either side of a blade of a nose, but it was a minor flaw in a countenance whose sharp definition made it arresting. "Miss Ann Shepard?"

He had a sensual mouth, wide and full, almost feminine in its line. It remained slightly parted after he spoke. *My dearest girl. My own sweet Olivia.*

Olivia realized that a dozen pairs of eyes were now turned in her direction, all of them expectant. They knew very well that she was not often at a loss for words and had never given any of them the cut direct. Mason sidled up to the table, but she expected no help from that quarter. He, like everyone else standing at hand, had not the slightest comprehension of the beast in their presence or its connection to her.

"I am Miss Shepard," she said politely, inclining her head. The faintest smile played about her mouth. He would crush defiance, but he would not understand amusement. Far better to give him a reaction he could not comprehend. "But you have me at a disadvantage, sir. You are . . . ?"

He did not respond to her inquiry. "It is a matter concerning your family that brings me here. A moment of your time, if you please."

Her family indeed. She pretended to consider, though she knew she would allow it. Sir Hadrien would not insist that she accompany him, not publicly, but he was perfectly capable of lying in wait. Aware that interest in her exchange had intensified, she darted a sideways look at Mason, assured him that the odd encounter was acceptable to her, then passed the deck of cards to him.

"Of course," she said, pleased that she could affect such ease in her manner. Where was Griffin? She cautioned herself against looking for him, unwilling to give Sir Hadrien the satisfaction of knowing he had put her off her stride. She rounded the table and the punters stepped aside for her, widening the breach that her father had made with his mere presence.

There were a few murmurs of disappointment as she left her station, but the pair of gentlemen cheats could barely contain their excitement. No one spoke to Sir Hadrien as he passed, and Olivia was struck again by the command he enjoyed in any situation. He was an unfamiliar face to those around him, yet he was shown deference by all. Sir Hadrien Cole did not frequent gaming hells, nor associate with those who did. If card play was his pleasure, then he arranged entertainments for his friends at Coleridge Park. He was rarely found in town, preferring country amusements to brushing shoulders with his current company.

He did not offer Olivia his arm, and for a brief moment she felt grateful toward him. The thought of taking his elbow, of touching any part of him, filled her with a dread so profound she experienced it as a sharp punch in her stomach.

"This way," she murmured, and led him toward the stairs to Griffin's private rooms. "Lord Breckenridge's study is available to us."

Upon entering the room, Olivia went immediately to the desk. She indicated the liquor decanters on the cherrywood table but made no offer to serve him refreshment. Except to raise an imperious eyebrow, he did not take issue with the slight. She watched him thread his way among Griffin's carefully arranged clutter to the drinks table and pour himself three fingers of whiskey. Her insides were wrenched again when she saw the depth of his pour. It was his way to nurse a drink, and Olivia prepared herself for a lengthy interview.

She waited, and in the end proved that her tolerance for the drawn out silence was greater than his own. What she did not anticipate was how quickly he would turn it to his advantage.

"I despaired that you would ever learn how very becoming quiet is to one of your kind." He raised his drink, watched her over the rim. "It seems you have. Kudos, my dear. It suits you well."

Olivia decided she would bloody her own tongue before she'd take that bait.

Sir Hadrien smiled. "Very well indeed." His cool pewter eyes traveled over Olivia slowly, the indifference of his public regard gone as he studied her with interest that was also insult. The cast of his features was no longer expressionless but bore the unmistakable stamp of attraction. "Miss Ann Shepard. The name is familiar, yet I cannot place it. How do I know it?"

"She was my nanny."

"Oh, yes. So she was." He rolled the tumbler of whiskey

between his palms. "I seem to remember you had some other name for her, though for the life of—"

"Honey," said Olivia. "I called her Honey."

"By God, that is it exactly. What became of her? I wonder."

Olivia did not respond, nor did it seem her father expected that she would. She was careful not to twist her hands together or fidget with the folds of her gown. He would see through both those things to the very heart of her fear.

"It is no matter, really. She was an unpleasant sort, as I recall, though you seemed to like her well enough. Is that why you're using her name?"

"Should I have used my own?"

Sir Hadrien ignored that. "You are under Breckenridge's protection, is that right?"

"I am his mistress."

"His whore."

"No."

"His whore," he repeated. "He knew who you were at the outset, and he still made you his whore."

Olivia wondered what she might say. *I was your whore first.* She pressed her lips together to keep that thought silent. "Perhaps you should tell me why you've come."

"Reparations, naturally. I confess, it did not occur to me that you didn't know. I'm here so amends might be made."

Amends? She could not help but frown. That her father should be speaking in such a fashion was unnatural. She was not so naive that she supposed he was bent on making amends toward her. Had he not just called her a whore? She settled on the only explanation that made sense. "So you are here to settle Alastair's debt, then. I should fetch Breckenridge. He has the full accounting of what is owed."

Sir Hadrien set his glass down hard. He had the satisfaction of seeing Olivia start. She had already taken one step away from the desk and toward the door, and now she stood perfectly still, wary and waiting. He gathered the threads of his composure because he could afford to be generous with her now. "Is it possible that you have become so foolish, my dear? You very much mistake the matter. I am here for what is owed me."

Knowing that Sir Hadrien fed on her fear, Olivia forced herself to fully face him. She set her hands behind her and curled her fingers around the edge of the desk. There was little she could do about the heat and color in her cheeks, but she managed to draw a breath through narrowly parted lips and release it very slowly. Her heart thrummed, one beat indistinguishable from the next.

She swallowed the bile rising in her throat. "I'm unaware of any debt that is owed you."

"I see I must say it more plainly, though it is a disappointment. I am here for the ring, Olivia. I will have it returned to me."

"Perhaps I am as foolish as you've noted, but I fail to understand how you mean to take it back without settling Alastair's debt."

"Your brother settled his debt twice over, once when he surrendered the ring, and again when he offered you in place of it. Now Breckenridge is in possession of both, and I find that insupportable." He took up his drink again and sipped. "The alternative is that you leave with me, but you can imagine I am reluctant to ask it of you."

Olivia was glad of her grip on the desk. Her knees felt as if they might give way. "I am of no value to you on the marriage mart."

"I believe you overstate it. Let us agree that it is difficult to gauge how advantageous a marriage you might make. I am fully appreciative of the effort that has been made to separate your behavior and circumstances from the family name. There is no blemish attached. That was well done of you."

"It was well done of Breckenridge. I was all for acknowledging my own name. It is a source of pride to me, after all."

Sir Hadrien did not miss Olivia's subtle ironic inflection and chose his response carefully. "Ah, yes, you would sacrifice your nose for your face. It was ever your way."

Olivia merely shrugged.

"I can think of several gentlemen of my acquaintance who would be willing to settle for a wife such as you might be."

"Truly? I'd always imagined your friends held the same lofty standards as you."

Showing impatience with her tone, his mouth flattened briefly. "Reginald Sewell, for one." When she looked at him blankly, he clarified, "Lord Pearce."

"The name means nothing to me. I have been out of society."

"So you have, but that was your own doing. Pearce might be a good prospect. He was recently widowed, and his children are grown with children of their own. He would not expect you to bear him a child."

"His expectations are of no account since I will not have him. You are mistaken also if you believe that I will not inform any prospective suitor of my association with Breckenridge. Our family's good name will remain above scandal as long as you do not force my hand."

"You are threatening me?"

"You may characterize it in any manner you choose. I am merely explaining what I will do. I do not desire marriage to any gentleman of your choosing and will expose your name to ridicule if you proceed along that path."

His eyebrows lifted a fraction. "You are changed, Olivia, but I cannot think that you are improved. Insolence is not attractive in a child."

"I am not a child."

"You are *my* child."

Olivia wanted to clap her hands over her ears. *My own sweet girl. My own. My very own.* The voices she heard, however, did not come from her father as he stood before her now, but as he'd stood before her once, and placing her hands over her ears had never served any purpose but to amplify the echoes of her past. *My dearest girl. Come sit on your papa's lap.*

"You look unwell," Sir Hadrien said. "Are you unwell?"

Olivia fairly recoiled when he took a step toward her. The desk at her back kept her from going into full retreat. She moved herself along its edge, ignoring the pain in her hip when she caught the corner, and stopped only when she was able to put the desk at least partially between them. "It is nothing," she said. "A slight megrim." And an urge to release the contents of her stomach at his feet. "I will take a headache powder before I return to the faro table."

"I suppose you are eager to do so, though I understand none of it. That you would use your considerable talent in the service of Breckenridge and his hell seems rather lowering, even for you. There are gentlemen's clubs, you know, where discretion is practiced as a matter of course, that would better suit you."

"I am content here."

Sir Hadrien shook his head, mystified. "Let us come to terms regarding the ring, then. I will expect it on the morrow. Your stepmother will be away from the town house the entire afternoon. It is then that you should come as she will not want to see you."

Olivia would have pointed out that she was of a similar mind, but coming to terms about the ring was more than deciding on the time of its delivery. "As I have said before, you will have to speak to Lord Breckenridge about the ring. It may be that he has decided to forgive Alastair's debt entirely and means to keep the thing for himself."

"He would not. That is unconscionable."

"Is it? I confess, I am not familiar with the gentlemen's agreements that cover such arrangements, but if you say that it is so, I will defer to your judgment. You should know, however, that Breckenridge will act as his own conscience dictates. Your opinion will not matter in the least."

Sir Hadrien stopped rolling the tumbler. His fingertips pressed the glass with enough force to whiten them. "Your manner is increasingly impudent. Does he permit you to speak to him in that fashion?"

"He encourages it." Olivia was not surprised to see she'd provoked her father's scorn, but it had the odd effect of steadying her. Before she thought better of it, she stepped away from the desk. The tightness in her chest eased, and she straightened, this time in a way that communicated confidence, not defiance. She folded her hands loosely together, presenting herself as a woman unbowed. "There is nothing about speaking my mind that threatens him."

Sir Hadrien set the tumbler down once more, this time softly. He covered the distance to Olivia in four easy strides. "Do you think I am threatened? Speak up, Olivia. Say what you think now."

A fine line of tension seized her, but she held her ground. "You are deserving of nothing so much as my pity, but I have none for you. I also have no rage. No fear. No disgust. Certainly no love. It's happened, I think, that I have no feelings at all to spare for you, unless indifference is a feeling. In that event, it is everything that I know. And, yes, I think you are threatened, doubly so that you cannot touch me any longer."

She'd chosen the wrong words. In retrospect, she knew it, but at the time they seemed to be exactly right. His arm came up so swiftly that she had no time to recognize the danger, nor react to it.

The blow was powerful. He caught her full on the side of her face with the back of his hand. She staggered sideways, tasted blood in her mouth, but managed to stay standing. Her vision blurred with the sting of tears. Bright bits of color floated in front of her.

"Shall I touch you again?" Sir Hadrien asked. He was breathing hard but perfectly in control. "Shall I?"

"You must do as you like," she said, facing him again. "I

will neither give you permission nor beg you to do otherwise." She did not look away from his cool, disdainful gaze, but held it calmly and without the rejoinder of a challenge. When he did not raise his hand a second time, Olivia was careful not to indicate her relief or gloat in her victory.

Sir Hadrien took a step back, then another, and this time it was he who put one corner of the desk between them. Olivia wondered at his retreat, whether the distance was in aid of restraining himself or protecting him from her. She hoped it was the latter, that he'd come to understand that she was capable of retaliation. Nothing had outwardly changed, yet Olivia did not think she was imagining there'd been a shift in power.

She had taken her own back.

"You should leave now," she said. "If you desire to speak to Breckenridge on the matter of Alastair's debt, then return tomorrow in the early afternoon. I will be gone from the house, and as I don't wish to see you again that time is also agreeable to me."

Allowing him no opportunity to protest, Olivia went straightaway to the door. She opened it and turned her hand in a gesture indicating his interview with her was at an end. She had no clear idea what she would do if Sir Hadrien stood fast, but it was not something she had to contend with. He did not surrender a fraction of his imperious air, but he took his leave nonetheless.

Olivia watched him turn toward the stairs and listened for the diminishing sound of his footfalls. When the noise from below covered them, she finally shut the door and leaned heavily into it. She closed her eyes against the rush of emotion and still she trembled with it. There'd been no running from him this time, no withdrawing into herself. She'd faced him down, and every part of her felt the effort now as a physical pain.

She had no idea how long she remained there, but she never

once felt any urgency to move. It was only when her heartbeat calmed and the wave of sickness passed that she pushed away from the door and went to the fireplace. She removed her wig and tossed it aside, then rubbed at her face with the back of her hand to erase the artifice of powder and paint. After plucking the pins from her hair, she shook it out and combed it with her fingers. A wave of ginger curls framed her face and fell softly over her shoulders. She caught all of it in one fist and ruthlessly pulled it back.

Olivia examined herself in the mirror, not for evidence of any injury that Sir Hadrien might have done, but to see if she was marked from her struggle with him in some other, more subtle way. She'd survived a battering, and the blow he'd struck was the very least of it, but what she observed in her face, in her carriage, was not a wounded warrior, but one already healed and made stronger by experience and sense of purpose.

And also so bloody tired.

She released her hold on her hair and smiled wryly at her reflection, acknowledging the limits of a healed soul and strength of character. Bone weary, she wanted nothing so much as to lie down. She picked up the rug lying over the back of a wing chair, removed a stack of books from the foot of the chaise, and lay down. Mason could manage the faro table for a while longer, she decided. It was her last thought before she fell deeply asleep.

Griffin found her there well over an hour later, though coming across her in the study was happenstance rather than planned. He'd removed himself from the gaming rooms only a few hours after they'd opened the doors to look in on Nat. The battle being waged in the boy's room was one that Griffin had discussed at length earlier in the day and rather than insist Nat resume Caesar's conquest of Gaul on the morrow, Griffin dropped to his knees and took up the cause of the soon-to-be-defeated army.

They'd positioned their men around the table and chair legs to lend the illusion of the forest that divided the Roman and Gaul forces. Nat's new major general was now Gaius Julius Caesar, credited to be a wily commander in the field. Griffin's men put up a good fight, but they were no match for the trained and disciplined soldiers from Rome. The end came exactly as history dictated it should, and after surrendering to Caesar, Griffin hauled Nat up, slung him over his shoulder, and dropped him on the bed.

He did not know how he'd been convinced to join the boy. Certainly his own father had never done the same with him, yet Griffin allowed that it was not an unpleasant task to keep the child company until he slept. What he had not anticipated was drifting off in a like fashion.

Griffin found a spot on the chaise where Olivia's bottom curved out and her knees curled in, and he sat. The rug was haphazardly drawn across her. Her feet poked out at the bottom and her shoulders were bare. He set his candle on the stack of books that had been moved from the chaise, then gently shook Olivia's arm.

She stirred but did not open her eyes. Her response was sufficient to make Griffin stop shaking her arm and stroke it instead. She liked that infinitely better and murmured her pleasure to make certain he knew it.

"Are you well?" he asked.

Olivia nodded. "Merely fatigued. Have I slept long?"

"I don't know." He explained the cause of his disappearance from the gaming rooms. She rewarded him with a beatific smile that made his heart trip over itself. He bent his head and kissed her cheek. "You were still at the faro table when I left and doing most excellently. Did William and Bennet Allworthy trouble you at all?"

She snapped her fingers. "Allworthy. Of course. I could

not recall their name. I'm afraid I left their comeuppance in Mason's hands." She cocked her head toward the mantel, opened one eye, and regarded the clock. It was gone midnight. That put her on notice immediately. She bolted upright, narrowly missing bumping heads with Griffin. "I need to get back. Mr. Mason must wonder what's become of me. You also."

"Not enough, apparently. He has not sent anyone to find us, has he? You know what explains it, don't you?"

Olivia shook her head as she threw off the blanket.

"Lady Rivendale."

She stopped wrestling with that part of her gown that was trapped under her legs and stared at him. "Lady Rivendale? You think she's come in?"

"It would not at all surprise. Would you care to wager?"

"I never bet against the house." She resumed tugging on her gown and allowed Griffin to assist her. "Would she know my father, I wonder?"

"I couldn't say. She knows who you are, though."

"She does?"

"I assume it occurred through her connection to Restell Gardner. Pray, do not ask. Her family tree is surprisingly full-branched in spite of the fact that she has no children of her own."

Olivia considered that, then offered a somewhat guilty confession. "I'm not certain, but I might have given myself away. She has a way about her, it's all I can offer as an excuse."

"It doesn't matter. She knows everything and is above all discreet." He frowned a bit as she turned her head. "Olivia?" He caught the underside of her chin with his fingertips and nudged it sideways so that he might have a better view of her cheek. "What happened? That is no pillow wrinkle. Your face is scratched."

She touched her cheek. "Is it?" She'd looked right past it when she'd studied her reflection earlier. "He wore a ring. I suppose that explains it." Her skin was faintly warm, but that was a consequence of sleep, not a lingering response to the blow that had pushed her off her feet.

"He?" asked Griffin, but he was already working out the answer. Olivia's offhanded inquiry about her father and Lady Rivendale suddenly made sense. "Sir Hadrien is here?"

"Was here. He's gone now, or he should be. I showed him the door, more or less. I do not imagine he is lurking in the gaming rooms. He was disdainful of them, Griffin, and suggested that I was squandering my talents here." Amusement laced her voice, and she smiled as she shook her head, inviting Griffin to find the humor as well. "He made reference only to cards, but he meant I should apply it to other things as well. Why work in the service of one man when I might work in the service of so many? You will know I was not tempted in the least, so he will likely arrive tomorrow and demand an audience with you. I will be gone, of course, because there is nothing left to be said that I did not already put before him."

Griffin stared at her. He spoke slowly, trying to make sense of the incongruity between what she said and how she said it. "Your father appeared without invitation or notice, suggested you'd make a better courtesan than a mistress, struck you hard enough to leave his mark, and you find cause there for amusement?"

"Do not forget he was disdainful of your hell."

"Yes, well, I shall plant him a facer for that," he said dryly. "As to the rest . . ." He paused, searching for a manner of death for Sir Hadrien that was outside the common mode.

"As to the rest," she said, "it is already done. My honor is satisfied." She took Griffin's hand in her own. "You did that for me, Griffin. I knew I could be strong because you expected I would be. I believed you first, then I believed in myself."

"I'm very glad to hear it, but it doesn't mean you should stand against someone like Sir Hadrien on your own. Good form requires that each participant choose a second. I would have been honored to be yours."

Olivia gave him a wry smile. "I had not realized you put such stock in good form."

Griffin shrugged. "When it serves."

"You will have your chance with him. Did you not hear me say he will probably return tomorrow? I suggested that he do so in the afternoon when I will be gone, though if you cannot promise that you won't challenge him, I will have to remain and act as your second, if only for the purpose of re-straining you."

"Restrain me? How do you imagine you might accomplish that?"

"Telling you would eliminate the advantage of surprise, and I will be counting heavily on that."

He chuckled. "Very well. I will allow that you can do what-ever you set your mind to and have done with speculation. Where will you be tomorrow if Sir Hadrien does indeed seek me out?"

"I am taking Nat to be fitted for some new clothes. Mr. Mason will accompany us, so have done pulling that dis-agreeable face."

"I can have someone come here to fit Nat."

"Then I wouldn't be gone from the house, now would I?"

"I have a suspicion that you've been planning this, and your father's arrival is a convenient reason to have it done."

"I frequently marvel at your perspicacity."

He could not think of anything to do about her saucy mouth except to kiss it. He felt the shape of her smile beneath his lips before she eagerly gave herself over. It was only with the greatest reluctance that he eventually pulled back instead of drawing her down on the chaise.

"I suppose we have neglected our duties long enough," Olivia whispered, searching his face. She leaned forward, caught his chin with her lips, then the corner of his mouth.

The tilt of her head invited him to linger a moment longer over the stem of her neck. She sighed. "I'll have to put the wig on again, paint my face."

"Mmm." He caught her earlobe, worried it. He felt her shiver ever so slightly. "God, but you tempt me." This time when he drew away he put himself outside of her reach by moving to the wing chair. He was only in it a moment before he realized the fit was not quite right. Lifting one hip, he reached beneath him and pulled out Olivia's wig. The string of seed pearls that had been artfully arranged in the auburn curls was twisted and drooping. He poked at the pearls, saw he was only making matters worse, and gently tossed the wig to Olivia.

Griffin slid into a casual incline in the chair and watched Olivia work. He observed her deft and nimble fingers while his mind wandered to certain details that had been left out of her account.

"Did you ask Sir Hadrien how he came to be here?"

She shook her head. "I imagine Alastair told him that he'd returned the ring to you. That would have brought him here straightaway."

"Have you had any correspondence from your brother?"

"No, but if he's been at Coleridge Park, then he hasn't yet received my letters."

Griffin considered that, wondering if the explanation was as simple as that. "Then Sir Hadrien's concern was all for the ring, is that right?"

Olivia glanced up, frowning. "I hope I did not lead you to believe it was ever anything else. He was grateful for the attention paid to keeping the family name well out of it. I told him he had you to thank, so perhaps he will." She bent to her task again. "Sir Hadrien had some idea that he would accept me in place of the ring, but I disabused him of that notion. He thought I might suit someone named Reginald Sewell, Lord Pearce."

"Pearce? Is he still alive?"

"So it would seem. Apparently he would not expect me to bear his children, so that is something."

Griffin's left eyebrow rose in a dramatic arch. "Indeed."

Olivia finished with the wig, then held it out in front of her for a final inspection. "You would not consider exchanging me for the ring, would you?"

"I hope that is not a serious question." But then he saw that it was, in spite of her attempt to say it lightly and put it before him as though it had only just this moment occurred to her. "Do you still trust me so little, Olivia?"

She'd hurt him, she realized, and rushed to explain herself. "No, that's not it at all, or rather I did not mean you should put that construction upon it. I am not so confident that I don't require reassurance now and again."

"You know," he said after a moment, "that marriage might improve your confidence."

"I thought we were done with Lord Pearce."

"Amusing."

"You have someone else in mind?"

"I will have to give it some thought." He saw she was in anticipation of yet another proposal and deliberately withheld it. There should be some small way of getting his own back after she'd turned down every one of his offers. "Your standards are perhaps too exacting for mere mortals."

She twisted her hair into a knot and slipped on the wig. "I have a particular fondness for mere mortals, so you are wrong there."

He stood and held out his hand to her. "I'll remain hopeful, then, that someone more suitable than Pearce will come to mind."

Olivia took his hand, rose, then allowed him to tug at the wig so it fit her head snugly. "Go on," she said when he'd finished. "I am still in need of a few minutes to apply my mask. Tell Mr. Mason that I will be at my station directly."

They walked out together, but before they parted in the hallway, Olivia stayed Griffin by placing one hand on his shoulder and turning in to him. The kiss she offered was hot and wet and deep, and served up to remind him that he teased her at his own peril.

Nat put his hand in Olivia's as soon as they stepped off the curb to cross Moorhead Street. They dodged a lumbering tinker's wagon, a single rider on a great cinnamon gelding, and a hack that would not give way to any of the pedestrian traffic. Mason led the way, urging them to hurry, then made a point of looking them all over when they reached the opposite side of the street.

"All of a piece, it seems," he said. "There's a good thing. My guts for garters otherwise."

"Guts for garters," Nat repeated gravely. "Too bloody right, Mr. Mason."

Olivia tried to be disapproving of both of her companions, but it required too much effort. "Let us continue, gentlemen, shall we? Nat is growing inches even as we stand here. The tailor will have to put twice the length in his knickers to account for it."

They started off again, this time with Olivia and Nat leading the way. They took the shortcut through the park, stopping from time to time to appreciate the budding trees and the occasional blooming jonquil. Nat was an agreeable companion, curious about everything he observed but politely restrained in the number of questions he put before them.

Why do ladies plant gardens in their bonnets? How do they wind the clock in the tower? How many ships fit side by side across the Thames? What did the hack driver mean when he yelled "bugger off"?

Olivia fielded some questions, tagged Mason to answer others, and in the case of "bugger off," ignored Nat completely.

Nat was cooperative while he was measured and fitted—more cooperative, Olivia recalled, than she had been when Griffin had arranged for her to be poked and pinned by Mrs. McCutcheon. When they were finished at the tailor's, Olivia suggested they visit the bookseller's. After that they went to a notions shop, the milliner's, and stumbled upon a place that sold all manner of pewter ware, including what seemed to be his majesty's entire army. Nat was pleased to leave with his first cavalry soldiers.

Mason offered to flag a hack for them, but Olivia wanted to be certain that she would not encounter Sir Hadrien at the hell and decided that walking, even weighed down with an armload of parcels, was just the thing to extend their time away.

They paused at the perimeter of the park to observe some children putting kites into the air. Their nannies sat on a bench, watching them, occasionally offering some encouragement, but seemingly more interested in exchanging gossip.

"It reminds me of the painting in your former room, Nat. You know the one I mean?"

He nodded. "I liked it very much, Miss Cole."

"Perhaps we should move it. I don't know why I didn't think of it before." She tipped her head back as one of the kites soared skyward. "Have you ever flown a kite?" she asked. "Look at the blue one. Oh, it's going to make a dive."

"I never have, have you?"

"Never."

Nat turned to put the same question to Mason, but the words stayed locked in his throat as a fair-haired gentleman appeared suddenly behind the valet and knocked him hard to the ground. Nat dropped his parcels and flew at the stranger, but he was swatted aside like a pesky insect. He stumbled, fell, and rolled on his back. He called a warning just as Olivia was struck between the shoulder blades by the villain's walking stick. The blow made her lurch forward and her packages tumbled out of her arms. She pivoted awkwardly, trying to find her balance, but before she could manage the thing she was lifted and slung over the man's shoulder.

Nat yelled, "*Bugger off!*" and started to rise to his feet. He took a kick in the side, fell back, and saw the same strike used to keep Mason down. Someone screamed, and Nat supposed it was a good thing except that no one really came to their aid. All but one of the children had abandoned their kites, and the nannies were urging everyone to huddle close.

Nat scrambled to his feet and took a step forward in pursuit of Olivia and her assailant. This time it was Mason who held him back. The valet gripped Nat's ankle like a vise.

"You can't, son, else I'll lose you as well."

Nat sunk back to his knees as Olivia was thrust into a waiting carriage. The villain followed, the door banged shut, and the carriage rolled forward swiftly, as though it had never been fully at rest.

Mason saw the same. "He was lying in wait for us," he said, pushing himself to his feet. His right shoulder was dislocated and his arm hung painfully at his side. He cradled it and directed Nat to pick up what he could manage and guard the rest while he hailed a hack.

A fat tear slipped free of Nat's lower lashes and followed the path of his scar. He bent to pick up Olivia's hat box. "It'll be guts for garters."

Mason nodded. "Too bloody right, it will."

Chapter Sixteen

Olivia stumbled and fell as she was given a final hard shove into the room that would be her prison. Just before the door closed, candlelight illuminated the windowless room, and she saw she wouldn't be alone. The door slammed shut, the light vanished, and a key rattled in the lock. A bar was shoved into place. By the time she caught her breath, the re-treating footsteps could no longer be heard.

"Alastair?" Olivia awkwardly pushed herself up on all fours, then sat back on her heels. "Alastair? Is that you?"

"S'me, Livvy. S'me."

The room's overpowering stench made Olivia gag. Sweat, urine, vomitus, and other human waste, all of it overlaid by something pungent and oddly fruity, assailed her. She grabbed the hem of her gown and pressed it against her nose and mouth. The fabric did almost nothing to stay the foul odor, and she could taste it on her tongue, feel it enter her lungs.

"Are you drunk, Alastair?" she asked through the folds of linen.

"S'wine cellar. Course I'm drunk. You will be, too. S'only way."

"Where are we?"

"I tol' you. Wine cellar. Good stock. She selects it, I think. Likes to."

Unable to stomach tasting the air any longer, Olivia lowered her hem a fraction and breathed carefully through her nose. The back of her head ached where she'd been struck. She rolled her shoulders and felt the knotty tension between them. She'd no chance to prepare for the attack and would not have known what had been used against her if she hadn't caught a glimpse of the villain and his weighted walking stick in the carriage. She'd feigned unconsciousness, hoping it would give her an advantage when they arrived at their destination. What it did, however, was give the villain an opportunity to bind her wrists before she knew what he was about. Her wild struggle came too late to be effective, and the hand he clamped over her mouth took away her voice and her breath. When she finally slumped against him there was no fight left in her. Her body jerked and shuddered, but it was in the throes of surrender, not in preparation for another round.

"She?" Olivia asked. "Who is *she?*"

Alastair groaned softly, held his head in his hands. "Mus' you go on and on, Livvy? She's she. A-lysss."

Mrs. Christie, then. More annoyed than alarmed by this intelligence, Olivia released her gown altogether and began to work on the knots of her wrist bindings. She used her teeth to loosen the fabric, nibbling and tearing at the knots until she felt one of them give. After that it was easy to pull one of the ends and make space enough to slip her hands free. He'd bound her with a length of lightly starched cotton. His cravat, she realized, as she folded it into thirds and tucked most of it under the sleeve of her pelisse.

"How long have you been here, Alastair?"

"Don' know. Wha' day is it?"

"Wednesday."

"Wednesday. The eleventh?"

"The eighteenth."

"Oh, well, then, s'been a week and a bit. S'easy to lose time here."

"I'm sure drinking helps." Olivia rose to her feet and carefully made her way toward the sound of his voice. She found him with the toe of her foot, then hunkered down beside him. "Have you been hurt?"

"My pride."

"Yes, that is always the deepest wound." She touched his forehead, brushed aside a lock of hair that had fallen over his brow. "You have not been treated kindly, I think."

"Not kindly, no."

She could not even be put out with him. He was so clearly gone in his cups that he was doing well just stringing a few slurred words together. The fact that he was still sitting upright had more to do with the wall at his back than his strength of will. Olivia removed her pelisse and made certain it was under her before she sat. Alastair, if he could have seen what she was about, would probably have rolled his eyes at her fastidiousness, but Olivia believed she needed to embrace dignity for as long as possible.

"Do you know why you're here?" she asked.

"Don' think she likes me anymore."

"Yes, it seems that might be the way of it."

"S'all right. I don' like her s'much either."

"Good for you."

"She wan's the ring, Livvy."

"Hardly surprising. You took it back from her, didn't you?"

"Did. I did. Heard wha' you tol' me. Thought about it. Thought I should give it back. Make things right. I 'spect things haven't always been right for you." He lightly bumped her shoulder with his own. "You really are there, aren't you? Wondered. Talk to myself sometimes, s'I wasn't sure."

"I'm here." She nudged him back. "Truly."

"How'd it happen?"

Olivia told him about the attack in the park. "Mr. Mason

would not have let anything happen to me if he could have prevented it. Nat, too, I imagine. I have to hope neither was seriously injured, that the gentleman villain wanted me too badly to do more than push them out of the way."

"Ain't a gentleman, now, is he?"

"No." Deciding that sparing Alastair the details served neither of them, she described her first encounter with the villain. Beside her, she felt Alastair's position shift and realized he'd drawn his knees up and was resting his head on them. "Are you feeling sorry for yourself, Alastair? I hope not, because I need you to help me to think our way out of this."

"You might have been killed," he said quietly.

"I might have been raped," she said. "Either or both can still happen, Alastair. I require you sober, not maudlin."

"S'right." He lifted his head, stared into the darkness. "Thinkin' now."

Olivia slipped her arm in his. "Good. Now tell me about this cellar."

Mason was unable to hold Nat back once they reached the hell's entrance hall. The boy dropped his parcels, bolted up the stairs, and was turning into the hall by the time Mason reached the bottom step. His ascent was much slower than was his wont. It was not only his shoulder that had suffered an injury but his ankle as well. He used the banister to support himself as he limped along.

Truss appeared, asked what was toward, and offered Mason help mounting the stairs. They were met just as they reached the top by Griffin, then in short order, by Nat and Sir Hadrien.

Griffin's face was tight. The scar shone whitely as a muscle jumped in his cheek. He looked Mason over, appraised his injuries as being painful nuisances, and assisted Truss with moving the valet to his study. By the time they had him settled on the chaise, Griffin had the whole of the story from him.

Remarkably, except for the fact that it was more easily under-stood, it was almost the same account he'd had from Nat.

"Did no one give chase?" Griffin asked.

"I wouldn't let the boy go, my lord." Mason hung his head. "And I could not."

"I don't mean the two of you. There were others in the park, weren't there? Passersby on the street?" He gave his valet no warning, supposing it was better that way, and fixed his hands in a position to wrench the shoulder back into place. "Not a single Good Samaritan?"

Mason bellowed as Griffin set his joint. Beads of sweat appeared in the crease of his brow and along his upper lip. He sucked in a breath so hard that it whistled between his teeth. When his eyes could properly focus, he saw Nat standing at the foot of the chaise, his eyes nearly liquid with alarm. "Sainted mother, but you scared the boy."

Griffin glanced at Nat, held out his hand. "Come. Sit here beside Mr. Mason. Don't allow him to so much as twitch. We have wounded on the field, and you must see to your men." He saw a bit of pink color return to Nat's ashen complexion as the boy nodded manfully and exchanged places with him at Mason's side. "Truss, send someone to fetch Pettibone."

Sir Hadrien stepped out of the doorway to let the butler pass. "What of the carriage?" he demanded, pressing his hands together. "What of its direction?"

Turning to look over his shoulder, Griffin gave him a quelling glance. "Your concern is misplaced, sir. Our inter-view is at an end." He turned back to Mason. "Was it the vil-lain, do you think?"

"Seemed as if it might be. I had a glimpse of blond hair. The size of him was what Miss Cole described before. Who else wants to hurt her?"

"A very good question." Griffin turned again to regard Sir Hadrien. "What do you think, sir? Who wants to hurt your daughter?"

The less than subtle questioning caused Sir Hadrien to bristle. "You are wrong, Breckenridge, and would do well to hold yourself in check. I have been with you, haven't I?"

Griffin caught himself before laying more blame. It was true enough that Sir Hadrien had been with him, but it was also true that Olivia had told her father she would be gone from the hell this afternoon. Griffin could think of no one else who knew about the change in Olivia's routine. The villain could have been watching, waiting for such an opportunity, but it was equally possible he had information to make abducting Olivia easier. From the description of events, it seemed the carriage had been lying in wait.

Griffin moved away from the chaise to stand in front of the bookshelves. He ran his finger along the books at eye level, stopped at Smith's *An Inquiry into the Nature and Causes of the Wealth of Nations,* and removed it. Having more than a little respect for Smith's work, Griffin placed it on the chair behind him. The next three books he removed were not given so much care. They were allowed to thud to the floor while he reached for the object of his search.

He carried the burnished mahogany case to his desk and opened it. Sir Hadrien had moved closer and stood in a position to see the pair of pistols lying against the dark blue velvet lining. Griffin ignored the disapproving noises coming from Sir Hadrien under the guise of throat clearing and examined each pistol in turn.

Both pistols were polished and primed. Griffin was glad now of his regular practice with them. They felt comfortable in his hand.

Griffin chose one pistol to secret under his frock coat at the small of his back. It fit snugly but did not limit his movement. Holding the other pistol aimed at the floor, he arched an eyebrow at Sir Hadrien. "Shall we? As I intend to take advantage of your waiting carriage, I do not mind sharing the space . . . overmuch."

Sir Hadrien frowned. "Very well," he said finally. "Naturally I will go, and I should have thought of lending my carriage at the outset."

"Good." He turned to Mason, who was struggling to rise. "Stay where you are. Nat, do not fail me."

Mason grimaced as he propped himself on his elbow. "Shall I send Foster to Bow Street, sir?"

"If I haven't returned in . . ." He considered the likelihood that things could be resolved quickly. "Let us say, two hours. Send for the runners and tell them to begin with Mrs. Christie."

"But you said she was gone from town."

"She has returned, I think." He turned dark, predator eyes on Sir Hadrien. "Isn't that right?"

Guided by Alastair's somewhat slurred and haltingly given directions, Olivia explored the confines of their prison. "Is this Mrs. Christie's cellar?" she asked as she paced off the length of the wall lined with wine bottles.

"Think so. Las' thing I recall before waking here was havin' dinner with her, so s'possible."

"She drugged you?"

"S'pose she did."

Olivia absently rubbed the back of her head where she'd been struck. She thought she might have preferred a sleeping powder to being clobbered. "Have you seen her since you've been here?"

"No. She ain't come around."

"What about the villain? Does he come around?"

"Now and again, just to take a poke at me with his stick."

"Who brings you food, takes the slop bucket?" When there was no answer, Olivia asked, "Are you shrugging, Alastair? Shaking your head? I can't see either."

"Shruggin'," he said. "Don' know who it is. Servant, I

'spect. S'not the one you call the villain. Seen him before, though. Not here. Somewhere else. Can't remember where."

Olivia sighed. "Tell me about who comes here. Same person or different?"

"Same."

That made sense, Olivia thought. Wherever they were, the fewer people who knew about it, the better. She turned the corner, ran her hand along the cool and damp stone wall. "Did you ever try to escape?" There was silence again, and Olivia had to remind her brother she couldn't see his reply.

"No," he said. "The villain tol' me you'd be hurt if I conceived any notions of bravery. Got drunk instead, but here you are so I s'pose I should've done something."

She came abreast of her brother and reached down to touch his shoulder. "You'll have to do something now, Alastair, no matter what he says will happen to me. He wants to hurt me." She paused. "He'll try."

Alastair drew in his legs as Olivia moved carefully around him and continued her search. "Won't let him touch you."

"I know." She bumped something with her toe, heard the slush of liquid, and grimaced as she stepped around the slop bucket. Her nose had gradually become numb to the worst of the odor, but tipping the bucket would have tested her resolve to keep down her breakfast. "We can also depend on Breckenridge to find us. If not today, then tomorrow, or the next day, but he'll come. I am not of a mind to wait for him, though, and he will not expect that I should."

"I fear you are being optimish . . . op-ti-*mish*-tic . . . op-ti . . . hopeful."

"It is not hope, but confidence."

"We do not know where we are. How will he?"

"He already suspects a connection between Mrs. Christie and the gentleman villain. Since none of us knows the identity of the villain, he must begin with Mrs. Christie, and I believe our father will know where to find her."

* * *

Griffin gave Sir Hadrien's driver Mrs. Christie's address, but as soon as the carriage began to roll, he set his eyes hard upon Olivia's father and pressed for information. "Will we find her at the residence?"

"I couldn't possibly—"

Griffin raised the pistol. "I *will* shoot. You've spoken to her. Your son would not have returned the ring to me, then run to you with news of it. He's shown some backbone of late, but not so much as that, I'm sure. If he didn't tell you what he did, then you came by the news in the only other way possible: Mrs. Christie told you. She must have been very angry with Alastair to take the matter up with you. So I will ask you again, will we find her at the residence now that you are also in town?"

"I cannot know." He thrust his hands forward as though his palms could ward off a pistol ball. "She might be gone shopping. Paying a social call. How can you expect that I will know if—" He stopped when the pistol jerked in Griffin's hand and sat back hard against the plump leather squabs. He could not quite contain the rise of panic. It edged his voice, lending it the slightest quiver. "She has Alastair, Breckenridge. She's taken my son. My wife is practically mad with grief and demands that I do whatever necessary to ensure his release. She cannot rise from her bed because of that woman. Do you think I would have debased myself by applying to you for the ring if not for the sake of my son and my wife?"

"I know you wouldn't have done it for your daughter."

"You don't know anything, except that you think you know it all. Olivia lies, Breckenridge. She always has. Embellishment. Exaggeration. Those are but the small ways she creates and re-creates her tales. Fancies. Diversions. One might name them such if one is of a mind to be kind . . . or forgiving. I am no longer of such a mind and have not been so for years. She is jealous of my wife, of my son. Even as a young girl she tried to turn my wife against me."

Sir Hadrien drew himself up and gave Griffin a considering look. "She reads people. Even someone like you who is remarkably good at schooling your features, Olivia is able to see something more. Have you never wondered why she is so good as a dealer? It is not only her expert handling of the cards. She watches the players, makes a game of supposing what they will do. She preys on them, not in an obvious way—not usually. I would venture to say that she's preyed on you, saw something that would make you sympathetic to some of her most virulent lies, and those are the ones she told to bring you around."

He paused, eyes narrowed. "I'll wager she crawled into your bed first."

Griffin lowered the pistol. "What did Mrs. Christie ask you to do?"

Sir Hadrien blinked, stared. A deep flush stole over his sharp countenance as he realized he was being dismissed. "That vile woman. She wants the ring, of course. She'd prefer the ring *and* marriage to my son, but as I would never give my blessing to the latter, and as Alastair cannot be compelled to enter into that arrangement, she seems to be willing to settle for the ring."

Griffin shook his head slowly. "There is more to it than that. The ring is valuable, to be sure, easily four or five times the debt that was owed me, but for her to risk so much to have it back seems out of character."

"How can you know?" Sir Hadrien asked flatly. "She has no character. No scruples. No morals." He thrust his chin forward, challenging. "Your association with women like her can be all that explains it. Mrs. Christie. My daughter. I did not know your wife, but she must have been so inclined. I understand that she presented you with a bastard before she died."

"There is nothing that Mrs. Christie likes less than leaving London," Griffin said just as if Sir Hadrien had never spoken. "A journey to Coleridge Park is a most unusual step for her when she might simply have written."

"A letter as evidence that she is holding my son for ransom? She is too clever for that."

Griffin conceded the point. "Still, she might have found another way to lure you into town. That she went to you speaks of some urgency on her part. Did she appear to be under duress?"

"She appeared to be quite mad."

Griffin realized Sir Hadrien would apply that description to anyone opposing him. He was incapable of seeing beyond his own nose. "How much time has she allowed for you to get the ring back?"

"She didn't say, although I had the impression that once I came to town she expected the thing to be done quickly."

"And yet you never once offered to pay Alastair's debt. Your reputation for being close-fisted is well deserved, it seems."

"The ring belongs to me," he said stubbornly. "To my family. I shouldn't have to pay for what is mine."

"That is between you and your conscience, in the event you have one, though it occurs to me that Alastair would have been better served if Mrs. Christie had negotiated with your wife." Griffin used the pistol to point toward a three-story brownstone town house with a wide entrance flanked by stone lions. "Ah, here we are. Before we go, let me explain the rules of engagement. You will follow my lead and do precisely as I say. The moment I determine you are a hindrance, I will shoot you. Whether or not I kill you depends on my mood of the moment. At the moment, I am feeling peckish, and that is not in any way good for you." He jerked his chin toward the door. "Go on. I will follow directly."

Cautious of the primed weapon in his hand and the pistol

at his back, Griffin was slower to leave the carriage. Sir Hadrien was already lifting the knocker when Griffin came abreast of him.

The housekeeper once again made noises about Mrs. Christie being gone from the residence. Griffin and Sir Hadrien were still ignoring her protests as they mounted the stairs. Once they reached the top, they followed the sound of another voice, this one issuing orders in tones both impatient and frustrated.

"You are leaving town again, Mrs. Christie?" asked Griffin. There were trunks and valises set out in the bedroom, and it was clear from the activity that they were being packed, not the opposite. "So soon? I was certain you'd only just arrived."

Alys's maid appeared from the dressing room with an armload of gowns and came to an abrupt halt when she saw the visitors. Alarmed, she looked to her mistress for direction.

Mrs. Christie snapped, "Those belong in the armoire, Linsley. They can be pressed later. Go! The dressing room." Her head swung around in Griffin's direction. "You mistake the matter, Breckenridge, as you are prone to do. I am coming, not going." Her gaze swiveled to Sir Hadrien, then back to Griffin. "This is still my home, and you have no right to assume you are welcome, let alone bring guests."

Griffin revealed the pistol that had been partially hidden against his thigh. He held it up without menace, merely to show he had it. "Have done, Alys. I see what is toward. Your pretense that it is otherwise is insulting. Send your maid out." He nudged Sir Hadrien forward enough to conceal the pistol as Mrs. Christie called to Linsley and ordered her out of the dressing room and then out of the bedroom altogether. He tapped the heel of his boot against the door and closed it behind her, then stepped away from Sir Hadrien so the pistol was clearly visible once more.

"Where is she?"

Alys Christie stepped behind one of the open trunks. Her hands played nervously against the lid. When she realized it, she forced herself to hold them still. She appealed to Sir Hadrien. "Do you mean to stand by and do nothing? It will not go well for you, you know."

Sir Hadrien recalled Griffin's clear directives and offered no reply.

"Where is she?" Griffin asked again. "Pray, do not dissemble. I promise I will not kill you, Mrs. Christie, but I *will* make you ugly. Give that a moment to settle in your mind before you answer."

She stared at him, her features sagging and her complexion going to ash. "By God, but you would do it."

"Most assuredly. Your answer."

"Johnny Crocker has her, has both of them." She pressed her hands together, imploring Griffin when she saw rage darken his eyes to black. "I swear I didn't know that he planned to abduct Olivia. I had no part in it. I only found out an hour ago, by messenger, what he'd done. It's about you, Breckenridge. He wants to ruin you. She is a means to that end, nothing else. I knew you'd come as soon as you learned of it, knew what you'd think, what you'd do. Why do you suppose I was leaving?"

Griffin let her wind down, made certain she did not intend to say more, then coldly reminded her, "I found my wife. Do you think there is anywhere you could go that I wouldn't find you?" He watched her, saw that she knew better than to answer, and continued. "And do not suppose for a moment that I believe you are blameless here. I know what Crocker is to you and you to him. The desire to ruin me did not necessarily begin with him. Now, does he have them at the hell?"

She nodded. "He wants the ring. Give him the ring, and he'll release them."

"I thought he wanted to ruin me."

"Yes," she said hastily. "He does. And wants the ring besides."

Griffin merely cocked an eyebrow at her, then waved his

pistol toward the door. "Come. There is room enough for you in Sir Hadrien's comfortable carriage. By the time we reach Crocker's hell, you should have the wrinkles in your story neatly pressed."

Affronted, Mrs. Christie drew her shoulders back. "I'm not going with—"

"Very ugly," Griffin said calmly. "Children will hide behind their mother's skirts when they see you."

"How often does someone come?" Olivia asked. A thin strip of light was visible around the door. She pressed her eye to it and tried to see activity on the other side. After a few minutes of varying her position, she gave up. She turned around and leaned back against the door. "Alastair?"

"Hmm?"

She realized he'd nodded off. "How can you sleep?"

"Always sleep when I'm in my cups. Have to."

"Not this time. I need you awake."

"Course you do. Sorry."

Olivia repeated her question.

"Don't know precisely," Alastair said. "Two times a day, perhaps. Can't tell by what they feed me. Soup mostly. Bread and broth. Drink helps. Fills the empty."

She understood that well enough. "Do you ever hear anything? This place seems to be so quiet, as if no one is around."

"Mostly like that, more or less. Voices come and go. No one ever answers me. Sometimes, though, the house fairly rumbles. That's a bit unpleasant, I can tell you."

"Rumbles?"

"Mmm. For hours. The bottles shudder, the door vibrates. I can feel it in my bones."

That's when Olivia knew. She was familiar with that sensation. "We're not at Mrs. Christie's at all, Alastair. We're in a hell."

"Too right, we are. In hell."

Olivia didn't correct him. At the moment she decided he had described their location better than she.

Mrs. Christie and Sir Hadrien shared the bench across from Griffin. He noticed they edged away from each other, taking up their respective corners as much as the space allowed once the carriage was underway.

Griffin held the pistol on his lap casually pointed toward the door. "How long have you and Crocker been partners?" Griffin asked, nudging Mrs. Christie's kid slipper with the toe of his boot.

"Partners with Johnny Crocker? I never have."

Griffin sighed. "I'd hoped you would not be tedious about it. Who is the gentleman villain?"

"Gentleman villain? I have no idea what you mean."

"We call him the gentleman villain," he explained, watching her closely. "Olivia's abductor. The same man who attacked her in my establishment not long after she arrived. The same one who tried to enter again through a window and succeeded only in frightening a child. Blond hair. Blue eyes. Slightly built, but athletic. By Olivia's account, a natty dresser."

"I suppose I might know half a dozen gentlemen who largely meet that description."

"I need the name of only one. The right one, of course."

Mrs. Christie shrugged her slender shoulders. "I don't know that any one of them is responsible for the things you said. It would be wrong to give you even a single name."

"I confess, Alys, that your stand surprises me. I had not thought you cared so much for principle and so little for your face." Griffin simply lifted the pistol in a way that suggested he meant to backhand her with it. He barely had any momentum built into the gesture when she threw up her own hands and blurted out a name.

"Burton. Neville Burton."

Griffin's attention swung to Sir Hadrien, but there was no recognition of the name in the man's face that he could see. For himself, Griffin tried to recall if there had ever been an introduction to Burton. The name was wholly unfamiliar. "Tell me about him. Does he work for Crocker?"

"Not in the sense that he's paid, I shouldn't imagine. I don't know the particulars. I'm *not* his partner. I suppose it's an arrangement like you have with Fairley or Varah. They step too deeply into debt, and you offer them an opportunity to clean the muck off their shoes in exchange for certain services."

Griffin lifted the hem of Mrs. Christie's gown just enough to make a deliberately insulting examination of her slippers. "What of the muck on your own finely shod feet? How much do you owe Mr. Crocker?"

Mrs. Christie yanked on the folds of her gown and drew her feet back under the hem. She glared at Griffin. "I don't owe him a farthing."

"Were you already beholding to him when you came under my protection, or did the debt occur later? I think perhaps it was later, around the time you began to steal from me. I can't fix the date in my mind without consulting my accounts, but it seems to me it was some four months in the past. Would that be about right?"

Griffin watched the full line of Mrs. Christie's mouth flatten. Her refusal to reply did not bother him in the least. "You stole the ring from me, replaced it with Alastair's marker, all of it done as if to help your young lover. Then you set him up to lose it to Crocker. I imagine Johnny was not entirely happy when you bested him by winning it back, or perhaps it was done of a purpose, and he meant that you should have it as a gift. He would have believed it was not entirely out of his possession if it was in yours, but then Alastair confounded you both by returning it to me. Have I got it right, Alys?"

She pressed her lips together, offered nothing.

Griffin stole a glance at Sir Hadrien. "At last I understand how quiet is becoming." Satisfied by Sir Hadrien's start of recognition at this sentiment, he returned his attention to Mrs. Christie. "The attack on Alastair's sister was in every way about you. Your petty jealousies. Your rage at being turned out. You conceived the notion that she was to blame. You sent Neville Burton to Olivia's room not only to punish her, but to punish me as well. Burton might be Crocker's man, but you had the use of him. It doesn't matter to me whether today's bit of business was planned by you or Crocker. Neither of you is blameless. Both of you are responsible."

Satisfied that she'd heard him, Griffin fell silent. Out of the corner of his eye he saw they were approaching Crocker's hell. He tapped the barrel against the roof to alert the driver that they were coming to their destination. The carriage slowed immediately.

"I expect nothing less than your cooperation," he said. "Both of you. You can trust that Crocker will see to his own well-being first and on no account will he be concerned for yours. As I am of a similar mind, you will precede me to the door."

Sir Hadrien alighted first, then Mrs. Christie. Griffin followed them up the stone steps and remained behind them while their knock was being answered.

Johnny Crocker's establishment did not cater to the fashionable crowd. They came, though, especially the younger set, to rub elbows with the rough trade. Too frequently it was because they had something to prove, either to themselves or their friends, or even more often, to the society of their parents. As a consequence, Crocker's hell served up regular brawls that broke furniture and jaws in equal measure. Crocker was known to tolerate opium smokers and did not fuss overmuch if that activity spilled out of the rooms designated specifically for it. He did not operate a brothel but allowed women to ply their trade within the house as long as they were comely and did not expect him to provide protection.

He paid the local constabulary well and expected little enough for it. He didn't call upon them to settle disagreements that arose at the tables and among the opium eaters, and he didn't welcome their interference when he settled such things in his own way. Doing nothing, it was the easiest money they earned.

Griffin and his companions were shown into the entrance hall by a man who would have seemed equally in his element on the docks. He had a thick neck and hands like paddles. He looked them over, nodded politely to Mrs. Christie, and asked Griffin, "What's your business?"

"Tell your employer that Breckenridge is here on the matter of a debt that's owed him. He'll see me."

The manservant nodded, turned his back to seek out Crocker, and was felled like the great oak he was when Griffin caught him in the back of the skull with the butt of his pistol.

"What was that?" Olivia asked. The bottles shuddered once and were still. "Did you feel it?"

Alastair's head came up. He frowned, realized Olivia couldn't see his confusion, and said, "Don' know. S'not the same as it usually is. Goes on for hours most times."

Olivia returned to her brother's side and sat down. "I've been thinking, Alastair. There's something yet that we might do."

Griffin directed Sir Hadrien and Mrs. Christie to drag the body to the front parlor and close the pocket doors. He didn't expect that the man would be coming around any time soon. His skull had cracked like the shell of a soft-cooked egg.

He gestured to his companions to climb the stairs to

Crocker's rooms. It was impressive that neither of them had done more than startle when the big man went down. Apparently he'd made himself convincing. All to the good, since he'd meant every threat.

Johnny Crocker was a large man himself, given to expansive gestures and raising his voice in a manner that made him seem larger. He jumped to his feet and threw his arms wide when he saw Alys Christie step into the room.

"Alys, m'love, so you've come. Couldn't stay away, could—" He stopped, thick, copper-colored eyebrows coming together over a pair of sharply leveled green eyes as Sir Hadrien followed on Mrs. Christie's heels. "Who's the toff sniffin' your skirts, Alys? Can't say that I like you bringin' him here."

"Sir Hadrien Cole," she said. "Sir Hadrien, Mr. Johnny Crocker."

"Cole? I'll be damned." He folded his arms across his chest so they rested comfortably on the shelf of his protruding hard belly. "I'm at a loss here, Alys. Damned, if I'm not at a loss."

Griffin stepped over the threshold behind them. "A loss? That is unlike you, Crocker."

"Bloody hell." He eyed Griffin's raised weapon. "For God's sake, lower your pistol, Breckenridge. I ain't of a mind to lay you out, though your manners make it tempting. What the hell do you want? If I have it, it's yours."

"Olivia Cole."

"Don't have it. Don't know precisely what it is."

"I am generally amused by your bluster. Not just now, though." Nonetheless, he lowered his pistol and made a point of looking around Crocker's study. The tidiness of the space was in perfect contrast to the man. Crocker's cravat was limp and slightly twisted, his shirt bunched around his waist, and there was a button missing on his waistcoat. His study, however, had no item out of place. The furniture was set at conversational angles and none of it held papers, books, or ledgers. There was room to walk in every direction without bumping into a stack of newspapers or tripping over a footstool. The vases, all four of them filled with expensive hothouse flowers, did not have to share a tabletop with mismatched porcelain and jade figurines and other odd collectibles. There were no decks of cards under the chairs or teacups and saucers lining the windowsill. No decanters were left out on the drinks cabinet, and the evidence that Crocker smoked the occasional cheroot or cigar was confined to the stale, smoky fragrance that lingered in the air.

"You welcomed Mrs. Christie rather warmly, I thought."

"Why shouldn't I? She's a right piece of God's handiwork and has a mouth what knows how to pleasure a man. You're familiar yourself."

Griffin saw his former mistress's back stiffen. At her sides her hands curled. "Have a care, Crocker, else she will launch herself at you. Don't depend on me to pull her off, nor to wager that you'd emerge the victor. She says she's not your partner, and neither is she in your debt, but something about her way of saying doesn't sit well with me. I thought you might entertain me with your version of the truth, but I'd like to see Olivia first. Sir Hadrien would like to see her brother. Explanations, as diverting as I'm certain to find them, will have to wait."

Crocker held up his hands in advance of his attempt to explain, his broad features suggesting confusion and innocence. "You mistake the matter if you think I know what you're talking about. You seem to be suggesting something that is beneath me."

"Since you'd crawl on your belly in the sewers if it would put a copper in your pocket, there's nothing that's beneath you." He raised the pistol, used it to nudge Mrs. Christie and Sir Hadrien a bit to each side, then kept it level on Johnny Crocker's barrel chest. "Show me where you're keeping Olivia."

Crocker shifted his weight, unfolded his arms, and held fast to the lapels of his frock coat. He took Griffin's measure, calculated the likelihood that he would use the pistol, and equally important, the likelihood that he would miss. The probability of the first was extremely high, the latter, extremely low. Johnny Crocker decided he could afford to cooperate.

"Do you have the ring?" he asked.

Ignoring the question, Griffin said, "Take me to Olivia."

Crocker shrugged his massive shoulders. "As you wish."

Griffin stepped back and out of the way so that all three could precede him. He explained to Crocker in his calm and careful voice what he would do if there was the least interference from the staff. Crocker simply nodded and took the lead.

They used the servants' stairs to enter the bowels of the house. The narrow passage confined their movements and made it easy for Griffin to keep them contained. When they entered the servants' hall, Crocker sent the cook and all three helpers out. A maidservant came into the hallway from one of the adjoining rooms, her arms extended and laden with laundry. A word from Crocker had her reversing her direction immediately. The hall was silent and still after that.

"Show me," Griffin said quietly.

"This way." Crocker turned the corner and stopped in front of a heavy oaken door. "Wine cellar. I have to get the key from inside my coat."

"Go on." Griffin noted the door was barred as well as locked. The combination was good for keeping people out *and* in. He felt more confident that he was being shown where Olivia and Alastair had been secreted.

Crocker removed the bar, set it aside, then used the key. They all stepped back as the door opened toward them and stayed rooted to the floor as the foul stench escaped the room.

Mrs. Christie gagged and stuffed her fist against her mouth. Sir Hadrien quickly found his scented handkerchief and pressed it to his nose. Crocker grimaced but stepped into the room, encouraged by the pistol pressed momentarily against his spine.

Griffin called for Olivia in the same moment she heaved the contents of the slop bucket into the crowded doorway.

Mrs. Christie pressed her hands against her stomach as she doubled over. Violent retching noises erupted from her followed by the remains of her breakfast. The delicate lavender scent in Sir Hadrien's handkerchief was obliterated by the sprinkling of body waste that attached itself to his hair, face, and clothing. At the center, where Olivia's aim had been most true, Johnny Crocker received no mere sprinkling, but a full shower of the bucket's foul contents.

"Christ! Christ Jesus! Holy Mother of God!" He slapped at his face with his hands, trying to wipe the worst of it away. The taste of it was in his mouth; the odor clung to the inside of his nose. There was no ridding himself of it. He gagged also, staggered forward, and bent at the waist. He never saw Olivia swing the empty wooden bucket back, around, and over her shoulder, so he didn't know when it reached its full height. The momentum carried it forward; Olivia supplied the direction. The impact with his head shattered the bucket and dropped him to his knees in the filth he was trying to escape.

Griffin could not recall that he'd ever thought much about the height and breadth of Johnny Crocker's shoulders, nor the way the man filled the space across a threshold. He thought about it now, and was grateful. Except for a few scattered droplets, Crocker's considerable mass had been an almost perfect bulwark.

Griffin stood slightly to one side in the doorway, allowing more light from the kitchen and the hall sconces to enter the wine cellar. He could see Olivia holding the rope handle of the shattered bucket. Two wooden staves still dangled from it. She was all of a messy piece, slightly soiled, a bit worse for the wear with her hair tousled and rents in her gown, but she was unbowed by the experience in any way that mattered. It was anger that flushed her face, not exertion or fear. She had a warrior's stance, not the still, guarded posture of prey. That she was armed only with the remnants of a slop bucket, well, he was hard-pressed to keep his lips from twitching.

He used the pistol to wave her over. To her credit, she didn't hesitate. When Crocker made a weak attempt to catch her skirts as she passed, she sharply slapped at his hand with the bucket staves like a governess disciplining an unruly charge. Griffin was not proof against that gesture. He was grinning as she came abreast of him.

Before she could comment, he moved her into the hall behind him. She came up on tiptoe as she pressed herself against his back. He heard her whisper her brother's name, and for the first time, he became aware of Alastair's presence in the cellar. Her brother was standing against the wall of wine bottles, his arms and legs spread wide as though he were holding back the tide of grape, when in truth he was being held up by it.

"Over here, Alastair," Griffin said. When Alastair didn't move, Griffin raised his voice. This time he managed to talk over the oddly syncopated retching of Olivia's three victims, and penetrate the fermented fog that clouded Alastair's thinking.

Alastair's head swiveled slowly toward the door. He grinned somewhat lopsidedly, then drew himself up almost straight and pushed away from the wall. He managed to grab the neck of a wine bottle in each hand as he did so and lightly tapped his father on the shoulder as he half sauntered, half stumbled past Sir Hadrien's heaving frame.

"Foxed," he announced, still smiling stupidly as he slipped by Griffin. "Couldn' help myself."

Griffin shrugged. "It's a wine cellar."

"That's what *I* said." Alastair struck the butt ends of the bottles together to punctuate his point.

Olivia tugged on the tails of Griffin's frock coat. "Can we go? I'd really like to go."

Griffin nodded. He stood, backed out, and closed the door.

The wooden bar stood precisely where Crocker left it. Griffin hefted it in one hand and slid it into place just as Crocker threw his considerable weight and one formidable shoulder against it. It shuddered, but then so did Crocker. The sound of his retching was muffled but easily identifiable.

Griffin felt his own stomach curdle. He took another step back and turned, giving Olivia a sideways grimace. "Clever and resourceful, indeed. A force of nature is more like it."

She managed a modest smile. "I supplied the force. Alastair supplied the nature, if you take my meaning."

Because the odor and contents of the slop bucket were still very much with them, Griffin had no difficulty comprehending. "I do." The door shuddered again as Crocker threw himself against it a second time. Griffin ignored it, though he saw Olivia and Alastair look toward it with some trepidation. "Your father's carriage is outside. You can take it back to Putnam Lane. We're not far from there, but I don't think walking is advisable for either of you." This time when the door vibrated, Griffin casually knocked back at it with the butt of his pistol. "They can't get out, any more than you could. Go on. I won't be long. Can you find your way?"

Olivia nodded. "Come, Alastair. Do you require my shoulder?"

"Have the bottles for balance," he said pleasantly. "Just the thing."

Rolling her eyes, Olivia turned to go. She'd taken only half a step forward before she felt herself being hauled back into Griffin's arms. She was wrapped in a hard embrace that nearly squeezed the breath from her lungs. What remained, he stole with a quick, hard kiss. She still bore the stamp of it on her mouth when he set her from him.

"Marry me, Olivia Cole."

She stared up at him, and because her balance was a bit off from the fierceness of that kiss and the perfect beauty of his smile, she said yes.

He nodded once, satisfied. "Now go."

Olivia turned, took Alastair by the sleeve, and began to lead him down the hall.

Griffin set his shoulder against the cellar door, rapped it twice with his pistol, and called for quiet. It took several moments, but it was achieved in the main. "Crocker!"

"You have my attention, Breckenridge."

It was a more reasoned response than Griffin had dared hope for. "Tell me where I can find Neville Burton."

"Don't know him."

"Not what I want to hear. Tell him, Mrs. Christie. Make him understand that it's not what I want to hear."

Trembling in the aftermath of being so violently ill, Alys Christie weakly raised her head. She was on her knees, nearly surrounded by her own sickness and afraid to move in any direction. "He knows about Burton. He forced me to tell him."

"I don't imagine there was much force involved," Crocker said, disgusted. "You have no tolerance for pain, Alys, above a bit of slap and tickle. Always been a disappointment in that regard." Crocker paid no heed to the sharp hiss of her breath and leaned against the door. "He's around, Breckenridge. I can't tell you more than that, and rest assured that I would, conditions here being what they are."

"Griffin?"

Olivia's soft interjection jerked Griffin away from the door. She was standing in front of him when she should have been gone. Alastair, too, was in the hall, listing slightly as he was no longer in possession of his wine bottles. Behind them was the young man instantly recognizable to Griffin as the gentleman villain.

"Mr. Burton's here," Griffin announced to Crocker.

"Is he? Not surprised. I don't suppose he ever left after bringing Miss Cole around." His deep rumbling laughter filtered through seams in the door. "Damned if he ain't made himself a useful sort. Get me out of here, Burton."

Griffin saw the villain shrug almost sheepishly, but his arctic blue eyes held nothing that could be confused for remorse. "What do you want, Mr. Burton?"

"Let us begin with your pistol on the floor."

Griffin hesitated. He saw Burton poke at Olivia with what he imagined was a pistol of his own. He put his weapon down slowly and raised his palms as he straightened. When Burton indicated he should slide it toward him, he did so with the toe of his boot.

Burton pushed Olivia forward, then set Alastair on the same path. Griffin now stood as a clear target for his pistol. The gentleman villain merely smiled when Griffin set Olivia at his back. "I only have to get through you," he said. "I'll take my time with her once I clean her up." He produced the cravat that he'd used to tie Olivia's hands. "She had this tucked in her sleeve. I believe she thought she might have use for it. Around my neck, perhaps. I think it will look lovely around hers. Did you know that cutting off the airway heightens the moment of crisis? I shall enjoy watching her then." He smiled at Griffin, then jerked his chin toward the door. "Open it."

Griffin lifted the bar carefully, aware of Burton's steady aim and fierce concentration on his movements. The distraction he provided was deliberately slow and calculated toward a single purpose.

He'd always admired the deftness of Olivia's touch, and no more so than when she neatly reached under his frock coat and lifted the pistol he'd shoved between his trousers and the small of his back. He stepped clear of her as she raised her arm.

Seeing the movement out of the corner of his eye, Burton twitched. It was enough for Griffin to seize the moment. He swung the wooden bar up hard, shattering Burton's wrist and knocking the pistol out of his grip. "Alastair!" he shouted. "The door!"

Alastair threw himself against it in time to catch the flat of Johnny Crocker's hand. Crocker's howl of pain was not loud

Jo Goodman

enough to mask the sound of crunching bone. Mrs. Christie screamed. Sir Hadrien shouted something unintelligible. Alastair opened the door a fraction, shoved Crocker's broken hand inside, and slammed it closed again. The cacophony continued, but the volume of it was lessened considerably.

Griffin set the bar back in place, pried the pistol out of Olivia's cold grip, and leveled it at Burton. The villain was curled on the floor, knees drawn up like an infant, cradling his injured wrist. His eyes were closed against the intense pain. Tears squeezed through his lashes. Unsympathetic, Griffin simply shook his head.

Alastair made a dignified surge forward, picked up both of the fallen pistols, and with one in each hand, found his balance again.

Olivia touched Griffin's sleeve lightly, exerting just enough pressure to encourage him to lower his arm. "You don't want to kill him."

"I do," he said. "I really do."

"Then I don't want you to."

Griffin weighed her wishes against his own, considered what it would cost them both to satisfy her honor and indulge his pride, and knew there was only one course of action. He lowered the pistol to his side, and with his free arm, started to draw Olivia close.

Watching them, Alastair Cole was contentedly aware that matters of honor and pride had been left to him.

He raised both pistols and fired.

Chapter Seventeen

June 1823

Alastair Cole offered his arm to his sister. "It's time," he whispered, nudging her gently with his elbow. "I made a promise, and I intend to see it through."

Olivia took up his arm but held it as one desperate to be pulled from the drink, not into it. "There is something to be said for going back on one's word. I don't think I fully appreciated that until now."

He chuckled softly, adjusted her grip on his arm, and bent his head to her ear. "You are simply making noises, Livvy. Your argument has neither passion nor reason. Chin up. Eyes front. Smile. There you go. You look lovely." He kissed her cheek. "He's waiting for you."

Olivia nodded, swallowed, and made to fall in step beside her brother. There was a moment's hesitation just as they would have started out. Faltering slightly, she disobeyed Alastair's eyes-front order and gave him her full attention. "I'm glad you proved to be such a poor shot. Twice."

He pretended to take umbrage. "I was drunk, remember." He patted her hand. "But I am glad of it, too. Now, shall we?"

Olivia squeezed his arm slightly, her grasp no longer as

fierce as it had been. "Very well." She took a calming breath, then set her eyes in the direction she meant to go. "This is not so different from the first time."

Beside her, she sensed Alastair's confusion, but also his relief that she intended to go forward. She did not try to explain herself. The memory that came to her was one that she embraced alone, and it remained more dear because of it. The same emotions surfaced: uncertainty, excitement, wariness. She'd stood in the entrance hall of Breckenridge's hell and accepted his challenge, in spite of everything she felt in that moment, to come to him.

No, it was not so very different now.

He was there once again, waiting for her, perhaps only marginally more confident that she would arrive to take her place beside him. Olivia suspected she was the only one who glimpsed relief in his eyes when she appeared framed in the alcove. She knew he didn't doubt she loved him, only that she loved him enough to run the gauntlet that was the center aisle of St. Michael's church.

It was not the march to the altar that was intimidating. It was the sea of faces on either side of it that gave her pause, and in this regard her imagination hardly stood up to the reality of the thing. She was aware of the gazes turned in her direction, of the assessments they made, of the encouragement that so many pairs of eyes offered.

His sisters were there, all three, husbands and children flanking them. Dr. Pettibone had a seat on the aisle. Lady Rivendale was among the attendees, and she looked on approvingly, supporting the rumor by her condescension that she'd been instrumental in bringing them all to this very place. Mr. Restell Gardner and his wife had come as well. They shared their pew with four gentlemen—four strangers who had once come forward to protect her. Guardian angels, really, whom Olivia would always think of as whiskey, gin, and two pints of ale. Mr. Gardner had brought them forward, had the story from them, and like everyone else, they were here now to wish her happy.

The faces gradually faded into Olivia's peripheral vision as Griffin filled the whole of it. He stood just to the right of the minister, strikingly handsome in his double-breasted black frock coat with the claw-hammer tails. Mr. Mason had done right by him, turning him out with nary a wrinkle in his trousers and waistcoat and having the good sense to insist on a pristine white neckcloth tied in the intricate Oriental.

His eyes were all for her, and she did not shy away from his glance. Mrs. McCutcheon and her entourage of seamstresses and dressers had done right by her as well. Olivia imagined they would be moved to more teary emotion if they were witness to Griffin's appreciation of their handiwork. That had been their response when they'd first stepped back to gauge the success of their efforts, and Griffin's approbation could not help but bring about a similar response.

The gentle, draping folds of her white satin gown brushed together as she walked, then rustled like whispers all around her. A band of pale pink silk edged the bodice, and wide ribbon bands encrusted with seed pearls bordered the hem and cuffed the short sleeves. Her hair, her *own* hair, was arranged off her neck in a knot every bit as intricate as the Oriental with the added touches of seed pearls and delicate white rose buds.

When she first saw her reflection in the cheval glass she'd wondered at the weeping response of Mrs. McCutcheon and her helpers, but now, seeing herself reflected in Griffin's dark eyes, she knew an urge to indulge in some teary emotion herself.

"Who gives this woman . . ."

Olivia heard the words, understood their import, and knew a certain peace in her heart that it was Alastair who stood by her. The irony that he should be the one to give her over to Breckenridge's care was not lost on any of them, but there was no desperation in the act this time, no avoiding responsibility to have it taken up by another. Alastair spoke his part with clear deliberation, honoring them all with his words.

"I do."

Olivia's hand was placed in the one that Griffin held out to her, and she knew the very rightness of it as Alastair backed away and she came to stand at Griffin's side. This man, this man who would be her husband, held her hand and all of her heart.

It was well past ten when they were finally alone. The guests, and almost all of them had accepted invitations to stay at Wright Hall for several days following the wedding, had retired to their respective rooms in the mostly renovated east wing. Griffin and Olivia had elected to stay in the part of the hall that was still largely a work in progress.

It was no particular sacrifice to take the lesser accommodations. Drafts were of no account on a night neither of them meant to enjoy long out of bed.

"That will be our supper," Griffin said, responding to the knock at the door. He stepped back, eyebrow lifted when he saw Nat standing uneasily in the hallway. "Here's a fellow I thought was all tucked in." He opened the door wider, ushered Nat inside, and gave Olivia a quizzing glance over the child's head.

Olivia had turned away from the dressing table when Griffin announced their supper had come. She waved Nat to her side and was as puzzled as Griffin when he fairly dragged his feet in coming to her. Clearly he had not arrived at their room in search of another bedtime story, a tactic he used from time to time when he wanted reassurance he could not quite articulate.

Olivia had undone her elaborately dressed hair and run her fingers through the waves. She pulled it to one side and began to plait it, aware that it was something Nat had observed her doing before and found fascinating. His eyes, though wide and fully alert, did not follow the deft movements of her fingers. "What is it, Nat? Has there been a dustup in the nursery?" She wondered at the wisdom of putting so many children in a suite, but Griffin's sisters were certain the nannies were up to the task.

"No, miss. Everyone's sleeping. I slipped away." He revealed this last with neither pride nor guilt. It was simply a statement of fact.

"So you did. You have some reason for it, I collect."

He nodded, said nothing.

Behind him, Griffin did not have to temper his smile while he spoke in grave and important accents. "I think her ladyship is wanting the favor of a reply."

Olivia noted that Nat gave a little start and his eyes widened a bit more. "He's teasing us both," she said. "Me more than you. He knows perfectly well that I am unused to the idea that I am suddenly become 'her ladyship.' Now, tell me. What is toward?"

Nat blurted it out. "Thomas says that we're married."

Olvia was so taken aback by this intelligence that for a moment she couldn't think who Thomas was. Griffin had it immediately and told her.

"Juliet's son. My up-to-every-trick nephew."

"Oh." She nodded. "Of course. The one with the cowlick." She stopped plaiting her hair and took up one of Nat's small hands. "It is never wise to place too much confidence in someone with a cowlick. Think of it, Nat—he cannot properly manage the particulars of his own hair." Griffin snorted, but she ignored him in favor of studying Nat's sober countenance. "We are *not* married, but I cannot tell whether it is a relief or of some concern to you."

He didn't respond directly but looked at the ring on her hand, a square-cut emerald in a bed of twenty-one diamonds, the gold band retooled to fit her slender finger. "Thomas says that since I gave over the ring, it means we're married."

Griffin approached and put his hand on Nat's shoulder. "Clearly, Thomas will have to answer for himself, but the facts are these: you held the ring for me and stood at my side. The vows that were exchanged were between Miss Cole and me, and bound us together as husband and wife."

Nat considered this. A crease appeared between his eyebrows as they knit. He caught his bottom lip, worried it. The trembling only marginally eased and the narrow line of his scar was stretched by the tension in his countenance.

Olivia sensed it first. She had Nat's hand, Griffin, his shoulder, and the child still had no idea how he was bound to them. She lifted her eyes to Griffin, saw he'd come to the same understanding. She nodded faintly, surrending the right to make the statement because it was for a father to say to his son.

"You stood for me, Nat, as Olivia's brother stood for her. I wanted you there because you are my family, my blood. I could think of no one who would better serve as my second than my own son."

"Your second? Truly?"

Griffin smiled, squeezed his shoulder. "Truly."

"That's all right, then." He nodded once, accepting it. The smile that edged his mouth faded as he turned to regard Olivia. "You're our family now."

"I am."

"But we're not married."

"No."

"Shall you be my mother?"

"If you like."

There was no hesitation. "I do."

"Good. It is the same for me." Before he could glimpse her tears, Olivia leaned forward and pressed a kiss to his forehead. "Go. Go with your father back to your room and see if you can't slip inside the nursery as quietly as you left it." She gave him a nudge into the shelter of Griffin's embrace, then sat back and watched them exit the room together.

By the time Griffin returned, their late supper of chestnut soup and warm French bread was laid out on the small round table pulled close to the hearth. Olivia had changed into a fine lawn shift and a deep purple Chinese silk robe and matching slippers made for just this occasion. She was sitting with her back to the fire, reworking the plait in her hair.

He watched her a moment, just inside the doorway, but when he caught her eye, he simply shook his head. She sighed, not disagreeably, and began to unwind the braid. Griffin approached, caught her hand, and completed the task himself. He sifted the silky threads of her hair with his fingers, each strand made more like molten copper by the leaping, twisting flames behind them.

"Beautiful," he whispered. He bent his head, found the curve of her neck and shoulder that she offered up, and kissed her. He touched his mouth to the corner of hers, then her cheek, and finally her temple before he straightened. Disengaging his fingers from her hair was done most reluctantly. He took up the chair opposite her. Her smile was soft, her eyes heavy-lidded. He would have abandoned his meal altogether if she had not broken off the heel of the bread loaf and offered it to him. Her hand grazed his; the touch was light but deliberate.

"He's asleep?" she asked.

"Mmm. Soundly this time."

"Good." Olivia drizzled a bit of honey on her bread. "I took it for granted that he understood what he had become to us. I suppose some things need to be said. He was delighted to learn he was your second. You showed a deft touch to place such a meaning on it. Battles. Duels. He understands all about those."

"He's never had a father. I suppose there is a great deal for him to learn in that regard."

"And you? What you said about Nat being your blood, have you come to know that it's true?"

"What I've come to know is that it doesn't matter. He's my son if I want him to be. You opened my eyes to that. I do want him to be, Olivia."

"That's all right, then," she said, just as Nat had. "You've a heart big enough for the both of us."

Griffin gave her a most significant look. "And more besides."

Olivia was having none of it. She pointed her spoon at him. "Your soup will grow cold. One suspects your ardor will not."

He laughed. "One would be right." He tapped her spoon with his own and encouraged her to eat as well. It had not escaped his notice that she'd eaten very little throughout the day. Every time he sought her out she was engaged in conversation with one, two, or all three of his sisters. He rescued her as often as possible, steering her toward Restell's wife or even the clutch that surrounded Lady Rivendale, but it seemed that Jenny, Kate, and Juliet invariably managed to separate her from others, just as if they were culling a lamb from the fold. It was little wonder that Olivia had no real appetite for their wedding feast and made only a pretense of eating what was placed before her.

"My sisters did not press you overmuch, I hope," he said.

"Press me? No. They were telling stories about you."

He almost believed her, then he saw the corner of her mouth curl ever so slightly. "No, they weren't. They were asking for every detail of our meeting, courtship, and engagement. Did I not predict they would?"

"I was not entirely comfortable lying to them."

"It's not your strong suit, I agree, but the truth will not serve."

"Then I suppose it was well done by you to protect my identity all these many months."

"Why, that is almost in the way of thanks, Miss Shepard."

He chuckled when she primly pursed her lips at him. "You realize there were very few guests who know the truth. Mr. Gardner, perhaps his wife. Lady Rivendale. Your brother. Your four gentlemen protectors. We know we can depend upon their discretion."

She nodded. It was enough that she knew now Mr. Rawlings and Mr. Rollins were one and the same. She was not certain that she believed he died by his own hand, but it was the only story that could be had from his friends. Neither Restell Gardner nor Griffin pressed to discover a different truth, and in that way her protectors were also shielded.

"As for your father," Griffin said, "he will never breathe a word of it."

"That's because he knows the ton sanctions this marriage."

It was because Sir Hadrien knew his life would be worth nothing if he spoke in less than favorable accents to anyone about his daughter, but if Olivia believed what she'd said, Griffin decided he could leave it alone. "Lady Rivendale lent our ceremony considerable consequence."

"It was kind of her to accept our invitation." Olivia chewed on a piece of bread. "You did not allow for much notice or preparation."

He shrugged. "I was afraid you would change your mind. You accepted my proposal under unusual conditions. It seemed best to go forward quickly."

"Unusual conditions." As she recalled, her father, Mrs. Christie, and Johnny Crocker had been loudly protesting their confinement while blaming one another for the cause of it. Innocence had probably never been claimed by such caterwauling. "Yes, that describes it nicely."

"I thought so. Neville Burton has taken himself off to the continent."

Olivia's head snapped up. "He has?"

"Some encouragement was necessary, but apparently he

believed he'd pressed his luck as far as he could when Alastair's aim went wide."

"The others?"

"Johnny Crocker booked passage on the *Fair Ariana* and is bound for Boston in two days' time. His companion, as I am given to understand by Mr. Gardner, is Mrs. Christie. They deserve each other, but I fear for the fine people of Boston."

"Do you owe Mr. Gardner another favor?"

He shook his head. "It was all done more in the way of a wedding gift."

"I am imagining that you had a hand in it as well."

"Merely as an educator. In geography, most specifically." When Olivia frowned at his cryptic reply, he went on. "I pointed out how small our island is compared to the length and breadth of the continent and the Americas. I told them that if they were desirous of living on an island, transport to Van Diemen's land could be easily arranged. Oddly enough, none of them chose the convict colony."

"You teach a good lesson. I've heard you with Nat."

"It seemed to speak to them."

Firelight glanced off Olivia's ring, setting the emerald center aglow, and capturing her attention. She raised her hand slightly, twisted it back and forth, and watched the diamonds wink at her. "Alastair told me it was fitting that I should have it."

"So it is." Griffin could have mentioned that Alastair hardly had any say in the matter, but he was feeling almost warm toward his brother-in-law of late and kept his tongue in his head. Having acquired both Olivia and the ring in one ceremony, well, he could afford to be generous. "I saw Lady Rivendale exclaiming over it."

"She did. Several times. Your sisters also." Olivia set her spoon down and pushed her empty bowl aside. "I refrained from telling them that your nature is to be so tightfisted that you presented me with my own family's heirloom."

"There is that, though I like to think it speaks more to romantic sentiment than the other."

Smiling, she rubbed her index finger over the facets of the emerald. "It did bring us together."

Griffin took up her hand, raised it to his lips. He kissed her knuckles, then turned her hand over and kissed the delicate underside of her wrist. She came to her feet easily when he stood and did not hesitate to step into his embrace. The fit was still there, the sheltering shoulder, the inviting arm, curve to angle, and she wondered why she had thought for even a moment that it might not be.

"It does not seem so long now," she whispered. "But when we were parted, I thought I comprehended the length of forever."

Griffin held her tight, stroked her back. He was of the same opinion. Five weeks, three days, had been forever, or just this side of it. The moment she accepted his proposal he knew everything about their arrangement would have to change. She'd argued with him, but in this he was intractable, and she moved back to her brother's home, stepped reluctantly out into society, and with the Countess of Rivendale's timely assistance and devilishly inspired planning, set herself directly in his path.

Their courtship supplied the most delicious *on-dit* as the London Season began, and when the ton realized a marriage was in the offing, the betting books opened for the date that their firstborn would appear. To the best of his knowledge, Olivia was unaware of the wagers or that certain wags were watching her belly. He did not know what she'd make of it and did not care to find out, at least until they exchanged their vows.

Sir Hadrien's absence during their brief engagement was the source of some speculation, but as he was known to have little enough use for town, nothing came of it. Alastair filled in nicely for his father, and his mother was sufficiently glad of his safe release that she willingly returned to Coleridge Park with Sir Hadrien.

"I wonder if you know how often I was tempted to visit Jericho Mews in the dead of night," he said.

"Perhaps as often as I was tempted to return to the hell."

"You were missed there. Faro revenues are most seriously compromised."

She pressed her smile against his cheek. "I am willing to return, you know."

"Perish the thought." He lifted her so suddenly that she gasped, though she recovered quickly enough to throw her arms about his neck. He carried her to the bed, dropped her inelegantly upon it, and while she was still laughing, he followed her down. "There is no going back, not even as Honey. I sent my mistress packing as I intend to be faithful to my wife."

She caught his face in her hands. "I am very glad to hear it."

He dipped his head when she nudged him closer, brushed his lips against hers. "There is another reason, though, that you can't return."

"Oh?"

"Someone has approached me about purchasing the hell. I am not going to sell it outright, but I will be acquiring a partner. He will have the running of the establishment day to day."

Olivia released his face and pushed herself up by her elbows. "What?"

"It's a good offer. I can collect a percentage of the house's profits simply by continuing to lend my name to the enterprise. He will have a larger share, but that is only as it should be."

"Do you trust him?"

"Yes. Yes, I do. And I have you to help me with the accounts and every confidence in your ability to know if something is off."

Olivia regarded Griffin carefully. "Are you certain you want to do this?"

"I am. Our income will be less, but perfectly manageable, and by choosing to live at Wright Hall, we will be able to oversee the development of the lands and finish the renovation of the house. The purchase price of the partnership will bring enough of the ready so that the family debt will finally be paid in full. It is an excellent compromise, so much so that it does not seem a compromise at all."

Olivia was still skeptical and took no pains to hide it. "It's not Alastair, is it?"

"Alastair?"

"Your partner," she said flatly. "You have not entered into an agreement with my brother, have you?"

Griffin's hard laughter weakened his position, and he was forced to roll away, else collapse fully on top of her.

"I suppose that is answer enough to my question," Olivia said. "Still, it is hardly complimentary of Alastair."

Griffin caught his breath, reined in his smile. "True, though I was thinking that your question complimented neither your brother nor me. I admit to a certain growing respect for Alastair, but I am not so witless that I would accept an offer of partnership from him."

Olivia turned, levered herself on an elbow, and walked her fingers up Griffin's chest, tapping the buttons of his waistcoat as she went. "If it is not Alastair, and really, Griffin, I am glad for all our sakes that it is not, then who?"

"Mr. Warner."

"Lady Rivendale's friend?"

"The very same."

"That surprises."

"It does, doesn't it? I am of the opinion that the countess has a vested interest. She is certain to have put the idea in his head."

"Your trust is not misplaced then."

"I don't think so, no."

Olivia's fingers had reached the top of his waistcoat. She

lightly traced the edge of the fabric. "The knot in your neck-cloth is impressive."

"The Oriental."

"I know. Mr. Mason told me. Do you know that the least wrinkle or crease means it could not be named such? It is a most particular art, the tying of neckcloths."

"At this moment, I am far and away more interested in the *untying* of them. Do you think you could manage it?"

Olivia tugged at fabric. "It's very stiff."

"You're still speaking of the neckcloth, is that right?"

"Is the other in a knot?"

"All of me is in a knot." He groaned softly when she pressed her hip against his groin. "Ah, yes, that is a good beginning."

She chuckled, but kept her hip exactly where it was. Tugging on the linen fall she said, "Allow me to deal with this first, then I shall see about the other."

Griffin gave himself over to her, and she to him. It suited them both, the sharing. There was no disguising the wanting, nor any need to. In a nod to their wedding night, there was an attempt at tenderness. He framed her face gently with his hands, kissed her mouth, her cheeks, the space just between her eyebrows. She buried her face in his neck, set a line of kisses along the cord, others at the underside of his jaw, and still more at the hollow below his ear. They exchanged endearments, whispered words that would have made them laugh, even roll their eyes in the full light of day, but here, now, seemed exactly right.

It didn't last, couldn't. Their long separation trumped what romantic notions they had conceived about their wedding night. Their kisses became more urgent, the caresses less gentle. Olivia's fingers tunneled into his thick hair, clutched his head as she pressed a deep, hot, hungry kiss.

The blankets tangled as their legs did. Their clothes, so carelessly discarded, slipped off the foot of the bed and onto the floor—except for Griffin's neckcloth, which wrapped itself sinuously around Olivia's thigh as though it had a life of its own. She tugged at it, produced it so triumphantly that it tickled Griffin's humor, then snapped it smartly against his hip when he dared laugh. He made short work of the piece after that, taking it from her before she set her aim at any other part of his anatomy, and flung it as far away from the bed as he could.

She watched it sail through the air, then turned on him, her smile so satisfied with this result that it was very nearly smug. She gave him everything, all of her, held nothing back. He answered in the same manner, as needy as she, equally generous, equally selfish.

Turning, twisting, he brought her to pleasure's finely honed edge and balanced both of them on it until no choice was left to them but to go on. He watched her face, felt the tension building, and seated himself deeply inside her as she came. Then it was his turn, and her body cradled him as he followed her.

Their breathing slowed, calmed. Olivia's yawn was wide enough to make her jaw crack. Griffin gave her a sideways glance, then drew her close and made a niche for her head against his shoulder. Neither of them said anything for a long time, content to let silence linger, even comforted by it.

What more, then, needed to be said?

It was Olivia who remembered. "How much have you wagered?"

"Hmm?"

"In the betting books. How much have you wagered?"

Sensing a trap was being laid, Griffin tread carefully. "You are speaking of a particular wager?"

"How can you not know of it? Alastair says it is all about."

"All about what?"

"Town, of course. A consequence of so much haste in regard to our wedding. We may as well have been wed by special license. Having the banns read was hardly any delay at all. Speculation is rife."

"Rife." Still practicing caution, he said, "What is the speculation?"

"That I am already carrying your child."

"I see."

"There are wagers. Whole pages in the clubs devoted to the date that I will deliver. It is unseemly, Griffin."

"I agree."

"You really didn't know?"

The trap yawned as widely as she had. His foot hovered over it. How to answer in a way that would keep him well out of it? "It seems I might have heard something."

She tilted her head back to better take his measure. "I thought so."

"I didn't wager," he said quickly.

"Why not?"

"Why not? I thought we agreed the speculation was unseemly."

"It is, but there is also a great deal of money to be won. Enough to renovate the library here at Wright Hall, I shouldn't be surprised."

She was probably right, Griffin thought. Still, he couldn't place a wager for the very same reasons he didn't play cards in his own hell. "It is generally accepted that I should have some inkling of such a date. It would hardly be fair."

Olivia turned over, levered herself up so that she could see his face as clearly as the firelight defined it. "I like that you have regard for certain conventions," she said. "Fair play. Honoring your vows. Appreciation of your responsibilities. I love all of that about you. Depend on it, really. That is why I made the wager."

"You?" He heard the trap snap, but his foot was well wide of its jaws. "You made a wager?"

"Lady Rivendale did. On my behalf. She was completely amenable."

"She would be. She will think of it as a very good joke on the wags. What date did you give her?"

Olivia told him.

"But that's nine months from now."

"It is, yes." She smiled, kissed the corner of his mouth, and settled herself comfortably against him, breast to chest. "Nine months exactly. You know what that means, don't you?"

He did. His hands slipped to the small of her back, then lower to the curve of her bottom. "It means we shall have to apply ourselves to just that end." He touched his lips to hers, whispered against her mouth, "My clever and resourceful wife. My dearest Olivia."